# All Over Again

by Grace Finley

Printed in the United States of America

ISBN (Kindle) 978-1-953781-00-0
ISBN (Paperback) 978-1-953781-01-7
ISBN (Hardcover) 978-1-953781-02-4

Finley Books
Phoenix, AZ

www.FinleyBooks.com

# FINLEY BOOKS

PHOENIX, ARIZONA

# 1

## answer

The first time Delaney Rhodes spoke to him, she had gone through significant effort to find him and she wasn't all that pleased about it. When he opened the door of the Anesthesiology sleep room, she was a blur of grey scrubs, lab coat and a dark ponytail. He slid his rectangular glasses on his face, squinting at her.

"How was it that you came upon my personal cell number?"

"You didn't answer your desk phone or pager."

"I don't often do such menial tasks when I'm sleeping, Nurse—?" It was in that moment that his vision adjusted and he recognized the young woman standing before him, the piercing crystal blue of her eyes.

"Not a nurse, actually. I'm here about Cole Pruitt. He's supposed to be the ring bearer for his big sister's wedding tomorrow."

"That's very exciting. Cole Pruitt is?"

"6 years old, blonde hair, dimpled cheeks, 5 inch scar at the base of his neck."

He raised his eyebrows. "Ah, the shunt revision."

"Sounds like a WWE wrestler." She scowled, shoving the tablet screen toward him. "You'll need to sign in."

He examined her employee badge as he waited for the software to load. She wore the required business formal wear in the staff photo—a wide collared buttoned shirt with a blazer, a small, professional smile. "PT, DPT, NCS, PCS" he read aloud, visibly impressed.

She nodded, staring at the tablet impatiently.

"What am I needing to do here, Delaney?"

"Sign off on Cole's discharge. Dr. Shah came by at eleven this morning with the resident and had him do a note, but he didn't co-sign it so it's holding up his discharge."

"Dr. Shah or the on-call couldn't handle it?"

"Dr. Shah apparently left for St. Bart this afternoon and--" She checked her watch. "I was told you were now on-call."

He reached for her wrist, twisting it gently to read the watch face. "Ah. I guess I'm handling it. Sorry. Alarm didn't go off."

"It happens."

"5:01—you didn't waste any time. Hold up—they've been waiting since this *morning*?"

She nodded, impatiently.

He shook his head. "I hope he steps on a jellyfish."

She pressed her lips together, preventing a smile. "I had Dr. Noland reroute the note to you for co-signature." Her eyes glanced to her wrist, where his fingers had been, a slightly confused expression on her face.

"How efficient of you," he said, smirking, and tapped through the appropriate screens. He handed her back the tablet. "We know each other, you know."

She dialed a number into her staff phone, arched her eyebrow at him. "I know."

"Your staff photo is much friendlier than one might expect based on this conversation--but at least you did give me the time of day."

"My wrist was coerced," she said quickly. There was a sudden glint in her eye, a flush to her cheeks, as she waited for someone to answer. "Hey—Dr. Mathison signed off. Tell Cole I'll see him next week. I will. Thanks, Allie."

"*Jack.*"

Delaney tucked the phone in her lab coat pocket, her body visibly relaxing.

"Delaney?"

She glanced up, sweeping her side bangs from her face, which revealed a cluster of freckles on her high cheekbone.

"Call me Jack."

She broke their prolonged eye contact, glancing into the sleep room and back. There was a stack of papers on the small desk inside, a copy of an open, half-read novel turned upside down. "I'm sorry if I was short with you before—"

"There was a mild level of justified hostility."

"Not toward you."

"Tell that to your eyebrow."

She tried unsuccessfully not to smile. "I'm a nice person, really."

"I remember." He let his words hang, waited for her to look at him again. He wasn't disappointed when she did. "We didn't get a chance to get to know each other back then." He smiled kindly.

She frowned. "You switched to supplemental to finish med school and then you left pretty abruptly," she said, tilting her head to the side inquisitively. "We didn't even get to have a goodbye potluck."

"That's the condensed version, yes."

"How long have you been back?"

"About a year now."

"You get the ideal call schedules obviously."

"Right? Yeah, I was on last night and had a surgery last until 2pm. Hoping for a lighter night."

"I'm sorry I had to wake you."

"It's not your fault."

"Oh I know. Still sorry. Beauty sleep and all."

His mouth fell open. "Are you saying I'm not beautiful?"

"Hideous," she said regretfully. "I'm *also* sorry I had to tell you that, but really, I can't be the first."

He gazed at her, mouth ajar but creeping into a smile. "Well I get stalked by pretty therapists—can't be all that bad to be me."

She rolled her eyes, resetting her position in the hallway. She had rotated her body as though intent to leave, but hadn't committed to the action. He was pleased to see that, along with the deepening shade of her cheeks. "Get some coffee, Dr. Mathison—then get your eyes checked."

"I can assure you that my eyes are fine, Delaney. It's not a subjective observation." He reached behind the door for his lab coat, checked for his badge on the lapel, then reached for the door behind him, shrugging. "I like the moderately disheveled look," he said, pulling on his jacket.

Her hand instinctively jumped to check the level of disarray of her hair. "Thank you?"

"I meant for me."

"Oh. Well then. Mission accomplished. Very trendy. You're just missing the skinny fit scrub pants."

He waved off the remark. "I don't have the hips for them."

She laughed as though in spite of herself—a snort really, then clasped her hand to her face. "It's a terrible fashion trend. An over-correction from the saggy pants look from a few years ago."

He let the door click shut behind him, then stopped short. "*Should I do something with the hair?*"

Her fingers had reached up to touch his blonde curls immediately, as though they had been awaiting an invitation. She fixed one rogue lock then retracted her hand slowly. "The hair works." She straightened her face, but found her mouth continuously turning upwards.

He watched her hand move away, amused. "Excellent." He started toward the elevators and she had no choice but to follow along. As they strolled down the hallway, it occurred to him what it might look like to an onlooker, emerging from the sleep room corridor together.

"Well this doesn't look scandalous at all," she murmured.

"I was just thinking the same thing—don't worry, it's not busy up here until later at night."

She nodded.

"I am *curious*," he began, holding the heavy industrial door open for her.

"About?"

"How'd you get in here?"

"It's not Fort Knox."

He followed her toward the elevators, catching sight of a cartoon sticker tagging a ride on her right pant leg.

"I borrowed a badge."

"Whose?" he asked, bending once she had stopped to retrieve the sticker--a one-eyed green monster. He held up his thumb with the sticker attached and walked it to the trash can.

"Ah. I wondered where Mike Wazowski ended up."

"Well?"

"I told one of the Pediatric Neurology residents I could resolve the discharge holdup in 5 minutes if he loaned me his badge."

He nodded, moving toward the elevator call button, his face contorted in amusement. "Cole is a cute kid."

Delaney's eyes brightened.

"He was a non-stop chatterbox about his dog, Rocket. Excellent with a frisbee."

"He loves *Guardians of the Galaxy*. Probably a little young for it though." She shrugged.

Jack tapped his leg twice and quietly sang a stanza of the Redbone classic.

Delaney bopped her head, joining in at the refrain. The click of a heavy door down the hallway silenced the m

He smiled appreciatively.

"You have a *remarkably* good singing voice, Dr. Mathison."

He grimaced and assessed the floor status of the elevators. "That's a fun movie. Except the first 5 minutes."

"Oh the first 5 minutes are brutal," she said, twisting her expression. "Actually, there's quite a bit of language and violence in that."

"Should we involve CPS?"

"It probably goes over his head, right?"

"*Nothing* goes over his head."

Her stomach clenched forward as she suppressed a laugh. "I heard it as soon as I said it."

"You follow him on outpatient?"

"I do." There was a fond flicker in her eye.

"You just did inpatient before, right?"

"Still do. It's just for him. We hit it off when he had one of his long hospital stays so they let me continue with him. I'd like to continue seeing more patients after they go home, but I stay pretty busy on acute." She broke eye contact to check her silver watch, fidgety suddenly. He took in her athletic hands, the defined muscles in them, an extra hair band around her right wrist, her long empty fingers. She noticed him staring and dropped her hands to her sides. "Sorry, I just remembered I told a patient's family I'd be by at 5 for caregiver training."

"You can blame me."

"Oh I plan to."

His instinct was to say something flirtatious, but thought better of it. "Do you still work on Rehab?"

"Occasionally they'll float me over when they have a pediatric patient or if they need vacation coverage. Usually I would have been seeing them already." She gave him a confused expression.

"You prefer working with kids?"

"It sounds bad, like I prefer cute puppies to a senior dog or something?"

"Peds patients can be tough. Going through so much, their outlook is so innocent and raw."

She nodded. "Yeah, that's true." There was more she wasn't saying. He could see it in the almost imperceptible drop of her shoulders, the quick flash of sadness in her eyes.

"Are you supposed to be off at 6?"

"No, was supposed to be off at 4, but I have a couple patients to go see. I just have to go borrow an adult walker for this teen patient I have. He's a big basketball player." She scanned the bank of elevators for the locations of the lifts, then eyed the stairwell.

"Wow, you're an early one, too, aren't you?"

"I am. They were going to be bumped because of staffing though. We have a new supervisor who thinks plans of care are just suggestions. I probably should—"

"Well if you're going to be around for a while tonight, maybe I'll see you again later," he said with casual suggestion. His audible change of tone seemed to trigger her to correct her posture. He checked her shoes for the presence of a heel. "Wow, you're tall. Most people end up looking up my nostrils."

She seemed to be suppressing another laugh. A sound that sounded like a half-sneeze emerged instead.

"It's okay to laugh, Delaney. Some might call it *therapeutic*."

She rolled her eyes and pointed to one of the elevators. "Okay, that elevator just flat out skipped this floor." She let her gaze drift across the empty corridor again, shifting her foot in the process, and as she did, she noticed him step forward and firmly push the dimmed call button.

He grinned sheepishly, stealing a glance out the corner of his eye. "Sorry. Can't blame a guy for wanting to get a couple more minutes with you."

She directed her body toward the elevators again, settled into her stance. "How do you like Anesthesiology?"

"I like it. I seem to only be tolerable in short doses so it's good that most of my patients get to fall asleep soon after meeting me."

She had only seemed half-resolved in her decision not to bolt for the stairwell, but she snapped to attention at his remark. "Why do you say that?"

"Well *you* can't seem to get away from me fast enough. For example." The elevator arrived and while Jack boarded right away, checking his pager, Delaney hesitated. He motioned to the space beside him. "I very rarely bite."

As she stepped on, he smiled to himself. A small victory.

"I didn't mean to be rude."

"You weren't. I'm the one who shamelessly kept you from your evening."

"Well, that's true."

"Do you work tomorrow?"

"*Yes.*" It sounded more like a question.

"I was thinking I would take you up on your offer of coffee."

She frowned. "Oh. I meant for *you* to get coffee."

"Alone, I know. What time do you start?"

"7."

"You're Type A so that means you're here at 6?"

"Typically, yes."

"The coffee bar opens about that time."

She frowned. "I don't think that's a good idea."

"Why's that?"

"Well--you're *married*, right?"

"So you're of the *When Harry Met Sally* mindset that men and women can't just be friends?"

Her face softened suddenly--to something mischievous and playful. "*When Harry Met Sally?* How old *are* you?"

He smirked.

"Actually I do love that movie, though I didn't see it until the 15th or 20th-anniversary release, I think. That must have been exciting for you to see it when it first hit theatres."

His head rotated slowly toward her, his cheeks tightened and red. "You're funnier than most millennials. Most are too busy being offended or Instagramming their food."

The elevator stopped on the 4th floor and a janitor with a very large bin nodded toward them. "I'll just wait for the next one."

She moved closer to Jack, her voice tight. "How *dare* you. My degree in safe spaces design could come in handy someday."

"Actually it could, the way this country is going. Of course we could be socialist by then—only the politicians and super rich will be able to afford safe spaces."

She shrugged as the door slowly closed. It immediately reopened as a new arrival tapped the call button. They simultaneously took a step back and a radiology technician stepped aboard with an ultrasound machine, uncaring about delaying their descent. He had his earbuds in and the music was blaring something likely labeled with parental advisories. Just as the doors closed, he examined the light panel and figured out he was on an elevator heading the wrong direction so he caught the doors just before they closed, stepped back off.

The janitor gave them an apologetic shake of his head.

Jack turned to her. "Going back to your earlier remark--I'm divorced. I was going through the divorce when I still worked on Rehab. Very little emotional baggage, I assure you."

She looked at him skeptically.

"I would very much like to get to know you, Delaney."

"Dr. Mathison—"

"Jack."

She sighed. "Jack—"

"I'll give you three good reasons why you should, then you decide."

The doors finally closed and the elevator was quiet, taking a painfully long time to continue its descent. "OK. 3 reasons. You have one floor."

He paused, just for a moment, to let her turn to face him. "#1: Coffee is a requirement at 6 am. #2: You're a tremendously hard worker and deserve a treat. The coffee, not me, but, you know—"

"Bonus?"

"Keep low expectations, I will be running on very little sleep after being on-call."

"Of course."

"#3--" He placed his fingertips on her cheek. He smiled when he saw her involuntarily take in a gulp of air and in a cool, soft voice, he said: "It's just coffee, Delaney."

She gazed at him until the elevator chimed. She waited for him to say something insinuating and immature, but his face remained resolved.

The doors opened on the third floor for Grant, one of the inpatient OTs. His eyes widened a bit seeing Delaney. "Hey lady. Aren't you supposed to be gone already?"

Then he noticed Jack's hand placement.

"Not yet," Delaney said, stepping around Jack's hand, glancing coyly over her shoulder as she turned toward the main inpatient therapy gym. There was a shimmer in her eye, accompanied by a hint of a smile. "Have a good night."

Grant and Jack exchanged an awkward greeting, as they both responded to her farewell.

The next morning, she came to her normal workstation and at first assumed someone had already claimed it. Of all the available computers, someone had placed their coffee at the one she always used. She tried to subdue her annoyance that she'd need to map to the network drive and printer. Then she looked closer at what was written on the side of the cup. "*Good morning, Sunshine.*" Below it was a sleeping face, captioned simply with "J."

"Seems you have an admirer," Julie said in a sing-song voice, taking a seat at the next computer. "*Another* one," she added in a whisper, eyeing Grant across the charting area, who appeared rather angry with the clinical notes he was reading.

"Good morning, Grant. You're here early," Delaney said politely.

He released some sort of gurgled greeting in response, rose up from his chair, gathering up his care cards, and left. "Mr. Caplan wanted to be seen early today," he explained under his breath.

Julie spun the next desk chair around and plopped down. "What did you *do* to that man?"

"I shouldn't have gone. It was just supposed to be a friend thing."

Julie raised an eyebrow.

Delaney sighed. "We were talking about movies one day, like months ago, and I mentioned how I was excited about the new Star Wars movie. He said he was, too, that he and a buddy of his were going to go--"

"Who?"

"Oh I don't remember. Drew, maybe?"

"No, who were you talking to about Star Wars?"

"Grant."

"Oh. You didn't tell me this--"

"Well he invited me along, his friend 'canceled' last minute, which was fine, but really seemed like a setup and then he tried to act like it was a date."

"Awkward."

"I didn't mean to hurt his feelings, but he kept looking over at me expectantly, he kept telling me I was 'pretty'." She fluttered her eyelashes.

"Man, I hate when guys tell me that."

Delaney rolled her eyes. "Here I was stuffing my face with popcorn and he's trying to make a move. I was so thrown off--like, sorry, I'm here for Harrison Ford."

"He's so old."

"Don't diss Han. That guy is the backbone of the whole Star Wars story."

"I thought it was Luke."

"Luke would be nothing without Han." Her eyes glazed over trying to focus on logging into the computer so she gave up, slumped back in the office chair. "And *then* they just killed him off. Lightsaber to the gut followed by a fall into an endless abyss--I mean, seriously? I'm sitting there mourning the loss and *he* was putting his hand on my leg." Delaney swept the imaginary hand off her leg. "The body's not even cold yet, dude."

"Um, spoiler?"

"It came out last year."

"I had no idea you were such a big *Star Wars* fan."

"My dad got me reading the books when I was in high school."

Julie's interest in the topic had clearly fizzled. "So what'd you tell him when he kept trying to turn it into a date?"

"I was honest."

"Uh-oh."

"Oh stop. I was nice. I told him I thought it was just a friends thing, that I didn't think it was the best idea for coworkers to date."

"OK, that's true."

"He avoided me a lot until I switched to Peds. Now he's been trying to talk more since we're not--wink, wink—" She nudged Julie's arm, imitating him. "--*really* coworkers anymore."

"And now you've got a doctor pursuing you."

"His name is Jack," she corrected, focusing on logging in again.

"Oh, sorry. Well, *Jack* is who I was asking about in the first place."

Delaney frowned, sitting back in her chair as the EMR booted. "What was the question?"

"What did you do to that man?"

"I didn't do anything."

"Really."

"Really. I woke him from a dead sleep so my patient could go home."

She pursed her lips. "Well, I think you should wake him up more often. He seems to like it."

"Stop it."

She nodded toward the coffee. "All he needed was to add a little puffy heart."

"You're obnoxious. 'It's *just* coffee,' Julie."

"Alright, then. I'm going to go get *myself* a coffee. I don't have a doctor delivering them to my desk like some people."

"It's *just* coffee," Delaney called after her.

"Then why are you blushing?" Julie said with a grin from the wide entrance to the gym.

Delaney grimaced, feeling her warm cheeks with the back of her fingers. She sighed, took a sip, and turned back to her computer. "Dammit, that's a good cup of coffee."

***

"I'm starting to think I enabled an addiction."

Delaney turned, startled, as she waited for her late afternoon coffee to be prepared. "Oh, caffeine and I go way back." As she fumbled a bit with stir sticks, she considered the hygienic concern of having them provided in such a way. It seemed irresponsible in a healthcare setting. She dropped the one she had picked back into the tub. "Who's stalking who now?"

"So, how are you this lovely day, Dr. Rhodes?"

"Delaney."

He gave her a sideways look.

"My name is Delaney...I'm not a doctor."

"You have your doctorate. Look—The badge people even had to shrink the font to fit your alphabet soup."

"Still."

"Fine, then call me Jack."

"Thank you for the coffee this morning."

He waited expectantly.

"Jack."

"You're very welcome, D." He perused the bakery case. "Do you mind terribly if I call you 'D'? I'd hate to be lumped into a group with the likes of Grant calling you 'Delaney.'"

"The 'group' being people who call me by my actual name, you mean?"

"I'd prefer to stand out in your mind a little."

"Mission accomplished."

"Excellent. My plan is working out perfectly."

"Actually, no one calls me that. It seems like the easiest way to shorten my name, doesn't it?"

"How many different nicknames do you have?"

She scrunched her nose. "Three? Laney is what most people call me, my dad calls me Dell or Dellie...well, now four with the addition of 'D.' Is that just the letter, or D-E-E?"

"Which do you prefer?"

She shifted her long hair behind her shoulder. It was a bit wavy from having it tied back. "Something is off-putting about D-E-E. I like the letter. It's more concise. And I have a stage name should my rap career take off."

He shuffled his feet. "I have a teenage cousin who calls me J-Dog. Maybe that would work if we collaborate on some songs."

"Oh, we might *collaborate*?" she said in a distinctly provocative tone. "And you've only just bought me coffee." She didn't quite recognize her own voice. "Wow. That was surreal."

He retrieved a stir stick from the tub, intending to present to her, but as she had turned away in embarrassment, he wound up presenting it to her ear. When she turned around, she was staring right at it, her eyes crossing reflexively. "This looks like a good one. I noticed you were indecisive about them before."

She glared at him, taking it.

"So what's the third nickname?"

"Oh I can't stand being called it." She retrieved her coffee from the counter when the enthusiastic Art History major called her name. "What kind of coffee *was that* this morning?"

"You liked it?"

"It was amazing."

"When do you work next? I'll bring you another."

"You're not going to tell me? I was planning to try to recreate it."

"House blend with coconut milk, but not the stuff they have here. It's too sweet. I keep a stash in the lounge of a brand that's more subtle. And a dash of cinnamon."

"No sugar?"

"Nope."

"You like coconut," she observed suspiciously, like this detail revealed something telling about him.

"Why do you say that?"

"Your hair smells like coconut."

"*Does* it?" He asked, crooking his eyebrow.

"You were invading my personal elevator space, you'll recall."

"Yeah, I believe I was," he said, approvingly. "I'm glad I had the good sense to shower that afternoon. Are you staying late again, or on your way out?"

"My sister's in town and she has my car. I'm supposed to be driving her to the airport, but she's running late." She sipped her drink and immediately scowled at it. "You've spoiled me."

He grinned. "I can take you to the lounge for the good stuff."

Her eyebrows jumped. "Oh, *can* you?"

"I did not mean that the way it sounded."

"She should be here any second anyway. I'll just deal with my mediocre coffee." She took another sip, equally dissatisfied. "You're here early if you're on call tonight."

"Meeting. It was canceled so I thought I'd caffeinate for the evening ahead."

"Here you are, *Doctor*," the enthusiastic Art History major said, his stubbled cheeks reddening a bit. "*You know* where to get the cream and sugar." He flipped his hair over his shoulder and turned to the next person in line.

Delaney stared at the side of Jack's head. He was grinning and motioned toward the corridor. "I'd prefer not to address that."

"Something tells me you routinely get extra punches on your loyalty card."

"That's client/barista privilege."

"I bet." She scrunched up her nose as she tried to restrain a laugh. "Wait, was mine the freebie?"

He shook his head, sipping his coffee. "No. But it earned me this one," he said, toasting her. "So, thank you."

"So we're even?" She was conscious of how large her smile had grown, how tight her cheeks.

"I wasn't keeping--"

"NeeNee, *there* you are." A woman with choppy blonde hair and noisy gladiator sandals descended upon them, her feet clapping against the marble floor. "I am going to *miss* my flight because you wanted coffee?"

Jack nodded appreciatively, as though to say--*and there's the missing nickname. NeeNee*, he thought silently, but he couldn't find any affection toward the name to be able to use it later, even in jest.

"You're an hour late, Caprice," Delaney said, her smile fading.

"I have the valet watching your car. You know, maybe if you had a car from this millenium I wouldn't have had to flirt with him so much to get him to watch it."

"First of all, I'm pretty sure you mean century--Secondly, it's a *valet*. It's their job to watch over cars."

"I'm out of cash." Caprice looked over her sister's shoulder and sucked in her cheeks.

Delaney stopped to take in her expression. "I know a five year old who would call that a fish face."

"Oh stop," Caprice said, waving her off. "Who is *this?*"

Delaney sighed regretfully. "Caprice, this is Jack. Jack, my sister Caprice," she said, starting toward the main entrance, uninterested in extending the interactions.

"Do you work together?" Caprice sized him up, glancing at his badge. "Wow, a *doctor?* What's your specialty?"

"Anesthesiology."

"*Wow. Anesthesiology,*" she said slowly, her eyes vacant of any understanding of what the word meant. "Wait—You're not dating though, right?"

Delaney shook her head, her hair following her head motion.

Jack found himself trailing behind her and Caprice followed, doing her best to touch him with each gesture.

"Dad mentioned the *other* doctor you were dating, NeeNee. If you're not dating *Dr. Mathison* here, are you still seeing *him?*"

Jack perked up at that, arching one thick eyebrow.

"You two are worse than Telephone." Delaney didn't turn around as she reached the driveway curb.

"I know what I heard." Caprice eyed his lab coat, feeling his shoulder. "That's not padded? That's *all* you?"

"Oh sweet baby Jesus," Delaney muttered. "Your flight?" She rotated on her heel. Her eye flickered over to Jack and her sister's hand now resting in the inside collar of his coat. She tilted her head inquisitively until he took notice. He didn't even see it happen.

She exhaled audibly, unimpressed by either of them and moved toward the valet station.

"So, heading home?" Jack asked, sliding surreptitiously away from Caprice, sipping his coffee.

"Yeah, I'm out in LA," Caprice said, nodding.

"What do you do?"

"I manage a lounge. Really upscale, members only. There's like a buy-in."

"Bars do memberships?"

Delaney performed a few heel lifts as she waited at the empty valet station.

"I only knew of the AHBA doing that—but membership was free."

"What's that?"

"American Honky-Tonk Bar Association? I was briefly a member."

Delaney paused mid-heel lift, glaring at him, mouth lifting on one side.

Caprice pressed on as his attention strayed. "So, I'm back in a few weeks."

This appeared to be news to Delaney. "I didn't get a reservation request."

"You have plenty of room at that new place of yours." She waved her hand dismissively. "It's really convenient to a lot of clubs, if you like dancing," she added, leaning more assertively into him.

"Is it?"

"The proximity to clubs was a huge selling point for me," Delaney explained, her voice channeling teenage snobbery.

He grinned. "It's a wonder it's not listed as a filter on Zillow."

"We should go to dinner, Dr. Mathison. I'm a lot more fun than my sister, right NeeNee?"

Delaney, a few yards away, narrowed her eyes. "What?"

"Aren't I a lot more fun than you?"

Delaney stared at her, then let her face go serious. "Oh yeah, my sister is infinitely more fun. A guaranteed good time."

Caprice play slapped his arm, having ninja-stepped into close proximity again. "See? She approves."

There was a disbelieving expression on Delaney's face. She turned around again, waving to the valet, who gave her a double take when he reached the podium. "Hi there, needing the keys for the Falcon in need of a paint job," she clarified. "Maximus Decimus Meridius over there drove her in." She motioned to Caprice, clapping around in her gladiator sandals.

Nick, the valet nodded, but he didn't pick up on the reference.

Jack watched Delaney gathering her hair at the nape of her neck. She released it in slightly tangled waves again once she realized she didn't have both hands free to tie it back properly. Caprice's voice was a buzz in the back of his ears.

Nick fumbled at the podium, continuously looking up at her. "I *just* had the keys."

"Take your time," she said, shifting her weight as she peered over her shoulder at her sister doing her best to inconspicuously draw attention to her breasts.

"Big into cars?" Nick asked, trying and failing to appear confident.

"Not really. My dad passed the car down to me, along with his big ears." She said this casually, then checked her watch. She suddenly felt a sense of dread if Caprice missed her flight. She was very much looking forward to a peaceful apartment again. She would need to wash linens and pillows--every fabric seemed to have soaked up the stench of nicotine despite Caprice claiming emphatically that she had given up smoking.

"No power steering huh?" Nick asked, trying to get a look at her ears, but they were covered by her dark hair.

"I was wondering how you got your biceps," Jack chimed in, taking several strides toward Delaney, his arm brushing hers. Caprice stayed back, pouting. She was incidentally much too old to be pouting for it to be remotely endearing.

The valet looked slightly offended to be removed from the conversation and started fishing around more deliberately for the keys.

"I'm going to go use the little girl's room since it seems I won't have time at the airport," Caprice announced in a huff.

Jack peered over his shoulder as she walked away, a bit of a stomp in her step. "Are you certain you two are related?"

"Half-sister."

"Is the other half Kardashian?"

Delaney peered over at him appreciatively, her face relaxing. She wore very little makeup, but she was easily the most beautiful woman he had ever seen. She blinked slowly, flirtatiously he thought, then turned her chin toward the sky. "It looks like we're getting rain tonight."

He shifted, deciding to accept her purposefully cliched topic. "Humidity is a bit higher today. There's a tropical storm down south that might be kicking some precipitation our way. I haven't checked the forecast."

She shook her head slightly, her lip turning up at the corner. "Yeah, okay, AccuWeather."

"They were in my pocket," the valet announced, jingling the keys before leaning in and putting them in the ignition.

Jack continued to watch her assess the clouds, the breeze sweeping stray strands of hair from her face, her eyes closing to enjoy the air on her skin.

"I do love the smell of rain," she murmured softly.

He made an effort to inhale deeply. The air smelled warm and thick. It's all he could manage to get from the effort.

"I would love to take you to dinner, D."

She opened her eyes, slowly turned to him. "You don't want to do that."

"Yes, I do."

"Why?"

"Why do I want to take you to dinner?"

"Yes." She seemed drained from the thoughts reeling in her head, her voice nearly a whisper.

He sighed, reached out and gently tucked a wild strand of hair behind her ear. "I've been told I make verbal lists a lot. Almost obnoxiously."

"You know, I've noticed that."

"Seems fitting in this case?"

She nodded. "OK, Jack. Let's hear your list."

"I could say you're brilliant, but that seems obvious to anyone who knows you professionally. I could say you're beautiful," he continued, noticing her eye flickered subconsciously at the remark," but that's also a given, *even* with those *gigantic* ears." He paused to examine them, moving the veil of hair briefly, then seemed to require a second look. "Good Lord, you must have *remarkably* good hearing."

"Tick tock." Her lips were pulled tensely into a smile.

"Right. #1: You responded more positively to the 'big ears' remark than to being called beautiful. I think there's a reason for that. I'd like to get to the bottom of it. #2: I already knew you were smart, but I think you're secretly quite funny, too." He raised his eyebrows. "And let me tell you--that is *insanely* sexy."

Delaney exhaled, waiting for him to finish.

"#3: I'm already looking forward to the next time I see you."

Her forehead creased. "I don't know if it's wise for me to fall for your charm," she said softly, leaning in as she spoke.

"So you find me charming?"

"It's not a subjective thing, Jack."

He grinned widely, letting a few seconds pass. "Are you *flirting* with me right now, D?"

"Well *that* was disgusting," Caprice groaned, wiping her hands on her shorts as she burst through the automated doors. "It's a *hospital* for Christ's sake."

"I don't think that was long enough for proper hand washing techniques," Jack whispered.

Delaney smirked, reluctantly stepped toward the driver side. "You're just carry-on, right?"

"Yeah, I read the air pressure is bad for bath products."

"Have a good night," Delaney said, nodding toward him.

"You too, D."

Caprice scoffed at him as she climbed into the passenger side. "You could have just said you were dating. Gross." As soon as she slammed the heavy door, he could see her making snipping remarks at Delaney, who looked past her to Jack, a thoughtful smile on her face.

It was six hours later that he was in the midst of a REM cycle when the click of the sleep room door lock caused him to sit bolt upright in bed thinking he'd missed a page. Being the Anesthesiology sleep room, he hadn't thought much about using the secondary deadbolt. He squinted in the dark as a tall figure approached him. With her, she brought the scent of night air, fresh laundry, and some sort of citrus. She traced the edge of the bed with her fingertips and once she touched his arm, climbed onto the bed. She found his face, gently leaned over his chest and kissed him.

"I'm sorry to keep disrupting your sleep like this, Jack."

"Who's Jack?" He said groggily.

"I can smell the coconut from your shampoo."

"I've been meaning to compliment you on that olfactory system of yours. It's very impressive."

"People don't appreciate it."

"People are idiots."

"Jack?"

The tips of her hair were damp--it must have been raining after all.

"Yes?"

"Kiss me."

# 2

# echo

Four years later...
Her throat felt like sandpaper, her mouth like it was coated in cotton balls.

"Laney, can you hear me?" a man's voice asked. He sounded like he was calling to her from down a  long tunnel. She didn't recognize his deep, jovial voice. Santa Clause. He sounded like how you would expect Santa Clause to sound.

Another voice, drawn out and garbled, like it was being played from a mangled cassette tape. A woman.

A leaky faucet, each water droplet bellowing around a stainless steel sink. Drip. Drip. Drip.

Drip.

Something had burned nearby recently, more potent than paper.

Her throat, coated in something antiseptic and raw, scraped, itchy. She tried to generate saliva, swallowing again and again.

She sniffed, her nostrils congested and useless, despite allowing the entry of unpleasant aromas--burning steel, rubbing alcohol, something foul and pungent.

She wasn't getting enough air. She gulped some through her mouth, but its contact in the back of her throat made her gag.

"Put the mask on her."

She flinched, hands from the right suddenly strapping something to her face. The mask immediately forced air through her impossible nostrils. It was concentrated and dry, like pressurized airplane air, but it eliminated the odors. She closed her mouth and took some deep inhales through her nose.

"That's it," a woman's voice murmured close to her right ear. The proximity and the clarity startled her. She recoiled slightly, her shoulder jumping to her ear.

"Give her some space."

She slowed her breathing, letting her dry lips part. She counted her breaths out silently—1 to 10, on exhale, 10 to 1. As she did this, she became aware of a throbbing in her head. It became so excruciating so quickly that the pain seemed to echo against the walls of her skull like church bells.

Her hands balled into fists and she beat at the sheets of the mattress, but it didn't feel satisfying or powerful. If she was making any impact, it was small taps at best and it seemed to make the throbbing inside her skull worse. Her body convulsed, every muscle group clenched.

The blanket was thrown hastily from her feet, cold air seeping up her legs.

"Just the left foot," Saint Nick observed. "Laney, wiggle the toes on your right foot, if you can." His voice was closer, clearer, less jovial.

*Right foot.*

Nothing.

The covers were tossed back in place.

"Laney," the fake Santa said, stepping even closer. "Can you open your eyes?"

*Stop talking. Stop talking.*

A steel tray dropped to the floor, spilling its contents, glass shattered, someone swore. It could have been 100 feet away, but her ears seemed to vacuum up the noise. The harsh clatter of sounds bounced wildly against the confines of her skull.

One syllable pressed through the chaos. One syllable made everything else fall away.

"D."

*Say it again,* she pleaded.

"D."

She turned her chin toward the source of the voice, away from the loud, foot fetish obsessed, white-bearded fat man. She winced as the other noises tried to force their way back to her consciousness. Her body seemed to be waking up. She felt every jolt of every nerve, every muscle, every joint.

Warm fingers on her cheek. *Jack.*

"Should she be feeling this much pain?" his voice was whispered, sensitive to her eardrums. An ally.

She took some heavy breaths, her nose and cheeks warm and sweaty beneath the mask.

His thumb wiped away a tear from her cheek.

Louder, sharper voices across the room. She squeezed her eyes, the overhead lights filtering through her eyelids, their voices piercing her eardrums.

Air forced toward her, the shadow of insistent arm gestures on her face. A darkened room. A small relief. She relaxed her closed eyes, breathing.

A presence close to her face. Fingers tracing her cheek. She slowed her breathing. She would not feel the pain pulsing through her brain. She would not hear the noises that clattered in her head so loudly she felt them in her bones. She would not think of how the right side of her body felt numb yet ached mercilessly.

She would instead focus on the gentle, warm fingers on her cheek.

A woman's whisper, harsh like the hiss of a snake--something about morphine.

Lips surrounded by prickly stubble pressed to her forehead.

The noises quieted, like an infant's cries as he eases into sleep. The pain ebbed, receding from her head, her body, like a wave flowing back to the sea.

And then, nothing.

# 3

# impact

When Julie first started working on Rehab, she had been shocked to discover that Delaney had, what Julie had determined, was an unsatisfying social life. Delaney had listed off all the things that filled her life--Work, gym, regular hiking and kayaking, reading, occasional movies, obligatory work events, monthly volunteering--and had argued that she felt fairly fulfilled, to which Julie had rolled her eyes like an insolent teenager. Julie argued that the only social activities in that list were the last two and volunteering didn't count because she only interacted with children. She had unsuccessfully set her up on a number of blind dates as a result of her assessment. She had begun to question her own judgement as each of these men, whom she had been fond of previously, suddenly had the charm of an assertive telemarketer asking about Delaney.

It was at a happy hour for one of the departing therapists that Julie decided she wasn't going to accept Delaney's conclusion about Jack, that he just had a temporary crush. They had stepped away from the group to play cornhole in the outdoor area, the outer perimeter lined with strings of globe lights.

"I really don't understand, Laney. I've set you up on dates—"

Delaney chucked the bean bag and it hit alongside the cornhole board. "I know, Julie. Dating is just not a priority for me. And these men—"

"No connection?"

"*No* connection."

"Try telling *them* that. You know, I get more calls asking about you than I get for myself."

"I doubt that."

Julie scoffed, not really wanting to confirm that it was the truth. "You must be really good in the sack."

"Julianna Beverly Patton."

"*Well*, have you? Slept with any of them?"

She grimaced. "I have."

"What's with the face? You're a grown woman. You're allowed." Julie's eyes widened. "*Who?*"

"Of the men you've set me up with?" She rolled her eyes. "Tom—and Mike."

Julie contorted her face. It was expressions like that which made her look about sixteen years old. "Who's *Mike?*"

"Sports medicine doctor? Michele Bordeaux."

"Oh. Right. I kind of regretted not keeping that one for myself. Not that he would have been interested."

Delaney shrugged. "Actually I could see you two having more in common. He's nice. We went out a couple times."

"Sloppy seconds?"

"You set me up with him."

"Yeah, okay."

"These guys don't feel a connection with me either."

"They seem to disagree."

"No, they just want to have sex. That's different." She chucked another bag. "How do you know?"

Delaney navigated her phone until she found Mike's most recent text—an animated gif of Austin Powers saying "You feeling horny?"

She studied the gif then giggled. "'You feelin' horny, baby. Yeah.' Oh come on! That's funny."

Delaney raised her eyebrow. "Here, I'll send you his contact info, in case you no longer have it."

"I guess Austin Powers isn't for everyone. Okay, so you're looking for more wooing, more romance?"

"Something other than Austin Powers. Not buying roses or writing sonnets, but--"

"*They* should try bringing you coffee," Julie said, her eyes wide.

"Coffee's a much better idea, but they'd use the wrong creamer *for sure.*" Delaney smiled to herself.

"Is that a euphemism?"

"Is *what* a euphemism?"

"*Creamer.*"

"You scare me, Julie." Delaney stared at her, Julie's cheeks reddening." No, it's not a euphemism. Seriously. Call Mike Bordeaux. You'll hit it off."

"Stop it. So why do you sleep with them? For extra cardio?"

"Funny." Delaney shrugged. "I guess I keep hoping it will feel different."

"You don't enjoy it?"

"Not really, no."

"Really?" She tilted her head, trying to find something in Delaney's expression. "Oh, Laney."

She shrugged. "I don't feel anything for them so I don't have the desire to be *intimate.*"

"Can't you just appreciate their--*physical* characteristics?"

"If I'm not attracted to them in any other way, I don't have any interest in what they look like." She fished the bean bags out of the hole and around the board. She decided not to share the panic that rushed through her when they touched her, how her skin seemed to retreat from their fingers.

"You're telling me you never lost yourself in the thralls of passion?" Julie's voice had become increasingly louder. Delaney was about to shush her when: "What about Jack?"

She found she couldn't inhale fully. "What about him?"

"Are you attracted to *him?*"

Delaney took an extended amount of time lining up her toss.

"You're not going to answer?"

"No."

"You *like him*," she said in a sing-song voice, smiling widely.

Delaney tossed the bean bag about a foot off the target. "Why are you on my case about this?"

"Oh my--you like *really* like him."

"Drop it."

Julie studied her, frowning. "No, I don't think I will. I don't think I'm going to drop it until I am matron of honor at your wedding."

"So you're getting married. Is it Mike Bordeaux? Did you already text him? Because you two really seem like a good fit."

"No, you and Captain Jack's wedding."

"Well 'matron' is only used if *you're* married." She raised her eyebrows. "You'd currently be referred to as 'Maid of Honor,' Miss Patton."

"You sure know a lot about weddings for someone who's supposedly not interested."

"It's common knowledge."

Julie tensed her lips, shaking her head. "You like him."

"Why won't you drop this?"

"Because this one seems *different.*"

"How?"

Julie sipped her beer. "You haven't even given him a chance."

"Yes I did."

"You slept with him?"

Delaney raised her eyebrows, gave her a quick nod.

"*And* how did you feel? My God, when did this happen? After the coffee? Before the coffee?" She lowered her voice, her eyes wide. "Did you feel the *thralls of passion?*"

Delaney exhaled, remembering his hands bracing her face with such gentleness—those strong, strong hands. She thought of how close he held her, how she had gasped involuntarily when he wrapped his thick arms around her, finding herself pressing their bodies together, unable to get close enough. "What?" She said, dropping her arms at her sides.

Julie shook her head.

"He's asked for us to get together. I'm assuming for--" Delaney noticed some younger teens approaching and stopped short. "Hey, were those guys in your graduating class for PT school?"

Julie glanced over her shoulder. "Laney, those guys are like 16."

Delaney smirked.

"Nice change of subject," Julie spat. "How do you know that's what he wants?"

"He's kind of a flirt, right? He's probably been a part of the sixth floor club before."

"This was in the *sleep rooms?*"

"You said I should wake him up again." Delaney sank a bean bag dead center and did an impromptu victory dance to the beat of the song blaring from the bar.

Julie laughed in surprise. "I'm impressed. That doesn't seem like you at all."

She stopped dancing. "You make me sound like such a dull person, Julie."

"You're not dull, but--"

"But what?"

"You're all business, Laney."

"I'm boring?"

Julie was thoughtful. "*No,* not boring."

"A b with an itch?"

"A what?" The statement registered in her eyes. "Oh no. You're not *'a b with an itch.'* You're direct, but you're friendly. You're kind. You're really giving of yourself--especially to your patients."

"Then what, Julie?"

"Just--*serious*. With anyone who's over the age of, say, twelve."

They stood quietly sipping their drinks, Delaney pondering sharing the knock-knock joke told to her by a six year old that morning, but decided it didn't support her case.

"He's not really a flirt," Julie finally concluded. "I heard about him with a few nurses when he came on as a doctor, but nothing for awhile--and who knows if that was even true? He keeps a low profile. Lower than you, you little sleep room temptress."

"It was one time."

"Exactly. You're constantly being pursued by men, right?"

"Not *constantly*."

Julie raised her eyebrow. "You are. My point is—You pursued him." She squinted at her, picking up on something in Delaney's expression, and dropped her shoulders conclusively. "You slept with him to see if he'd be like the others and only be after--"

Delaney thought about his strong, capable hands around her back. Other men would suction their hands on her breasts, seem to develop all out tentacles, hiss in her ear asking if it felt good, only wanting one response, not really caring about anything but it adding to their own enjoyment. With Jack, it was like their bodies melted together, like she lost sense of where in the world she was. He didn't want one or two parts of her--he wanted all of her.

"I don't know what you're thinking about, but do you know, I just have to mention him and you smile?"

"No I don't."

"That wasn't a question. You do. And not like that bizarrely silly therapist you are with kids. A *real* smile." She let that sink in. "Maybe that means something."

Delaney sighed. "Well, what if it does? Yes, I'm attracted to him. I was attracted to him two years ago--" She frowned when she saw Julie's eyes bulge in their sockets. "I should *not* have said that. Forget I said that."

"I will not."

"Yes, it felt different, but what difference does that make if he doesn't--"

"Doesn't what?"

She lowered her eyes.

"How can someone who looks like you--" Julie seemed exhausted by her, waving the thought away.

"What?"

In a wise voice that sounded much older than she appeared, she said: "It means you should *try*, Laney." Then she toasted her with her frothy beer glass, the youthfulness returning and headed to the bar for a refill.

***

It was as she finished in the weights area and was heading toward the locker rooms to change into her bathing suit that Delaney spotted a familiar figure with unkempt blonde curls stretching against the wall just outside the racquetball courts. It was as though Julie had planted him there. She shook her head, pulling out her earbuds as she approached him.

A woman in a moisture wicking ensemble that featured a lightsaber-esque pattern straight out of the eighties bent down to pick up her Fiji water bottle. She did this slowly and deliberately, peering back at Jack like the start of a low budget porn film. Then she stretched toward the ceiling, parading herself in a small circle so she'd have to pass him.

"It's warm in here today," she said, patting her sweaty cleavage.

"Is it?" He raised his eyebrows and walked the opposite direction, looking a little cross.

The woman continued her swagger toward the ellipticals before determining it wasn't a love connection.

"That's some tattoo—I thought lower back tattoos had lost popularity."

Jack made eye contact with Delaney, dropping his expression once he realized he probably looked too happy to see her, given she hadn't so much as replied to his text--a simple one line:

*I miss your smile, D. -Jack*

"I wouldn't know. What was it?" He pulled the disinfectant spray and paper towel from the wall, double backed to the rowing machine.

"WWJD."

He stopped mid-step. "On a tramp stamp? That just seems wrong."

Delaney assessed the roped off group of rowing machines. "Wow, what's this about?"

"Marathon training group, apparently. They block those off certain days of the week."

"That's inconvenient." She took a sip at the drinking fountain between the rowers and basketball courts to give herself something to do other than watch him clean the machine.

"Well I'll tell you—Jesus would have wiped down the machine after He used it," he said, returning the cleaner to the wall and throwing away the paper towel. "Although I could only dream to sit in the sweat of our Lord and Savior."

She smirked, her lips tight, then found herself doubling over where she stood.

"Your laughs always seem to take you by surprise," he observed, releasing his neutral expression.

She stood upright again, composing herself. "Well of all modern cardio equipment, I do think this would be Jesus's machine."

"I know he can walk on water, but maybe he prefers rowing for longer distances."

"Keep the robes from getting wet," she suggested, adjusting her stance, searching for casual conversation. "I'm surprised I haven't seen you here before--I didn't realize you were a member here."

"Maybe if you stayed the other night, you would know." He was glad to see she had picked up on his playful tone.

"That would have come up in conversation?"

He grinned, checking over his shoulder for any eavesdroppers. The closest gym occupant was two rows up with earbuds in. "You know—'that was incredible, how do you bend like that, I love the feeling of you in my arms, maybe we can get some food...and oh yeah, I just joined Gains, maybe we could work out sometime.'" He frowned. "Had somewhere you needed to be?"

"I stayed until 5, there was no offer for food between rounds of snoring--you know, you really might benefit from a sleep study--and I had to get ready for work."

This information seemed to please him. "That was *very* rude of me not to offer you a snack or perhaps a beverage from the vending machine."

She scanned his face, deciding something internally it seemed.

"Can I make it up to you?"

"I had a good time, Jack," she said quietly.

He crouched to the seat of the rower with an exaggerated groan.

"Oh stop it. You're not that old."

He moved much more fluidly, getting himself positioned. "Would you like to get some food after you're done here? I was planning to grab a smoothie and watch *Biggest Loser* at the cafe. I find the weigh-ins life affirming."

She frowned, processing his remark.

"I guess that's not 'food,' per say."

"I had a late lunch anyway. They make pretty good smoothies?"

"They do."

"I don't do kale or wheatgrass."

"You forget, I know how you like your coffee."

She smiled tightly, looking across to the empty basketball court and back. "Yeah, I suppose you do."

"I'll come up with something you'll like. I was going to work off some pudge here first though." He patted his toned stomach. "Unless you're done?"

She smirked and tried not to have her eyes linger or think of four nights earlier when she gained some intimate knowledge of his body, including that washboard stomach, which she had kissed repeatedly at one point. "No I still have laps to do."

"Ah you're a swimmer."

"Michael Phelps is a swimmer. I don't think he'd appreciate being categorized with me." She checked the wall clock. "7:15 maybe?"

"We'll miss the recap, but yes."

"Okay then. I'll leave you to fight the non-existent flab." With that, she strolled to the women's locker room, her dark ponytail flopping against her back, her turquoise racerback tank accentuating her tan, well-defined shoulders. She unexpectedly caught her reflection in the mirror after changing into her racing swimsuit in a restroom stall. Her cheeks were certainly red from the earlier workout, but they were also tensed into a wide smile.

"Oh, shut up Julie. I see it."

45 minutes later, Jack watched her re-emerge from the locker room, wearing black capri leggings and an oversized gray pullover. Her dark hair was wet and pulled on top of her head in a haphazard knot. He stood as she crossed the cafe flooring change threshold.

"You weren't kidding," she said, eyeing the flat screen centered on the wall over the seating area. "You really watch this?"

"It's the only reality show I'll watch. Well, *Amazing Race* has some appeal, too."

"Yeah, I like that one."

"Early evening tends to be quiet when I'm on-call. They're a few weeks in so their workouts are getting more impressive." He pulled back the chair opposite him, but she stopped short.

"Couch is open," she observed, motioning to the boxy black leather sofa.

"It seemed too--intimate? I didn't want to presume--"

She grinned at him fondly. "Unpadded chairs are a killer for me--bad hip." She cocked an eyebrow at him and made her way to the couch. The show went to commercial just as she took a seat. "I have to be honest—this is not the social life one imagines for an attractive single doctor."

"I shall have to make myself attractive so I can find out first hand." He grabbed both red-orange smoothies and joined her.

"Oh stop it. You look like a young, blonde James Garner and you know it."

"'A young, blonde James Garner,'" he repeated slowly. "No, I didn't know that. That's a good thing?"

"Oh God, yes." She pursed her lips. "I mean, *yeah*, you're alright." She gave him a sideways smile.

He placed the drinks on the coffee table and followed her lead to sit on the couch. He noticed that she tucked one of the throw pillows under her right hip so he sat on her left side.

"What's the story on the hip? This isn't a traditional PT compensatory strategy, is it?"

"Not exactly ergonomic huh? Don't tell the other PTs on me. The pressure helps with the pain."

"Your secret is safe with me."

"So it's your night off—why aren't you living it up at a bar or club?"

"Why aren't *you*?"

She reached for one of the cups. "I've never really thought of myself fitting in somewhere like that. I'm also anti-social."

He chuckled. "Makes two of us. In my mind, I think I have the potential to be this really outgoing person, living it up, but it's just not me. I feel like *Grey's Anatomy* gave me unrealistic expectations of a career in medicine."

"Well except for the sleep room."

He grinned. "Actually the sleep room, as of a few nights ago, far exceeded any Hollywood expectations."

"Not before then?" She peered over at him as she let her hair loose, a cascade of dark waves.

He was temporarily dazed, seduced by the action. It look him a moment to realize she had asked him a pointed question. "What do you mean?"

"Rumor has it you've been quite social with some of the nurses?" Her face wasn't judgmental. It was inquisitive, as though she'd asked where he grew up.

"Is that right?"

"It's a rumor. I learned early on that just because someone says something, it doesn't make it true, but I do think it's something I'm going to want to know your answer to."

He frowned. "Honestly, I let the doctor thing go to my head when I first got back. It probably didn't help that I was rebounding from my divorce."

She processed this. With her fresh, makeup free face, he noticed she had more freckles than he had realized. The cluster set on her high cheekbone drew his interest. It looked like a constellation. She narrowed her eyes and gave the smallest of shrugs. "OK."

"OK?"

She rotated back to retrieve her cup. "Yeah."

"Does it bother you?"

"It wouldn't do much good to be bothered by something I can't change--right?" Delaney turned her attention to the television.

His mind went to the remark her sister had made about the "other doctor," but he decided against asking.

She relaxed into his chest as the show returned from commercial. He was pleased with his decision to have a proper shower and change into clean clothes, though he wasn't fond of the faux woodsy aroma of the body wash provided in the showers, particularly since she seemed to have such a keen sense of smell.

She burrowed gently into him. "No offense, Doc, but you smell funny."

"I'm sorry--I don't normally shower here and the gym has evidently decided men should smell like Pine Sol."

"Ah. Pungent." She peered up at him, her mouth curling up on the side closest to him.

"Whatever they have on the women's side smells much better."

Her body tensed momentarily. "Oh I bring my own stuff. The women's side has something with peppermint and tea tree oil. It's a little strong for my taste."

"Ah." He sniffed her neck. "Oranges?"

"Grapefruit and lavender." She had one hand strewn across his knee and the other relaxed in her lap, like this was a frequent occurrence, like they'd sat together like this a thousand times before.

It was as he had become terribly amused by this that he noticed a pale, puffy scar on her right wrist. It was a jagged line that extended up her arm, disappearing under the gray sleeve.

"You know, I would probably *be like* Jillian if I were a coach, but I'd much prefer Bob if I were on this show. He seems to tend to emotional needs better."

He snapped to attention as she looked over at him again, but it was too late. She glanced down to her exposed wrist, adjusting the sleeve thoughtfully.

He felt both shock at what he had seen and guilt that he'd imposed on something she wasn't prepared to share. He fully expected her to leave.

She moved to the edge of her seat, setting down her cup. He tried to quickly come up with something to say, an apology of sorts for what she'd gone through to want to hurt herself.

Rather than leaving, she wiggled her arm out of the sweatshirt as modestly as possible and presented it. The scar became much more jagged higher up, but where one might expect it to end if it were truly a suicide attempt, it continued, splitting in several places, and ending just above the inside of her elbow.

"I have a lot of these," she said softly. She silently pulled the hair back at her right temple to get to her scalp, revealing a thin, cleaner looking scar that stretched far into her dark hair. "I have some across my stomach and legs, too. They're a little rougher looking than this."

His eyes examined her skin, his fingertips gently tracing the scar on her forehead, then the long branch-like scar that stretched from her elbow onto her palm. It was as though they had materialized out of nowhere. He'd gazed in her direction on a number of occasions and he, honest to God, had never noticed them. "Jesus, D. What happened?"

"Car accident."

He stroked the tender skin on the underside of her arm.

"They thought I'd lose my arm, or at least lose any usefulness in it, there was so much damage. My right knee and most of my leg shattered and I had a serious head injury."

His attention was drawn back to her forehead, her temple, trying to imagine what she must have looked like when the wounds were raw and gaping. It hadn't been a plastic surgeon doing the stitching--it was too sloppy.

He frowned. "This happened recently?"

"No, when I was 15."

His eyes widened, questioningly. "I never noticed them before."

"Oh. Well we only really saw each other in passing."

"You were 15?"

"My mom and I were a few miles from home when this guy ran a redlight and t-boned us. His car hit my mom's side and a pickup truck with a pretty solid grille guard hit mine, hence why I'm a swimmer now instead of a runner."

He tried to absorb this information. "Your mom--"

"Died before they could get us out."

He shook his head, exhaling. "I'm sorry."

She watched him examine the scars, but was focused on the tingling the light touch of his fingertips was causing throughout her body.

"How long were you in the hospital?"

"5 months. Almost 2 at Horizon."

"Dr. Schuler used to work over there before he came here to start Rehab."

"That's how we met."

He could recall seeing Dr. Schuler hug her with paternal affection. Now it made sense. "No wonder he's so fond of you."

"Papa Schuler."

"Pardon?"

"Oh it's a joke. We had dinner and someone called me his granddaughter."

"They thought you were his biological granddaughter?"

She smiled.

"I'm surprised he ever let you switch from Rehab to Peds."

"They were short-staffed on Peds so they kept pulling me and I really enjoyed it." She pursed her lips, squinting one eye. "I'm going to put my arm away now."

She slid her arm back in her sleeve, sat back a little. "He tracked me down over there one day in the pediatric gym and watched my session. After I took my patient back to his room—Alexis. 8 year old heart transplant recipient. Smartest kid I've ever met—I swear that girl is going to be the next great inventor— *anyway*, he met me out in the hallway, smacked me on the back and told me I was fired from Rehab."

"Sounds like him."

She nodded absentmindedly, then exhaled. "Do the scars—change anything?"

"Why would they change anything?"

"They freak some people out when they see them."

"Honestly, I never noticed them," he replied. "I was too distracted by your gargantuan ears."

A laugh escaped her mouth, like a half hiccup, her cheeks tightening into a broad smile.

"I need to tell you something," she said, her eyes glistening a bit.

He waited, mind still reeling from what she had told him already.

"My mom had me in modeling from the time I was a baby."

This was not what he was expecting, but he nodded, noticing how she suddenly looked more uncomfortable in her own skin than he'd ever seen. Still, it was an unusual change of subject and his face reflected that. "I can't say I'm surprised," he finally said. "I mean, you're absolutely the most beautiful woman in any room--"

He intended the remark as a compliment, but it seemed to make her uneasy. She shook her head. . "I look like *her* and I think she always regretted a little not reaching her full potential with it." She winced, shifting her leg, turning toward him.

His eyes drifted to the scar by her temple again.

"I had finally worked up the courage to tell her I wanted to quit the day of the accident."

He frowned. "You didn't like modeling?"

"Hated it."

This brought him some relief, but he wasn't sure why.

"The conversation didn't go well at first. We were on our way to a photoshoot--wedding dresses--"

"15 year olds model wedding dresses?"

She crooked her eyebrow.

He found himself both appalled at this practice, but he was admittedly curious to see some of her modeling photos.

She stared at her hands and this led to him seeing the puffy white scar again. He no longer felt as curious. "After the shoot, she was more understanding. They usually discouraged parents from watching the shoot, but she came in toward the end."

"What did she see?"

"One of the photographers didn't realize I was 15--or he did—based on what he was asking me to do. Either way, she was OK with my decision after that." She swallowed hard. "We'd just stopped to have burgers and milkshakes, something I'd *never* been allowed to have, sort of a celebratory dinner to end that chapter."

Jack smiled lightly, imagining the relief she must have felt.

"I remember we were talking about the ridiculous accessories they had me wear. One headdress thing they raved about was literally half a peacock on my head. Poor bird." She rolled her eyes, dropping her gesturing hands to her lap. She seemed to be visibly changing the direction of the conversation as she adjusted her position on the couch.

Jack gazed at the tender pink of her fingertips, her long thin fingers. He very much wanted to reach out and take her hand.

She took a breath before continuing, her eyes meeting his again: "I was never allowed to smile." She let that statement hang. "Fourteen years, I was never allowed to smile. Apparently my look was more 'high fashion' and they made it sound like if I smiled, it would make me ugly."

He narrowed his eyes at the suggestion.

"No, that's inaccurate. They didn't 'make it sound,' they told me I was unattractive when I smiled and smiling would make me ugly--lines, wrinkles, all that."

He shook his head.

"I guess it's a tough habit to break. Sometimes it's like I still expect to get scolded anytime I smile. I feel self-conscious about it."

He thought of a particularly strict teacher in school. During exams, she'd float around the room, as though on wheels, carrying a meter stick, tapping it rhythmically against her opposite palm, weaving in and out of the desks. If anyone's eyes lifted from their paper, the stick would whip down and snap the corner of the desk. Even when he took his board exam, when he raised his chin to glance out the window, he jolted, hearing that whipping noise in his head. He tried to imagine feeling that anxiety every time he felt even a small bit of happiness.

As he thought about it, he realized that when he'd observed her when he was an OT, she didn't smile much. There'd be small friendly expressions of acknowledgement, but very little, if any, actual smiling. Some of the therapists had interpreted this as snobbery, despite her kind and encouraging nature with patients—at that point, rehab patients.

"It's different with my Peds patients," she said, reading his thoughts. "I laugh a lot with them. That's why I love working with kids. They want you to be silly. They like you more if you make crazy ugly faces. Older patients don't care for that much," she added, joking he decided.

He could imagine her posing in one of those dramatic photographs--her piercing blue eyes gazing out with haunting intensity from the pages of a magazine. The image, though beautiful, suddenly made him uneasy.

"The point I'm getting to--I hardly know you so this might sound a little-- forward?"

He straightened up at that, involuntarily.

Her big eyes focused on him. "You make me smile--and I don't even think twice about it."

He inhaled reflexively, taking in the details of her face--her thick eyelashes, her high, prominent cheekbones, the constellation of freckles. "I'm pretty sure that's the best compliment I've ever received, Delaney."

"I thought you weren't going to call me that because of Grant," she whispered.

"*Who?*" he replied with a confused grin.

Her face softened, her eyes seeming to brighten by a shade or two as she turned back to the television, her head resting again on his chest.

When the show went to commercial, he spoke quietly toward her ear. "I'm off this weekend--was planning to go up to Havasu Canyon and camp out, but would gladly cancel that to do just about anything with you."

It's one place she had seen in pictures, with its turquoise water and red rock walls, but had never gotten around to visiting. "Don't cancel your plans."

He furrowed his eyebrows.

"Would you take me with you?" She asked, watching the car dealership commercial without hearing a word of it.

His smile was audible next to her ear.

They watched the rest of the show in casual bliss, remarking on the workouts, both drawn to the same couple of contestants, annoyed by the contestant that thought she "knew her body best" so she didn't want to listen to the nutritional advice. She lost the least amount and was eliminated. The update at the end showed her still struggling, reaching a plateau after losing 27 pounds on the show. As the credits rolled, Delaney frowned. "I hope she didn't gain it all back." Her shoulders slumped. "She was really irritating, but for her daughter's sake?" She stretched as she stood. "*This* is why I can't watch reality shows."

He motioned for her drink cup, which she handed over after taking one last slurp of mostly air, and he dropped it in the recycle bin. "Madam, may I walk with you to retrieve your sweaty gym bag?"

"Why yes. Yes you may."

He stopped her abruptly. "D, I'm curious about something."

She rolled her shoulders, tilting her head inquisitively toward him.

"What *does* a crazy ugly face look like?"

She immediately grasped both ears, pulled them out as far as she could, bugged out and crossed her eyes, and contorted her mouth into a deformed fish face, tongue out.

He burst out laughing.

"That one's my favorite," she said, smiling broadly.

# 4
# day four

Dr. Schuler was never great at disguising his feelings. He could keep a flawless poker face when he was jesting in good fun, but when it came to things that mattered to him, his emotions radiated off of him. If a patient had made remarkable progress, if one of the "cuties"--typically 80-90 year old women had just gushed over him or insisted on giving him a kiss, his face would light up with a boyish smile. If medical status had declined for a patient that had been doing well, it felt like the unit was enclosed in a thick, dark cloud.

It would be a gloomy day on Rehab. He rubbed at his smooth, almond face, his eyes heavy, his fist pressed into his cheek as he began team conference.

"We have a lot to go over, everyone. We have a couple new patients, which we'll review first. There's a name on the list everyone should recognize so let's review her first--Ms. Rhodes in 88. Delaney is a transfer from acute. 29. Eight weeks ago, a stroke alert was called in the employee cafeteria after she was observed to have had facial drooping, loss of speech, and weakness in her limbs. She was taken immediately to Radiology for a scan, observed to have suffered an intracerebral hemorrhage from a weakened blood vessel, likely from traumatic head injury she suffered about 14 years ago. Surgery was done almost immediately and seemed to be successful, but Laney remained in a coma for several days. She awoke spontaneously, but due to concerns of swelling and fluid accumulation in the brain, she was put into a medically induced coma to allow her brain to heal and swelling to subside. She had EVD placement and a couple days later, it was removed. She also experienced deep venous thrombosis, recurrent fevers--finally released from ICU to Neuro on the acute side after a 47 day stay."

He stared down at the stack of papers before him, speaking in a flat voice. "With the acute stay, she's at 68 onset days. We had neuro patients down to, what, six?"

The care coordinator nodded, regretfully.

"Those early days are so critical," he reflected, rubbing at his face again. "We've been doing pseudo-rehab on the acute side, but so far, not as much progress as I'd like to see." He chose not to share what everyone knew—that ICU had suggested discharging her to a skilled nursing facility because they didn't see her potential to recover. "This is likely due to medical complications and from her becoming really deconditioned so we've had to dial it back. She was finally medically cleared and now she's ours."

The team had already heard how he fought leadership to reopen a room that wasn't slotted to open again for a week because of the yearly deep cleans. He had been holding a bed for her ever since she was admitted on acute, but the day before she was to come over, they had forced through an admit when he had a day off. A few staff members had been startled by the bellowing of his voice against the office walls after the administrator had disappeared inside. Some had said he had punched a filing cabinet during the conversation, which was all very uncharacteristic of him. He typically internalized his frustration, indicating his inner thoughts with a flicker of something in his eye.

"All of you have had a chance to work with her for a couple days now, I'm assuming. How's she doing?" he asked the room.

Julie leaned forward apprehensively, her thick blonde hair clipped back in a half updo. She wore far less than her typical amount of makeup, seemingly applied to serve no other purpose than making her look less tired. "She looks quite a bit better than when I first saw her after the bleed. I know the right side of her body is affected, but I notice some deficits on the left, especially that arm and hand. It looks a lot like the right, with that clenched, claw shape. Decreased grip strength. Not quite as severe as the right, but still, I wouldn't expect it--"

"I noticed that, too. She just had a CT that looked normal six days ago so Neuro isn't wanting to do another brain scan yet. Something about 'best practice.' We'll just keep close watch on these symptoms."

"She has some serious spasticity in the right leg--and numbness, I think."

"Do you think it's numbness or inattention?"

"It's tough to say. She can't really express herself, but I haven't noticed any visual-spatial deficiencies on that side."

"OT? Speech?"

Alice shook her head, tucking her bobbed red hair repeatedly behind her ears. "Lots of other things, but no, no vision issues that I've observed."

Grant perked up from fumbling with his care cards. "Uh--no, I really didn't. I'm not sure if—Jack--has though."

"It's not on the card?"

"Ah, there. Yes, he did do some visual testing with her. No, about as good as it gets."

There was a knock at the door. Dr. Schuler waved toward it. "Speaking of whom--back from slumming it as a lowly Anesthesiologist—Jack Mathison, everyone."

Jack stepped inside wearing navy blue scrubs. His dark blonde hair was a bit overgrown, curling on top, white hairs sprouting up over the past few weeks in his sideburns. There were dark circles beneath his eyes and he only smiled out of politeness, moving to take the seat beside Julie.

"This is a bit unorthodox, but to put it bluntly, I just don't give a damn about going by the book when it comes to one of our own." Dr. Schuler's voice broke. He cleared it purposefully.

A few of the staff members looked at each other, confused. Most looked sympathetic.

"In case you've been living under a rock, Dr. Mathison is *Delaney's--*" Dr. Schuler paused.

"Caregiver," Julie offered.

The social worker jotted something down.

Dr. Schuler stared at Julie, shook his head. "Significant other." It wasn't clear which terminology offended him.

Jack nodded, staring blankly toward the physiatrist.

"As most of you know, he was an OT in a former life. I believe that has proven--and will prove--to be beneficial in Laney's rehabilitation. If there are things she can be working on when she's not in therapy, he can help make that happen. Let's be sure not to overwhelm her though." Dr. Schuler peered over at Jack, who was sitting rigidly in his chair. "We want to give Delaney rest and healing time and not work her 24/7, though if she were in charge, she'd probably do just that."

There were some affirmative shakes of heads, some stolen glances to Jack.

"If you have concerns, you can sidebar with me. If it makes you feel better, think of Dr. Mathison as a highly qualified--" There was that hesitation again. He glared at the table. "Of all people, she shouldn't need--" He swallowed. "Just sidebar with me if you feel strong objections. Just know that you won't change my mind."

The tension in the room eased at his familiar bluntness.

"It's good to see you, Jack. Sorry about the circumstances," Sandy, one of the veteran nurses offered with a kind smile.

Jack made a superhuman effort to smile. "Nice to see you, Sandy."

"For now, we were discussing spasticity in Delaney's right leg versus neglect," Dr. Schuler continued. "Jack?" There was a bite to his voice. He shook his head apologetically, began searching the pockets of his lab coat.

Jenna slid the tissue box across the table.

"I did the visual screening with her in the hospital. I know Teresa did some as well--" Jack began, his voice strained and raspy. He frowned when he saw

Alice sitting across the table instead of the Neuro specialized speech therapist that normally worked on Rehab.

"Teresa had a family emergency. Just happened last night," Julie said quietly, reading his thoughts. "She'll be gone awhile."

He grimaced before continuing. "No issues there. That leg is very, very tight, but I suspect there's a lot of numbness. I did some pin prick tests--it's the knee down that seems to be impacted. The upper leg is tight, but she can feel it just fine. Her right hip has caused pain for many years--she has a few screws in there, so just be mindful. She definitely needs a cushion if sitting for longer periods."

"She's had hip surgery?" Sandy asked. "Injury?"

"Car accident," Dr. Schuler said, swallowing hard.

"She might be hesitant to use that leg because of the numbness, but also because of some referred pain from the hip. Try not to have her sit too long in one position."

Dr. Schuler nodded. "That's a good point. Go on, Dr. Mathison."

"Please call me Jack." He looked uncomfortably over at Grant. "I'll defer to Grant for his assessment."

"We'll get to Grant. Go on. You have more insight on Laney than anybody else at this table."

Jack took a deep breath. "There seems to be a disconnect with her being able to control her body, particularly her arms. Her left leg seems okay--perhaps deconditioned at this point--her right, I think it's more so the other issues. Her arms are just tough at this point. They're like lead weights for her brain. You can ask her to lift her arms and she just stares at them, like she's silently ordering them to move, but nothing is happening."

"She understands though? Instructions? Other things you're saying to her?" Dr. Schuler prompted.

"Definitely. She can't respond at this point, not much visible expression there, but I feel like the message gets through. If you watch her eyes, you can see she understands." Jack took in the sad, sympathetic faces around the table and his confidence broke.

"I agree," Julie said.

"So do I," Dr. Schuler said firmly.

"Dependent for self-cares and ADLs," Jack continued, motioning across the table to the nurses, both of whom nodded. "If we can re-establish the connection between her brain and her body, I think she'll make a lot of progress really quickly."

"I was just saying, bleeds seem to have spontaneous recoveries, like all of a sudden they start doing really well. Remember Frank in 74?" Julie added, her question directed toward Grant. "Well I guess we had him earlier on. Like the week after the bleed, but even so."

"Let's stay on our current patient, people," Dr. Schuler said quickly. "Mobility-wise, where is she?"

Julie adjusted her lab coat. "We have a long way to go. We're working on loosening up the right leg through gentle stretching. She's only toe touch on that side so we haven't been able to do balance testing or any of our standard stroke measures really. Terrence is getting her in aqua therapy this afternoon to see if we can get her walking in the pool first."

"Good idea. She's a swimmer, you know," Dr. Schuler said, stuffing the used tissue in his pocket.

Julie smiled. "I know."

"Speech?"

"Flat affect. Very flat. There's just no obvious recognition that she understands. You all know her better than me, but as a clinician, I wasn't able to identify any cues. Couldn't rate her for comprehension." She picked up a packet of evaluation materials and immediately placed them back on the table.

Dr. Schuler cleared his throat. "I certainly respect your opinion, Alice. You just saw her this morning?"

"Yes. Just finished with her."

"She's improving. Slowly, but improving," Julie said defensively.

"What kind of things did you get to do with her?"

"Communication board, object identification, sound generation—" she held up the picture board that looked like something taken from a board book for toddlers. "She could point with her hand—" she made a claw shape of her hand, "you know like this—when I asked her where, say, the train was on the board, or if I told her to point to the red car. She could do it, as long as the board was close enough to her. Eventually, she just didn't seem to want to participate anymore."

The room was silent.

"So I suppose she did comprehend a bit," Alice retreated. "She wasn't able to produce sounds except for a gurgle noise in the back of her throat. We can work on that."

"It was probably a growl," Julie whispered to Jack. He exhaled deeply, but his eyebrows jumped a little in agreement.

"Now I understand she has some memory issues? She can't remember the past few years?" Alice asked.

"That's right," Julie said, glaring at the speech therapist.

"Well how did you assess *that*?"

Jack exhaled through his nostrils, saying nothing.

"Believe me, Alice, we'd love if you told us otherwise," Julie answered. "There wasn't any official testing because of her inability to speak at this point, but—"

"Oh I don't doubt the findings—"

Dr. Schuler raised his hand to silence her. "She's eating and drinking okay?"

Alice sat nervously organizing her visual aids.

"Alice? No swallow issues?"

Her chin jolted up. "Swallow? No, no issues remarkably. Regular diet."

"Not a great eater," Sandy assessed. "She doesn't like being spoon fed."

"I wouldn't expect she would."

Jenna sat up. "She likes smoothies. She can obviously drink through the straw on her own."

Jack could feel the weight of Delaney's head on his chest, sitting in the gym cafe when they first started seeing each other. He could see her fingers absentmindedly tapping on his knee. He could smell the gentle citrus of her body wash. He remembered the wide neck of her pullover sweatshirt, which kept sliding off her shoulder, how he felt drawn to kiss the smooth, creamy skin on the back of her shoulder.

"Is there anything we can give her for homework over the weekend?"

Alice glanced around the room before realizing the question was meant specifically for her. "Right, no speech coverage this weekend. Probably just basic sound production, humming, facial relaxation to help the right sided paralysis. We use a couple apps—" she said, presenting the tablet. She showed the voice generating app, typed in the message and the device said in a computer voice straight out of *War Games,* "I am hungry."

"Well that could sound more natural," Grant remarked.

"She's able to use that?" Dr. Schuler asked.

"She should be. It's just a touch screen. It just might take her longer because of limitations with her hands. How far back is her memory? Would she have used a touch screen?"

"Can that stay over the weekend?" Julie asked, ignoring the questions.

Alice pulled the tablet toward herself, territorially. "Oh. We have to hang onto it. It's our only one. The apps we have were expensive and took forever to get approved."

Julie cleared her throat. "Can you recommend some apps? We can get another tablet set up?"

"Like a list?"

"A list of apps, yes."

"Oh sure, absolutely. I don't know how well she'd do with it given the limitations of her hands, as I mentioned, but worth a try!"

Julie and Grant exchanged glances.

Dr. Schuler coughed. "Nursing?"

Sandy motioned for Jenna to report.

"Appetite is low. She struggles obviously with utensils--and distractibility--and she doesn't like being spoon fed, as Sandy mentioned. Sandwiches and finger foods work better since she can pinch a bit on the left hand, but it's hand over hand assist to get her to be able to do any of it." Jenna glanced at her notes. "Down a few kilograms since her admission to acute."

"Pain?"

"I think more than what she can express. I was in with her just before conference--her whole body was *tense*, she had tears in her eyes—"

Julie and Jack sat up simultaneously.

Dr. Schuler glanced briefly to Alice, then back to Jenna. "Could it be depression?"

"I wouldn't blame her if it was, but no, she actually did motion to her right shoulder when I asked." Jenna demonstrated by tilting her head toward her own shoulder.

"Well there's some non-verbal expression!" Alice said optimistically, perhaps regretting her harsh assessment.

"Did you give her anything for the pain?"

"I gave her the highest dose of Tylenol we're allowed without an order and I got her a hot pack. I thought the moist heat might help, figuring I'd check with you for a pain med order first thing."

"Heat is good. She's been prone to chills recently so while I think ice would help better, let's stick with moist heat, say 30 minutes on, 30 minutes off, round the clock."

"Why her shoulders, do you think?"

"CPSP."

"Pardon?"

"Central post stroke pain. It causes that spasticity we talked about, as well as significant pain in the muscles and joints. *Especially* the shoulders. I'll prescribe something for her, but if she gets sleepy or dizzy during sessions, let me know. We want her as comfortable as possible, but still alert for therapy, so she can still get something out of it."

"Yeah, the night nurse said she didn't sleep at all."

Dr. Schuler dropped his pen abruptly. "Strange that the nurse didn't inform me since I was *here* and could have done something about it."

Jenna shrugged apologetically. "She's been lethargic this morning. Participating but—"

"Not to Laney level?"

"No, not at all."

"Do me a favor. Go give her 300 mg Gabapentin. Schedule TID to start. Please. We'll increase as quickly as she tolerates."

"Now?"

"Unless you can give it to her an hour ago."

"Yes, Sir."

"Thanks, Jenna. Anyone else?"

The room was silent.

"OK. I like the aqua therapy idea. Maybe work on her hand flexibility under the water, use the resistance to open up her fingers?"

Grant nodded. "Yeah, that should help a lot."

"You all are the experts, I just thought it might be good--"

"It's a great idea, Dr. S."

Dr. Schuler frowned, struggling with some inner-conflict.

"Would help if we get her using a tablet to communicate or something," Julie said.

"I'll work on a tablet this weekend," Jack replied, his voice still scratchy.

"Jack, I understand you're leaving us for a few days?"

"More like a day and a half. It's my sister's wedding in Chicago." He tried to look resolved about going, but his nervousness was apparent.

"We'll take good care of her. Who's on this weekend?"

"I'm here," Julie began, "Terrence, too."

"I'm working," Grant said.

"And we already established no speech coverage," Dr. Schuler concluded. "OK, Jack, no need to keep you. I know you have a flight to catch and we have a few other patients to discuss."

"Thanks everyone," Jack said, stepping into the hallway.

Jenna was just leaving Delaney's room and made a beeline for him. "Hopefully that will help. I had it prepped, thinking he might prescribe it."

"The problem is that it can make memory worse."

She looked regretful. "Maybe if the nerves start working again, the pain will ease up? So she doesn't need to take it?"

"Yeah."

She dropped her chin. "She remembers you."

"No, she doesn't."

When she originally woke, she had pressed her cheek into his fingers, comforted by his presence. He had wished she had opened her eyes before succumbing to the medically induced coma. He wished he had seen her look at him again.

Three weeks later, when they resolved that the swelling had receded enough, they woke her again, pulled her from what had the outward appearance of a deep, content sleep. She woke too quickly, it seemed, and looked immediately distrustful of her surroundings. He had moved toward her, hoping his presence would calm her, as it had the first time--he had been confident it would. She hadn't even been looking at him, her eyes tensely scanning the room. When he placed his hand on her arm, she jolted away, her chin whipping toward him, all familiarity with him gone from her intensely blue eyes. Her glare remained, defensive and uncertain about why he was touching her.

"Then why does she light up when she sees you?"

He sighed. "Because I look like a young, blonde James Garner?"

She laughed, then tilted her head to the side. "Wait, isn't James Garner dead? You actually remind me of Harvey Specter in *Suits*. Only scruffy. And taller."

"I'm probably starting to look like Nick Nolte's mugshot."

She frowned. "Who?"

*I'm only thirty-four*, he insisted silently, thinking of Delaney teasing him about being old.

"She smiles with her *eyes*, Jack."

He had to admit that it was comforting to have this validation. He had thought it was his desperation to see something that told him she remembered him.

His chest ached with guilt about leaving. "Are you working this weekend?"

"I am tomorrow. Jeff will have her Sunday."

He combed his fingers through his hair. "She likes Jeff."

Jenna smiled. "Before the stroke, they had this snippy repertoire with each other."

"Mutual disrespect."

"But in a fun way."

He nodded, distracted. "I don't want to leave her this weekend."

"You're leaving?"

He'd forgotten she missed that part of conference. "My sister is getting married."

"*Oh*, then you have to go—are you in the wedding?"

"I was going to be a groomsman, but our dad had knee surgery a few weeks back and now I'm walking her down the aisle."

She studied his face then said firmly: "Jack, you have to go. Laney's covered. Sarah has her scheduled for meditation, art, tai chi, her therapy calendar is packed--I'll probably tell Sarah to lighten things up."

"Yeah, probably soon for art and tai chi. Is there a therapy dog on this weekend? She'd like that."

"I'll find out. Even if we have to trek over to the main hospital."

He nodded, appreciatively.

"Did you tell her already that you're going to be gone?"

"I did, but--" Delaney had listened to him, but without a way to respond, she had appeared--unaffected by the news--and there was little way to know what information she was retaining in her short-term memory. "Would you remind her? So she doesn't think—"

"Of course."

"She was crying? Before?"

Jenna rubbed at her nose. "Honestly, I think it was the pain, but she *was* frustrated with Alice. How could you not be?"

"That board was--surreal."

"That's a good sign though, in a way, right? If she's frustrated by it she must understand. Frustration *is* expression, right?"

He considered that. "Yeah, that's true."

"I was going to ask Dr. S to prescribe a sleep aid for her. I think sleep would benefit her as much as anything else right now."

"She didn't sleep at all last night?"

She shook her head. "I didn't want to elaborate in there. It felt like I was throwing the night nurse under the bus, but she should have paged him. During morning report, she told me Laney woke up around midnight and didn't get back to sleep. Because she didn't complain, she let her be. 'She can't even grab a book to entertain herself, Shawna. That's really neglectful.'" She frowned. "I shouldn't have said that probably, but it makes me so angry."

Jack silently wondered how long it would take Tabitha to forgive him for bailing on her wedding.

"Why aren't you staying in there with her instead of in 92?"

"She doesn't remember me—it wouldn't feel right."

"And sleeping across the pod does?"

He shrugged it off. "I didn't want to push anything on her. I usually stay with her until she falls asleep anyway." That thought didn't help. He usually let nursing handle bathroom rituals before bed—using the toilet, brushing her teeth, washing her face, but he'd been reading to her until she fell asleep since she had come out of the coma. Though she couldn't express it, she seemed engaged in listening to him. The thought was that movies would be too stimulating--and stroke survivors were thought to be more at risk for seizures. He'd been reading her the first of a series by JoJo Moyes that she had bought in recent months.

Jenna studied his face. "Well she's going home with you, right? Otherwise, who else does she have?"

Jack's heart lurched.

"I'm sorry. That was--"

He cleared his throat. "She has me--regardless."

There was the sympathetic head tilt he had come to know so well.

She frowned. "When do you leave?"

"I fly out this afternoon and fly back tomorrow late." He omitted the fact that his flight back was actually at 5:00am Sunday so he wouldn't arrive back at the hospital until Sunday mid-morning. He checked his watch. He had 20 minutes before he needed to be in the truck enroute to the airport.

"*Dr. M*, she'll be OK. This is what we do here."

He looked over at her closed door, unable to grasp that he'd be thousands of miles away that night and having to put on a pleasant face for his sister's sake at the wedding rehearsal. That Delaney would have little means to communicate with anyone.

"She'd want you to go."

That made him snap to attention. It was the truth. "Thanks, Jenna." He pointed toward Delaney's room. "I'm going to check in on her."

Only the bedside lamp was on. The overhead lights had been too harsh for her eyes since the craniotomy. So far, word had gotten around Rehab and staff had been conscientious about keeping light in her room dimmed. In ICU and Acute, he had resorted to duct taping the light switch in the off position after multiple instances of staff flipping on the lights at all hours, usually just after she'd managed to fall asleep.

Some of the therapy staff had taken the liberty of decorating her room. Silk leis streamers stretched loosely between the edges of the large window. Vintage replica Hawaii travel posters were gummied on the walls. A bouquet of bird of paradise, ginger and palm fronds filled a vase on the table by the window. Real.

*Schuler.*

The staff thought it would be motivating--a goal, a light at the end of the tunnel--that when she got out of the hospital, they would finally take the trip. In reality, she'd have no idea why the room was decorated that way, that she and Jack were supposed to have left for Hawaii the day after her stroke.

The decorations just reminded Jack of what he had left unsaid, undone. He thought of the plans he had for the vacation. He thought of lying on a quiet beach beside her, pulling her to him in the cold waves, breathing in the suntan lotion on her skin. He thought of the cushion cut ring he had planned to give her during a sunset stroll on the beach, still in its small navy velvet box zipped inside the inner compartment of his carry-on bag. It seemed so insignificant now, so meaningless, all these things he *planned* to do. He wished he had proposed any of the dozens of other times he thought the words might explode from his mouth.

Delaney was turned onto her right side, to apply compression pressure he realized, a heating pad tucked under her shoulder. He wondered if she had positioned herself that way, or if it was Jenna's doing. Either way, despite the tense expression on her face, she had fallen asleep--a heavy, desperate sleep.

Her long hair was wild from humidity and neglect, the surgical site hidden beneath the unkempt strands.

He thought of the night a few weeks before the stroke. He was returning from a conference and due to a flight delay, hadn't arrived home until 2am. He had crept into the bedroom and found she had left the nightstand lamp on. She had her glasses on and her thumb holding her place in a novel with a navy cover and vibrant red lettering (the one he was currently reading to her), her opposite hand pulled up by her chin. Much like now, the right side of her face had been mashed into the pillow, but her left cheekbone was clearly visible—the contour unmistakable, along with the constellation of freckles.

Closing the distance to the hospital bed, he wished she would stir awake, smile sleepily, and breathe his name the way she had that night. He wished she had achy muscles from swimming laps at the pool rather than excruciating pain scorching her joints and muscles from her brain desperately trying to make connections with her body.

*Please wake up and say something. Tell me to shave. Make some reference about me being old even though I'm only five years older than you.*

Her breathing deepened, the tension in her muscles easing a bit.

"Sleep is good, too," he whispered, kissing her exposed cheek.

***

Chicago offered a cheerful early summer day and substantial traffic. The Cubs were home and had a late afternoon game so the drive from Midway that shouldn't have taken longer than 30 minutes had taken double that. He peered out the window of the Uber SUV, the street bright in the vibrant mid-afternoon sun. It was Pride month, he recognized, storefronts displaying rainbow flags, stickers, and messages of support.

"There's a parade tomorrow?" He asked once he saw a sign advertising it.

"That's right," the driver, Nick in the black Tahoe, a bald man who looked like his regular job was as a club bouncer, replied.

"Damn."

"Not a supporter?"

"It's not that. My sister is getting married this weekend."

"She gay?"

Jack chuckled. "No. Should make getting around tomorrow a bit more challenging though."

"Ah, I got you," Nick said in his thick native Chicagoan accent. "She having it at the hotel?"

"The reception, but the ceremony will be at Fourth Presbyterian Church."

"Oh that's just down the street from the Drake. You can walk it in two minutes, no problem."

Jack felt some relief for his sister, leaning into his headrest as the car crawled away from the lakeshore. "I have a flight Sunday morning—am I better off taking the train?"

"To Midway? Nah. You'd have to take a bus to the train. Everybody will be sleeping it off by Sunday morning. Roads should be clear. You have my details. I'll get you there. What time?" He made a quick lane change, cutting off a taxi cab.

"Flight's at 5."

"AM? Damn, Chief, have someone you have to get back to?"

"I do, actually."

"Fair enough. She didn't come to your sister's wedding though?" he asked gruffly.

"No, she couldn't."

"Had to work or something?"

Jack considered that. "Yeah."

"How long have you been dating?"

"3 ½ years."

"That's a good stretch. You gonna marry her?"

Jack felt his cheeks tighten, but his eyes stung suddenly. "That's the plan."

"Good for you, good for you. Just watch out at the wedding--single women get a little crazy at weddings."

"You have personal experience with that?"

"Nah. My cousin, though. He got black out drunk, woke up married to a twice-divorced woman named Pepper."

"Wow. What did he do?"

"Oh, they're still married."

Jack frowned to himself.

"Marrying the right person: that's the most important decision a person makes."

Peering over the driver's shoulder, Jack spotted a simple gold band on the man's thick left hand.

"My Paula was the only one for me. Life hasn't been easy, but at the end of the day, I'm blessed."

"Is that her there?" Jack asked, leaning forward to motion to the photo on the dashboard. The woman pictured had shoulder-length blonde hair and was snuggling a fat pug.

Paul nodded, then wiped at his eyes with his left hand. "Lost her 19 months ago next week."

Jack found himself unprepared for this turn in conversation, but he listened as his driver, a stranger just 40 minutes earlier, shared how he and his wife had never been able to have children and they were denied for adoption because he had a prior drunk driving conviction, despite being sober several years. They did end up fostering a teenager, who they were later able to adopt. Their son had been in the Army and deployed to Afghanistan. They got word he would make it home for Christmas so Paula had taken it upon herself to decorate for his homecoming. She went up on a 16-foot ladder while Paul was on an errand even though he said he would take care of hanging the lights on the top roof.

He returned from picking up their son from the airport to find her dead in the driveway.

"I'm sorry to unload all that on you. I don't know what came over me."

Jack felt the lump in his throat clear and suddenly the pent up words fell out.

"Well that proves it," Nick said when he had finished.

"Proves what?"

"There's always someone who has it worse." He read Jack's confusion in the rearview mirror as he accelerated through the light. "I got 25 years with my Paula. You and this young lady--"

"Delaney."

"Delaney. You're only a few years in. You just got started. To have this thrown at you? It's not effing fair." He shook his head, taking in the crowds of people swarming the streets. "Do you have a picture?" The SUV jolted to a stop at the next light.

Jack opened his Favorites album on his phone, swiped to a photo of the pair of them at the top of a summit, an expansive, lush mountain range and lake in the background. They both wore broad smiles, each with an arm outstretched at their side. The next photo he took when she had stood at the edge, gazing out to the horizon. He had gone to relieve himself and had been careful to be quiet on his walk toward her. She had her eyes closed, as though in meditation, sighing deeply. It was just as he was lining up a really artistic profile photograph that she turned suddenly, roaring, and he had stumbled backwards. His thumb accidentally hit the shutter button and the camera captured her mid-laugh as he landed hard on his ass. She had a difficult time composing herself, managing to stutter out breathlessly between laughs that he had the funniest look on his face. He swiped to the next one where they had nudged together, sitting on the rocks to take another photo together. She had relaxed into him, tilting her head against his, a content little smirk lifting the left side of her face.

He held the phone out for Nick, who smiled silently at the photo. He didn't speak until he made the next turn after Jack had reeled back his arm. "I'll keep her in my prayers."

Jack slid out of the SUV in front of The Drake Hotel, surveying the towering buildings that surrounded it. Just down the street, he could see a tour group drifting down Michigan Avenue past Gucci and Bloomingdales. He gave a cordial wave to Nick and closed the door.

"Oh my God. You look like a hobo."

He rolled his eyes as he turned toward the unmistakable voice of Tabitha's best friend. She was holding a padded hanger above her head, trying not to drag the thick canvas bag on the sidewalk. Her red hair was pulled into an updo, her makeup caked on to cover years of teenage acne.

"Always nice to see you, Sam."

She ruffled his hair, wrapped one arm around his neck in a half-hug. "You're scheduled for a boy's spa day tomorrow. I'm sure they can make you pretty again." She squeezed his face in one manicured hand, frowning at his appearance, then kissed his cheek. "It means a lot to Tab that you're here, Jack, with all that's going on"

He felt his throat tighten. "Let me get that for you," he offered, taking the hanger from her, pushing his overnight bag toward his back. "Tab went with the lead weight one, huh?"

"Right? Lots of tulle and hoops. Very poofy and girly."

"So she'll be a very beautiful cupcake."

"Essentially, yes." She turned toward him quickly. "Do *not* tell her I said that."

They started toward the gilded awning, his eyes drifting to the art gallery window and an ornate dragon light fixture. He couldn't stop his mind from silently observing--D would love the colors of that painting. She would love the architecture of this building. As they stepped across the lobby, he found every observation referenced back to her. The deep midnight blue of the lobby carpeting reminded him of her eyes in dim lighting. It was also her favorite color. He could see her stealing a touch of the huge white bouquet of orchids perched atop a carved circular table, checking if the flowers were, in fact, real, her eyes bright and sparkling in the light of the grand chandelier. She would beam at the ornate woodworking, the weight of the tapestries, likening it to an old historic library.

While they waited at check-in, she would have dropped onto one of the tufted golden chairs, summoning a modeling pose while contorting her face or flapping her eyelashes at him. He would shake his head, walk to her, draw her up to stand, his arms wrapped around her waist, saying something like: "Can't take you anywhere." They would be tangled in each other as they made their way to check-in.

Instead, he had already disappointed an eager bellhop when he told him he just had the one bag--and he could handle carrying both it and the wedding gown unassisted. Then the desk man clarified that it was just the two of them and gave him an irritated glance when he told him it was actually just him. He made a point of explaining how he would need to adjust that in the reservation—for security. Then came the credit card on file.

"The credit card taken to guarantee the reservation was issued to Delaney A Rhodes--" he looked across the desk, his face stern. "That's *not* you."

"No. You can put the room on this," Jack said, sliding out his American Express.

Once that was resolved, probably following a script, the man asked him how many keys he would like.

"Just the one should be fine," Jack replied, avoiding Samantha's sympathetic gaze.

"Here, I can take that," she said, motioning to the gown. "I'm going to go put it in Tab's room. Rehearsal starts at 5 and I need to go change. Do you know how to get to the church?"

"The concierge can provide directions, Sir." The man said with a dismissive perk of his eyebrows, still focused on typing something on his computer.

"So can I," Samantha said. "Turn right out of the front, cross Michigan, turn left, then walk a block or two."

Jack carefully handed her the gown. "I'll shave, don't worry."

"I wasn't going to say anything," she called over her shoulder, gliding toward the elevator bank.

"We have you in a park view suite, per your request, on an upper floor."

Jack decided not to mention that it wasn't his request.

"Room number is printed there. Just take these elevators." He did a double finger point toward the elevator bank where Sam had gone. "Let us know if we can do anything to make your stay more pleasant."

The elevator featured similarly ornate woodwork as the lobby. He avoided his reflection in the tall mirror as he boarded and found himself glancing back at the armless couch throughout his vertical ascent. Delaney would be unable to resist plopping down, throwing a long leg up in the air as she did, no doubt playing out a scene from *Pretty Woman*.

He found his room without incident, but as he pushed open the door and took in the expansive lake view through the sheer curtains, his eyes fell upon a pair of plush waffle robes folded on the bed, a pair of sleep masks, two pairs of slippers. The coffee table held a gift basket signed from the happy couple, the handwriting a loopy cursive, likely the work of one of the bridesmaids. It was addressed just to him and was filled with comfort items and chintzy Chicago tourist garb like a snow globe featuring the skyline and a Chicago Cubs keychain, as well as a water bottle with the wedding info printed on it, a bag of Garrett's popcorn, and a wedding itinerary.

When Delaney first made the reservation, she had them arriving on Wednesday, to allow some time to explore and be available for any "catastrophe" leading up to the wedding. She had said this with a hint of sarcasm. She wasn't the big wedding type--too much grandeur. Despite whimpering through ordering the $275 bridesmaid gown, she had been genuinely moved to have been chosen.

She had bought them Cubs tickets for Wednesday evening, justifying that the proximity of Wrigley Field was reasonable enough for any such catastrophes. He could see her in a ball cap, leaning back into her seat, watching as he stole sips of her beer after he'd finished his.

Delaney had been enthusiastic as she talked about doing a *Ferris Bueller* checklist, visiting the same places they had in the movie--the art museum, the stock exchange, going to the observation deck of the Sears Tower, now the "What-cha-call-it" building. She teased that he could even lip sing on a parade float. He reasoned that the chances of a parade happening during their visit was slim. He could imagine the look on her face when she found out there would, in fact, be a parade, playfully smacking his leg in the back of the Uber, her eyes pleading with him to play along.

He shed his clothes and showered quickly, deciding against using one of the hotel provided disposable razors in favor of his electric one. He decided to iron his wrinkle-free dress shirt, as well as his pants and jacket. Besides underwear, a plain t-shirt and pair of cargo shorts for the flight home, it was the only outfit he had brought. He would be picking up his suit in the morning and Tabitha had insisted on matching bridal party shirts for the "prepping" time before the wedding the following day. It was in the basket.

Delaney would have insisted on a backup outfit and the luggage would have been impeccably organized. She always did balance spontaneity and practicality with skillful precision.

As he checked his reflection, he noticed how tired his face had become, how drained of color. In the mirror was a man he barely recognized.

She should have been there, slipping into the navy blue shift dress all the bridesmaids were instructed to wear for the rehearsal ($120 + shipping), having him clasp her necklace. She would have taken his arm and he would have felt that familiar sense of pride, to have a woman of her caliber beside him. She inevitably would have done something silly like blow a raspberry or hum the *Mission Impossible* song as they waited for the elevator when she'd caught him staring too long.

He walked to the church in silence, contrasting the symphony of city noises surrounding him. When he arrived at the church, Tabitha appeared to be having trouble taking full breaths. Upon seeing him, she had sighed, walked purposefully toward him and gave a small smile. "You don't look like a hobo," she said reassuringly.

Her hair was pulled into a side braid, tight curls bouncing against her cheeks. She had more makeup on than he'd ever seen, her round eyes outlined, her cheeks contoured, her lips intentionally lightened and glossed.

"The makeup artist had a family emergency so I did a trial with this other lady today. I am *not* using her tomorrow."

"You look beautiful," he said, kindly. Actually, she looked like a blonde Kardashian. It wasn't a look he cared for in general, but especially not for his little sister.

"I'm glad you're here."

She looped her arm around his for the walk down the aisle, tension rising from her skin. She watched helplessly as the ring bearer repeatedly tossed his pillow in the air and twice lost it in a row of pews.

Tabitha was startled when Jack began spontaneous bouts of sprinting, a silent game of red light/green light—tugging her along and stopping abruptly. By the time they reached the altar, she was giggling, despite calling him an ass.

During rehearsal, he found himself glancing to the bridesmaids, imagining Delaney standing among them. She'd be the tallest by a half-foot, standing in her statuesque manner, her shoulders taut and sun kissed. An engagement ring would be glistening on her hand. It would have been wonderful and surreal to be standing at the front of the church, across from his future wife.

In her place was his teenage cousin, Hailey, with her choppy blonde hair, dark roots, and petite frame, looking lost without a smartphone in her palm, fidgeting with her chevron pendant necklace.

It was once they arrived at the upscale steakhouse an hour later and he sat beside his dad that the ache in his chest began to overwhelm him. They sat at one end of the long table situated in a private room featuring dark, carved wood and architect lamp lighting.

He instantly became aware of the time. Delaney would be having dinner soon, as well. Julie was going to dine with her in the cafeteria to give her a change of scenery.

Jenna would then help her get changed and ready for bed, staying after the usual 7pm nurse change. He had left an old phone on the nightstand with a pair of headphones, the audiobook version of *Me Before You* queued up to where he had left off. Speech hadn't been able to fully assess if her reading ability was impacted so he thought an audiobook was a safer option.

"You can call and check in. I won't tell," his dad said, having watched him stare at the menu upside down for a solid two minutes.

"I called after the rehearsal. She was in the pool for PT."

"Hey that's a great idea for her. No impact and she loves swimming."

Jack nodded tightly.

"Still not talking?"

He shook his head. "She's getting a bit more dexterity in her hands though. I'm getting an iPad set up for her--hopefully that will allow her to type out messages. And I have some contracture gloves on order to help strengthen her hands. We have exercisers there, but nothing like these. These should help. I don't know anything about Speech though and the therapist that specializes in neuro had a family emergency so she's just not getting the therapy she needs right now." He rubbed at his face and the corners of his eyes roughly.

"So. You're here, but you're there."

"I'm trying, Dad. I want to be here for Tab."

"But--"

"I feel like I'm missing--" He found his hand motioning to his chest.

"Your heart."

"I know she's in there--in her mind," he clarified. "I know she'll recover--" A care management supervisor had just that morning mentioned having brochures available for group homes, 'just to keep your options open.' "She's going to get better." He recognized the desperation in his voice.

His dad removed his reading glasses after deciding on his entree, squeezing the bridge of his nose. His eyes glistened a bit even in the low lighting.

"I keep wondering what happens if—" He couldn't say it. He couldn't doubt that she would progress beyond her current state—not out loud. He couldn't ponder living options for her, couldn't accept the chance that the world would continue on without her as she was.

"When I met her, I felt like I finally woke up—"

"Literally and figuratively," his dad added, blinking purposefully.

The image of her standing at the door of the sleep room drifted before his eyes. Rigid, tensely all business—then softening incrementally to the woman he knew with her radiant eyes that danced when she spoke and her easy smile.

Jack gave a convincing smile to Tabitha, her blurred image in the distance coming into focus. She was discussing a problem with the wedding coordinator. The groom was arguing that this was just the sort of issue they were paying for her to handle unbeknownst to them. Tabitha frowned regretfully across the room at her brother.

"Tab is really stressed with things, huh?"

His dad raised his wispy blonde eyebrows. "It's all nonsense. All of this. Expensive, anxiety-inducing nonsense."

"It means a lot to her."

He shrugged. "Maybe. But it's not what matters. It's fluff. Whether the vows stand the test of time or just turn out to be hollow words matters."

"They seem to love each other, right?"

His dad tilted his chin toward Tabitha, who was engaged in debate over manners with her future husband, now defending the wedding coordinator. "I wish they'd focus as much of their energy on each other as they are to seating charts and DJ playlists."

"Are you still doing physical therapy?"

"Two to three times per week."

Jack nodded. Delaney would be angry with herself for not being able to evaluate him, give him exercises, size up the therapist working with him.

"She's still there, Jack."

"Yeah, I know, Dad, but—Even--" He took a breath. "Even with everything she's going through, I can't help but think that I need her more than she needs me." He stared off to the private room entrance where the wait staff were propping open the doors in preparation to serve appetizers. "His family paid for tonight, right?"

"They did. Drink up."

Jack chuckled silently. "That's not--"

"Alcohol doesn't solve anything, but you've had a hell of a few months. Have a drink."

"Only if you join me."

"For one, yes."

A few minutes later, they each had a low ball glass filled with a burnt umber colored liquid. Jack clinked the ice around his glass, smelling the rim. "I smell coffee."

"You do. Coffee liqueur. Haven't you had a Black Russian before?"

"I'm a beer guy. There was a time I was a shots and beer guy."

"You can linger over this one, Kid."

Jack nodded, sipping slowly. As he swallowed the simultaneously sweet and bitter drink, he closed his eyes. He could see Delaney standing in his industrial kitchen wearing a pair of his boxer shorts, the waistband rolled down to keep them up, a worn in white v-neck t-shirt, sipping her coffee gingerly. He had just come in from covering a night shift. With her hair messily tied on top of her head, she had turned around, smiled broadly as she wrapped her arms around his neck and said: "You know, if you were coffee grounds, you'd be espresso because baby, you *so fine.*"

He could taste the fresh coffee with its coconut milk creamer on her lips.

His dad sighed. "She'll remember."

He scoffed involuntarily, gazing across the room. Tabitha was staring intensely at her husband-to-be, who appeared to be justifying a remark or joke. "She's having to deal with so much right now."

"Delaney or Tab?"

Jack shook his head. "Learning to walk and talk again is nothing compared to *this.*" He intended it to be joking, but he found himself increasingly somber. He frowned as he finished off the drink, the ice rattling a bit in the glass as he set it heavily on the table.

His dad slid his glass toward him, waved to the server for another.

Jack swallowed hard and kept his eyes lowered as he felt them rimming with tears.

"She'll remember," his dad said, a little more forcibly.

Jack thought of sharing all the statistics, all the medical jargon about memory loss, but he was captivated by the confidence of his dad. He had a similar matter-of-fact expression when he told the story of how he met his mom in elementary school and knew immediately he would marry her. "Dad, how can you be so certain about things?"

"I have faith, Son." He perked his eyebrows, tapped his glass, and the bride and groom kissed. Tabitha looked far more relaxed after being dipped by her husband-to-be, her round cheeks red and dimpled.

# 5

# change

Quinn sat upright in the hospital bed staring at the sheets and blanket pulled tightly across his legs that he was unable to feel, aside from sharp, shooting pain that seemed to be brought on spontaneously by no action of his own. Every morning he woke up and wished in vain that it was all a bad dream--the accident, the extensive hospital stays, the humiliation of being entirely dependent on strangers. Most days he felt like if this were truly going to be his reality, he'd prefer not to wake at all.

"Did you scare everybody away?" Nurse Ann asked, fresh from her dinner break, standing in the doorway. She meant it as a joke, but if she hadn't already, she'd hear later about how Quinn had thrown his parents out of his room, figuratively, of course. Once they left, he confronted his girlfriend, a slender woman with shoulder length blonde hair and an apparent love of high heels, who left crying a short time later. The clopping of her heels drowned out her sobs.

"Something like that," he said. "Did the transfer paperwork come through?"

"Oh good, you decided to go! It's really a great facility from what I hear."

"You would have known this if you had simply checked in with your coworkers before gracing me with your presence," he muttered.

"Oh I'm going to miss that rapier wit so terribly. Let's check your vitals and change our your bags and I'll be on my way." She crossed the room, not easily persuaded from her cheery disposition. "Oh looks like you're having good output. Keep up with the fluids." She patted his shoulder.

Quinn rolled his eyes, running his right hand over his thick, wavy black hair in exhausted annoyance. He knew very well he had a catheter, but he most certainly did not need reminders, nor did he need to see the full bag, which Nurse Ann proudly presented with her blue gloved hands, pointing out that the color wasn't too dark.

As the heavyset nurse with sandy colored hair and 80s bangs zigzagged across the room completing her tasks, Quinn scowled at his phone. Being left handed, it was a bit awkward trying to navigate, let alone type out a message with the cast in place down to his knuckles. He tried using his right hand more. He would become ambidextrous if he had to, but he needed to work. He preferred the laptop, but all his visitors were dismissed before he could coax them to retrieve it and he did just snap at Nurse Ann. He wasn't about to admit how helpless he truly was. He'd just wait until next shift. It should be Nurse Beth, who he didn't mind watching work. He was suddenly grateful Ann was taking care of the ostomy bags before shift change. Beth was fresh out of school, maybe 22, long dark hair, upbeat little voice, and she wore modern, slim fitting navy scrubs that hugged her curves. He was actually surprised the hospital allowed them.

He checked his email and found a message from his boss. Evidently they were transferring his accounts temporarily to Corey--preppy, asshole little Corey, until his "situation" had "resolved." His dad was CC'd, which told him that his dad was consulted, if not involved in the decision.

"You might want to edit your language. I've heard they're less tolerant for behavioral issues," she said, turning on her heel to leave. "Rehab beds are coveted. I wonder who put in a good word for you."

He was about to fire off a retort when he noticed she had placed his laptop on the bed beside him.

The door clicked shut.

With no reason to use the laptop, he slid it on his empty food tray and rotated the arm of the tray away from the bed. He stared at his legs again. His tailbone was throbbing, which they said was referred pain from the compressed part of his spine. He wanted to kick free of the covers, which they said were important because of it being crucial for his recovery that he didn't get sick, but the taut angle of the covers was starting to feel more like a straight jacket holding him prisoner in the hospital bed. Honestly, people were saying a lot of things these days he didn't like.

He had overheard his attending physician mutter that Rehab wasn't the right place for him--something about lack of evidence that he'd progress beyond his current functional status. Apparently it was rare for the rehab facility to accept outside transfers—and on a Sunday, no less. The physician had rambled on about a prior patient who would have done tremendously well there, but the rehab  facility wouldn't accept the transfer. 99% of their referrals were internal, fed to them through their own inpatient hospital. His doctor had wondered aloud "what Dr. Schuler was thinking" and why, of all the patients, he had practically recruited "that pompous asshole" as a patient.

Quinn had chosen not to share his connection with Dr. Schuler when he was asked repeatedly. He had initially been surprised he even remembered his name.

The transfer took place the following morning. Beth was, in fact, working, but he was not as pleased to see her as he thought he would be. She helped gather up his belongings and had offered to get him set up to shave, but he declined. He had prided himself on his appearance for work, but since there was no work, some stubble wouldn't hurt. His mother arrived just before the transport van. She was dressed in navy gaucho pants and a flowy white blouse, accented with a delicate strand of pearls, a beautiful Stepford wife. She seemed a bit cautious with him, her eyes lowered more than he was accustomed. She moved carefully, making as little noise as possible. He had witnessed this sort of behavior when it came to his dad who had moments of rage, usually accessorized by a chunky glass of bourbon, when everyone knew not to trigger him further, but she had never been this way with him. They had connected about their mutual dislike of his father's drinking habits. They were very close up until he finished college and started at his father's investments firm. Before the accident, he hadn't seen her since Christmas. The accident happened the week prior to Easter.

As the transport people transferred him onto a more portable looking gurney, she stood in the corner, her thin arms folded and clutching her stomach, sweater tied loosely over her shoulders. She nodded occasionally, to herself it seemed, and took his hand before they left the room.

"I'll make sure we haven't left anything here. Would you like me to meet you at the new hospital, help you get settled?"

It sounded like he was moving into dorms at college, rather than moving into an intense rehab facility in hopes he'd somehow be able to walk again, if not, be able to live without caregivers 24/7. It was a shallow consolation, really. "Thanks, Mom. I'll manage. Maybe stop in tomorrow--if you're available?"

That seemed to lift her spirits.

The transport was bumpy and he felt nauseous by the time they arrived. He wasn't sure what he expected, but the exterior looked like a luxury boutique hotel. They parked in the circular drive out front and were greeted by the admissions supervisor, a very polite, but to the point lanky woman with gray shoulder-length hair. Quinn didn't get much of a read on her personality, good or bad, but she reiterated constantly that outside transfers were rare occurrences, seemingly to excuse the appearance of dishevelment.

A young energetic therapist popped onto the scene to further add to the chaos.

"You must be Mr. Harwell."

"Yes, I must be. And who must you be?"

"I'm Julie Patton, I'll be one of your physical therapists."

"You're the one who's going to get me walking again."

"Well you wouldn't think that's your goal based on how they brought you in. What's with the stretcher?"

"You wanted me rollerblading alongside the van?"

"That would be impressive, but I doubt we would have gotten insurance auth if you could manage that."

"Self-pay then."

"Corey, could you grab a wheelchair?"

He glared at the assistant, who had done nothing more to him than have the wrong name. "That's a fun coincidence."

"See? You're already having fun," she said, undeterred. "I'll give you a little tour while they take care of paperwork."

"Yes, I'm pleased to check this tour off the bucket list."

"Thanks Corey. OK, Mr. Harwell--"

"Quinn. I know it's a professional thing, but it really irks me when people call me Mr. Harwell."

"Quinn. So just this once, we'll do the heavy lifting. I just need you to hold on to Corey and myself."

Once he was situated in the chair, she tucked the catheter bag in the pouch on the side of the chair. "We'll meet ya'll back at the room?" She didn't wait for an answer. "Now I read that you have feeling through your waist into your hips a bit?"

"You read correctly, Julie. 'Feeling' being pain."

"Is it safe to say you can feel your groin area?"

"Depends on why you're asking."

"To try and figure out why they cath'd you."

"Of course you were."

"Have you had continence issues?"

"The cath has been in the whole time so I don't know."

"I'll talk to Dr. Schuler. Okay, so this is our lovely lobby/atrium." She motioned across the lobby to a large entrance closed off like a Brookstone store in a shopping mall. "They're closed on Sundays, but that's where the integrative medicine area is. They do massages, some naturalistic treatments, modified yoga, therapy dogs--"

"Now this is former NFL player, Martin Schuler, right?"

"That's him."

He nodded.

"Down this way is the cafeteria. I recommend the brick oven pizza."

She didn't look like she ate pizza regularly.

"They do flatbreads sometimes, but even the plain pepperoni is pretty tasty."

The cafeteria was a bit institutional looking, but the walls of windows were lined with trees that challenged the desert setting. It looked more like Florida. Being between breakfast and lunch, there weren't many people.

"This hallway connects with the main hospital. There's also a coffee bar."

"I know someone who used to work with Dr. Schuler--I wonder if she--"

A woman in a floral dress and lab coat waved to Julie from where she sat at one of the handicap accessible tables. She was tucked in beside a patient who appeared to be slumped a bit to one side in a wheelchair, dark hair wild and unbrushed.

Julie waved back. "How's she doing?" She whispered, exaggerating the words on her lips.

The other therapist shook her head, shrugging.

"Come on, Laney, I know you're in there," she said, turning the wheelchair around.

Quinn froze. "Who's that?"

"One of our speech therapists. I'm not sure if you'll work with her."

"Speaking well is low on the priorities list, Julie."

"Well they handle cognitive, borderline psych stuff, too."

"I might use her services after all then, eh?"

"She's used to working with children," she said, absentmindedly. He couldn't tell if she meant it as a jab. They returned to the lobby and she said hello to a wiry-haired woman in a robe pushing a four-wheeled walker, her husband beside her. "Doing great, Madeline."

"Who's the patient she was working with? Did you say 'Annie'?" he asked, even though he knew she hadn't.

"Oh--" The wheelchair slowed as Julie hesitated to answer.

"Patient privacy or something?" He peered over his shoulder to see Julie was gripping her cell phone in her right hand.

She pulled him into one of the conversation areas. "I'm sorry. I need to make a quick call."

He didn't answer, preoccupied as he stared toward the cafeteria. The speech patient didn't seem to be paying attention to her therapist, her chin turned toward the coffee bar, the left side of her face perpendicular to him. Her profile was familiar, her high cheekbones, her well-defined jaw. Half of her head had been shaved at some point, the short hair poking out in every which direction.

"I know, Jack. We're making progress--well for PT. She's getting stronger. Pool is helping *so* much, even in the past couple of days. It's really loosening her muscles. Grant is focusing on hand exercises." She swayed a bit, gnawing at her fingernails. "No, they're still pretty clenched. Yeah, Speech is what worries me. Alice isn't cutting it. No, Schuler pulled strings and Alice had to come in one day this weekend. The other supplemental wasn't available. Teresa's dad is doing better so she's coming back Wednesday, thank God. Oh you have? See? You're making use out of a flight cancellation. What time do you take off? Jack, you've got 11 hours. Use your big fat doctor's wallet and stay at the airport hotel, get some sleep. Lord knows, you won't sleep when you get back here. OK, I'll see you tomorrow then." She tucked her phone back in her lab jacket. "Yeah he's not going to sleep," she concluded, then seemed to remember Quinn was there. "Sorry."

"Jack seems pretty concerned. Friend of hers?"

She snapped to attention, glancing toward the cafeteria. "Yeah, he is."

"And she *is*?"

"Well you'll be seeing each other in breakfast group and some of the rec therapy activities--I guess you'll find out."

"I won't tweet it out. Is she famous or something? You said her name is Laney?"

"Yeah, Laney. No, she's not famous. Stroke. She had a stroke."

His stomach clenched. "A *stroke*?"

"Yeah and she's only 29. Same as you, actually, right? We've got some young patients right now. Well, being young, we should be able to make some really great progress for both of you. Young brains, bodies tend to bounce back better."

The therapy session seemed to be wrapping up.

Julie checked her fitness tracker watch. "Unbelievable. You still have 10 minutes, Alice," she huffed and shoved the wheelchair forward.

"I thought only old people have strokes."

"No. Sadly even kids can have them."

"She's not doing well?"

"She wasn't making much progress on acute and the first few days here, but in the past day or two, it's been better. We didn't know she was in so much pain and that was keeping her from sleeping, which was, in turn, keeping her from doing well in therapy." She turned the wheelchair around, having been circling to glare at Alice, and started pushing him down the main Rehab hallway.

"Patients need sleep to heal," he said, quoting his last nurse.

"Yeah, so since we started to get a handle, as far as we can tell, on her pain, she's really turned a corner."

"That's good, at least."

"Hey, we'll get you moving in the right direction, too," she said, redirecting. "Out this way is our therapy courtyard."

"Looks--serene."

"Around the other side is our breakfast room, rec space, and just down this hall is our gym." The walls were lined with picturesque scenes of ocean, beach, and other tropical flowers.

"Y'all know it's the desert outside, right?"

"Dr. Schuler picked the style. He grew up in Miami. It's sort of spa-like though, right?"

"Oh yeah, very zen," he said sarcastically, but he did find the ambiance aesthetically pleasing.

They entered an expansive gym space that featured a wall of windows, lined, of course, with an abundance of tropical foliage. "This, dear Sir, is where the magic happens. Mostly. We have an endless pool in the back, too."

"Julie, did you kidnap the new patient?" A spiked, spiral-haired young man with deep toffee skin asked, smiling widely as he approached from the hallway. "Case management is in a tizzy looking for him. Apparently they don't want to sign off on transport until they actually lay eyes on him."

"Wow, way to make a guy feel like a Fed-Ex package."

"Just giving him a tour."

"Hi, Mr. Harwell, I'm Terrence. Julie and I will probably be the two main PTs switching off with you." He held out his hand, which Quinn shook apprehensively, partially because the therapist's fingernails were painted glittery blue.

"Terrence works on the Pediatric wing sometimes. One of your admirers, Ter?"

He finished off the handshake and retracted his hand to examine his nails. "Oh yeah. Sorry about that. Just trying to fill Laney's shoes over there. One kid asked if I was Frozone. She thought blue would go with my Super Suit."

"It suits you."

Terrence was distracted, looking off to the entrance. "*Hey*, there's my sister from another mister--"

The speech therapist had already made her way to the gym, slightly winded with her bag full of oversized materials hanging on the handle. By the look on her face, she was apparently unable to rid herself of her patient fast enough. She had swung the wheelchair around as soon as she entered the gym, as though parking a shopping cart at the front of a grocery store. Delaney seemed to be sitting up straighter in the chair than he had seen her in the cafeteria, more engaged in the setting, despite being parked facing a wall and a bunch of therapist license certificates.

"How did it go?" Terrence asked, approaching them.

The speech therapist contorted her face. "We've got a long way to go."

Terrence rolled his eyes as he reached the wheelchair, out of Alice's peripheral vision. He whispered something to Delaney, then spun the chair around. Her eyes seemed happy when she made eye contact with Terrence. Relieved. As they passed Alice, Laney scrunched her nose like she had just picked up on an unpleasant odor. The rest of her face was inexpressive, the right half with a slightly warped appearance. She quickly looked down at her hands to avoid making accidental eye contact with anyone else.

"Delaney," Quinn blurted out.

She jolted to attention. Her familiar eyes were kind and had a piercing aqua color. She recognized Quinn immediately, looked him up and down questioningly.

Terrence had been working out a scheduling issue with Julie, but suddenly had a friendly, but protective stature. "Yes, Sir. This is Laney. Laney, this is Quinn Harwell. New admit today. Dr. Schuler brought him over from University."

Her face remained expressionless, but her nostrils flared a bit and her eyebrow flinched.

"Laney isn't much of a talker right now," Julie chimed in.

Delaney scanned his appearance--his scruffy face, his sweatpants and t-shirt, flip flops, the ostomy bag tucked into the pocket of the chair. She suddenly looked far more alert than even seconds earlier, thoughts seeming to race behind her eyes.

"Well, not to be rude," Terrence began, "But Miss Laney and I are hitting the pool. You've got your suit on under there, right girl?"

"She does. We put it on at the end of our session," Julie called after them. "Hey--braid her hair beforehand so it doesn't get more tangled."

"Yeah, I know how to do that."

"*Terrence--*" Julie threatened.

"I got you, I got you. So, your suit--Is it an itsy bitsy teeny weeny yellow polka dot bikini?" Terrence whispered loudly, then dramatically swatted at the air. "Nah, I wanna be surprised. We'll see y'all later."

Julie retrieved Quinn and started for the opposite exit.

"Friendly bunch," Quinn commented when they reached the patient room hallway.

"Oh, well, that was probably not the best thing to say in the gym with other patients present, but yeah. Laney's pretty special to us."

"I can see that."

"She's one of our therapists."

The last time he saw her, she had just been accepted into the pediatric residency program.

"I shadowed her when I first started. We became really good friends," Julie explained.

"That must be hard to see her go through this."

Julie caught herself staring off toward Laney's empty room as she pushed the wheelchair toward the nurse's station.

"How does a 29 year old have a stroke?" he asked quietly.

"One day she had a headache and *boom*."

"A headache?"

"Well Laney had a pretty bad concussion when she was a teenager. Evidently that can damage blood vessels and increase your chances of having a stroke."

He shook his head, angrily. "She's going to get better, won't she?"

"Physically, I think she'll get much better. The other stuff--speech, memory-- is beyond my expertise."

"She has memory loss?"

"Best as we can guess, she doesn't remember the last few years."

A twinge of guilt slithered up into his throat as he hoped this meant she didn't remember their last encounter. "She's a pretty girl."

"You should have seen her before. I guess she modeled as a kid."

He nodded. "No kidding."

"Hey, don't look now but your nice guy side is showing."

"No, it's just the lighting."

"Oh OK, well, I think you'll like it here."

"No place I'd rather be--you know besides home, work, the middle of the desert with no water filtering my own pee to drink—"

"Oh there's that charm again. You better watch it or you'll have all the ladies swooning."

"Yeah life-altering spinal cord injury. I should take it all in stride."

"Pun intended?"

He frowned. "That was insensitive, Julie."

"You would be Quinn Harwell?" A man's voice greeted, matter-of-factly.

"I *would* be Quinn Harwell. And you are?"

"Jeffrey, I'll be one of the nurses taking care of you."

"I have a *male* nurse?"

"Oh good, he's latched his fangs into you," Julie said, passing off the wheelchair. "Sorry Jeff, Mr. Harwell reports he does *not* have a nice guy side and whatever you do, do *not* ask him about his penis." She was already spun around and jogging down the hall. "Hey Dr. Schuler--I have a question about my friend Quinn--"

Quinn rolled his eyes, as he was certain his catheterized penis was being discussed. Down the corridor, he saw the outline of Dr. Schuler turning to speak with her. "So, you go by Jeff?"

He cleared his throat. "My name is *Jeffrey*," he said with an annoyed tilt of his head.

Quinn looked in the direction Julie had gone. "Julie called you Jeff."

"*You* may call me Jeffrey, or Nurse Adkins."

"Can I call you Jeffrey in a British accent and ring a little bell?"

Jeff tightened his jaw. "That's funny."

"You think so?"

"No."

Quinn dropped his chin, giving him a sideways look. "Jeffrey, did we just become best friends?"

# 6

# endure

Quinn had claimed the end locker just across from the gymnasium restrooms and drinking fountains for the second year. It helped when your mom was on the school board and tweaking locker assignments was the least of her capabilities. He did not seek out her assistance to get him out of detention, however, and he had spent the last hour scrubbing paint off surfaces in the art room with mineral spirits. Despite wearing gloves, his hands still felt dried out and he was sure he would be smelling mineral spirits for the next few weeks. He decided that if he could smell it, his mom certainly could, and then he'd be forced to explain why he felt compelled to chuck colored pencils at the ceiling tiles and wound up in detention in the first place. That is, if he wasn't able to come up with a semi-believable lie. He was pretty terrible at lying. It was going to be tough enough to "uh-hmm" his way through a conversation about the soccer practice he missed because he was in detention.

The empty building was suddenly flooded by the ruckous of a group of senior boys, who paid little attention to him and disappeared into the locker rooms. It struck him as odd that they turned into the girls' side, but was relieved that he might have avoided having to deal with them when he went to scrub his hands. He shoved his backpack inside his conveniently situated locker and took several whiffs of his hands, confirming that they did, in fact, need a scrubbing. He dropped them immediately upon seeing his childhood crush appear through the double doors from outside. She was slightly out of breath and her cheeks were red from exertion. He was about to ask her if she had track practice, something that should have been obvious by the gray t-shirt she was wearing. Then the boy who had held the door for her, who Quinn recognized as her sister's boyfriend, ran to match her pace.

"Thanks so much, Delaney. I don't know what's going on with her."

"She's crying?" Her dark ponytail thumped against her neck as she walked.

"Yeah, totally distraught over something. She doesn't want to talk to me, but she asked for you."

Delaney made eye contact with Quinn, her blue eyes bright in the late afternoon sun streaming through the doors ahead. "Where is she?"

"In the back there, by the showers," Jeremiah said, sounding concerned, following her inside.

Quinn thought of the other boys who had just gone in.

He thought of her eyes meeting his, just for a moment.

He could hear her call out to her sister just as Jeremiah locked the door.

*** 

Delaney was surprised to find her dad home—almost as surprised as he was to have her walk through his door. There had been a schedule, years before, but he kept having things arise with work and due to a bad deal made, he had desperately needed to retain his clients. Delaney's mom had taken him back to court—to get more child support and to modify the parenting plan. As time went on, things had been better with work, but she insisted Delaney was at too critical an age to have more changes brought on her—she added that Delaney had expressed not wanting to see him, that she was too busy. As a result, she hadn't set foot in his house for three years. Their visits were meals or outings that didn't require a sleepover.

He had just poured a glass of scotch, the ice clinking in the short tumbler, when he heard the keypad on the door. The setting sun flowed around her and flooded the room.

"Dell, to what do I owe--" He set the glass down on the coffee table with a thunk. "What happened?"

She slowly navigated the steps, her eyelids like lead weights. The backpack slid off her shoulder of its own accord.

He rushed to her side and placed his hand on the side of her face, examining the side of her head. "There's blood--"

"I hit my head. I'll be alright."

"Did you get in a fight?"

She blinked slowly, gave a small nod.

"What about?"

The last thing she remembered was running. Running had become like a drug to her. Her mother appreciated the calorie burn, but was concerned it would turn her legs too muscular, her skin uneven with sun—and then there was the potential sun damage. She would have preferred Delaney run on a treadmill, but she reluctantly agreed. After a short time of running on her own, she had joined the track and field team. She was phenomenal at hurdles, with her long ballerina legs, but she loved long distance running the most. The coach wanted her to do some short distance races after seeing her finish her laps by sprinting from the final turn. No one reached that speed after running that far. He estimated she'd be even faster once she acquired more muscle in her legs. She had beamed when he said this and for once she didn't slink at the thought of the photographer, the director, her mother, lecturing her about staying thin. Delaney found herself craving the wind in her face, the sun on her shoulders, the rhythmic crunch of the track dirt under her shoes. She had already decided that the next photoshoot would be her last. She would face the disappointment of her mother. No one could make her model.

That was the last thing she remembered—peering out over the horizon, the mountains looking soft and almost carpeted with the red and orange light, the crunch of gravel under her shoes, the steady thumping of her heart, the pulsing of each stride through every muscle in her leg as her foot made impact, her slow controlled breathing.

The next thing she knew, she was standing in the parking lot with Quinn, a boy she barely knew--no, not standing--wrapped in his arms, stirring to consciousness in a slurred, confused state. Her hair was dripping wet. She was no longer wearing her track outfit, instead changed into her regular school clothes without underwear or a bra. Her body ached in unfamiliar places, places it shouldn't. Her head throbbed. It felt as though the blood vessel in her forehead was pulsing into her skull. She had reached up near her ear and found blood, the area around it swollen. She remembered thinking that she didn't know the tight skin had the ability to swell so much. It was unbearable to touch, but she kept finding her fingers drawn to it.

She had concluded quickly that they must have been walking through the parking lot together, though she had no idea why that might be the case. Her next thought, other than suppressing the impulse to scream, a seething pain spreading from her temple, was: Mom can't see me like this. It was clear without seeing herself that there would be bruising, possibly a wound, and that could put the modeling job at jeopardy. Hopefully there would be some veil, some sort of bizarre headdress to hide it. Perhaps they'd frizz her hair in some Bride of Frankenstein fashion, or use some dramatic makeup application. She was going to quit modeling, yes, but she needed to give her mother one last shoot.

She had noticed the boy who was holding her upright as an afterthought. He was clearly concerned and was saying something about going to a hospital.

*Doesn't he know I need to clean myself up? If Mom finds out I got injured at track, she'll make me quit. It's the only place I feel happy, Quinn.*

On the excruciating walk, it had become clear that this wasn't simply a track injury. She thought to ask if someone had punched her in the ribcage, but the pain emerged from all angles--like she was being unbearably constricted. She wasn't sure what a broken rib felt like, but she suspected the pressure in the lower right side of her chest might be just that. It made her labored breathing all the more painful.

"Delaney," her dad said, his voice bellowing in her ears. It sounded like the large body of water he had been speaking through was being drained.

She looked up, trying to look more alert. "Don't tell Mom," she said quickly.

"Why?"

"The shoot."

"You're concerned about a photoshoot? Dellie, you look--"

"I'm quitting."

It looked like he had been shot backwards. "What?"

"I'm quitting modeling, but after tomorrow. I'm going to tell Mom."

He didn't imagine that conversation would go well. Edie had so much of herself invested in Delaney's modeling, but there was a part of him that felt validated. Edie was quick to point out that he was an absentee father, but even if that rang with truth, he knew his daughter hated modeling and was only doing it to please her mother. He also felt proud of Delaney for speaking up for herself. "If that's what you want to do, I fully support you, but Dell--" He looked over his daughter, moving the clumped wet hair from her eyes. She looked like she had been mangled by wolves. "What *happened*?"

She stretched her back, exhausted, then winced.

"Sit down. Come in here."

She dropped to the leather couch with a thud and very much wanted to lie down and sleep, but she stayed sitting upright, her dad joining her with a washcloth and bag of peas from the freezer. When he asked again, she knew better than to tell him she couldn't remember. It would sound like a lie or he'd believe her and she'd wind up in Emergency. The story fell out in surprisingly concise detail. She told him about the pack of girls that hated her for modeling. They tormented her for it. They said she was "doing things" to keep getting these gigs. That part was at least. She had been changing after track and they confronted her. She had to cut her shower short. She threw on her clothes and had bent down to tie her shoelaces. When she stood, she slammed her head into a locker door. It was an accident.

He listened intently, nodding along, and pulled her into a hug when she was done.

He believed her.

She asked to use the bathroom to clean up and he felt guilty with relief to have a few minutes to digest everything. It was as she trudged toward the bathroom that his ears picked up on an unfamiliar noise echoing down the hallway. *I bent down to tie my shoelaces*, she had told him.

The sound was the unmistakable clapping of cheap flip flops.

He dried her clothes while she cleaned up in the bathroom. He placed her clothes outside the door for her to retrieve, feeling uneasy, an impulse to take her to the hospital. Listening outside the door, she was running the sink, gulping water from her hands, by the sound of it. He wondered if she had vomited. *Concussion*, a voice in his head said urgently. He was about to take a parental stand and had leaned into the door to say her name when the door opened. She emerged in dry clothes, her backpack slung over her shoulder, her hair parted to the side, as to cover her injury, and pulled into a distracting, messy knot. For good measure, she seemed to have applied some light makeup. He felt ridiculous insisting she go to the hospital now so instead, he sheepishly asked if she wanted something to eat, knowing very well he didn't have anything she was allowed to eat in his fridge. Actually, he was quite certain there was little more than butter and a carton of half and half in there.

"I won't involve you. I don't want Mom getting mad at you when you didn't do anything," she said, looking at the floor.

It sounded as though she should have said: "didn't do anything *wrong*," but she didn't.

"Would you be able to drop me off closer to the house? My head does hurt a bit."

He nodded and went to search for his car keys.

# 7

# carry

"So tell me about your marriage," Delaney said suddenly, having just finished her bite of hawaiian tuna. She and Jack were having lunch on the outdoor patio of a poke bowl restaurant close to the hospital. Jack had just proudly determined they had been together exactly two weeks. She had squeezed his stubbled cheek, smiling widely, and said: "Aww, you're so precious. I think I'll keep you around for awhile."

She chased this wry remark with the prompt about his marriage.

Jack didn't talk about his marriage much. He could typically deflect conversations about it with anyone else by saying they were two different people, etcetera, then immediately toss in a joke about ending things when he was student loan poor, thus avoiding alimony payments. This attempt at humor had fallen short of impressing his lunch companion. She had paused chewing, the space between her eyes creasing, her crystal blue eyes focused on him.

"List three of Gillian's good qualities," Delaney challenged, after she had swallowed her food.

He chuckled nervously. "Uh—she's outgoing. She's health conscious. And she is kind to animals."

"See? Everyone has their good traits."

"Hitler?"

"Extremely charismatic. This made him a very effective public speaker."

He nodded. "Clearly."

"He also had strong convictions."

"You missed your calling in PR."

"He also seemed to like his dogs a lot." She took a moment to take a bite, chewing thoughtfully. "It could very well have just been propaganda, but it still pokes holes in my belief that dog people are inherently good."

"There *are* a lot of dog people that are total jerks."

"The ones that pretend their dog is a service dog?"

"The ones that don't clean up after them?"

"You know what? Dog people are total assholes," she whispered with a shocked grin.

He found himself smiling when she did.

"Three reasons it didn't work with Gillian?" Her face remained inquisitive and kind.

He cleared his throat. "I was only *physically* attracted to her; there was no other connection. Her mini dog liked to pee in my shoes. She sided with the dog."

"'Irreconcilable differences' really covers a spectrum of reasons. And *another* example of a dog person being a jerk." She seemed to recoil a bit. "I shouldn't call her a jerk. I don't know her."

He raised his eyebrows in an indiscernible way. "*And*—I only married her because she was pregnant."

Delaney nodded slowly. "I don't want to be insensitive, but you know that needs context."

"The baby wasn't mine."

She frowned, but there was some relief in her eyes that she hadn't uncovered a greater loss.

"The baby was biracial. Half-Asian. Some investment guy she worked with."

She raised an eyebrow, reached across the table, and removed his eyeglasses from the chest pocket of his linen button down shirt. She slid them up to the bridge of her nose. "You're not Asian? I really need to get my eyes checked." She squinted. "How are you seeing right now?" She slid the glasses off, handing them back to him, blinking repeatedly.

"I have contacts in. I grabbed these thinking they were sunglasses." He slid them on briefly. "Do I look studious?"

Her cheeks tightened and she attended to her food, her long bangs falling in her eyes.

"That dorky, huh?"

She sighed, her lips pursed and upturned. "I am actually self-conscious of how physically attracted I am to you, Dr. Mathison."

"Is that right?" he said, clearly amused. He tucked away the glasses, glad they had managed to get a table with an umbrella to provide shade from the sun.

"I'm a big believer in paying attention to the inner beauty and all that," she asserted, dropping her shoulders, "There's just one major problem with that."

"What's that?"

"Your inner beauty is also a tall, chiseled doctor with a great personality. It's *really* distracting."

He shook his head, grinning.

She ignored his remark. "Your inner beauty doesn't snore though. *By the way.*"

"Do I need to worry about you two?"

"No, you would be wise to get a sleep study though. It's a shame you have such a phobia of your own kind." Something seemed to register in her mind and her eyebrow furrowed. She shook her head almost imperceptibly, releasing the thought. "OK, so while you *are* incredibly attractive--*incredibly* attractive--" She paused to place her hand on his cheek and sigh dramatically, as though beholding a beautiful piece of art. "You are incredibly *not* Asian."

"I am not Asian."

She imagined him holding a newborn, looking into that sweet face and realizing the truth of the situation, of having anticipated the moment for months and months, preparing his life, his mind for this new life, his new role, only to discover that none of it was to be. She felt a knot in her stomach. "That must have been—"

"A waste of time."

She clearly wasn't fond of his statement.

"I mean if the baby had been mine, I would have made the best of the situation, owned up to my responsibilities."

Delaney sat stunned by his statement for an extended few seconds. At last, she released a breath. "Wow."

"What?"

"Such *indifference*." She leaned forward, lowering her voice. "It's just my opinion that a man who would have simply 'owned up' to his responsibilities doesn't keep a newborn sized Cubs jersey in his dresser drawer."

"Snooping?"

"I was looking for socks. You told me to make myself at home." Her eyebrows challenged him to question her, while her eyes were glossy, making him wonder if she was holding back tears.

"It wouldn't have been the greatest situation, but to think you're having a baby and then have that taken away? Kind of tough to—adjust." He started loading his fork without any clear objective to actually take a bite.

"I'm sorry you had to go through that, Jack."

He nodded with reluctance.

"Was the baby a boy or girl?"

"Girl," he said, lost in a memory. "Sabrina."

She watched him as he processed the memory. She could practically see the images pass before his eyes. "Did you hold her when she was born?"

He froze, then nodded slowly. "The doctor handed her to me right away."

She pictured him, hair tousled, perhaps wearing a casual outfit similar to what he was wearing now holding a swaddled pink bundle, looking into the sweet face of a baby who carried no trace of his genetics, but who he had invested so much in already; a baby he already loved.

"While I was holding her, one of the nurses made a remark about Asian babies being so beautiful and asked about our donor." He sighed. "I was just lost in seeing how beautiful she was, how something could go from a tiny bean to a healthy, perfect little baby girl."

Delaney's head tilted involuntarily.

"She was beautiful. I mean, she was all red and angry at first, but--" He swallowed hard. "I didn't even notice that she was *clearly* not my child."

"So you--" her voice broke. "Was Gillian the one to--"

"A baby, as it turns out, is good leverage to try to get a man to leave his own infertile wife."

When Jack looked for her reaction to that detail, anticipating shock or disgust, he found something else. Her face was blotchy and pinched, her eyes glossy. She winced, lowering her gaze. "I'm sorry, Jack."

He shrugged, but he could sense an uneasiness grow within her. He wasn't sure which part she had the most issue with.

"Sabrina will never know all she missed out on not having you as her dad. She would have won the parental lottery."

Jack stared down at his plate, smiling lightly. "Thank you, Delaney." He was about to add that purchasing a miniature jersey wasn't a clear sign of fatherly abilities, but then she followed up with:

"Children being used as pawns is one of the things I dislike most about the human species." Her face was terribly sad as she said those words.

His mind raced over things he could say, but then he heard himself say, with no foresight of the thought: "Some species eat their own children."

Delaney jolted forward as she laughed, slapping her hand to her face. The tears that had been filling her eyes poured out with the motion. She made eye contact with him, her smile broadening. "Jack Fitzpatrick Mathison. Believe it or not, that doesn't make me feel better!"

"It got you to laugh."

"Totally inappropriate," she grumbled, shaking her head. "How dare you make me laugh about something like that."

She twirled a bit of seaweed salad around her fork like spaghetti and held it out for him.

"You think my middle name is Fitzpatrick?"

"It just came out. Was I close?"

"Lucas."

"Jack Lucas Mathison."

He accepted the bite, his eyebrows jumping as he tasted it. "That's less slimy than I thought it would be."

"I actually ate a bowl of just seaweed salad. It wasn't a small bowl either."

"Unless you're on *The Amazing Race*, why would you ever eat a plate of algae?"

"Because it's delicious?" She made an exaggerated expression. "Actually, nothing is delicious in such large volumes. There may have been a language issue on my part."

"Was this in Japan?"

"Hai."

"Hi yourself," he said in a low, flirtatious tone, which caused his intended reddening of her cheeks.

She had shared stories of some of her travels on their first camping trip together. While he had traveled quite a bit domestically, she had trekked to some bucket list destinations.

"Where's your next dream place to travel?"

"Your bedroom—Um, I don't know. What was the question?" Her smile tightened.

"Well, alright, alright."

"You're a bad influence, Jack Mathison."

"I can live with that."

"I bet you can." She rolled her eyes. "Iceland."

"Iceland. Good choice. Interesting choice."

"Alright that's a half-truth. I want to go to Iceland, but that's an active trip, Iceland. Lots of outdoor stuff, going from place to place. I'd actually love to park it on a beach in Hawaii with people bringing me $16 drinks in hollowed out pineapples and gorging on poke from Foodland."

He nodded approvingly. "What would gorging look like?"

"Straight out of the deli container, just grab a plastic fork and chow down until you get a little food pooch bell-ay." She patted her own flat stomach.

"That sounds amazing."

"Yeah but I have an ingrained need to do something—so maybe, get up early, go walking or on a paddle board, watch the sunrise, and *then* turn into a sloth for the rest of the day."

He loved her animated way of storytelling with big gesturing hands and exaggerated facial expressions. She could make an outing to the grocery store sound compelling.

He considered what it would be like to vacation with her, but as soon as he added Hawaii to the equation, he felt a lump in his throat. His one and only visit had not been a pleasant one. He had gone to spread his mom's ashes off Oahu's north shore. She'd never gotten to go, but always wanted to. His dad had tried to keep it together for Jack and his sister, but he had let out a horrific wail when he saw his wife's ashes being carried away by the sea, parted from her for the first time in 32 years. If he allowed enough space in his mind, Jack could still hear the desperate wail of his father just as clearly.

"So you've mentioned your sister, Tabitha, and your dad a little--" she said, inquisitively. "What are your parents like?"

He furrowed his brow, wondering if she had mind-reading capabilities. His reply fell out smoothly. "My mom used to sing all the time. Everything. Lullabies, classic rock, Frank Sinatra, Ella Fitzgerald. She had so much talent, but she never pursued it." He paused at that. "She and my dad would randomly dance together. She'd be cooking dinner, singing 'Fly Me to the Moon' or something and he'd sweep her into a dance."

She smiled dreamily. "That's a great image."

He nodded. "He adored her. They were just one of those couples. No one questioned if they loved each other."

She watched his eyes light up as he spoke about them, then picked up on the moment his face filled with a sadness that seemed to radiate off of him.

"She was diagnosed with breast cancer when I was 10. By the time they found it, it had already spread everywhere--her spine, her lungs."

She gazed into his eyes, which suddenly looked subdued, a bit less sure of himself. She tried to picture him at 10 years old. His blonde hair was probably shaggy, his chiseled face with a bit more youthful roundness. She reached for his arm, letting her fingers slide back and forth gently on his wrist.

He shook his head. "I know you understand. More than most."

"How did your dad cope?"

"My sister tried to get him to date a few years back. He has no interest in it. I wouldn't say he's unhappy--he works a lot, he travels, he gardens, but seeing him, he just seems--"

"Incomplete."

"Yeah." His eyes narrowed as she thought of the exact word he was seeking. "He's a romantic, a true believer in 'the One'." He tried loading his fork, then rested it back in the container. "My sister thinks he needs to get remarried, fill that void."

Delaney tensed. "I get her point—but—even if there's someone else in the role as his wife—" she seemed to notice the discomfort in his face. "The void will always be there."

"He once told me not to bother with any relationship that felt like if she left, I could just carry on the same as before." He thought of the rest of what his dad had said: *Love changes you, son. If a woman doesn't reach the very core of who you are, it's not worth it. It's not love.* "I think that's what bothers me about my marriage. I married Gillian because I couldn't stand the thought of not being in my child's life the way my parents were in mine. Even then, I felt like I was disappointing him--and missing out on something--*extraordinary*." He looked up at Delaney, who was still stroking his arm.

He smiled to himself, thinking of the day his dad came to town, just after his divorce was finalized. He expressed these things to him as they sat in the stands at a baseball game. His dad, gazing out to the game, shook his head. "Everything in its time, Son. When it's the right time for you, the right time for the woman you're meant to be with, she'll come knocking on your door." He doubted his dad meant it so literally, but he had some amusement over it when Jack first told him about Delaney. "Well what did I tell you, Son?" he had said, slapping him on the back.

She frowned. "I'm sorry about your mom. She sounds really special."

He gazed across the restaurant. "You know, when you invited me to lunch, I didn't know I was signing up for a therapy session. I hope you're in-network." He seemed to be trying to will the tears back in his eyes.

"Oh I don't accept insurance, but I think you'll like my payment plan."

He made eye contact again. He couldn't help but smile when he looked at her.

He wanted so badly to tell her he loved her, but it was too soon--wasn't it?

"Do *you* sing?"

He groaned.

"You *do*." She leaned forward, eyes wide. "Wait, were you in a Hanson tribute band? Actually was that too recent for you? What was a popular band from when you were growing up? Something and the Sunshine Band?"

"KC and the Sunshine Band was before me, thank you." He grinned.

"What do you sing?"

"I *used* to sing. I did some plays, a little acapella."

"Why did you stop singing?"

He swallowed hard. "When my little sister graduated from high school, she had gotten really emotional, that she wished Mom was there. I don't think I had allowed her not being there bother me--because there wasn't a point, right? But seeing Tab like that--it opened up some wounds for me, I guess. Things that reminded me of her--it just stung. I just didn't want to sing anymore."

She nodded slowly. "*Well*," she began, waiting for him to meet her gaze. "If you ever felt like singing again, I would like it very much if you sang to me." She said this quietly, matter-of-factly, leaning back in her seat. "You know, if I'm sad I think that would make me feel better."

"I don't ever want you to be sad, D."

She looked over her shoulder toward the family just entering the patio area, the toddler with spiky black hair flying a die cast plane from surface to surface, a chubby faced infant asleep in her carrier. She smiled to the exhausted looking parents, then turned back to him. Her expression was affectionate and reflective. "I've found that sadness makes happiness mean something. I don't like feeling sad, but I appreciate its purpose."

*I love you*, he said silently.

"Anyway," she said, waving her hand. "I'm terrible at small talk. With grownups at least." She stabbed at the seaweed salad, giving a small smile. "And *by the way, you* invited *me* to lunch. It was practically a kidnapping."

She had a point. He had walked straight into the charting area, taken control of her mouse to lock the computer. She had been poking a fork mindlessly into a very dry looking salad, which he discarded in the trash, took her hand and led her out of the gym and down the hall.

"If you feel that way about it, it'll never happen again."

She grimaced. "Actually, I kind of liked it."

He perked up.

"It was a little *Officer and a Gentleman* minus literally sweeping me off my feet, you being in uniform—" she took in his appearance. "Although this casual look really does something for me." She sat back in her seat. "The other difference is I do have to go back to work." She checked her watch. "And soon."

"I still have you for eleven and a half minutes. What else do we need to cover?"

"Is there a checklist for this lunch date? Cover before *what* exactly?"

He ignored the questions. "Really though--what's left? How many kids to have?" *Too soon, Jack.*

"*Oh.* I don't want kids."

"You don't?"

"Oh gosh, this could be a problem, I knew I should have brought it up sooner," she said, shaking her head. "But it's just weird to bring up things like that so early on."

The setting started to whirl around him.

She sighed dismissively. "Good thing I hadn't gotten too attached to you. This could be a tough breakup for you though."

"You don't want kids? You work with them all day."

She winced. "Exactly."

He was motioning with his hands like he couldn't fathom how he had overlooked something so obvious.

She shrugged. "I can't *stand* children, actually." She looked up at him, trying almost successfully to keep a straight face.

He stared sternly into her sparkling blue eyes, thinking how it should be a crime to have that genetic bloodline end while silently scolding himself for being so blinded by disappointment not to pick up on the obvious sarcasm. "Crazy ugly face."

She instantly contorted her face, bugged out her eyes.

"I love it. It's like a hypnosis trigger phrase. How many do you want?"

"Three," she said, snapping her face back to normal and dropping her napkin into her plastic bowl. "You?"

"2 or 3."

"You looked worried about the breakup, Jack," she said quietly, consolidating trash into her bowl. "Some might even say *'distraught'*." Her eyes got deliberately wide. "You're done, right?" She stood and started toward the trash bin with both of their containers.

Jack got to his feet and followed her. When she turned around, she bumped right into his chest. "I love you," he said, framing her face with his hands. It was the first time he'd said the words and he could feel his heart pulsing through his veins.

"You know, I was *wondering* about that."

He kissed her, dropping one hand to tickle her stomach under her scrubs.

Delaney flinched, laughing, pulling herself close to his ear.

"I love you, Jack."

***

Dr. Schuler closed the ledger sized folder and tucked it behind a 3 inch binder of Medicare regulations in the corner of his desk. He checked his phone to find several dozen dating app notifications and direct messages. He hadn't figured out how to turn off notifications despite seeming to have deleted the apps successfully and grumbled as he dropped it into his back pocket.

He scratched at his forehead and got to his feet, stretching as he emerged from his darkened office.

"How's the new kid?" He asked Jeff.

"Having dinner," Jeff replied. "He wasn't impressed with our menu so he had sushi delivered. UberEats."

"I've heard he's a challenge?"

"He's tamed since this morning. He even offered me his California roll."

"Really?"

"Cheapest roll there is, but I appreciate the gesture."

"You turned him down?"

"I'm low carb, but Liv jumped at the free food."

"How many months pregnant is she now?"

"Fourteen, I think?"

Dr. Schuler attempted a smile, patting the counter conclusively.

"He had me put a specialty roll aside for Laney. What's that about?"

Dr. Schuler shrugged.

"She's in the pool."

"Who—" he coughed. "Laney?"

"Second pool session today."

"Good." Dr. Schuler nodded thoughtfully. "Going to get some dinner and get some rest. I'm available on my cell phone." He turned around and started for the main corridor, angling his stride at the last moment to cut through the gym.

The air in the back corner of the gym had a distinctly chlorinated aroma. Patients and their families inevitably had to comment in the back hallway about the increase of humidity in the air, the thick warmth. As he made his way down the short hallway, he prayed that she was making some improvements and wasn't just bobbing helplessly in the water. He pictured her like other patients—choked by an imposing life vest, kicking and flailing erratically.

When he reached the windowed door, he prepared himself for the worst, but as he peered inside, he found that she wasn't wearing a vest at all--and she wasn't flailing. She was floating, her body appearing to drift atop the water, her arms outstretched, her eyes blinking slowly toward the ceiling.

"Alright, girl. Push those legs down into the water."

The motion was slightly unsteady, but with only a small disruption of the water, Delaney was standing upright. She held onto a floating barbell for balance, her attention focused on her therapist.

"That's it, that's it. *Step.*" Terrence smiled broadly. "That's my girl—such determination in those eyes—I *like* it!"

Delaney steadily paced forward and soon she was across the pool and making a turn, her expression serious. Terrence guarded her on the right as she continued.

"Well let's start wrapping things up, okay Laney? We can pick back up tomorrow."

Laney slowed, her jaw tightening.

Dr. Schuler glanced at his watch. 6:30. It was far past when Terrence should have been there. He thought of the photo Terrence kept at his workstation of his baby girl with her dimples and open mouthed laugh. He pushed open the door, met with resistance from the thick humidity in the pool room. Both therapists turned to him abruptly. "I'll keep working with you, Laney. Looks like you're doing the Daytona 500."

"Going to the right, but that's alright."

Dr. Schuler slipped off his cross trainers.

"I have an extra pair of board shorts and a rash guard back in my—" Before Terrence could finish, the physiatrist was stepping into the pool, his scrub pants soaked up to his knees.

He thought better of stepping in any deeper before removing his phone from his pocket. "We have a stash of scrubs in this restroom, I'll be fine. You can get on home," he said, patting him on the shoulder.

"You know, I don't care what anybody says about you, Sir. You're alright."

Dr. Schuler nodded. "Nothing they say would surprise me."

Delaney paused to stretch her leg, rotating it in a large circle under the water.

"Is the Gabapentin making a dent in the pain? I was hoping by now it might be helping."

She blinked slowly and continued moving around the perimeter of the pool. For once, the fact that she couldn't speak and that many questioned her cognitive capacity gave her an advantage on this particular topic. She simply acted like she hadn't heard the question. In the meantime, she considered her choice of hiding place for the pills--on the bedside table behind the picture frame Julie had placed on the table a couple nights prior. It was a group photo with several hospital staff at a bowling alley. Most were striking random silly poses-- Julie and two other nurses posed like Charlie's Angels, a line up of men behind them in aviators looked like either Secret Service or Super Troopers, and a trio of men had women riding piggyback who were assisting them do "See No Evil, Hear No Evil, Speak No Evil." It had been surreal to see herself hoisted on Jack's back covering his eyes, their smiles equally broad.

She wasn't quite sure what transpired as she thought of how this other version of herself had wrapped her arms around Jack with such familiarity. What she did know was that suddenly her toes didn't touch the pool bottom properly and her heel slid quickly as she overcompensated in recovering. Her face slid underwater for less than a second before Dr. Schuler's thick arms were pulling her back to the surface. In that moment, she heard her own voice in her head shouting "no" and she forced her feet solidly into the bottom. She stood upright, her shoulders drawn back with impeccable posture, water pouring down her face. Dr. Schuler released his hold on her back, his hand slowly moving away and nodded toward the pool length ahead. "Don't get lazy on me now, Rhodes."

Laney had made two passes by where his phone sat on the edge, her eyes scanning to the glowing screen before she stopped to examine it more closely, passing it off as an opportunity to stretch. Despite the restrictions in her facial dexterity, she successfully executed a side eye.

"Oh, so you're gonna judge me now, are you?"

She exhaled, started forward, dragging her hands through the pool, combing the water with her fingers.

"I'm going to delete the apps. I just can't figure out the damn phone. I don't have time for that stuff."

Her strides through the water made her head naturally bob so it appeared she was nodding along in agreement. So he continued.

"Do you remember me telling you about a woman named Vivian?"

Laney stopped, peered back at him.

Dr. Schuler grinned. "She wrote to me." If the timeline they had figured for Laney's memory was correct, she would recall lecturing him over a Mexican lunch about pursuing Vivian too soon after her husband died. Vivian was a childhood sweetheart, though he never fully expressed to her how he felt. When he was drafted into the NFL, her father had forbidden her from seeing him, saying he'd only break her heart. She had eventually married an insurance salesman and had three children.

"This was a tragedy. He was your age--that's too young. You can't sweep in there. Give her time."

"We don't *know* if it was a 'tragedy.' He could have been a real jerk."

Laney had held up the phone from which she was reading his obituary. "He was in charge of the food pantry at their church."

Dr. Schuler shrugged. "He could have been a real jerk running the pantry."

"He did charitable work in Haiti."

"The Clintons claim the same thing."

Laney squinted one eye. "OK, that's a fair point, but it's *too soon.*"

"What if I sent flowers?"

"That might be nice, but it says 'in lieu of flowers, family requests donations be made in Al's name to St. Jude's Research Hospital.' See? That's nice. Al was probably a good person."

"Why in *his* name?"

"Martin."

His dimples deepened.

She exhaled, releasing a partial growl. "Do not make his death about you. Pay respect to the man who probably really loved Vivian, gave her a good life, three kids."

"Fine."

She narrowed her eyes. "You *already* sent the flowers, didn't you?"

"Maybe."

"What did you send?"

"Daffodils and orchids."

"Why those?"

"Daffodils are her favorite and orchids are expensive."

"Showing off the pocketbook, huh Doc?"

His cheeks reddened. "That's disrespectful."

"*I'm* being disrespectful? The body isn't even cold yet."

They both reluctantly laughed.

"And what was on the card?"

He shrugged.

"Tell me you didn't let the florist attach a generic card."

"No. It was simple, but short: 'Although it's difficult today to see beyond the sorrow, may looking back in memory help comfort you tomorrow.'"

Delaney blinked.

"What? I thought it was nice. It even rhymed."

"Looking back on *what* memories?"

He considered this and his mouth fell slightly ajar. "I didn't mean me."

In the pool, though her face lacked its typical animated quality, Delaney's eyes confirmed she remembered the woman. She waited for him to continue.

"About a month ago, she started sending me postcards. She's been traveling."

Laney began circling the small pool again.

"She said she was giving herself time to grieve, but she had been thinking about me." He pictured her loopy cursive, how his name looked in her handwriting. He thought of the beach on the opposite side of the postcard with its quiet sand dunes and expanse of the ocean beyond. Though it was just a stock image, he could practically see her walking along the ocean's edge, wearing a white sleeveless linen dress, her fair skin tanned, her short honey blonde hair impossibly blowing in her face. He exhaled. "I haven't had a good track record with relationships. I don't know if I trust myself not to screw something up."

When he looked up, Delaney was staring at him, her face indiscernible.

"I wish I could know what's going through your head. I'm sure you'd knock some sense into me, tell me what to do."

Beside her, his phone screen lit up again. She moved closer to it, peering at the notifications.

*Well, she can read,* he thought, relieved that she didn't have that speech therapy mountain to climb. He was about to make further excuses for the presence of the app, the notifications, the private messages, as he could only imagine what was on his screen, but then he watched as Delaney swiped her elbow across the pool edge and the phone plopped into the chlorinated water, sinking like a brick to the shallow pool floor.

Delaney continued forward, meeting Dr. Schuler's gaze.

He smiled.

# 8

# unwanted

D r. Schuler pushed the sliding glass door gently, opening it just enough to pass through, and closed it behind him. The curtain was pulled back a bit, allowing light to flood half of the room, so he tugged that closed, as well. The room wasn't nearly dark, but his eyes still needed a few moments to adjust so he stood blinking, listening to the steady beeping of the monitors, the breathing of the machines. Finally the room started to come into focus.

Delaney had been turned on her left side in a deceivingly natural pose of embracing a pillow. It was all an effort to prevent pressure sores and to move her body, even in its comatose state. Her team of doctors hadn't ordered therapy yet, saying there wasn't a point since she was asleep, but Julie had reported coming to see her at least once or twice a day to stretch her body a bit, help get her repositioned. Jack, of course, was doing the same.

He stepped around the base of the bed, glancing up at the recliner tucked in closely to her bed rail. Jack had positioned himself to be as close as possible to her. It appeared he had been sitting upright, a darkened tablet slid into the chair arm. He had fallen asleep with his neck slung uncomfortably toward his shoulder, his arm over extended to the bed so he could keep his hand resting on hers.

The Anesthesiologist had stopped shaving, his full facial hair giving him the look of some sort of lumberjack. He had been ineligible to take FMLA due to the fact that he and Delaney weren't related, but Human Resources had been sympathetic to his "situation" and advocated for him to be permitted to take a leave of absence unpaid. By what Dr. Schuler had been told, Jack had spent the weeks thus far in the confines of the hospital, at her side nearly constantly. Shaving had clearly not been a priority, despite there being very little to do otherwise to pass the time.

Martin Schuler sighed as he took in the scene. Since the pair had started dating, he had felt sadness tied to a strange persistent thought that she no longer needed him. It was asinine, he had decided, in that he wasn't her father or family; he was her mentor. Then he had scolded himself for being so dismissive of her. He truly did think of her like a daughter (although having no children of his own, he didn't know if his interactions with her were particularly fatherly).

The blankets were loosely draped over her. Even if he didn't know she was in a medically induced coma, he would know the blanket placement was not her own doing. During her time in the hospital as a young teen after the automobile accident that killed her mother, he remembered her sleeping habits being a struggle for Nursing. They said she twisted in her sleep, attempting to turn on her side, wrapping the blankets tightly around herself. It had surprised him given the extent of her injuries and the pain such movement would inflict, but he had gone into her room, found her as they had described. Her face had been tensed, her grip on the blanket tight. He had wheeled the rolling stool beside her and sat.

She hadn't had many visitors. He had seen her dad around a few times, but he didn't seem as up to the task as one would have hoped. He seemed receptive enough to helping, but he became insecure when asked to make any decisions about Delaney's care. When Martin had come in to consult about bringing her to Rehab and presented the options, either a) extend her acute care stay then do home health, b) send her to a skilled nursing facility (which Martin essentially eliminated by his detailed accounts of their deficiencies), or c) bring her to Rehab for intense therapy, excellent nursing with the goal of having her be able to do outpatient therapy on discharge, her dad had seemed grateful he had made the answer so clear.

Other than her dad, Laney had five other visitors. 1 & 2: Paternal grandparents who sobbed upon seeing her, having not seen her since she was a young child. Social work had provided their synopsis--that her dad had been uninvolved with Delaney for most of her life so the grandparents hadn't seen her for 7-8 years. 3. An overweight, dented faced man had slipped by Nursing and stood at her bedside as she slept. When the nurse had gone in to check on her, he was staring at the teenage girl with disgust and the nurse had questioned his relationship. He had muttered a response mixed with expletives as he left so Security had been put on alert, though he hadn't attempted to return. 4. A sister who seemed angry with the world had spent all of 15 minutes in the hospital. She had no other in-state family.

Finally, 5. A teenage boy named Quinn, lanky and nonthreatening, had apparently been showing up since early on in her ICU stay. He would typically come in after school hours and stay until dinner. He would usually spend the bulk of Sunday after early church service with her as well. The team had concluded that he wasn't a boyfriend, but were grateful for his presence. Her lack of family support was a frequent contention of team conference and had justified an extension in her stay in order to allow her to discharge with modified independence or setup for most activities.

The scars on her face were still prominent, a deep pink. Wound care had just started applying an ointment to help them fade. Her long hair had been hastily shaved back from her wounds when she was first in Emergency. The rest was messy and strewn across her face. Her jawline had sharp edges made more prominent by her disinterest in eating. Her admission weight was well into the underweight category to begin with.

Her sleep had been strained and filled with dreams, her body twitching on occasion, her fingers clenching into fists. She flinched when he placed his hand on her cheek, though she continued to sleep.

"You're safe, Little One," he said softly. He stroked her cheek, careful to avoid her scars. "The worst is behind you." He remembered watching her shoulders ease with his words and her eyelashes flutter open. She gazed toward him, her crystal blue eyes piercing deep within him.

In another world, he would have a child her age.

The thought was surreal and haunting. Before him was a girl with fair skin, blue eyes, freckles--a child of his own would certainly look quite different--but there was a correlation being drawn in his mind of two children discarded by those who were supposed to love them most. Delaney had been abandoned long ago by her father and left behind when her mother died. Her pain was more lasting than that of his own child, but both were tragic.

He had barely remembered the name of the woman who approached him as he walked to his sports car in the covered parking lot over 15 years earlier. He had received the upgrade in parking accommodations after the conclusion of his residency and had been thinking fondly of the marvel of his life's success. She had walked toward him with nervous resolve and he had pondered how he could excuse himself by saying he had a speaking engagement to attend. Two words were enough to silence him.

She was keeping the baby. It would be a challenge, but she would find a way to make it work. She understood that they were two grown adults so it was as much her fault as his that they were in this situation, but talked about how important she thought it was that the baby have both parents, in whatever arrangement they worked out. She was really quite reasonable. By countering with the same sort of logic and supportiveness, they had parted on good terms.

For the next 3 months, he did what he could to avoid her. He had learned that she drove a compact white Honda so before exiting the building each night, he'd scan the parking lot for signs of it. His secretary had learned not to pass him phone messages from her anymore, though she was struggling to hide her disapproval.

It was when the calls stopped that he became curious. There was something about having a child coming into the world and wanting them to be supported. It was less parental responsibility and more that he didn't want it to get around that he was the father of a juvenile delinquent. At least he could set the child up on a path for success, perhaps check in from time to time to guide them.

She didn't return his calls. He thought to let things go, but he found himself redialing her number routinely after work for several days. When that didn't work, he stopped in where he had remembered she worked—at a lounge downtown. It was an odd day when he wasn't dressed in scrubs, having had to attend a late afternoon conference. He walked in confidently in his business suit with gray and yellow striped tie and situated himself in a leather club chair at one of the coffee table conversation areas where he knew he couldn't be missed.

He sensed her approaching from the direction of the kitchen and raised his mouth at the corner as she circled in front of him. "Martin, what are you doing here?"

She did not look pleased to see him.

"We haven't been able to get in touch and I wanted to see how you're doing." He motioned to the opposite chair. "Can you take a break? It's not busy yet."

She glanced toward the bar and quickly took a seat.

"How are you, Cassidy?" His eyes glanced to her apron, which was not protruding in the way one might expect for being 6 months pregnant.

"I'm--fine, Martin."

"How's the baby? Healthy?" he asked, reaching coolly for his low ball glass.

She frowned, her eyes widening. "There *is* no baby."

He retracted his hand. "Something happened? During the pregnancy?"

"I started looking into daycare, insurance, and it was just too much. I had planned to start school next year and since it became obvious I would be raising the--" She redirected. "Since I wouldn't have any help, I decided it wasn't a good time to take on--all of *that*."

It felt like someone had punched him in the chest. "I said I would help."

"Yeah and then you didn't return any of my calls." Her coiled hair bounced as she made her point.

"My secretary didn't give me messages that you'd called," he said, hating how lies had become automated.

Cassidy dipped her chin forward. "I wasn't born yesterday, Martin."

The phrasing "wasn't born" echoed in his ears. His heart started to ache. "If I had known--"

"If you had known," she scoffed, shaking her head. "Well now you know."

Martin sat back in his chair, trying to process this new information. "How long ago?"

"Two weeks ago," she said firmly.

*5 months*, he said silently, his mind reeling all the things an unborn baby of that age is capable. What they feel. "I didn't think they allowed 2nd trimester--"

"I traveled out of state where they do."

"Oh."

"I presume we don't have anything else to discuss?" She stood, fixed her apron and walked quickly away.

15 year old Delaney's eyes blinked slowly and watched him touching her cheek. "You seem like a good person," she whispered. "I don't understand why you have such a poor reputation."

He raised an eyebrow, but tried to maintain a kind expression. "I do? Who have you been talking to?"

"If you don't say much, people tell you things they probably shouldn't."

"People must tell you a lot."

She nodded slightly. "Do I remind you of someone?"

The question startled him.

"I get that a lot, too," she clarified. "Mainly it's in the context that they're so relieved what happened to me didn't happen to their similarly aged child, relative, neighbor."

"They say that to you?"

"They say it around me. People seem to think if you don't speak, you don't hear."

He lifted his eyebrows in understanding. "I have the test results you asked about."

Her body tensed.

"It was negative. Both for pregnancy and for STDs."

She closed her eyes for a moment, slowly releasing her breath.

"I can prescribe a contraceptive temporarily until you can see a primary doctor if you have plans to--"

She shook her head. "I won't need it."

He nodded, then frowned. "Was it the skinny kid who's here all the time?"

She sighed. "No. It wasn't Quinn."

"Well I hope whoever it was--I hope the experience was nice. I do think you're young to--" he paused, waving off his remarks. "I'm sorry, it's not my place."

"Probably not, but it's nice to have someone care." She said quietly. "And I happen to agree that I'm too young."

He glanced around at the darkened room. "You know, it's only 8:30."

"One can only browse a 144 square foot gift shop so many times. I'm on low sensory due to seizure concerns, as you know, so movies are out, and the book I was reading put me to sleep."

"What book?"

"*Lord of the Rings*. It's on the reading list for next year. Figured I'd get a jump on it."

He was thoughtful a moment. "Have you ever had a cuban sandwich?"

"If it's not raw vegetables or lettuce, probably not."

Nursing was pleased to see Delaney outside her room, but they couldn't hide their surprise that Dr. Schuler was wheeling her, leg extended out before her. It was the night crew so they weren't accustomed to seeing too much of him and they were out of the normal day-to-day enough not to feel comfortable questioning him when he announced they were going on an outing.

It was as he reached the parking lot that he was especially grateful for having switched over to a larger capacity vehicle. There would be no way she would have been able to keep her leg at extension in the Lotus. His Mercedes was still meant to impress, but it actually had a backseat.

He found himself glancing to his rearview several times throughout the short drive. The sight of the outside world seemed to have captivated her. She had her head leaning against the window, staring across the backseat toward the stripmalls and dark neighborhoods beyond.

"It just occurred to me I probably needed to get your dad's approval to take you for an outing."

Disappointment filled her eyes. "Probably."

"Should I call him?"

"No, we wouldn't want to bother him. Just don't get us in an accident or reveal yourself as a serial killer and we should be fine."

He made a mental note to ask the social worker if she'd had any contact with Delaney's dad. "Reveal myself as a serial killer?"

"Yeah, I don't need to know what you do in your spare time."

"Well rest easy."

"I tend to be a decent judge of character. I also reasoned that if you did end up murdering me, part of me would be relieved." She made eye contact with him in the rear view mirror. "I'm not about to kill myself, I don't want to take any medication for it, and yes, I'll say something if either of those two things change."

"Okay," he concluded, frowning.

She nodded. "So unless I'm mistaken, you seem to have a vested interest in my case."

He chuckled slightly. "You're bolder than your silence would imply--and of course I want to see you do well."

"I don't mean it in any negative sort of way. Do you have a child around my age? Niece? Nephew?"

He swallowed hard. To say no would feel like a lie. "I lost a child who would be about your age."

"I'm sorry," she said, her eyes meeting his again. They were the brightest shade of blue he'd ever seen, even only illuminated by street lamps. She rested her temple against the headrest, exhaled. She was quiet for the rest of the drive.

"Oh good, they're still open."

Delaney ducked her head to look out the windshield. The line was still 10 people deep at the white food truck covered in customer messages and artwork in colorful markers.

Once parked, he rounded the front of the car, opened her door, and hoisted her in his arms in the same manner he'd loaded her in the car. He carried her toward the slightly graded hill. At the base, they were playing a movie, dozens of attendees sprawled out on blankets and sitting in lawn chairs.

"I thought no movies for me."

He slowly lowered her to the silky cool grass. "You're probably passed the point where it's a concern. I'm just going to put in our order. Oh it's *Seabiscuit.* I heard this was good," he said, motioning toward the projection screen down the hill.

He returned with their beverages a few minutes later. She was focused on the movie, leaning back onto her hands, but sat up to take her drink cup. "You'll of course add this to my bill?" she said facetiously.

"Obviously. How's the movie?" he asked, settling into a spot beside her on the grass.

She sipped the beverage, her eyes fixed on the screen, the fresh fruit slices bobbing around in the ice. "It's a tale of the ultimate underdogs rising up against all odds to victory set during the Depression. You will ugly cry."

14 years later, he found himself studying that same profile, her right hand curled up by her cheek. The anesthetic seemed to be an appropriate dose. If not for the oxygen mask, she would have the appearance of a deep, peaceful sleep.

"Tomorrow's the day?" Dr. Schuler's raspy voice asked, noticing Jack sitting up in his chair.

Jack nodded toward the bed and Delaney's youthful face. "That's the plan."

"Do me a favor before then? *Shave.*"

# 9

# gone

S he was back in Alaska. At least she assumed it was Alaska. She was sitting on a snowy lake bank, her body surrounded in what felt like slush. There wasn't a logical reason why she was sitting in slush and she lacked the ability to remove herself from it, but she wasn't chilled like she expected. Her core seemed to be generating an abundance of heat so the contrast was refreshing and she found herself gazing across the water to the white mountains in the distance, set beneath a crystal clear sky.

*"There we go. That temperature is coming way down."*

Delaney peered around at the setting that now seemed quite familiar. She'd visited at least a few times in recent days. To her right was an expansive forest. An arctic fox flitted about at the edge of the forest, glancing repeatedly in her direction with its black beady eyes. The trees were tall and narrow and were holding more snow than they seemed capable. In a clearing just beyond the fox, who appeared to have uncovered something savory in the icy snow, she half expected to find a lamppost and a fawn carrying packages back to his burrow. Each time she found herself in this exact spot, she checked.

To her left was a small cabin with smoke emerging from the chimney. She tried to smell the wood burning, but found her nose only picked up on something that smelled like an antiseptic nearby.

Suddenly the skin on the left side of her head sizzled.

*"See? That staple isn't holding."*

The pain subsided quickly. "Jack? Is that you?" she called toward the cabin, waiting for him to appear at the door. The cabin had expansive windows on the lake side and a wrap around porch that, in total square footage, probably matched that of the cabin itself. There was a double wooden rocker set beneath the overhang and protected from the snow. On the railing was a navy blue enamel coffee mug. She could almost see the steam from the hot liquid billow up from it.

There was some conversation--no, arguing, in hushed tones--in the distance.

"Jack, come sit with me, it's so beautiful," she called. She ran her hand through her hair, her fingers searching for the source of what was causing the left side of her head to feel so exposed. Her eyes focused on the bright blue, cloudless sky overhead. The air was thinner than what was comfortable to her, but clean. As she sat, she felt her body temperature starting to fall rapidly. Her body shivered within the insulated jacket. She resolved that she'd go inside in a few minutes, wrap herself up with Jack in a red plaid blanket next to the fireplace. She imagined he'd probably have a stubbled face. Depending on how long they'd been at the cabin, maybe a full beard. The coarse hair would tickle her skin as she snuggled in close to him. She saw her fingers tracing the bone structure of his face, glowing warm in the firelight. It was a welcome thought as the chill of the snow seeped further into her body, her muscles numb, her bones feeling more rigid.

*"You can remove those. We don't want her body temperature to drop too much or it will overcompensate."*

She frowned over her shoulder at the arctic fox standing at attention at the edge of the forest, the direction of the voice she didn't recognize. "Did *you* say something?"

Suddenly her body didn't feel quite so numb, her skin and muscles in the painful state between asleep and awake. The snow around her legs spontaneously started to melt, draining into the lake. It was gradual at first, then all at once, the snow was turning to water.

As soon as she found she was able to move her legs, she scrambled to her feet, taking off for the cabin. It was as she was reaching the door and she was about to burst out with a joke about "an inconvenient truth, part 2," that she felt her body being pulled away from the structure. First it was like moving against a strong wind, then a magnetic repulsion, and then she felt herself being pulled backward, as though into a vortex.

The lake, the mountains were gone.

There was silence and then the slow rhythmic sound of ocean waves. She was on her side, arm draped across the tan abdominals of her favorite Anesthesiologist. She ran her fingertips over his appendectomy scar, smiling at the comfort she felt of lying so close with him. She listened to his voice echo through his chest, her cheek resting against his rib cage. He was reading to her, but she wasn't fully taking in the words.

She had a hat resting on her head, to shield her from the sun it would seem. Her head, her body felt a few degrees overheated. A dip in the ocean would feel tremendously refreshing, but she was content where she lay and she somehow understood that she lacked the ability to tell him or even move.

Rather than fight the claustrophobia of immobility, she embraced the setting and how safe she felt in his arms. His hand was stroking her arm, as rhythmically as an ocean wave glides upon the shore. His skin smelled of suntan lotion and saltwater.

It could have been minutes or days that she stayed on that beach in his arms. She was content and that's all that mattered.

Then came the rush of air in her chest. She startled awake, terrified. She was floating in space, unaffected by the limitations of gravity. She stretched her legs, let them flutter back and forth, propelling her through the air tunnel she found herself in. The chill of the air made her skin shiver a bit and the billowing of the fabric made her question how much clothing she was actually wearing, but she was effectively distracted by the patterns of colors swirling around her. She reached out her hand and watched in wonder as her fingers split the color streams as though gliding through water. In the distance were bright blue flashes of light. She kicked her feet, moving toward them.

And then came the pain. Her muscles writhed and ached. The skin around her ears felt pulled too tight. Her stomach grumbled angrily. There was most certainly a catheter tube in her urethra. Her back was pinched from poor positioning. Her skull pulsed. Her hip burned.

And then her senses returned. There was the smell of antiseptic, of bodily fluids, of sweat, of unsavory foods, and someone in the room was wearing a strong cologne. She squeezed her eyes closed, sensing how intense the lights around her would be. She could hear their buzzing in her ears.

She pictured Jack and how she imagined he looked sitting upright on their beach, where they'd spent what seemed like weeks. His skin would be tanned and glowing, his hair disheveled, his eyes set behind a pair of mirrored aviators, his smile easy.

She had been focused on his smile, the slant of his lips, when she felt a tension in her temple. She reached up near her right ear, dazed by the sensation.

As the tension eased, the space before her was suddenly empty.

Someone had been there, she thought, but she found herself alone in what remained of the image. It was replaced by darkness provided by her eyelids.

The noises continued and her eardrums found them intolerable. The lights were dimmed and the voices, the noises were quieted, but her brain had done enough of an assessment to know three things:

1.  She had no recollection of what might have caused her to be hospitalized.

2.  Her deficits were severe, obvious when she wanted to shield her face with her hand, but nothing happened. She couldn't conclude based on sensation whether she still had all of her limbs.

3.  She had no desire to be woken. She longed for the dream she could no longer remember.

"Wake up, Delaney," Dr. Schuler whispered and she slowly opened her eyes.

The overhead lights were still too bright so she kept her eyes lowered. The first thing they settled on clearly was her hands. They were curled in the oddest of positions in her lap, knuckles braced upward like she had recently had a laptop there and she was bracing her fingers over the keyboard as she pondered something to type. They were also tremoring pretty severely.

*Stop,* she ordered, but nothing happened.

She was positioned in a semi-reclined position. Her neck was positioned too far forward so that her neck had improper alignment and despite some trepidation about her motor function, she was able to flex her shoulder blades and someone helped with the bed controls and pillow placement. As she settled back into the pillows, she peered over to who had helped her.

*But Jack Mathison left to finish med school,* she thought, confused.

He was clean shaven and smiled kindly, but he looked exhausted. Since it would be very strange for the hospital to have the occupational therapist on hand for her situation, if he was just working supplemental, she reasoned that perhaps he was already acting in an Anesthesiologist role.

*I must have just had surgery and he was one of the doctors...residents...* She wondered how long she had been there.

Six people surrounded her in varying proximity. Delaney let her eyes float away in search of someone she'd recognize as one of the surgeons. Based on the pulsing in her head, she knew she was probably looking for a Neurosurgeon. She gleamed over a nurse, a nursing administrator, swallowing continuously, trying to clear her cottonmouth. Her throat felt raw against the dryness. There were two men in dark blue scrubs. One looked like he should be delivering newspapers in the fifties. He looked the appropriate age to deliver newspapers--and he wore Clark Kent style eyeglasses. He peered past the shoulder of the much more confident looking doctor in front of him, a human shield. Delaney tried to focus her eyes to see the doctor's name badge, but her eyes were fuzzy and uncooperative. She slowly turned her chin toward the last occupant of the room, Dr. Martin Schuler, who had a heavy hand on her arm.

*What happened to me?* She pleaded silently. *It hurts so much.*

The sound of the IV drip alarm pierced her eardrum and her body retracted from it, turning on her side with no conscious effort to do so. After a bit of struggle and loud voices, the alarm was silenced.

She found herself breathing heavily toward the bed rails, relieved to not have to look at the prying faces. Dr. Schuler's hand rested again on her arm, gently sliding the length of it.

*He was on the other side of the bed*, she contemplated. *Who--*

She could feel she wasn't blinking, her eyes wide, as she looked up to see that the hand belonged to Jack Mathison and he was leaning in close to her. *Too close.*

"I'm here, D."

Before she knew what was happening, her body jolted and hastily tried to sit up.

Jack helped her with the pillows again, but as he did, he seemed to recognize the tremor in her hand getting worse.

*Why is Jack Mathison here? Why is he tending to me like this?*

"Blood pressure is elevated," the delivery boy doctor pointed out. He regretted speaking as soon as he found Delaney had turned to look at him. She was immediately distracted by Jack's hand returning to her arm.

*Jack Mathison is married. Why is he touching me?*

There was a wave of uncertainty floating up the length of her body. When it reached her head, she felt dizziness and pain. The pain was so strong and from so many directions, every part of her body throbbing, she didn't know what to focus on. She squeezed her eyes shut.

She intended to cry out for relief from the pain, but when she expected to hear her own voice, she heard only her chest convulsions, rattled from congestion. She tried again, but her mouth wasn't moving. Her eyes flew open and desperately scanned the attentive faces.

"Delaney, I'm Dr. Cobach."

She looked toward him without moving.

"You're in the ICU. We've had you in a medically induced coma for the past 14 days to let your brain rest."

*I've been in a coma for 2 weeks? Brain rest from what?*

"I keep telling my wife *I* need a medically induced coma myself just to catch up on some sleep."

*Oh hell. You're that Dr. Cobach.*

Dr. Schuler cleared his throat.

"Do you remember anything about the accident?"

*Accident?*

"She wasn't--" Jack Mathison began, his hand resting on her wrist, his position defensive of her. She paid close attention to this, how between Jack and Dr. Schuler, she felt like she had a personal set of bodyguards.

Dr. Cobach took the tablet from the resident and scanned the text on it. "Oh, I'm so sorry. I have another young patient, looks a bit like--" He waved it off. "You weren't in an accident."

"How are you feeling, Kiddo?" Dr. Schuler interjected.

She met his gaze, her chest still rising and falling heavily.

"Laney? Can you understand me?"

She found herself incapable of answering. Of speaking. Of blinking in morse code. Of moving her hand out of its current positioning.

"Blink if you can understand."

She heard her own desperate inhalation.

"Can you shake your head? Nod?"

Delaney felt her left hand become warmer and then she was looking directly at Jack again, her head turning instinctively and not of her own direction.

Of all those to occupy the room when she was woken from a coma, Jack's presence confused her. Dr. Schuler made sense. She was close to him and he was a doctor at the hospital, but Jack would only be there if--

She watched her hand pull away from him forcefully.

*I didn't tell it to do that.*

Dr. Cobach was waving his hands around. "This is all overwhelming, I'm sure--"

Delaney stared at Jack, watched him retreat by a half step, his head tilting, as startled and confused as her. No, there was more there. She had unintentionally inflicted pain and now she had no way to relieve it. She hadn't meant to move her hand. Actually, she had quite liked the warmth the contact had produced. Dr. Schuler didn't even like him. He wouldn't have let him be there unless he should have been. Unless she would have wanted him there.

The empty space was beckoning her back. She could see the streams of color seep into the scene.

*No*, she said silently. *No. Reach for his hand. Make it better.*

She desperately sent instructions to her hand to move toward Jack, but she saw it lying empty, useless, and impossibly clenched on the bed.

"BP is coming down," a nurse remarked.

"Is that better? We've given you a light sedative."

*What the—I just woke up and now you're going to put me to sleep again?*

"Slow the drip a bit." One of the nurses instructed. "There. That should do it."

The nurses had moved to tend to the drip and then had left the room with the resident. Before her stood three men: Jack appeared to be fighting the emotions thinly veiled behind the concern in his eyes; an observer now. Dr. Cobach had moved closer with his wild, white cotton candy hair blowing gently in the airflow from the ceiling vent. Then there was Dr. Schuler trying to look stoic. He touched her arm, but didn't make a show of it, seemingly to be conscientious of Jack.

Dr. Cobach patted her leg through the thick blankets. "Delaney," he began, his voice less jovial. "Can you touch your nose?"

*Of course I can.*

Both hands stayed in position on the bed, despite her attempts to order them to move.

*Oh.*

*Shit.*

He nodded. "Wiggle your toes. Sorry, I'm not normally Dr. Seuss. If the toes are too tough, try shaking your foot. First the left." He tapped her left foot for further clarification.

She watched as she successfully instructed her left foot to move. It seemed to please the room's occupants.

"Oh that's right, the left had worked before," he murmured. "Try your right?"

Nothing.

"Ah, I thought not. That's OK. Delaney, I'd like you to use your left foot to help you answer questions, OK?"

She shook her foot.

"Good. Now, do you remember what happened, why you're here?"

She stayed still.

"You had a hemorrhagic stroke."

*Shit.*

"Luckily it was treated almost immediately," he said, nodding to Jack.

*Did this happen at work? How severe? Wait, did Jack save my life?*

"Even so, you had some complications and we felt it best to put you into the coma, give your brain a chance to heal."

*What do you mean by 'complications'? Why can't I move anything except my left foot?* She glanced over to the empty space to her left, Jack standing just on the opposite side of the bed rail. *Where's Dad?*

"The swelling has decreased significantly. Are you in pain?"

She wiggled her foot like ringing a dinner bell.

He went through her body parts, asking for an affirmative response for each that had pain. "I'm really sorry you're so uncomfortable. We were hoping a lot of that would have passed. We'll get you something soon, OK?" He glanced over to Dr. Schuler, then to Jack. "Delaney, I'm going to ask you a few other questions. Would that be OK?"

She begrudgingly agreed.

"Do you remember this man?" He put a hand on Dr. Schuler, who appeared to stand a little straighter.

Delaney gently shook her foot, knowing what was coming.

"And this man? Do you remember him?"

She wiggled her foot.

Jack was breathing rather heavily. He swallowed hard.

"I'm going to list off some years. Wiggle your foot when I list the current year."

*Oh.*

*Shit.*

"2000." Pause. "2001."

"I think we can skip ahead a little," Dr. Schuler remarked. "I met her in 2005."

"2005." Pause. "2006." Pause. "2007."

The process seemed to be excruciating for everyone in the room except Dr. Cobach, who rhythmically listed the years. Finally, he received a response. "Good," he said, though she sensed that it really wasn't. "Now, we've had you sleeping so we don't expect you to know precisely, but if you had to guess, what season would you say we're in? Winter?" Pause. "Spring?" Pause. "Summer?"

Delaney apprehensively shook her foot.

Dr. Cobach sighed. "OK. Summer 2015. That's good information." It all seemed conclusive, like he was going to leave it at that.

She peered over to Jack, noticing how the color had drained from his face. He stared at his hands, the floor, seeming to be processing this information. Her heart clenched in a way she was unfamiliar. She swallowed hard. He glanced up, his eyes wide and bloodshot.

It was as the air flow from the vent overhead reached her face that she realized her face was streaked with tears.

Jack stepped forward a bit apprehensively, reaching for a tissue from the bed table. He sat down beside her and gently wiped the tears from her eyes. She didn't flinch away, her gaze constant, but the flow of tears thickened. He braced her face with both hands, wiping the tears away with his thumbs. "It's going to be OK," he said solidly, confidently. "You are the strongest person I know."

She took some deep breaths, studying the gradients of his blue eyes, his strong jaw, the scar on his nose. She thought of the brief, friendly glances they'd exchanged. More so than any other of her fellow therapists, she seemed to pick up on his moods. She could feel them like a palpable presence in the department. He was mostly a happy person, charming, funny--so when this had started to shift, it was evident. She felt it. In her mind, it was just a few weeks ago that she had left him a "humerus" mug of coffee to cheer him up, only to find out the following day that he had resigned from his supplemental position.

On one hand, she was scared that she couldn't remember--years maybe?-- and the physical impairments were legitimately terrifying, but there was a small part of her that was curious about what had transpired to go from not being worthy of a goodbye from him, to having him at her bedside.

She couldn't think of all of that. Her brain, the sedative, were having a seductive dance and she found herself being pulled into darkness.

# 10

# articulation

Delaney had never been instructed to squeeze her butt so many-- actually, no, scratch that. She had never been instructed to squeeze her butt. Never one to partake in group fitness classes, there had never been a setting that called for such instruction. When she went through physical therapy as a teenager, squeezing her butt would have been ill-advised given the severity of her hip recovery.

Hoisted up in the litegait, making the rounds through the halls and gym, she had heard it at least fifteen times so far.

This was progress considering after the stroke, she required a two person assist for most tasks. She had been reduced to using a bedside commode. She had been desperate to ask what had become of the Sara Stedy, scanning corners in the hallways, in the gym, hoping to locate it. She suspected it had been loaned out and never returned. Most staff didn't realize it cost several thousand dollars.

"Come on, Laney. Squeeze that tushy. Squeeze that tushy."

The instruction had become a sort of mantra that Julie chanted in the rhythm of "I think I can--." In an effort to minimize the reminders and to, of course, make additional progress, Delaney repeated the phrase in her head nearly constantly, but found herself distractible. Any loud noise, distant conversation, pain, chill, itch, smell would derail her mind enough and inevitably Julie would remind her to squeeze her butt. Again and again and again.

It became intolerably annoying after just half a session, but despite this, she did notice a significant difference when she followed the instruction.

The hallways were still quiet. The nursing staff had just changed shifts so the fresh faces were busy getting settled, reviewing vitals, sipping coffee. Julie was in her room at 6:30 on the nose with her cheerful, motivated demeanor and her two sidekicks—the aforementioned litegait, a contraption that hoisted her up like a doorway baby jumper, and a technician helper, to assist. On this day, it was a clean cut man with a friendly smile, dark, tousled hair, and a leather wristband with a cross on it.

"Did you sleep okay, Laney?"

Delaney was zeroed in on the leg strap digging into her pelvis. She meant to nod, but her brain had forgotten how to properly deliver the message to her neck muscles. Actually, she *had* slept well. The second pool session had helped. By the time Jeff had helped her change from her swimsuit and set her up with dinner—he had sensed how tired she was and hadn't pushed for her to sit in the recliner—it was all she could do to keep her eyes open. He presented a tray of misfit foods: salmon with mashed potatoes and asparagus (one of the room service items that was surprisingly good), two slices of sausage pizza (he explained that Julie had said it was the best variety they served), and a specialty sushi roll topped with crispy tempura (for which he gave no explanation). He used the remote attached to her bed to turn on the television and settled on an episode of *Friends*. Delaney yawned widely as she reached for a piece of sushi, opting against using chopsticks or a fork. It was an instinctual movement--they'd been happening more frequently. I'm hungry=grab the nearest food. Follow-up bites were more challenging because her conscious mind was overthinking how to do things.

"Bon appetit," he said kindly, sitting in the recliner and mostly keeping his attention on the television. He wouldn't have stayed at all, but due to safety concerns, she required at least supervision to be sure she didn't forget she had food in her mouth and inadvertently choke.

Weighted utensils had significantly helped her tremors, but she struggled with grip and controlling her movements.

"Some cultures encourage eating with your hands, Rhodes. Go for it."

Her nose flared, but she set down the fork, and she focused on the sushi, working to grip each piece with the proper amount of force as to not have it crumble in her fingers. She had the hang of it after two pieces, taking several long sips of water, gazing up toward the television.

"The PC police hate this show, but I do enjoy it," Jeff remarked, settling into the chair. The last thing she remembered before falling asleep was Chandler boarding a plane to Yemen and Jeff turning to her to remark about the change in airport security since the air date.

She had dreamt that night of sitting in a kayak in the middle of a turquoise river, smooth red boulders on either side. She much preferred that to the restless night she had the day before--at least she thought it was the day before. She did a quick recap, going backwards. Last night was definitely the river dream. Saturday and Friday nights were heavy and dreamless thanks to the addition of a pain medication. Thursday night was restless due to pain. Her entire body had ached—no, it had felt like various parts were on fire, scorched by a branding iron or some other torture device.

She had always been cautious about opioids, but given the wonder of a restful sleep, she certainly understood their appeal. Then again, about twenty minutes after taking them, her head felt like it was filled with helium so despite Dr. Schuler prescribing them TID, she had self-reduced and only took them at bedtime.

"Steady there. Your mind wandered, didn't it?"

Delaney straightened her posture, determined to stay focused. *Don't say it. Don't say it…*

"Now—squeeze that tushy, squeeze that tushy…"

*If you had done this during your residency, I would have failed you.*

"It's heating up out there," Julie said, motioning with one arm toward the wall of windows on one side of the hallway.

Much of the landscaping had grown enough to cover the bottom part of the windows and the lush trees provided good shade in the afternoon, but through the middle, the orange tint of the morning sun cast luxurious shadows over the nearby mountains. The mountains looked like they would have vegetation, unlike the mountains in her dream, which were smooth and coated in beautiful red dust. They looked like something she'd seen in photographs of Havasu Canyon, though she had never been there herself. She gazed out at the mountains in the distance and wondered how far away her dreams had taken her.

"That's excellent standing, Laney. Oh my goodness you're doing so well standing. Much more steady than you have been. You're relying a bit too much on the left leg though. Do you feel that?"

The mountains fell out of focus and as Delaney adjusted to her immediate surroundings, her right knee buckled. The litegait frame rattled.

"Easy. Get your bearings."

Delaney wiggled her legs around awkwardly until at least her left leg straightened up and she was comfortably upright again, relying on the litegait straps and left leg equally. Her right foot was turned in at an awkward angle, the leg doing little to support her. Her hands, which had been useless at her sides jolted forward, grabbing the handles before her for stability. Their grip strength was not particularly helpful, but Julie stared at them nonetheless.

"Did you just do that?"

*Nod*, she thought. *Say 'yes.' And squeeze your butt.* She looked over at Julie, furrowed her eyebrows. She wasn't sure she'd gotten that much expression from her face since prior to the stroke. It felt a bit surreal. She furrowed her eyebrows over and over again, simply because she could.

"Is something uncomfortable?" Julie looked over the contraption. "This strap looks twisted. That hurts?"

Delaney released the tension in her forehead. *Yes.*

"Yes?"

She perked up her eyebrows, though she suspected she probably looked more surprised than anything.

"Don't worry, we'll fix that when we get to the gym. Is that OK?"

She repeated the gesture. *Yes.*

"Screw the picture card speech wants to use with you."

Julie didn't catch it, but Delaney grinned. "Shall we continue?"

Delaney could picture being five years old and running full speed at a swing, letting the rubber seat catch her. She would throw her arms out and pretend to fly--back and forth, back and forth. She wondered what it might look like to push off and try something similar in the litegait. Her mind settled on the litegait being tipped over, her swinging comically upside down, Julie frantically screeching for help…

"Shall we continue?"

She exhaled. *Yes.*

"OK, let's fix that right leg. It's just kind of being dragged along right now, eh?"

Delaney tried to correct it, but the numbness in her right foot made it difficult to gauge placement.

"The AFO should be here this morning. I think that'll really help you utilize that leg better."

Delaney concentrated on straightening her right leg, wobbled her foot until she found the currently working nerves, then firmly pushed the bottom of her foot into the floor. The pressure made the painful tingling more manageable. *You're neglecting the right leg. If you don't use it, it won't get better.*

"Good, let's keep going."

Delaney focused back on directing her legs to take turns propelling forward. The natural gliding motion of the monstrous contraption helped this be less of a painstakingly slow process. Once they had turned into the expansive gym, she was a bit overwhelmed by the bright natural light, the morning sun reflecting off the shiny floors, freshly buffed, the multitude of therapists congregating around the wall in the back, who all looked up when she entered. Some whispered amongst themselves and became very expressive with their eyes and hands. She recognized a few, but she had no way to acknowledge them.

"Hey Buddy," a familiar friendly voice called from the charting office that lined one side of the gym.

Not wanting to sidetrack her brain too much and forget the task at hand, she focused a bit of her brain power on trying to make her face look friendly. Since the injury, she had a tendency, according to overheard commentary, to have a stern expression.

Julie and the technician ensured she was seated safely and unhooked the overhead straps. She peered over her left shoulder, searching for the source of the voice. She could see a figure beyond Julie moving toward her. A surge shot up her neck.

"I tried my hardest to get back—I hear the weekend went pretty well?"

Delaney concentrated on doing a step above the surprised expression Julie had now established as an affirmative response.

"D, you're *smiling* now?"

Julie's chin snapped around to check. "Laney, you're smiling!"

"This is new, like this morning?" Jack asked, perplexed, half skeptical it was staged for his benefit.

"Like *right now*. I noticed she had more expression in her face this morning. You're even smiling a little on the right."

This information deflated the victory a bit. *Smile,* Delaney ordered the right half of her face. She found her frustration had creased her forehead and didn't want it to be misinterpreted as pain. That happened with Nursing over the weekend and the dose of Oxycodone had been practically forced down her throat leaving er head foggy throughout Speech. At the point that Quinn showed up, she thought he could have easily been a pharmaceutically induced hallucination.

"Hey," Jack said softly, capturing her attention as he moved well into her comfort zone. "Little steps forward is still forward."

She relaxed her face and gazed into his eyes. They were the type that looked a slightly different shade in each type of light--eyes of a different color, she decided. She thought dreamily of Emerald City in *The Wizard of Oz* and the horse of a different color, amused by the connection. Her grandpa had played the Scarecrow when he was in high school and college theatre. She had surprised him on Halloween when she was six by dressing as Dorothy. That was the year her parents divorced and she had spent the months that followed repeatedly clicking those sparkly red slippers together, wishing they would reconcile. She convinced herself if she just believed and wished hard enough, it would happen.

She didn't have ruby slippers during her recent hospital course, but she recalled feeling that same sort of trapped desperation.

Worse than that.

She had wanted to die. Most of her time in the hospital was a blur, but there had been a few moments that were very clear and had stuck firmly in her brain. One was that she had wished whole-heartedly that she would die.

If that would be her life—in pain and unable to communicate and unable to function without an invasive level of assist, having other people bathe her, toilet her--she certainly didn't want to live.

It was with painful irony that she had started to think that way. She had been firmly against the wave of support of assisted suicide that had swept into the political arena, arguing ardamently that it discounted the value of life. It was eerie and disconcerting how open she had become to the thought of it for herself.

Her brain had not seemed capable of allowing her out of the miserable thought loop--then again, when she had managed to light any optimism or motivation, it was immediately snuffed out by someone insisting on dressing or undressing her like a doll. In ICU and acute, outside of limited therapy sessions, she wasn't given the chance to attempt a task before being briskly rushed through it, an invalid. It was more efficient for them. First she'd try to distance herself from the moment, pretend someone wasn't cath'ing her or having her use a bedside commode, sponge-bathing her, and then the darkness, the solitude of death seemed welcoming, a retreat even. The logical component, the permanency of death, evaded her thoughts. She longed to close her eyes and drift away to nothingness.

Jack had been there around the clock, but had distanced himself after a few weeks. Because her short-term memory wasn't reliable and her brain only seemed to want to encode useless information like the popularity of stethoscope covers among hospital staff--tropical seemed to be the most popular, followed closely by cartoon owls--she couldn't recall if there was a particular event that prompted Jack to start coming around less frequently. His absence saddened her in ways she didn't understand. She felt sorry for him, burdened with the impairments of a woman who didn't even remember having dated him, trapped in his own way. Was he only staying because he felt obligated? There had been coworkers who had stopped in to see her, but no one who would provide the level of care expected of a significant other. Did he know if he left she would likely go to a SNF or group home? Did that add to the obligation he felt toward her?

She had no way to tell him to move on from her and if she was being honest, she didn't truly want him to move on. A part of her feared that he would. She wanted to be better, but if she wasn't going to get better, his unfair situation and burden just added another dimension to her mind's justification that dying would be better for everyone.

The tortuous thought cycle broke the night before she transferred to Rehab. Nursing had just completed evening ADLs--it was appropriate they referred to them in this way rather than "self-cares" since they were not "self" anything. She was assured repeatedly for days that this would change once she transferred to Rehab. She was familiar with Rehab so she knew the remarkable progress some patients made, but her mind doubted that she would be so fortunate. Instead, she anticipated it would be more of the same stagnation, but with staff she was more familiar, which seemed to make it worse. They'd encourage her to do tasks independently, but she worried that she wouldn't progress.

The nurse, a sweet grandmotherly type, had just left the room. The persistent thoughts telling her she was better off dead had started to cocoon her. She expected them. They would incrementally constrict around her until the nightly meds took effect. That was enough in itself, but then the sadness would start to fill her, the meds numbing any defenses she had left. Each night it seemed to be a competing force if she would be suffocated by her entrapment in her own body, or if she would drown in the sadness of being trapped in her own body. That night was no exception. She wondered silently if she could will herself to die, since she lacked the physical capability to do so. People died of heartbreak, they said, right? She laid in bed and found that despite her sinking depression, despite the numbing medications, there was a part of her still clinging on, telling her not to give up. This only added to her feeling of being trapped. *Why?* She silently demanded. *What do I possibly have to live for?*

That's when Jack stepped in her room, a resolute expression on his face. He started speaking as though they were mid-conversation.

"So they got rid of my favorite sushi roll. They replaced it with something called a Fashionista Roll. What the *Sam Hill* is that?" He had slipped into a southern accent. He was carrying a paper bag in one arm, duffel crossed over his body, and he had shaved.

She watched him cross to the table and chair to the right of her bed, feeling the pressing urgency to burst out laughing, but her body seemed incapable of it, like how a sneeze can suddenly get stuck and vanish.

"Apparently it's low carb and it contains kale. *Kale.* I'm afraid we might need to find a new sushi place. I just don't trust their judgement anymore." He dropped the duffel and the food bag on the table and sat down in the chair with a purposely dramatic sigh. He turned to her, smiling lightly. "Hi, D."

The room was quiet, but more significantly, her mind was quiet. She felt her shoulders ease, her breathing steady.

Knowing she had no means to answer, he omitted asking about her day. "I also thought since you're on a no-TV protocol, I would provide some after dinner entertainment." He nodded. "I've been working out my interpretive dance routine between patients. It's like Lord of the Dance meets MC Hammer. I'm pretty stoked about it." His eyebrows were raised in faux propriety.

*I should remember those eyes, that smile, that charm, all being directed toward me.* Delaney gazed at him--in her mind, it was affectionately, but on the outside, given the constraints of her expression, she feared she looked too solid and unamused. *I'm sorry, Jack. You should never be forgotten. You deserve better than this.*

He tilted his head, his eyebrows furrowing, as though he had heard her thoughts. His tensed expression released in an instant, perhaps after he became aware he was staring. He pulled a book from the duffel. "*Alternatively*, I did bring another book to read to you, if you'd like." He paused, reconsidering this. "I suppose I could just get you an audiobook read by Liam Neeson or maybe Sean Connery. They're more my generation though, I suppose. Maybe Chris Hemsworth as Thor? '*I am Thor, son of Odin, and as long as there is life in my breast... I am running out of things to say!*'"

She meant to shake her head, laughing silently at his Thor impersonation, but she couldn't link the desire with the proper muscle movement, and the moment passed.

He watched her, dropping his shoulders with a sigh. That sigh seemed to carry a thousand words he wanted to say.

It was difficult to tell, but Delaney was just as surprised as Jack when she spontaneously mimicked his sigh.

"Has Caprice been calling you?" Julie asked, then observed Delaney slow her arm rotation on the NuStep, unable to effectively multi-task eavesdropping and moving her arms. "She's been sending me texts."

"Yeah, texting. Legal stuff," he replied, shaking his head.

"Like power of attorney?"

"Like, financial access."

Delaney came to a stop and grunted dismissively.

"She's a class act, huh, Laney?" Julie said, including her and excluding her simultaneously.

She vaguely remembered Caprice coming to visit her when she was in ICU-- she wore some God awful perfume and loud, chunky jewelry. Of course, Delaney was recovering from brain surgery--she very well could have been sensitive to those sensory irritants.

Delaney frowned. Caprice actually visited twice. The other time she had read to her from *People* magazine about an actress turned princess causing friction in the monarch, and seemed curt with Jack, particularly when she suggested he fetch her lunch moments after determining with surprising authority that they should name her as respite care so the state would pay her. Unless Caprice had gone through a dramatic personality transformation, it was highly unlikely she planned to actually provide any respite care at all, which was apparent when she suggested a "backup" respite person.

It occurred to Delaney that she couldn't remember her dad visiting. There were some friends, work colleagues, but actually, very few family members. Her dad was not one among them.

He would have come to see her. He would have slept in the recliner in her room.

Jack placed his hand on her shoulder, squeezed gently.

It was like coming to full consciousness after just dozing off for a brief second. She resumed normal breathing and didn't quite understand why her chest felt so hollow. She tried to recover what she was just thinking about. It seemed important, but she found it had dissolved into the air. She could almost see the particles floating around her.

"Did you bring the tablet?" Julie asked him conspiratorially.

"Of course I did," Jack replied, still focused on Delaney's face. Her frown ceased and she got herself set on the machine again.

"Good, maybe Speech can ditch that picture card from the 80s."

"When is Teresa back?"

"Thursday night now. She'll be into work on Friday. Thank God."

Their conversation turned to a buzz in the back of Delaney's ears as she adjusted her hand placement, focused solidly on the machine before her.

Across the gym, one of the supervisors waved to Jack and said something about having gotten some sun.

Her brain tried to process the phrasing. She wondered who first coined the phrase, as it depicted an image of physically acquiring sunshine, as though in buckets. She found the image a little funny, picturing Jack with his large stature, scooping up sunshine and skipping down a hillside with a bucket in each hand, arms swinging gleefully like in a nursery rhyme. For extra comical impact, she pictured him dressed as Thor, since he did certainly embody a Thor-like aura, the image complete with chest plate and cape blowing in the breeze. She giggled internally.

Then she toppled sideways off the seat.

Delaney appreciated the fact that she'd fallen into Jack, truth be told. She took her time pushing off him, his arms enveloping her in warmth. She inhaled deeply, picking up on a light, somewhat tropical scent. She examined his skin tone for herself and had determined, regardless of whatever prompted someone to coin the phrase, getting some sun had a decidedly agreeable effect on Jack's appearance. Even so, he still looked drained of energy reserves.

As he helped her find the center of the seat, he sensed her hesitation to let go of him. He crouched down beside her and she made eye contact again—still with a bit of trepidation, but more attachment than even days earlier. He placed his hand on her cheek instinctively and she didn't flinch away, as she had early on. She looked tired, but her eyes seemed to focus better. They didn't have the glassed over look they had for much of her acute stay. He wondered about her pain keeping her awake, if she was having side effects from medications she couldn't express. There hadn't been much two-way communication since the day they woke her from the coma. She had stopped responding to prompts with foot movement, despite nothing changing on her scans. Her reluctance to make eye contact when questioned led him to believe that she had made the decision not to respond in this manner.

She was never one to wear a lot of makeup, but without it she looked younger and more vulnerable. He wanted to ask if she'd remembered something while he was gone--she was certainly more alert and there was something questioning in her eyes, but Julie, who had been waiting to get her back on her therapy track, cleared her throat.

"I still have a few things I'd like to do with Laney here before breakfast group."

He nodded approvingly, smiling at Delaney. "You're doing great." He moved away slowly, his hand grazing her arm. "I'll come get you after breakfast."

She watched him over her shoulder for as long as her peripheral vision allowed. Her heart felt heavier in her chest the further away he was, each beat causing her shoulders to rise and fall slightly.

"It's good to have him back," Julie said, turning back to the machine. "I think he had his sister's wedding?" It seemed to be an intentional prompt.

Delaney was still distracted by the lingering scent of his hair. It was subtle, but her sense of smell seemed to have been heightened since the stroke. Most of the magnified aromas were unwelcome. A hospital is filled with pungency of all kinds, mostly bodily fluids or wafting grease from the cafeteria, but he was an escape from all of that. He smelled of something sweet and exotic. Tropical. It felt as though images were trying to make their way to her consciousness, nudging firmly against the center of her brain, but unable to get through. A beach. A man with a solid jawbone in aviator sunglasses smiling at her. Hands. Strong, tan hands.

She suddenly became aware of Julie staring at her, trying to be patient. This effort was obviously causing her much stress, her knuckles white with force as she held the grip on the console, other hand on her hip. Her breathing was heavy. Beside her stood Sarah, the Recreation Therapist, who appeared to be speaking to her, probably checking in about breakfast group, though Delaney couldn't hear her.

Beyond them, one of the therapists, a minute little thing who looked two weeks out of school, was making photocopies. Delaney watched the papers glide out into the tray, listening to the process of papers being fed in, looping inside the machine noisily, likely signaling an impending paper jam, but for now, printed softly below.

*The hippocampus, the neocortex and the amygdala all play a role in episodic and semantic memory storage. The neocortex stores generalized concepts, the hippocampus stores information about one's own life events, the amygdala stores emotions and feelings about those memories.'* She could see the very therapy gym where she found herself now, but filled with therapists munching on their lunches, listening to an educational in-service from a Neuropsychology resident. Delaney had run late working with a patient and had rolled in a balance ball to use as a seat, getting some smirks from coworkers, including Jack, who was casually resting against that very copy machine.

"Should we get back to it?" Julie asked. "Sarah will get the other patients seated and come back for you so we have a little more time."

Delaney stared at her a moment, trying to recall what she was just thinking about. She snapped her eyes shut, tried to block out noises around her. *Focus,* she told her brain. In turn, the image of the red rocks, the turquoise water, the waterfall came to mind. The steady stream of cool water thundered off the highest rocks.

"I'm pretty sure it was his sister, Tabitha, who got married?"

Another prompt that received no response. Delaney's eyes scanned over to her, like a dental patient with a mouthful of tools, water pik, and water sucker being asked a bunch of open-ended questions, wondering how a highly-educated person could be so oblivious to the fact that she couldn't answer.

"Let's get those arms working."

Delaney tried to press on with her circles with more deliberate force of her left hand, but as though forgetting it was there, she realized the right pedal was empty. She stared at her right hand still useless on her leg, as usual not wanting to release its curled, hook-like position.

Corey, the technician, moved to assist. "No, let *her,*" Julie said a little too firmly.

Delaney let go of the left pedal, used her clenched, but functioning hand to force her right arm up. She pushed her palm around the handle.

"Those fingers are stubborn."

She glared at them, ordering them to grab the handle.

"Your thumb was cooperating before--try that."

Delaney easily wrapped her thumb unassisted, pushed her other fingers into contact with the handle, but one by one, they drifted off the handle like strips of tape that had lost stickiness.

"Does that feel alright?"

*No*, she said silently, but on seeing that it was drifting past the top of the hour and sensing this was probably making Julie physically ill, she gave a jump of her eyebrows. *Yes.*

"Oh this is great. I think I can figure out 'no,' but how about we establish something--just in case you're utilizing your hands and can't easily flip me the bird or something?"

*Laugh.* A low gurgle came out. Not exactly the sound she was aiming for.

"Was that funny? Yeah I'm sure you've wanted to do that--you know, they call me General Patton."

"They do that for a reason," Corey chimed in from over Delaney's right shoulder, spotting her in case she fell that direction.

"What, because I'm bossy?"

"You're tough, mostly in a good way."

"Now, Laney. Squeeze—"

Delaney clenched her butt, glaring at her.

"I think that was a 'flip the bird' moment, General," Corey remarked. "I'll get a wheelchair."

At breakfast group, Delaney discovered they had forgotten to remove the litegait harness and the thigh strap was still digging into her pelvic bone. She spent much of her chewing time eyeing it.

Eating left-handed had proven challenging and there was too much stimulation to allow the necessary level of concentration to enhance her skills. There was too much chatter about weekend happenings, current movies, and a short rant from one of the other patients about the President. She didn't know what he was talking about exactly, but she sensed she disagreed with it. She recognized his use of male pronouns so she narrowed the field in her head. There had only been three female candidates so it didn't narrow things much. The newspapers were stacked beside the male patient at the far end who seemed keenly unaware of their presence, or of anything or anyone else. Probably for the best. The current date, whenever it came to her attention, had a way of startling her. It was fortunate, in that way, that she struggled to remember it.

There was also a puzzle on the far end of the table, partially put together. The box appeared to depict a cityscape. She actually wouldn't mind the quiet solitude of a puzzle, but no one had offered it as an activity option and she had no way to request it.

They had brought her into the group the previous week, but she had felt sedated and hadn't looked around much. Suddenly, there were too many things to look at. The lights were turned too bright. The patient art pieces that filled one wall were too busy, too many colors, brush strokes going in competing directions, unbalanced compositions. The flat screen television offered a frequently rotating spectrum of motivational screensavers. She found she couldn't get through the quotes fast enough before it switched to the next.

With all of this stimulation, combined with the sensation of the strap cutting into her bone, she found focusing on breakfast particularly difficult. She also found her body aches were steadily increasing. She kept picturing the pain scale, the cartoon faces. *4*, she said silently, *creeping toward a 5*.

She repeatedly attempted to load her fork when it already had a bigger bite than she could handle. At one point she had left the fork lingering in front of her mouth as she tried to remember again how the election turned out. How long had it been since then? Julie had said it was heating up outside, which would imply it was nearing or already summer. Her last memory before the stroke, which she didn't remember, was in 2015, mid-summer. She was sitting cross-legged on the balcony in her newly acquired condo, muscles sore from a tough workout, stack of boxes in the corner, teriyaki chicken bowl in her lap, gazing out toward the mountains, glowing orange in the setting sun.

She bought the high rise apartment for its maintenance free lifestyle, which suited her schedule, but also because she loved looking out the window and seeing water. It was not a river she'd want to swim in, but she appreciated the glistening of the water in the sunset, the old fashioned street lamps that lined the bustling bridge, cued by the hour. Her dad had also advised her that it was a good investment.

She dropped her fork, startling the entire room. The elderly traumatic brain injury cursed.

"Calm down everyone, it's just a fork," Quinn muttered. She had and hadn't realized he was in the room. She saw him quickly when Julie wheeled her in, but without a way to acknowledge him, or communicate, she mainly kept her eyes lowered. "Is this the *only* way to get breakfast here? I don't know how everyone else feels, but I don't care for the forced social hour. No offense."

"No, this is our breakfast group. We like for everybody to attend, but you can have breakfast in the cafe, in your room…"

*In a tomb, with a broom. You can have it here or there. You can have it anywhere.*

She shook her head at the bizarreness of her thought patterns. She sympathized with him--she didn't care for the mandated social hour--in fact, she had resolved that should she return to work and should she work on Rehab again, she would not push it on patients so forcibly. The distractibility of her mind had made it somewhat tolerable, but also made the experience exhausting.

"Am I right?" he asked, looking directly at her, but with a softened expression. Prompting. Offering solidarity. *Quinn.*

She relaxed her face, closed and opened her eyes, hoping to signify an affirmative response.

"She doesn't know how to speak anymore," the traumatic brain injury said bluntly.

Quinn watched Delaney closely as her eyes darted up to the woman with frizzy black hair and a "Kiss Me, I've been to Ireland" shirt under her robe, then to the table. She focused her attention solidly on the table, trying not to think about the harness, trying to ignore the relentless ache in her chest.

"How are you this morning, Laney?" His voice was friendly and familiar.

*Quinn.*

*Quinn.*

*Quinn.* She looked up, intending to try out one of her new facial expressions, but Speech therapy stepped in and retrieved the brain tumor patient. Delaney watched them leave, wondering when Teresa was returning and mentally preparing herself for another day with Alice.

Suddenly she realized she was absentmindedly holding an English muffin, having determined she didn't have the dexterity to apply jam, and Quinn was staring at her. She dropped it unceremoniously back on her plate.

"Do you remember me?" he squinted at her. "I thought you may have yesterday?"

"Her name is *Delaney*. Strange name. Doesn't remember things from years ago...or a few seconds ago. It's fascinating, really. And sad. So young." Traumatic brain injury explained. Delaney couldn't remember having ever had a conversation with her and she honestly didn't know if the woman was telling the truth. Her remark about the strangeness of her name suddenly came to the forefront of her mind and she allowed her face to glare. Actually, she wasn't sure it was coming across as a glare, but she did know she looked, at minimum, irked.

Quinn frowned. "I'm pretty sure she can hear just fine."

*Yes. Yes she can.* She leaned back in her chair, thinking of how he looked when they first met--scrawny, lanky. She thought of how he reignited a love he had for playing baseball just after they met and had bulked up a bit junior year. She distinctly remembered being impressed by the girth of his bicep as she took his arm walking into prom. She thought of the last time she remembered seeing him--meeting for lunch downtown, trying to look confident in his tailored business suit.

"Strange, strange name—Delaney."

"Janice, are you causing trouble again?" Julie appeared from just around the corner, finishing an apple and chucking it into the trash can as she entered. "'Delaney' is a beautiful name and it fits her perfectly."

"I guess we know who *her* favorite patient is," Quinn whispered, winking at Delaney. He looked remarkably like himself, but with a broader jaw line, overgrown hair—and the wheelchair, of course.

"The only other patient in here I'm currently working with is *you*."

*I think that was rude, Julie.* Delaney reviewed the dialogue and confirmed that yes, yes she was being rude.

"Now I thought we bonded over the catheter removal. I expressed genuine gratitude."

"What does 'Delaney' even mean?" Janice scoffed.

"I actually don't know," Julie said, pulling her phone from her coat pocket. "Ah, here we go--'Alder grove.'" She paused to nod approval, flashed a photo of what was apparently an alder grove forest to Delaney and Quinn.

"I think there were trees in that photo," Quinn observed.

"*Oh--'dark challenger.'*"

Delaney hadn't looked up the meaning of her name before. She'd always been satisfied by the story shared by her dad—that he had spent some time in Ireland in his travels as a young man. He loved the country, the scenery, the drinking. Her name was derived from the River Slaney, where he had spent weeks reading and fishing. He cited it as his favorite place in the world, winning out over flashy places like Paris and Tokyo, luxurious destinations like Bora Bora and the Swiss Alps. Ultimately, if he had the choice to live anywhere in the world, it would be a small stone house along the banks of the River Slaney.

She felt her chest inflate with the memory and then, suddenly, her heart fell.

Julie shifted her weight. "I heard a rumor you cursed at the night nursing staff."

Laney looked up, her mind quickly emptied again.

"How many times do they have to turn on the damn lights while I'm trying to sleep?" Quinn stated bluntly.

*Seriously. What are all the vitals monitors on your computer for?*

"Fair complaint. Maybe try a sleep mask?"

Quinn pressed his lips together, considering that. "That's not a bad suggestion, actually. So who have you come to torture? Oh please let it be me."

"It *is* you. Laney worked hard with me already today."

*Walked 450 feet. In the litegait, but still. Speaking of which,* she thought, glaring at the harness. No one seemed to notice.

"Excellent."

"I see that smile again, Laney."

*Not a smile, Julie.*

"You did good. Jack texted that he's on his way, alright Hon? Terrence and I are going to thumb wrestle to see who gets to work with you this afternoon."

*Eyebrows up.*

Julie smiled.

"Can you write? You need a little whiteboard or something."

She automatically raised her clenched hands, then stared at them as though they were foreign objects. They had moved when her brain intended without having to think her way through the action. Still clenched, but even so--progress.

"We're working on that, aren't we, Laney?" Julie was so busy picking up some discarded trash from the floor that she missed the spontaneous motion. By the time she looked back at her, her hands were back on the table, though Delaney was still staring at them.

"God, that must get annoying, having people talk to you like that," Quinn remarked.

*You have no idea.*

He touched her elbow as Julie wheeled him out of the room. "I'll see you in awhile, Delaney Adara. For your sake, I hope Terrence wins."

"I'm going to pretend I didn't see that smirk, Laney." It was just as they rounded the corner that Julie questioned him about what he had just called her.

*Delaney Adara*, she thought fondly. Her dad used to call her by both her first and middle names. His voice would wander rhythmically through the syllables. Quinn had once told her that it was a good thing her last name was a single syllable, or it would really be a mouthful. *Delaney Adara Rhodes*, she said silently. Her mind automatically echoed another name: *Delaney Adara Mathison*. She felt her cheeks tense. *DAM*, she thought, amused by the double entendre.

"You're not Julie," a case manager observed from the doorway.

Delaney could do nothing but look at her.

"Hey *Laney*, it's been awhile," she said loudly. The woman had a black bob and reading glasses propped up on her head. "Are you treating a patient in here?" she asked, looking around the empty room.

Sandy stepped in suddenly from the hallway, pulling the social worker, who only worked on Rehab a couple of times a year, aside.

Margie turned to her and in a hushed voice, something Delaney was used to at this point, inquired about what was wrong with her. As was the case with a nursing manager, a therapist who had been on maternity leave, and a dozen others, as soon as Sandy mentioned "stroke," there was a reflexive gasp, her hand covering her face, her eyes expressing her horror.

Delaney let her face turn stern, then let herself be distracted by the morning sky through the windows.

"You hang in there, OK?" Margie said, her voice rising at the end like she was asking a toddler to eat vegetables.

Delaney didn't look up. She sat alone, letting her hands, now resuming their clenched shape, fall in her lap. She appreciated the quiet and found herself gazing out to the courtyard.

It had been something built into Dr. Schuler's contract with the hospital that there be an outdoor space that was both functional and offered an in-house outing for patients. The courtyard had been designed with four "Zones." There was the serene water wall "Reflection Zone" with a park bench, surrounded by potted plants, which had been put together through the occasional gardening workshop. There was a mosaic tiled water wall on one side, muted shades of blue and green. The "Golf Zone" had a small putting green, as well as a catch net. The far corner was typically set up, ready for workshops for visiting artists, a gathering space for the therapy dogs, and for a small audience when musicians came and played. Across from that was a bridge set over surplus potted plants with a ramp on one side, steps on the other, varying walking surfaces, gravel, cobblestone. It was useful in safety training for patients.

Sarah swept in to retrieve some abandoned trays and touched Delaney's upper arm delicately. "It's pretty outside today, isn't it?"

It felt right to offer a smile, but Delaney found herself solemn--and she lacked the energy for the inevitable overreaction to a simple twitch of facial muscles.

She knew that courtyard. She'd spent a lot of time working with patients on the bridge, easing them into a comfort with uneven pavement, having them practice their stance on steps, fueling their confidence with occasional affirmations, reminders to keep a light grasp on the rail instead of a death grip.

She blinked, as though resetting her mind to her new reality, that she was one such patient now.

"Hey Buddy, how was breakfast?"

Delaney glanced down at her plate and was surprised that there was so much still there, including the hastily discarded english muffin.

"Not hungry?"

She was confused as to whether she should answer with a yes or a no. Yes, not hungry. No, not hungry.

"Bad phrasing. *Are* you hungry?"

*Yes.* She suddenly pictured pancakes before her--a big stack of fluffy golden pancakes topped with butter and maple syrup so hot and fresh she could steam her face as she cut into the stack. She wanted to devour them and then sink into a late morning slumber.

"Lots of distractions in breakfast club, I bet."

*Yes.*

He examined the cold food, trying to hide mild disgust at the food quality. "What if we visited the coffee bar?"

*Yes.*

"They're going for a gourmet donut theme these days, but they also have the savory ham and cheese croissant, if that sounds good to you."

*Yes.* She glanced down at the harness, hopeful he would finally remove it.

"Oh, well you don't need that contraption on right now, do you? Let's get that off." As he unclipped the harness and gently removed it, he met her gaze. "You did a lot of walking with Julie this morning I heard. How about we take one of the wheelchairs for a spin, let your muscles have a rest?"

His hair was freshly cut--shorter on the sides, slightly tousled on top. She wanted to ask him about his weekend. He was obviously outdoors a lot, the line from his sunglasses apparent. *A wedding. He was there for a wedding. Tabitha's wedding.*

She'd had moments that she worried he was gone because he'd distanced himself again, but Julie and Jenna had provided some updates—with each reminder, each update, she felt better capable of encoding his whereabouts to memory to the point that when she woke up that morning, she knew he was returning.

"I won't pop any wheelies, I promise."

She sighed, as she eyed the wheelchair over her shoulder. *I hate that I need that effing thing.*

"Delaney, you're clearly expressing disdain for an inanimate object."

She maintained her resting "flip the bird" face.

"This calls for something with a whipped cream dollop."

She raised her eyes and stared forcefully at him, but she felt her new smile creep across her face.

"D, the wheelchair is *temporary*," he said solidly, but tenderly.

She inhaled and exhaled, softened her expression.

"Actually, this isn't the one I had in mind anyway." With that, he went to fetch a wheelchair from around the corner.

She recognized that he had called her "D" for the second time that morning. Usually it was 'Buddy.' She remembered years ago (she assumed) hearing him in the hallways calling people that. She wasn't sure yet how she felt about being called "D," but it felt infinitely more intimate than "Buddy," which seemed like something you call someone when you can't remember their name. That wasn't the case, of course. It had probably been well-meaning.

When he returned, he cheerfully wrapped a gait belt around her waist—she tried not to equate it to how a dog must feel when they're leashed up for a walk. He effortlessly slid her chair back from the table with her still on board, her legs toward him. It felt familiar, this close proximity.

"Hey, when she stands, could you slide out the chair and put the wheelchair behind her?"

"You bet," an unseen voice replied.

She stared down at the arms of the chair, grasping the left armrest and pushing herself up to stand.

"Focus on your balance. Rely on the left leg if you need, but try to keep it even. We're working to rebuild strength on your right side. If you don't use it, it won't get better."

Delaney distanced her feet a bit and she felt less wobbly, though her right foot was less solidly planted. His grip on the gait belt tightened. A phantom person behind her dragged the chair away loudly and after a gush of air, she could sense the wheelchair moving closer. She waited until she felt the seat against the back of her knees and heard the brakes click into place, then reached back with her left hand and slowly lowered herself to sit. Jack kept his strong arm wrapped around her waist until she was seated.

"Nicely done," he said, tucking the gait belt onto the wheelchair. "Thanks, Corey."

"Getting some java, huh?"

"We are," Jack responded, unlocking the brakes and wheeling her out into the hallway. He leaned in by her ear as they moved through the hall, humming as they went. It took her a few strides and a few odd stares from onlookers to realize it was the wheelchair with the bar between the wheels (for some reason no one in the department could figure out) and he was riding the wheelchair like a shopping cart.

*Jackass*, she thought, but found her cheeks were increasingly tensed.

The cool rush of air in the front lobby sent a chill through her. She was working up a sweat in physical therapy earlier so the light t-shirt and soft cotton capris were enough, but she found herself shivering as they crossed toward the cafeteria.

He wheeled her up to an empty table, locked the brakes, and immediately pulled out a tablet. As it started up, he took off his lab coat and held it out for her, the sleeve ready. "It's below 78 degrees in here. I know you've *got* to be cold."

She was certain she was smiling as she slid her left arm into the sleeve. He assisted with the right side, gently guiding her right hand through. The coat immediately surrounded her in warmth. It smelled distinctly masculine. She could also pick up on a light lavender smell. Laundry. There was that tropical scent again as well.

*Coconut.*

"Better?" He asked, once it was on properly. He rubbed her arms before taking a seat.

She stared at the neutrality of the bamboo laminate tabletop, then closed her eyes, as the muscles in her right leg constricted and twisted, like a rag being wrung out. The pain pulsed through her calf, moving up into her hip and back. If she told him in whatever sad, nonverbal way she could figure out, he would likely take her back to get pain meds, a muscle relaxant and oh how she wanted the relief, wanted the piercing pain to subside.

His hand touched her wrist and as she opened her eyes, still gritting her teeth, she stared at the balled up fist that had once been her right hand. She stared at the puffy white scar on the underside of her wrist just beneath his hand, the deep contrast with his sun-soaked skin. She focused on the warmth of his hand, the tenderness of it.

She wanted him to reach up and touch her face again. She could practically feel the thickness of his palm, the smoothness of his fingers, folded and running lightly across her cheek. Despite her hand easing from a fist, it refused to relax beyond a claw, a backwards C, *a damn Lego hand*, she thought angrily.

She fought her frustration, fought her desperate anger, pulling in her breath. The twisting of her muscles had stopped, only a dull soreness remained, but the ache in her chest was almost unbearable now. She had no way to tell him that her mind had been sadistically circling the same thought all morning, that memories were coming to her in fragmented bits, and just when she felt her brain piecing some parts together, they were gone again, swept away by boisterous laughter of nearby staff, absorbed in a cold whirl of hospital air.

Jack was watching her. It wasn't with the bored acknowledgment of a child observing a monkey at the zoo like Alice. It wasn't with an analytical stare, fueled by substantial internal pressure to have her progress, like Julie. It wasn't with the uneasy, widened eyes of a person fearful of breaking some sort of artifact, like Grant.

Jack simply looked at her like he wanted to know more, his eyes captivated and patient.

When she had taken a few steady breaths, his eyes narrowed just slightly. She glanced across to the tablet sitting idly on the table. Something caught her attention on the screen and she leaned forward briskly. Her left hand moved toward it without her consciously telling it to do so.

It was a communication app. She'd heard of them in the past and it would have been very pre-stroke Delaney to scold herself for not thinking of one sooner. Post-stroke Delaney did not care. Post-stroke Delaney was too distracted by the prospect of communicating with more than just eyebrow raises.

# 11

# connection

J ack indecisively swiped through a couple of menus on the tablet. She
noticed the furrowed concentration of his eyebrows, his rugged but
polished appearance, his substantial hands, freshly tanned. She was quite
taken by those hands. They periodically distracted her from the screen, her
eyes following each gesture.

"Alright, so let's give this a try." Finding her watching him so intently
temporarily sidetracked his mind, but he pressed on. "So this app gives you some
shortcut responses and requests. Like a high tech communication board. We're
crossing into speech territory, but Alice assured me she doesn't mind."

Delaney released what sounded like a growl, but zeroed in on the tablet
anxiously. The main screen was simple with a lineup of icons in the middle:
PatientTALK, PatientPLAN, PatientTEAM, & PatientPRACTICE.

"OK, so we go into PatientTALK and we can view the menu as a bunch of
pictures, we can switch to common phrases--'I'm hungry,' 'I'm having pain,' 'I
need to use the little girl's room'--"

She glanced over at him, narrowing her eyes. It sounded purposeful and
rather bizarre coming from him. It sounded like something Caprice would say.

"There's also this screen, which has frequently used conversational phrases,
another for ADLs, you can switch to a keyboard, or a blank screen where you
can write--once your hands start cooperating a bit better that'll be easier. I
ordered some gloves to help with the spasticity. There weren't any locally."

Delaney studied the phrases screen, which he had left up for her. She raised
her left hand to the screen, still clenched in a hook. "*Right on!*" Said the two

thumbs up stick figure. The volume was turned up comically high and the voice startled her.

Jack smiled, adjusted the volume. "Let's switch to the female robot voice while we're at it."

She switched to the words screen, which changed each time she chose a word, trying to intuitively guess what she intended to say. It was a peekaboo game, jarring as the program enthusiastically tried to predict her thoughts.

When it was clear it was more frustrating than anything, he tapped the blank notepad icon. "How about just free text? If the keyboard is too much, we can switch back."

Her movements were a bit rigid, but as she moved her hands back, the screen read: "*who wrote these phrases bill and ted*"

He actually laughed so loud it echoed through the nearly empty space. She was already working on her next message at impressive speed, even utilizing the uppercase key.

She stared at him matter-of-factly as she moved her hands away. "*With the voice quality of the female robot and my search and peck typing I fear any attempt at humor will fall flat*"

"It's good to know your concern is with your comedic delivery, D."

"*I would do much better with the guy from Monty Python.*"

"John Cleese would be ideal." He smiled tightly.

*I knew you'd know who I was talking about. You're about the same age?* She felt the pressing impulse to type the words, but she looked at the man before her and felt the palpable gap--of what she could remember and what she felt for him. The first time he tried to embrace her, when she was first pulled from the medically induced coma, she had flinched away. It was involuntary, a response to receiving affection from someone she had never known in that context. She recognized him only as a distant coworker.

The scene was made worse by the fact that she couldn't utter a word and her face was frozen in a state of indifference, at best. She regretted her actions, both because he looked utterly destroyed by it and because ever since, while memories had only returned in bits and pieces, emotions she couldn't quite explain had swept through her. She longed for him to be near, to touch her face, put his arm around her, hold her. Watching him keep a respectful distance made her heart writhe and ache.

She gazed at his hands clasped together on the table.

"That can't be all you have to say."

She hesitated. She couldn't very well tell him that she wanted him to touch her more. For one thing it would sound really creepy in the robot voice.

"Hey, I didn't see this before," he said, pulling up the sleeve of the lab coat and grazing the deep purple bruise on her forearm with his fingertips. It was several inches wide and seeped across the width of her arm. "Did this happen this weekend?"

*Yes.* She watched him touching her arm so gingerly, hypnotized by it, by his thick fingers, muscular hands. She was sure her pulse was racing.

"What happened?"

His fingers were smooth and soft...and warm. She could feel his body heat run through his fingertips, radiating into her skin.

"D."

She looked up at him, breathing deeply, looking unintentionally stern, caught in her thoughts. She shook her head suddenly, which surprised her enough to soften her expression.

"Your body is starting to figure things out, Buddy."

His use of "Buddy" visibly deflated her.

"You don't like me calling you that, do you?"

She controlled the rate of her head shake.

"What do you prefer?"

"*D,*" the female Stephen Hawking said quickly.

That singular letter seemed to have a deep impact on Jack. He sat a little stunned.

She pulled up the Settings menu and muted the voice before presenting the screen. *"Will you work with me on shower self cares?"* It occurred to her that he could have misread what she was asking, given how she kept getting caught staring at his hands. She allowed herself the thought of being in a shower with him. Not there, though. In a much more luxurious shower--without a shower chair, the constant dinging of alerts from the nearby nurse station, without the clinical expectation of cleaning tasks and instruction, or God forbid, a code blue alert. It wasn't just for the fact that she felt a magnetic pull to him. The clinical manner taken by other staff to the self-cares and shower routine in particular made her uneasy. The helplessness, having someone else in so intimate a setting, the clattering of the water against the tile—it made her shrink into herself.

That wasn't even accurate. It had made her jolt toward the bathroom door so spontaneously, an instinct to run so strong, she had forgotten she was currently reliant on a wheelchair. She planted one bare foot on the tile then tumbled when the weakness in her leg gave way. If it hadn't been for Grant's quick response and effort to catch her, his hands with an uncharacteristically firm grip on her arms, things would have been much worse. When she caught her breath, she found herself a nose length away from the vanity. Grant had pulled her back toward him and she had looked directly in his green eyes, wild with shock. She started to cry silently. She rotated on her throbbing hip, assessing the shower, breathing heavily as images flashed across her vision.

She was grateful to Grant, but she did not want his hands on her. He seemed to sense this and pushed himself off the floor. "Come on, Laney. You probably need a rest anyway," he had said, guiding her into her wheelchair. "Maybe Jenna or Julie can do something with you later for showering."

She couldn't tell him why. Even if she could speak.

She snapped herself back to attention.

It was clear she had missed Jack's response so he repeated himself: "Yeah of course I will. How'd things go this weekend with Julie?"

*"PT was good. Worked in the pool a lot between Ter and Dr. S."*

"Dr. S helped?"

She nodded, her eyes brightening.

"What about shower stuff?"

*"I had Grant."*

"You had Grant for all your self-cares? Julie was supposed to cover for at least the shower." His eyes darted back to the bruise on her arm.

*"Julie's a PT."*

His eyes didn't register the implied question.

*"OT usually does showers." You know that. You were one.*

"I know, but--" he began, hesitating to give too much detail. He scratched at his eyebrow then found Delaney studying him, as though trying to decipher if he was bluffing in a poker game.

*"Julie wasn't happy either. Is there something I need to know about Grant?"*

"No—I mean, he had a crush on you at one point—but he's a good therapist." He took a few forced breaths. "Julie just didn't tell me. How did it go?"

*"I fell—so it could have gone better."*

He stared at her, unamused.

*"It wasn't Grant's fault."*

"How did you fall?"

*"Gracefully. Obviously."*

Jack chuckled, shaking his head. "This sense of humor has been in there the whole time?"

*"No. I was decidedly unfunny up until two days ago."* Her eyes were bright and focused.

He had a surreal reality as he adapted to the idea that she was actually joking around with him. As recently as a week prior, there had been discussion about 24 hour assistance, skilled nursing, group homes. He felt his shoulders relax a bit, some weight lifted from them. "What happened in the shower?"

*"I had a cognitive episode."*

"Clinical, but vague, D."

*"Say that again. That last syllable."*

He gazed at her, resisting the impulse to ask if her memory had returned--or get his hopes up. "D."

She smiled, breathed deeply like inhaling a sweet aroma, and then she was back to typing. *"I had a flashback."*

"You remembered something?"

*"Yes, but it was from a long time ago."*

"I thought your long term memory was OK?"

"*I hadn't forgotten it exactly.*" She shrugged, then acknowledged her first shrug with a jump of her eyebrow.

"Yeah, I saw it." He smiled kindly, instinctively stroking her cheek for a split second before thinking better of it and trying to pass it off as sweeping hair strands off her face. Then he dropped his hand to the table.

She watched his hand fall away then focused her attention on the tablet. She took a long pause before deleting the message and starting again. "*How was the wedding?*"

"You don't want to talk about the flashback."

She seemed to be waiting for him to fill in the blanks, to know what she saw in those flashbacks. When he didn't, she dropped her eyes to the tablet. "*I do not.*"

"Well," he began, "It turns out I'm not nearly as good at small talk as I once was."

"*Me neither.*"

He half-frowned, half-grinned. "Smart ass." He presented his phone and pulled up a photo of himself in a vested tux with the newlyweds. He wore a vibrant, wide smile and mirrored aviator sunglasses. The bride had loopy blond curls and wore a traditional and frilly ball gown and slightly tense smile. The groom was tall and lanky with a thick, scraggly beard and tattoos poking out from his collar. Delaney stared at the photo, trying to remember the girl. What came to mind was a photo of a four year old with the same curls standing in a field of sunflowers wearing ladybug rain boots, a rainbow striped skirt and a yellow *Curious George* shirt. *Tabitha*, she thought, trying to solidify it in her memory. The light pungency of orange blossoms filled her nasal cavity.

Delaney swiped through the next few photos, a little indifferently, but stopped when she reached a photo of Jack with a very pretty, perky looking woman wearing a short black dress and a large amount of makeup. "Short" was generous. Delaney suspected that had the photographer captured the shot from too low an angle, she could have confirmed her suspicion that the woman wasn't wearing underwear. She was particularly curious about the placement of the woman's hands—both on his chest, one pulling suggestively on his tie.

When Jack saw her staring, her nose scrunched on one side, a bit of a territorial glare in her eyes, he couldn't help but smile slightly. "That would be my ex-wife, Gillian. Tabitha accidentally invited her. Outdated address list or something went to the calligrapher. I suspect she's the reason couples steer away from having an open bar."

Delaney appeared incapable of moving past the photo. Her eyes continuously scanned the fine details—Gillian pressing her breasts into him while simultaneously criss crossing her legs to give herself a slimmed look, her smug smirk with those beet red lips, no teeth showing.

Finally Delaney settled on Jack's face. His eyebrows were crooked and you could hardly call the expression on his face a smile, more like bewilderment. His arm was around her, but his palm was open and didn't seem to want to touch her, his hand levitating over her hip.

Delaney relaxed her shoulders and swiped to the next.

The next photo was the curly haired bride with, who Delaney could only imagine, was her dad. He had a shorter version of her curls and when he smiled, his eyes were swallowed by creases. She immediately felt the warm weight of arms squeezing her gently, kissing her forehead. He'd smell of the outdoors, of potting soil, of lumber.

Suddenly their kind smiles, not terribly different than Jack's, were too much of a sensory overload: remembering, but not at the same time. She slid the phone back, closed her eyes, trying to hold off the tears that she felt filling them.

When she opened her eyes again, she focused on typing a message on the tablet, her fingers moving at a surprisingly rapid pace. She typed, then stopped to delete lines at a time, finally settling on: "*It looks like Tabitha had a beautiful wedding.*"

He was caught up in her knowing his sister's name. He was sure Julie had probably mentioned it, but clearly her short term memory was making big improvements. "Everyone sends their love," he said hesitantly. "Dad, Tab--*not* Gillian."

A laugh caught in her chest and she released a sort of hiccup. When she looked up at him, her eyes were filled with tears. She looked down at the tablet again.

*"Gillian reminds me of my sister a bit."*

Jack smirked. "A bit."

Delaney nodded conclusively. *"Strange to go from a woman like that to someone like me."*

He shook his head. "Strange would be going in the *opposite* direction."

She furrowed her eyebrows for a long time, long enough for him to regret being so bold. Then she turned her attention to the tablet and slowly tapped out a message. *"Do you have photos of us?"*

He sat back slightly. "Of course I do," he replied, starting to navigate his phone. "Clothed ones?"

*"Jack. Ass."*

"Okay, I deserved that. Well, here, I'll start you at the beginning."

When he slid the phone toward her, there was a vibrant photo of the pair of them with their faces smashed together, backdropped with a rich blue sky. The next was taken by someone else, a full-length shot. She saw herself standing in front of Jack, his arms embracing her in a playful hug from behind, her arms tucked around his. He smiled widely, his head tilted towards her, while she was caught mid-laugh. In the background was a turquoise waterfall, cascading from beautiful, but jagged red rocks.

The setting wasn't very far where she imagined her dream had taken her. She pictured herself once again sitting in the kayak looking over the blue water. Suddenly she sensed a presence behind her in the boat.

She sighed, started to type. *"I remember but don't remember at the same time."*

He nodded.

*"You could tell me about before--about us--"*

He read the words carefully, nodded again.

*"I assume there's a strategy to not telling me everything I've forgotten?"*

"Some say." He scratched at the back of his neck.

*"People say a lot of things, it doesn't make it true."*

"Selfishly I'd prefer if certain memories don't come back quite so clear."

"*Well that's comforting.*"

"I don't know why I said that. Clearly I am without faults."

"*Clearly.*"

She stared at him. She had never been the type to date too seriously. She was committed to work and her patients and typically found activities to fill the rest of her time. It wasn't that she didn't want to be in a relationship, but she had never met someone that she had felt a connection, that made her feel at ease.

They hadn't known each other particularly well from what she could remember. He was friendly, but seemed distracted much of the time. Married at the time that Delaney came on staff—to the woman in a tiny black dress—she had already forgotten her name. One morning, she recalled, she had been working in the charting area long before anyone else arrived. She emerged and found him intently organizing the patient lists on the whiteboard. Something in the weight of his breath as other therapists continuously entered his space and how he seemed to be inhaling more than exhaling told her it wasn't the time to make friendly chit chat. She wasn't the small talk kind anyway. She offered to help and he grunted out a "No thanks." Undeterred, she went to the nurses lounge Keurig and returned with a borrowed mug filled with Hugh Jackman's Laughing Man Coffee. "Thought you might need this," she had said quietly, placing the mug at the corner of the counter as she left to see her first patient. She remembered catching him smirk as he noticed the clipart of the arm bone on the mug and its caption: "I found this humerus."

Delaney inhaled deeply, fond of the memory, but frustrated by not being able to recall years with this man. How did they go from distant coworkers to dating? Did she play a part in his divorce? He was supplemental back then, attending med school. Maybe the stress of that was too much for his marriage.

She looked across at the coffee bar as she felt the effectiveness of her bedtime pain meds finally ebbing away. She winced as she rolled her shoulders, the joints seething and angry. She felt a similar ache in her hip and dreaded having to put weight on it, but sitting wouldn't be an option for very much longer. Perhaps she could slither into bed, rather than attempt a legitimate transfer. As long as Julie didn't descend upon them to insist on proper techniques, that is.

In the back of her mind, she heard muffled words, something about coffee, but she found her attention focused on her hip and the pain that was radiating into her buttocks and back. She would definitely be insisting on working with Terrence in the pool. Thanks to the tablet, now she could. Her body had clearly had enough weight bearing activity.

Jack watched her lose her focus. Her presence had shifted from being attentive and curious to being tense and closed off. This had been a bit of a pattern--two steps forward, three steps back--and he couldn't help but feel disappointment. He studied her in the wheelchair as she stared off into the distance.

The hair on the left side of her head was starting to grow back. He looked at the surgical site, the fishhook shaped seam. He had suspected early on that Dr. Cobach had the resident do part of the surgery. It didn't look as clean as it should have. During her recovery, the staples hadn't held in place as they should have, as they had been placed unevenly. He should have known. He should have insisted on having Dr. Isaac.

After reprimanding himself silently for a few minutes while she stared out the windows, he decided he should probably get her back to her room to rest.

Her chin snapped to attention just as he stood up and she frowned, typing: *"I was told there would be food. And coffee. And a whipped cream dollop."* She smiled in her new lopsided way. Her crystal blue eyes were suddenly as focused as before.

"You know, I *did* say that." He leaned in close to her shoulder, unlocked the brakes and wheeled her over to the display case.

The woman who ran the counter at this patient cafeteria was in her late seventies. She remembered most people's orders if they were regulars. She certainly remembered Delaney and had likely been updated a bit on what was going on. She smiled sweetly at her. "Hi Sweetie, it's nice to see you."

Jack was pondering how to explain covertly that Delaney wouldn't remember her (she had transferred from a different campus about 18 months earlier) when Delaney unmuted the tablet and it read: *"Hi, Phyllis. How are you today?"*

"I'm doing quite well." She exchanged a look with Jack, answering his questioning expression by pointing toward her name badge. "What can I get the two of you?"

Delaney scanned the baked goods greedily, but the rumble of a cart delivering dining plates effectively caught her attention. At least one wheel was severely off-alignment. The noise echoing against the tiled floors seemed painful to her.

Fortunately, there wasn't a line, and fortunately, Phyllis was patient. Once the cart had returned to the kitchen, Delaney turned her attention back on the display case. She seemed unaware how much time had passed.

"You should hear the floor buffer. Awful. I guess they have to do these things sometimes though," Phyllis said.

Delaney nodded, but she was struggling to focus back on her menu selection. The pain in her joints was reaching an intolerable level. She knew she'd have to cut their time short so she could get a pain med. That pain med would likely make her tired and she probably wouldn't do so well with typing once it really kicked in. She wanted desperately to talk to him, even limited to a tablet.

"I've been told I order really well—do you mind if I order for you?"

She was slightly startled, her mind caught up in its own world, but she shook her head.

"She'll have a chocolate croissant and a slice of pumpkin bread, both slightly heated, grande blended mocha, 1 pump vanilla, 2 pumps milk chocolate, as much whipped cream as you can stuff in one of those dome lids—and a chocolate drizzle if you can manage it."

"For you?"

"Black coffee. Banana bran muffin."

Delaney eyed him, letting her face remain stern.

"She's right. I'll have what she's having."

As he paid, he noticed her concentrating on the tablet screen. There was a solid few sentences so far. She stopped mid-message to scowl at her right hand, managing to get the fingers to flex a bit. She seemed to be shielding the screen to keep him from reading her message, but with a sigh, she erased what she had worked so hard to type, turned off the screen and closed her eyes, willing her body aches away.

The rumble of the blender filled the nearly empty cafeteria space. Delaney kept her eyes closed, trying to block out the noise.

"Is it the muscles, nerves, or everything?" he asked, his face close to her ear.

She opened her eyes, taking in the details of his face.

He nodded, reading her expression, and retrieved their items from Phyllis, thanking her sincerely. He held out her cup so she could take an indulgent sip, then tucked the cup in next to her hip. "Here's what I'm thinking--it's unconventional, but hear me out: caffeine, opioids, pastries, and a mid-day reading from that British book, followed by a rest for you, a lineup of screaming women in labor for me?"

*** 

At 3:16pm, Quinn propelled himself through the threshold of his doorway, peering down the hallway toward Recreation Therapy. Sarah had expressed her intent to make him go to Art, but he had claimed an upset stomach. He had been convincing enough with his complaints about the food quality that she had let him be and now he figured it was far enough into the activity that he wouldn't be roped into going.

It was then he spotted Sarah pulling open the door to the Rec Room. She waited for the door magnet to activate then emerged pushing Delaney in a wheelchair. Delaney was overtly slumped in the chair, eyes strategically positioned toward the floor. He quickly spun the wheels backward on his wheelchair and disappeared into his room.

A few minutes later, he covertly maneuvered from his room to Laney's. Once inside, he found Delaney sitting up in her bed, focused on the tablet resting on her rolling food tray.

"I knew you were faking," he chimed with a smile.

She glanced up, her face illuminated by the tablet screen in the otherwise shaded room. Despite overhearing that she had been seen smiling, her expression was neutral, if not serious.

"I can leave if you wanted to be alone?"

"*No, stay,*" a female British voice said.

"Hey, she speaks! Sort of."

"*Do not judge me on my spelling or grammar. The auto-correct is obnoxious.*"

He smiled. "You forget. I barely passed English."

"*That I remember.*"

"But thanks to you, I did squeak by in the end."

"*So what happened, Quinn?*" Her eyes pointed toward his wheelchair.

He shook his head. "I was being stupid."

"*Ah. I'm told I was getting breakfast.*"

"You don't remember?"

She frowned.

"What's the last thing you remember?"

"*Sitting in my condo eating dinner. I had just discovered a rogue honey walnut shrimp in my teriyaki chicken bowl.*"

"What is the significance of that, I wonder?"

Her mouth curled up slightly.

"When was this?"

"*The same day you ditched me at the Greek restaurant.*"

"That day is your last memory?"

"*Yes.*"

"I regretted my behavior that day--how I dealt with your rejection."

Her eyes narrowed at the screen. "*I didn't reject you. I rejected a date with you.*" She took a breath. "*I didn't date, Quinn. Not anyone.*"

"Why?"

She lowered her chin, looked at him with her big, blue eyes. Then she started tapping the touch screen keyboard firmly. "*You know what happened in that locker room.*"

He felt like he'd been punched in the chest.

She added: "*It's not something you just walk away from emotionally.*"

He swallowed. "I wasn't sure if you remembered--"

"*I didn't think I'd ever settle down, get married, any of that.*"

"Something changed since then."

She nodded. Whether she meant to or not, her eyes looked decidedly brighter, as he could only imagine she was thinking of Jack.

He thought of the call Julie had with Jack the day he first arrived. How concerned he had been. "Tell me about Jack."

Quinn thought it would be torturous to be told, even in writing, how wonderful this other man was, making it clear how Quinn could have never competed, but as she shared details about Jack, he found he couldn't summon those feelings. Perhaps he was impacted by the fact that most of the memories were limited to the time she had been hospitalized, that he sympathized with her inability to recall anything from their actual relationship. Perhaps he was impacted even more by the fact that despite this fact, as she typed, her mouth turned upward.

This was a woman, after all, who didn't smile, even when she was joking around and in her present state, struggled to express herself. Whatever prevented the sinking feeling of rejection, he found himself gazing at her in wonder. When she had finished typing, he sighed deeply. "So just a fleeting attraction to Dr. Jack then."

Delaney's smile tightened.

"I can't imagine having a woman speak--or type--about me so fondly."

*"I'd speak about you fondly if I could speak, but I don't imagine many women around here would do the same. Then again, you're not an asshole to me."*

"I have that reputation?"

Her left eyebrow jolted upwards. *"I get it. The situation sucks."*

"Truth be told, I was pretty much an asshole before the accident, too."

*"Why do you think that is?"*

"Shall I lie down on the couch for this therapy session?"

Her face remained firm.

"Things were going well. I don't know. Maybe I just became arrogant?"

She exhaled.

"What?"

*"You're unhappy."*

"Well, can you blame me?" he asked, motioning to the wheelchair.

She shook her head slightly. *"When we ran into each other--you seemed unhappy."*

Quinn frowned. When she saw him, he was wearing a pressed suit, was driving his sports car, and dining at fancy restaurants. She didn't know, but he was quite popular with women. With all that, if a man couldn't be happy, there must be something seriously wrong with him. He laughed uncomfortably. "I'm not sure what you were picking up on. Maybe the sting of rejection or whatever, but I had been doing very well for myself before the accident. If I could just get out of this chair, I'd be right back at it. You don't have to worry about *my* happiness, Laney." He had just placed both hands on their respective wheels and stopped, looking back up at her. Her face was morphed from the stroke, but he could still see the girl he had adored for all those years. Her impossibly blue eyes were not judgemental or angry as they watched him.

"I'm sorry."

She blinked slowly. Twice.

"Hey Laney, as long as you're awake, let's have you use the restroom, okay?" Jenna said cheerily from the doorway. She crossed the room, weaving around Quinn.

Delaney discarded the tablet to the bed, waiting for the bed rail to be lowered. She seemed to be purposely avoiding eye contact.

"I'll leave you to it," Quinn remarked, wheeling himself toward the hallway. "Let's talk later."

# 12
# home

Delaney's dad pushed open the front door, retreating to help his fifteen year old daughter manage the two step descent into his ground floor condo. The steps were the result of the complex being constructed on the side of a hill, common of the area. There were also steps required to get to the sunken living room area, as well as the master bedroom and one of the spare bedrooms. The doctor had advised that she avoid steps, as her hip was still healing and her balance was still unsteady. Her dad resolved the issue by relocating his study to the living room, moving the television and leather couch to the front room just off the foyer. He had determined the sunken bedroom would be Caprice's, if she changed her mind and decided to stay, leaving the other spare room for Delaney.

The condo was distinctly male, a cliche really. There was minimal furniture and most of the wood tones clashed. The only photos were contained within outdated heavy brass frames--most of the photos looked at least twenty years old. There was one frame that stood out among the mix. It was natural wood tones, as it was made with popsicle sticks. There was a big tree colored on one side, puffy clouds around the top and "#1 Daddy" written across the other side with about eight exclamation points. Delaney gazed at it and the photo inside the frame, which was the pair of them at Disneyland, on the teacups it appeared. It was the last time they had spent such a long span together—a whole three days. She was six.

Nearly a decade later and they were cordial and awkward with one another. After losing the custody battle, he never anticipated he'd ever have her living with him, not even for sporadic evenings. The fact that he hadn't done much to prepare besides have the cleaning lady come by an additional time the day before demonstrated how disbelieving he was that his fifteen year old daughter would be living with him permanently. It seemed far less likely that his stepdaughter, Caprice, would be living with him. She was weeks away from turning eighteen and she had a generally dismissive and detached attitude toward him.

The kitchen table was piled with papers, its days of being used for its intended purpose seemingly gone. There were exposed cords everywhere, stacks of magazines, and it smelled stale.

"That's my project for tonight," he explained. He seemed to mean the table. "Your room is right this way," he said, carrying her luggage like he was a bell boy rather than her own father. He opened the door to what was to be her bedroom, tucking the luggage next to the old dresser. He examined the space, as though for the first time. The walls were empty aside from a few nail holes, the bedspread a dated plaid, probably from his childhood bedroom by the look of it. "I'll get more of your things from the house--maybe your regular bedspread rather than this old thing."

She shook her head. "It's fine." Her voice was raspy, having not been used very frequently in five months. "Mine wouldn't fit anyway."

"Would you like your bigger bed, maybe?"

She took notice of the bed size. She wondered if her feet would hit the baseboard. "Maybe that wouldn't be such a bad idea."

"You've gotten so tall."

*I mean it*, her agent had scolded. *Half an inch more and you won't be desirable as a model anymore.* Her mom had looked over at her in desperation, like she could will a stunt in her daughter's growth.

*Mom*, Delaney thought, picturing her at that burger dive, toasting with milk shakes. Suddenly there was the shrill screech of tires skidding, the crushing of steel, the shattering of glass, her mother's body wedged in positions incompatible with survival, bones jutting out of her fair skin that would turn gray before firefighters were able to pull her from the car.

"I should have had this set up already. Things have just been so--" He let his voice trail off, glancing across at his daughter leaning against the wall, wincing as she stretched her leg, the hip having been pinned back in place through two separate surgeries. There were deep, dark circles beneath her eyes and he'd never seen her look so thin. "What's your favorite color? We can paint the walls when you're feeling up to it. It used to be purple, right?"

She frowned.

"I remember you used to wear purple all the time." He surveyed her outfit-- jeans and a worn-in navy blue t-shirt. "Maybe that's changed now. Is that your little league shirt?"

She glanced down at the shirt, nodded.

"That was a long time ago--you just played the one season?"

One ball to the cheekbone, which almost got her fired from a coveted modeling job and her mom had pulled her from the team. She gave a slight tilt of her chin. "When I was eight."

"It still fits. Not many people can say that." He seemed understandably more concerned than impressed. "So--you just decide the color and I'll pick up some paint." He tried to lighten the mood, adding: "But probably not purple."

"I never liked purple," she said, her voice crackling.

"Oh."

"I like green," she offered.

"Me too. Must be the Irish in us."

She seemed to be having a tremendously difficult time keeping her eyes open. "Would it be okay if I slept?"

He felt a slight bit of relief, running his hand through his sandy colored hair, but then he assessed the window and its lack of any covering. It was the brightest room in the condo. "I'll have to pick up a curtain. I need to run out to get your prescription. I can stop off at Target. Or we can go later together, get some things for in here?"

"Maybe another day? The curtain would be nice though."

"You've got it," he said, pointing awkwardly toward her. He moved for the door. "Do you need anything before I go?"

She shook her head. "No, thank you."

"Lunch? I can pick something up on my way back? The fridge is--a little limited right now."

She blinked tiredly. "Lunch would be nice. Thank you." She pulled back the covers, finding the pillow beneath was dressed in a stiff sham cover, rather than a regular pillow case. She said nothing, tucked herself under the plaid bedspread, and slept for the next 18 hours.

When she trudged out toward the living room, she wondered if she had been asleep longer. It looked like he had been working non-stop for days. The kitchen table was cleared with the chandelier on, expectantly, a jar candle burning as a centerpiece. It smelled like engineered fresh linen. The stacks of magazines were gone, the shelves under the television lined with books she recognized as her own.

"Those can move to your room, once I tackle Swedish furniture assembly," he said, motioning to the stack of boxes by the front door. "Or they can stay out here, if you prefer."

"You took on IKEA? Some people go in and don't come out for days."

His eyes widened optimistically. "I believe it. I went a little overboard. Everything was just so practical and reasonably priced." He crossed the room, pointing out the plain brown boxes and rattan storage boxes filled with smaller items. "I can take back anything you don't like--I just got the sense--" He hesitated. "Maybe having new things would be nice."

"That was a good idea, Dad. Thank you."

He smiled, then gestured sharply toward the kitchen. "I got groceries, too, but I didn't cook anything yet."

"That's OK."

"But I picked up a pizza about an hour ago. I'm trying to keep it warm in the oven."

She started to follow him into the kitchen, her hip stiff and achy, but he raised his hand to stop her.

"No, I'll bring it to you. I haven't dug out the chair cushions yet and these chairs would feel awful on that hip.

"I rented the latest *Harry Potter*. Then I realized I hadn't seen the first two and they didn't have them to rent anymore--so I bought all of them at Target."

She smiled at her father as he retrieved the pizza box from the oven, burning his hands in the process.

"This pizza is supposed to be the best around. It's thin crust without being too crunchy. Homemade sauce and everything." He darted around the kitchen like a mad man. "I got new plates, but they're all in the dishwasher. Paper OK?"

"No. I insist you hand wash a plate."

He stopped what he was doing, peered over the half wall that separated the living room from the kitchen. "I can do that." His mind was obviously reeling, wondering first and foremost, if he had the proper kind of soap to do that. The blatant rudeness of her demand didn't seem to enter his thoughts.

"Dad? I'm totally kidding. Paper is fine."

He grinned, rounding the corner from the kitchen. "And you do like *Harry Potter*? I wasn't snooping, but I saw the collection in your books."

"I do." Delaney started for the leather sofa in the front room, across from the television set on the blue screen for the DVD player.

He set their plates on the cleared coffee table and jogged back to the kitchen to get their drinks. "What would you like to drink? Once upon a time you liked lemonade so I made some, but I also bought soda, juice, Gatorade--I have bottled water, though they say our tap water isn't all bad."

"Lemonade is great." She hadn't been allowed to have lemonade in at least seven years. It didn't go particularly well with pizza, probably, but she didn't care.

He placed a beveled glass before her, filled to the rim with ice and lemonade. Through the side, she could see the price sticker still on the bottom.

"Did I forget anything?"

Delaney surveyed the spread. Napkins. There were no napkins. And she was well overdue for a pain pill, evident by the throbbing ache of her hip, the pulsing of her temple, but she looked across the couch at her father, who was adjusting a new throw blanket on the back of the sofa, and shook her head. "You did good, Dad."

***

"You look like the Terminator with those on," Quinn teased, propelling himself across the courtyard. He still hadn't shaved since he arrived a few days earlier and with his pre-existing scraggly facial hair, he was starting to have the appearance of a freshly sponge-bathed hobo.

Delaney reached one hand toward him, donned in a high-tech glove. *I was going for Iron Man*, she said silently. In her head, she had blasted a hole through the wall into a utility room along the corridor.

"Seems to be helping?"

She gave him a small nod before continuing to toss a bean bag back and forth between her hands, purposefully squeezing it between throws to give her fingers a better workout. For the past couple of days, he'd been trying to make light chit chat. The efforts were strained. She remembered he had an outburst, but she didn't remember what it was about, or what had been said. Given his strategy to pretend nothing happened, she didn't anticipate that an apology or further explanation was on the horizon.

"Where's Nigel?"

Nigel was the name the pair of them had given to the tablet after she had decided to switch the voice to a cordial British man. She nodded toward the bench behind her, waved her fingertips.

"Ah, Terminator hands aren't compatible with touchscreens?"

She shook her head.

"Thought we could have breakfast in the piazza here? I have the General at 7. You must have Terrence?"

She disliked the gesture and she had no interest in eating, but gave a thumbs up, returned to her OT homework. She had appreciated the familiarity of Quinn, despite the awkwardness. With all she didn't remember, it was fortunate really to have someone she did, but the early morning silence was as much peace as she'd managed all night and his presence felt imposing.

"You're up early, even for you."

She shrugged, hoping it didn't come across too dismissive, but just enough to hint to him to leave her alone.

"It's really nice out here."

Despite the unseasonably cool morning, her skin was already coated in sweat and she desperately wanted her hair pulled back off her neck.

A flood of anxiety and depression threatened to drown her. She told herself last night she could push through the emotions. She just needed to ride it out, but every heightened sensation—every itch, every ache, every noise now threatened to give away her calm exterior as a farce. She found herself cringing internally at lights that were too bright, staff that were too loud in their friendly greetings, and aromas, regardless of pleasantness, that were too robust for her to process.

She had known about the multiple surgeries, but the sensation of having a large patch of the left side of her head shaved recently had just made its way to her awareness. She really couldn't care less about what it might look like, but it was an additional distraction she couldn't block out, the unevenness of the temperature, the prickle of the shaved hair against her ear.

The racing thoughts were enough to deal with. She didn't need amplified sensations on top of them. She had spent the past few hours trying to silence her thoughts, tame the sadness, the frustration, the anger that overwhelmed her. She had fallen asleep the previous night, lulled by Jack reading to her, and a muscle relaxant that wore off by 2am. She woke with a hollow burning in her chest, like someone had shot a hole through her. She fumbled to an upright position, forcing off the sleep mask Jack had brought in to help her sleep. As usual, Jack had gone and the room was empty, the glow from the nurses station framing the door, the only light in the room, and the sound machine filling the room with the echo of ocean waves.

*You had a stroke. You're going to be okay. You're getting better each day.* She tried to steady her breathing, practicing the relaxation techniques Sarah had taught her. It worked as well as to be expected, slowing and lengthening her constricted breaths subtly, but enough. Then a sobering thought came to her consciousness: *Dad is dead.* Over and over. *Dad is dead. Dad is dead. Dad is dead.*

She didn't feel the tear streaming down her right cheek until it splashed to her bare shoulder. Her hand instinctively shot up to wipe her eyes, but the metal of the finger extensions over her knuckle jabbed her in the eye socket.

It was impeccable timing for Grant to step out onto the courtyard, messenger bag slung over his shoulder, sipping a coffee, just on his way in. "Laney, how are those gloves treating you?" he asked.

"They're not kind to eye balls," Quinn remarked.

"Oh damn," Grant said, rushing across the courtyard. "You okay, Laney?"

Delaney looked across at Quinn from behind the glove. He was dealing with his own limitations, trapped in a way. He could relate to some of what she was feeling, but she didn't suspect he knew about her dad. He'd know it was strange that he hadn't visited, but he seemed to be avoiding any conversational landmines, which pretty much covered anything of substance. He didn't seem to want to discuss his own circumstances--she'd asked about his family and he'd been vague, negative--so that had left small talk, generalized safe topics. It was excruciating. If she'd been able to speak, she would have been tough on him, challenged him, helped him perhaps. Instead, she was stuck, unable to help him, herself, or anyone else. She couldn't even escape the torture chamber of her own mind.

Grant sat on the bench and rotated her wheelchair toward him—more precisely, away from Quinn. He gently tugged her hand away from her face, examined her red eye rather intimately. "That's probably going to bruise, kiddo." He laid his cool palm flat against her upper eyelid and brow. "I can get you a small cold pack?"

Delaney was startled by this sudden onslaught of proximity, pulling back instinctively.

Grant still lingered a bit, looking over her face with curiosity. It happened a lot. People she knew staring at her, studying her. Catching himself, he looked immediately to her hands. "So other than the solid design, how are the gloves working out?"

She nodded generally toward her hands, flattening her fingers then flexing them again.

"That's good, Laney. Really good." He sat back on the bench. "So I heard you opened the gym this morning? 4am?"

"I didn't know anyone besides nurses were here at that time." Quinn added.

"Someone used her badge," Grant said, eyeing her employee badge lanyard on the handle of the wheelchair.

Quinn tilted his head to see her photo at the proper angle. It was much more casual, despite the business attire, than her fashion photographs. There was a shimmer in her eye, a genuine enthusiasm in her smile. He wished he could have seen her in her element like that. He wondered if there was any chance of her returning to work in some capacity, but given the fact that she couldn't support her own weight, it was unlikely she'd be able to support anyone else.

"So how long have you been wearing these?" Grant asked, lifting her gloved hands. There was a lengthy pause filled by the sound of the water feature.

Quinn noticed her nose flaring as she breathed. She looked like she was about to cry. He wouldn't blame her, given the circumstances and how irritating some of the staff were when they spoke to her, but she wasn't one to break down emotionally. Something had happened and close talker Grant was not helping.

"How long would you say, hmm?"

"Are you waiting for her to blink the number of minutes?" Quinn snipped. "Can you get her a stylus or something so she can still use the tablet *with* the gloves, maybe?"

Grant looked over at the tablet then back to Delaney, who had tears trickling down her cheek. "I'll try to track one down, OK, Laney?"

She nodded slightly.

"You seem tired. Would you like to postpone our session until later? Do you want to go sleep for awhile?"

Delaney inhaled in constrained frustration, limited from wiping the tears from her eyes.

"One question at a time. *Jesus.*"

Grant looked taken back. "Mr. Harwell, I'm working with Miss Rhodes right now. You wouldn't appreciate someone cutting in on your time would you?"

"See, that's perfect. You ask a question, then allow me to answer."

Delaney closed her eyes, her bottom lip quivering as she tried to hold back more tears.

"Laney, would you like to postpone our session?"

She nodded.

"Would you like me to take you back to your room to sleep more?"

She shook her head.

Quinn tried not to look too smug since Grant was clearly already embarrassed.

"How about we take these off for a bit? If you wear them for breakfast, it might help though."

She nodded.

As soon as she slid her hands from the gloves, they resumed a semi-clenched position.

Grant watched this. "This was a workout for your fingers so don't be surprised if they're achy. They're getting stronger." He placed a hand over hers as he stood. "I'll schedule us for just after lunch."

He leaned in close by her ear, speaking just for her to hear. This time she didn't flinch away. She simply gave a small nod and he moved away again. As he left, Quinn wheeled himself next to her.

He looked around thoughtfully. "Has the cruise director dropped off our activities schedule yet? I'm hoping to get some bingo time today."

She smiled weakly, out of politeness.

"You ready Quinn? I have an awesome workout planned for today." Julie said, appearing in the doorway, hands dug into the pockets of her lab coat, hair volumized with large beach waves.

"Oh Christ," he muttered under his breath. As he turned himself toward Julie, he matched her excitement. "Julie, darling, I don't care what anyone says, you look lovely at 6:45am!"

Delaney turned her face away.

Julie looked confused as Quinn approached her. "Someone's had caffeine today. I like it!"

Just as Quinn managed the door frame threshold, Jack passed by him in the opposite direction. He walked briskly, oblivious to his presence. He crouched before Delaney in his dark blue scrubs, speaking closely. She didn't seem to mind the proximity like she had with Grant.

He quickly retrieved the tablet, offered it.

She couldn't have typed more than a single word. As the automatic door closed, Jack had placed the tablet aside and was helping her stand. He immediately wrapped his arms around her, her shoulders shaking as she cried into his chest.

Quinn stopped inside the windows, mesmerized.

"You were so energized. What happened?" Julie questioned.

"You know I'm not a morning person. I was trying to cheer up Laney—she was having a rough day." Delaney seemed to be relaxing, her visible facial features softening, though still, unbearably sad.

"She was?" Julie peered out to the courtyard.

At first he assumed Jack was whispering in her ear, but then he began to ease her into a sway. Quinn shook his head. "He's singing to her. Of course he's singing to her," he scoffed.

Julie smiled tightly. "Oh my goodness, they're so sweet." Then she frowned. "Use the *right* leg, Laney," she said into the window.

Quinn looked at Delaney's leg, which she was barely using, touching the ground with her toes at best. She was taking some deliberately long breaths.

"Maybe we should hook her up with e-stim on that leg during her downtime today," Julie said. Quinn assumed correctly that she wasn't talking to him.

"He seems to care about her a lot."

Julie's eyebrows perked up. "That's an understatement. Six weeks in ICU, he was there around the clock. He wouldn't be working now except he has to. Something with HR because they're not married so he can't use FMLA. We need therapy time with her anyway, I suppose." She shook her head. "Let's get to the gym."

"So what caused the stroke? They're usually blood clots, right?"

"Most strokes are clots, but she actually had a blood vessel burst right by her brain stem. Nobody thought she'd make it. Most people wouldn't."

"You said on my first day that it was because of a concussion?"

"Could have been. Traumatic brain injuries could easily weaken blood vessels."

"Like dealing with that the first time around wasn't bad enough," he muttered under his breath, pushing the wheels a bit harder, then stopped. "The brain stem is on the back?"

"What was that?" Julie asked, distracted as she was typing something into her phone.

"Therapists shouldn't text and treat."

She absentmindedly agreed with him and continued inputting something.

"Boyfriend?"

Her cheeks reddened. "*No.*"

"You're a terrible liar."

"You had a question?"

"The stem is on the back?"

She nodded.

"The blood vessels are OK by her right temple though?"

"As far as I know. Why wouldn't they be?"

# 13
# filter

Quinn lowered his eyes as he gathered the car keys from the wall hook. His mother looked up from a stack of bills, her glasses resting low on her nose. "You going to Laney's?"

"I am."

"Are you going to ask her?"

He rolled his eyes. "She probably doesn't even want to go."

"It's the prom. It's a rite of passage."

"We're just friends."

"*Friends*. OK," she said in a sing-song voice.

They were spending most afternoons and weekends together. It seemed like less of a conscious decision and more of a habitual routine once the school year started. Delaney had seemed resolved, but uneasy about returning to campus, so he had made himself available. Despite being in the hospital for the better part of sophomore year, she had made up work, and her schedule consisted of mainly AP courses, which gave them no shared classes. She planned to graduate a year early, which was feasible considering she was no longer involved in a grueling modeling schedule, her hip injury left her unable to do track and field, and she seemed to have little impulse to do much beyond attend school and her therapy sessions. She would attend his baseball practices on occasion, usually reading something in the stands. She'd sit with his mom for games. On weekends, they'd typically see whatever was new at the movie theatre, dine at a casual counter restaurant. She had a subdued presence, saying little in front of anyone else. Occasionally he'd pick up on some humor, but it was a deadpan delivery so he wasn't always confident she was joking.

On the first day of school, he met her in the parking lot. He had offered to pick her up at her dad's condo, but she had reasoned the walk was good for her. He arrived early to school and had leaned against his compact car, watching the hilly road that circled the perimeter of the school for signs of her. She appeared at the exact time they had specified, wearing dark wash jeans, frayed at the heels, black Converse, a plain black v-neck and a dark gray hoodie. She had given herself bangs since he saw her the day before. It was strategic, he had determined, to cover a bit of her surgical scarring. As was the hoodie, since it was a scorching August day, despite the appropriately moody looking sky.

She crossed the parking lot, her fists dug into the pockets of her hoodie, legs rigid and determined. He thought he could see her eyes repeatedly panning to her right, to the gymnasium, as she approached him.

"First day," he said, imitating typical teenager angst.

She raised her eyebrows beneath her bangs, scanned the faces around them.

"What do you have first--AP English, AP History, AP Economics, AP Underwater Basket Weaving?"

The corner of her lip flinched. "AP Lego Robotics."

"I must have missed that one. Probably has a prerequisite?"

Another flinch, a shuffling of her feet. She motioned toward campus with her shoulder. "Should we go? I want to make sure I claim the good pieces."

That's how it began--he walked her to her class (AP Advanced Calculus), even though having that as a stopping point made the path to his own class nonsensical. Afterwards, they met by their lockers, which he had secured side-by-side on the southernmost building since that's where all but one of her classes were located. The pattern would repeat until lunch. She never seemed particularly hungry so he would typically meet up with friends at the cafeteria or off-campus while she went to the library. After lunch, they would pick up where they left off--at their lockers, and the pattern would continue until the end of classes.

On that first day, she had told him she would just walk home after her AP Chemistry class, but after class, she had approached him at his locker from across the bridge that connected the campus over the desert wash. Her face was ashen, her prominent upper lip parted from the lower.

"Do you need anything out of your locker?" he asked.

She shook her head, almost imperceptibly, her eyes straining against the limits of her peripheral vision to see something behind her.

He closed his locker loudly and moved toward her. "Shall we?" he said, offering his hand.

She surprised him when she took his hand immediately. Despite having been clenched in her pocket and despite the 105 degree outside temperature, her skin felt like it had been in a freezer.

Quinn stepped toward the parking lot, tugging her gently along. He thought he saw people taking notice of the pair of them, like they were spotlighted in the scene. Then again, he had dreamed of holding Delaney Rhodes' hand for nearly five years.

The novelty of it was invigorating.

Delaney moved into him, seeming to shield herself. It was then he noticed her hand was trembling. He squeezed it gently. "Did you eat anything today?"

Her eyes had tensed as they passed the bridge, her pace slowing slightly. Just to their left was a classmate he recognized from countless school assemblies, one of the celebrated football players. Even at just 16 years old, he towered over most everyone with his husky frame. That day, he bowed his head when Delaney met his stare.

Meanwhile, her fingers squeezed Quinn's hand with surprising force.

"Did you eat anything today?" he repeated, starting on the path toward student parking.

"No," her voice said quietly as she redirected her eyes to the sidewalk before them.

"Well it's about time for my second lunch. Drive-thru burgers?"

She nodded, seeming to calm the further they got from campus.

Each day, she got a little bit better, or at least, the setting became more familiar. Most days, he felt the inclination to ask her if she remembered that day in the locker room. In particular, he was curious about the boy on the bridge-- Timothy--perusing past yearbooks concluded that the pair had been friends as kids. Each day, he found some cognitive loophole justifying why he shouldn't bring it up. If he were honest, the fear of her suddenly rejecting him if she really didn't want to talk about it was enough.

From the outside, they appeared to be a couple. There weren't any platonic friends in high school that held hands--well, there were the obnoxious, bubbly girls that did, though that seemed to be more geared toward getting attention from boys. There was something about the physical contact between two girls that led teenage boys to believe that at any given moment they would witness lesbian behavior.

Through some natural progression, they had started kissing the other on the cheek when they said goodbye. Quinn had initiated this on the anniversary of the attack when he felt particularly resistant to let her walk to classes alone. She hadn't reacted negatively, but she hadn't reciprocated until a week or so later. They had done it ever since.

"Why don't you just kiss her?" his mom said suddenly. "None of this cheek business. Just kiss her square on the lips, see what happens?"

"Mom."

"What? You like her. *Right?*"

He couldn't explain to her why he felt like he couldn't push things too far with Laney. He couldn't explain what had happened to her. Somehow he didn't think the explanation for why nothing was done to prosecute her attackers would sit well with his mother. She wouldn't accept that nothing could be done because Laney didn't remember. She would read his face to know that there was doubt in his mind whether she truly had amnesia around the incident.

"What time will you be home?"

"11? We're going to get some dinner and go to the new Denzel Washington movie."

"The Jim Carrey one I heard was good. Something about *Sunshine?*"

*Strategic erasing of bad memories,* he thought. *Probably not.* "When is dad coming home?"

"Next Thursday."

"Are you going to be okay?"

She gave a knowing tilt of her head. "Ask her."

He circled around to where his mother sat at the granite bar and gave her a sideways hug.

The decision to go to prom together happened in a way similar to how they became friends in the first place, which was simple proximity. They were walking onto campus one morning and Student Government was selling prom tickets, soliciting at the entrance like Girl Scouts selling cookies. The VP/cheerleading co-captain, Ellie Rogers, had approached them, or rather, she had approached Laney, talking surreptitiously about an English assignment. Ellie complimented her on an analysis she had given of one of their recent reads. Quinn had assumed it was a sales tactic, but she had let them pass with a small smile, calling to Laney that she would see her in class.

When they reached the lockers, Quinn had mentioned the prom, saying something about: "I don't know if you had thought about maybe going with me? I mean if you don't think you want to go, but if you do, maybe..."

Laney had slid out her chunky Calculus book, closed the locker door, and waited for him to stop stumbling over his words.

"Did you get any of that?" He asked, wincing.

"Start over," she said, squinting one eye.

"Would you like to go to prom? With me?"

"No. And yes."

Quinn's mother beamed as she helped him with his rented tux. "Did Laney pick out the tux? I'm sure she has good fashion sense, right?"

"I think prom tuxes come in bow tie, regular tie or *Dumb & Dumber*."

"I bought a few extra copies of that style magazine she's in. I know she doesn't do it anymore, but not many people can say that they modeled professionally. Have you seen it?"

"Nope." He pictured images like what she had done most recently--wild, larger than life hair and dark eyes, seductive stares, provocative poses, typically involving an arched back and parted lips.

She finished looping his tie and retreated to flip to the marked page. The first photo was a moody shot through a glass pane reflecting trees. Her big eyes, which seemed to reflect the atmosphere of some distant, breathtakingly chilly planet, stared straight over her bare shoulder into the lens, lips slightly parted, the camera a friend that had betrayed her.

"My God, she's a beautiful girl," his mom observed. Then she pointed at her bare skin. "I'm sure they'd have her wearing something, right? Probably a sleeveless dress?"

"You'd hope," he said, doubtfully.

She pointed a slender finger at the next photograph. "That's her too, isn't it?"

It was another black and white shot of a young woman dressed in only a voluminous tulle skirt, leaning forward over the skirt and what appeared to be a bed. Every rib was visible, nearly every vertebrae of her spine, her pointy shoulder blades prominent. Her arm was stretched upward on the bed, her hair fallen forward. A heap of stunning sadness.

Another: Her long dark hair loose and blowing gently behind her. She appeared to be walking down a wooden beach path toward the wide open sea, her back to the camera. She was wearing a gauzy, undone dressing gown that floated in the breeze and ornate six inch heels that extended her already lengthy legs. Her heels were crossed, as though walking a narrow balance beam, her right arm extended to brush the dressing gown as it billowed out. The material was sheer, the outline of her backside evident. If he didn't consider her age, or what only he knew, the photographs were incredible and artistic. She looked like an earthly goddess. His mother was a bit thrown off by the subtle nudity, but captivated by the drama of the images. She clasped at her heart, remarking again about her beauty. In her mind, she was envisioning how beautiful her grandchildren would be.

The last photo of her had her standing before the ocean, waves crashing over her feet. Her hair was larger and wind blown, her chin high, her face filled with desperate neutrality. She wore a beautifully textured wedding dress that collected at the bottom probably meant to look like a billowy mermaid tail. Her shoulders were pulled back, but her arms had a quality of yielding, dropped to her sides, framing torn, fraying bits of the dress. Half the dress had strips ripped away, as though it had been mangled. The damage left very little coverage over half of her bare chest. He focused on her face in its braced, pensive state.

"When you said she was modeling wedding dresses, I kind of pictured David's Bridal catalogs."

He nodded, touching the glossy page.

***

When the door opened, Laney's dad was standing inside, tall and slender. He patted Quinn on the shoulder with a lengthy arm, smiling tightly, his eyes and forehead lined more than they should have been at his age, his sandy hair a bit wild.

"She's almost ready," he assured him, knowingly. His eyes were simultaneously blue and green. Given Laney's mother's desire to have her model, he wondered if part of her choosing to be with Laney's dad was for his appearance. "Want something to drink before you head out?"

"No, thank you, Mr. Rhodes."

He nodded, locking his gaze with a protective intensity. "I can't believe she's graduating this year. You still have another year?"

"Yes. I'm not a brilliant mind like Laney."

Thomas Rhodes smirked, his face filled with pride. "There's a lot going on in that brilliant mind, you know?"

Quinn nodded.

He peered down the hallway. "You'll take care of her tonight? Get her home safe?"

"I will, Sir."

"I always thought there'd always be more time," he said distantly, his eyes still fixed down the hallway. "When she was little. When her mom and I divorced and I started traveling more and more for work, I just--" His voice broke. "She grew up so fast."

Quinn watched him try to summon the tears back in his eyes.

Mr. Rhodes' eyes were fixed on a black and white photo framed on the wall. It was a closeup of Delaney at probably four years old, her eyes impossibly big, her face contorted in a sort of half fish face. "I supported it when she was little—the modeling. She had fun with it. She could be a kid. Then it seemed like all of a sudden they had her--" he motioned blindly to his desk, situated in the front room. On it was a stack of the same magazines his mother had also stockpiled. "She's still a *kid.*"

Quinn placed his hand on the man's shoulder, drawing his attention to the emerging shadow down the hallway. Mr. Rhodes wiped roughly at his eyes and managed a smile.

Only by looking at the obligatory doorway photo taken by her dad could Quinn remember the exact detailing of her prom dress. It had sheer, beaded sleeves, a glistening, beaded torso, and she had referred to the color as blush. The skirt was flowing tulle. She had done her own hair in an updo with whimsical braids. Her makeup was light, barely perceptible.

What he did remember was that in a sea of trendy two piece cropped prom dresses and mini dresses, the latest teen fashion craze, she was an effortlessly ethereal being.

He watched her throughout the evening, struck by how she contrasted the presence of the other girls her age. While most of the other girls vied for attention, obsessed with appearances, constantly adjusting straps, checking their plentiful makeup, Laney seemed to simply exist. She took in the ballroom, decorated as a winter forest, with childlike wonder. She spoke with him with captivated interest. He never saw her eyes pan around the room to assess any threats to her ego, like he saw with some of the other girls, devastated that someone else would dare to also wear a similar color. There were couples having arguments, clearly enebriated early in the evening, packs of girls who had vowed to not have dates, gossiping and infuriated when the guy they had hoped would ask them arrived with someone else.

In the middle of all the drama, they danced. The playlist seemed to be recycled from weddings. The obligatory group dances gave them an opportunity to be silly. The slow dances felt unnatural and awkward. She didn't embrace him like he imagined she might--it was all very *platonic.* She carried the conversation. She asked him what was going on with the internship his dad was setting up for him, listening intently, watching his facial expression as he spoke. He eventually asked her what her plans were for after graduation. Despite having spent most days together, watching her work so tediously, he found he had been entirely in the dark as to what she intended to do. He had assumed she would go directly to college. She had vast interests, but she seemed to be centering on Physiology, Health--she had appeared to him so frail after the accident, but recently she had started swimming, pilates, building long, lean muscles.

It surprised him that he was unaware she had shadowed therapists at the Rehab center where she had been a patient, but he was blindsided to find out that while she did plan to go to school to be a physical therapist, she didn't plan to start for over a year.

When he asked what she planned to do in the meantime, her lips had turned up at the corners. She painted pictures with her words of places around the world: the split pinnacles in China, a cherry blossom lined path along a river in Japan, a castle backdropped with the snow-capped peaks of the Swiss Alps, a tranquil river in Ireland, an ice hotel in Norway. Her eyes shimmered with enthusiasm and excitement.

He remembered staring at her, dumbstruck, as she disappeared out the large, arched doors to find the restroom. They had spent so much time together and here, he felt like he knew nothing about her. She had isolated herself, coping with what had happened to her those 16 months earlier, broken, scarred. He had kept watch of her, supported her. It was unfathomable to him that she would consider going to college outside of the city, let alone travel halfway across the world.

She appeared then, a waiter holding the carved door open for her. She floated inside, familiarizing herself with the layout again. He was about to wave to her when he saw Ellie, the Student Government VP descend upon her. To his bewilderment, the spiral haired blonde hugged her, gushed at her dress, and even more surprisingly, Laney seemed genuinely happy to see her. They spoke with large gesturing hands and when they parted, they hugged again.

The truth of the situation was simple and it stung him with piercing intensity: All along, he had viewed her as a victim, raw and vulnerable, needing him, but the young woman walking toward him in her ethereal gown, slight smile and crystal blue eyes was not a victim. She was a survivor.

# 14

## eve

I n medical school, Jack had an instructor who said it was inevitable that each and every one of them would face death in their career. Someone would die before their eyes. He had two suggestions to prepare for this: Have a good mental outlet and have good malpractice insurance.

The case was an interesting one. The patient was a thirty-one year old woman who had chosen to carry on with her pregnancy after doctors had recommended a critical, life-saving brain surgery. When she reached 38 weeks, she had agreed to have a c-section followed immediately by the surgery.

When she was wheeled in, Jack greeted her and was met with the sweet melody of a southern accent in return. He told her about his role and how things would progress. Her eyes lit up when he mentioned the baby.

"She's a *girl*," she had gushed, tears welling in her eyes. "We have two boys already and of course I love them to pieces, but I always dreamed about having a little girl."

He couldn't tell if the tears were excitement or fear or some combination of the two.

As he set her up on the drip, checked the monitors, she asked him if he was married or had kids. He looked into her bright blue eyes. He and Delaney had only been seeing each other for a few months so he wavered in his answer. "No, not yet."

"But you want to?"

He checked the setting he just adjusted since his attention felt split, took a deep breath to re-center himself. "I do," he said, nodding.

"There's someone you have in mind. I can see you smiling behind that mask of yours."

He chuckled. He went through his checklist, making sure everything was as it should be, then turned to his patient, Samantha Ellis, who appeared to have been waiting for him to finish what he was doing.

"Text her and tell her you love her."

"I can't. It's a sterile environment."

"Is it in your pocket?"

"Maybe."

"Use Siri."

The room was void of people other than the pair of them and the nurse setting up the surgical trays, who raised her eyes expectantly.

Jack leaned toward his chest pocket. "Hey Siri--" Beep. "Text D."

"*What would you like to say to D?*"

"I love you, comma, capital D, period."

"*Your message to D says: 'I love you, D.' Ready to send it?*"

"Yes."

"*Message sent.*"

"What is D short for?"

"Delaney."

She smiled. "That's a pretty name." Her eyes moved to his pocket, lit up with a reply. "Siri can read it out loud," she offered.

"I wouldn't put it past her to send a 'We need to talk,'" message in response as a joke." He shrugged. "Hey Siri, read new text."

"*D sent you a text message that says: 'So sorry. Bad reception in the elevator. Could you please repeat that?' Would you like to reply?*"

He shook his head. "Yes."

"*What would you like to say?*"

"I love you more and more each day, period."

There was a short delay, then: "'*Thanks. I'm very fond of you.*'"

He shrugged. "Told ya."

Samantha smiled. "I like her."

Jack resituated the pulse monitor on her index finger, sat back in his seat. "Yeah, me too."

The team of Neurosurgery nurses started to file into the operating room and he immediately sensed her body tense. "So have your boys gotten to meet their baby sister yet?"

Her eyes focused on him, glistening in the light. "Yes. They love her. My younger son, Cole, said she looks like a baby doll. They took me straight from the c-section so I haven't gotten to see them altogether in person. It was through texts."

"Soon you will."

She nodded. "I can't wait to kiss my husband, hug my boys, snuggle my baby girl." Her eyelids started to drift. "My husband thought it was so silly what I wanted to name our daughter. He teased that he was going to put 'Leia Organa Ellis' on her birth certificate instead."

"Well that's fan loyalty."

"Right? Oh, there's nothing like holding your newborn baby."

He felt a twinge of pain in his chest, remembering holding Sabrina, not realizing she wasn't even his daughter. "You'll get to hold her soon."

Samantha smiled dreamily.

Jack lifted his eyes to the nurse approaching his patient. "What did you want to name her?"

The woman's lips indicated she was speaking, but the clatter of surgery prepwork drowned out her voice--and then Samantha was silent, her eyes closed.

"She's had a tiring day already," he explained to Paula, who promptly began the process of attaching protective shields over Samantha's face.

It was the third time he'd participated in the surgery and for the first two and a half hours, things were textbook. The surgeon had chosen Frederic Chopin for background music, his slow blinks following the melody of the music, his safety glasses reflecting the red intricacies of Samantha's brain. Jack had checked and rechecked the monitors, continuously re-engaging. He had just stretched out his back, holding in a yawn.

First he noticed a spike in her pulse, then a quick drop. He adjusted the monitor on her finger, at which point he noticed her hand had rolled, her palm facing upward.

"Call Dr. Jennings," the neurosurgeon said flatly.

It was then Jack noticed the blood splatter across the man's safety glasses. His direction had caused an uproar of movement in the observation gallery, several staff furiously scrubbing in at the sinks.

An hour later, he found himself sitting on the opposite side of a partition wall, shielded from hallway traffic staring down at his hands, the patterns in the carpet. The space was used for the lab, which was currently under construction so there were very few people who ever occupied the waiting room chairs.

There was a light squeak of a tennis shoe on the opposite side of the wall-- and then Delaney stood before him, slightly winded. Her eyes were already welled with tears, lip quivering.

He eased himself to stand and she immediately wrapped her arms around him.

*** 

When Jack arrived to Rehab at 5:37pm, he was told that Delaney was out in the pool. He strolled the long hallway, stretching and twisting out his tight back muscles. At the point he expected to hear the lapping of chlorinated water, at a minimum, he heard silence. Then he picked up on some airy instrumental tones. He peered through the glass panels to the left of the door.

Delaney was floating in the center of the small rectangular pool, arms outstretched at her sides, eyes closed. Sarah stood on the opposite side of her, speaking quietly, rhythmically. When she saw Jack, she waved him in.

Terrence turned around from the edge of the pool closest to the door and gave Jack a silent fistbump. Jack sat beside him, surveying the scene. "Is she asleep?" he mouthed to Sarah, who nodded.

"Sarah did a little voodoo on her and zonked her out," Terrence whispered.

"Just some light hypnosis to help her relax."

"She agreed to it?"

Sarah glared at him. "Of course."

Delaney's body floated, as though on a cloud, her chin pointed upward, eyes closed delicately. Her skin had lost its tan pigment in the time she had been hospitalized, her arms and legs lean, but no longer well-defined and muscular. She once emerged from taking a post-workout shower, dressed in comfy loungewear, her damp hair already crimping itself into waves, staring at her feet as she walked. When he asked her what she was doing, her face beamed with pride as she said: "My feet have muscles!" and she had gone on to flex them to demonstrate. He smiled at the memory, how bright her eyes had been, how natural and comforting it was having her in his house, yet also surreal that she was there, that they were in love. "How long has she been in there?"

"Two hours, right Sarah?"

Sarah nodded again.

"Two *hours*?"

"I didn't want to wake her. I had to trade off with Cory earlier."

"I came out here to see about doing a session, but as you can see, she wasn't feeling up to it," Terrence explained.

Jack's eyes scanned the space, the outside windows at the roofline providing a gentle sunset glow. "It's nice out here."

"Actually I am feeling far more at peace than 20 minutes ago," Terrence conceded.

"I told you." Sarah's forehead furrowed. "She must have been so tired. I heard she didn't really sleep last night?"

Jack shook his head. "Last night was rough." He pushed away the guilt that he wasn't there to comfort her, that he had to be informed something was wrong by Grant this morning. Mercifully, Sarah didn't pry. She just looked at Delaney's peaceful face and smiled kindly.

Terrence started to rise to his feet. "You two can handle little Laney. Actually, that girl is *tall*. Look at her all stretched out. How tall is she?"

"5'11"."

"Maybe we'll work on some postural exercises. *In the meantime*, I'm gonna get myself home."

"Thanks, Terrence." Jack leaned back on his hands, took a few deep, cleansing breaths as he watched Delaney looking as relaxed as he'd seen her since before the bleed. The water outlined her body with perfect definition, while her dark hair drifted out behind her on the surface of the water. He watched her chest rise and fall with a steady rhythm--up…down…up…down…

"Laney," Sarah said, raising her voice a bit. It was enough to jolt him from his own trance.

She motioned to Jack to pick up her phone. "Would you just hit pause?"

The gentle spa music stopped.

"Laney?" she said, a little louder. "Time to wake up."

Delaney's eyes opened reluctantly.

"I guess you needed that," Sarah said softly. "I hate to wake you, but I need to get over to Noelle's Happy Hour."

There was a moment of calm as Delaney's eyelids started to drift closed. A split second later, they flew open again, startled--and her midsection dropped into the pool as though attached to lead weights. There was a chaotic splashing and she sank beneath the surface. Sarah kept missing her when she tried to grab for her arm. Suddenly, Delaney flipped her body upright, slammed her feet into the bottom of the shallow pool and her head shot through the surface of the pool. The overcompensation sent her falling toward the entry stairs.

Jack wasn't sure of the physical steps he had taken to thrust himself into the pool. One second he was sitting along the side of the pool wishing Sarah would allow Delaney to continue to sleep, the next his back was slamming into the metal steps, Delaney was lying on top of him, and he was surrounded by bath temperature water, potently tinged with chlorine.

Delaney was breathing heavily, her hair suctioned to her face. Her face was braced in bewildered shock. He could feel her hand reaching to see the placement of his back in relation to the corner of the step, making sure he hadn't struck his spine on the landing.

"Are you both OK?" Sarah asked, finally clamoring to them.

Jack felt Delaney's hand slide under his shirt to touch his skin directly, her eyes squinting.

"I'm fine," he said softly, trying to shift the veil of wet hair from her eyes. "Are you?"

She glanced to the center of the pool where she had been floating, her eyes widening.

"Grant was right. I should have used the float," Sarah conceded.

Delaney exhaled, giving a short nod.

Jack started to feel the same calm he felt watching her float, having her so close. Their positioning reminded him of a much colder setting--when they traveled to visit his dad in Chicago and she started a snowball fight in the Cloud Gate park against his rowdy cousins. When the tide had turned, she had run full-speed toward him, her neck rotated to see behind her, and she tackled him to the ground. Her back was immediately pummeled with snowballs intended for him. There was a prolonged moment where they just gazed at each other, her eyes smiling at him, his arms tightly around her.

"Aw, sweetie," he had said as they rose to their feet and he found her coated in snow. At that point, everyone was out of breath and laughing. "Did you just take 97 bullets for me?" He started brushing off her back.

"I did what I had to do," she said, grinning.

He nodded in appreciation, holding her arms, looking very serious. "I shall avenge you." He raised his eyebrows, pointing his eyes toward the unsuspecting trio of ironically bearded young men, and took off, scooping up snow along the way.

In the much more tepid setting, he let his hesitation melt away and embraced her, kissed her forehead.

It was one of those moments that, under normal circumstances, would have led to a more intimate tangling of limbs. Instead, there was an echo of voices of therapists in the hallway, making their way to the back exit, and the recreation therapist standing over them, anxiously checking the wall clock.

"Great reflexes, Jack."

Delaney dropped her gaze, seemingly lost in her thoughts, suddenly uncertain of her hand placement.

"Should we get out of the pool, Laney? I don't know about you, but my fingers are pruny," Sarah suggested.

Jack guided Delaney to sit on the step beside him so he could pull himself to stand first. She was still entirely dependent to climb up the shallow steps, though this seemed partly due to her wanting to continue holding onto him. He helped situate her in the wheelchair, his own scrubs soaked up to his shoulders, his shoes sloshing.

Sarah wrapped herself in a robe and fetched one for Delaney, which she more so used as a blanket. "I can take Laney back. Nursing can do her shower while you get changed."

Delaney immediately looked defeated. It was visibly wearing on her to be spoken about like she wasn't there.

"Yeah I suppose all the OTs are gone for the day," he replied.

Sarah checked the time again. "What about you? You're still an OT. They're giving you a hard time?"

Delaney glanced up, inquisitively.

"Leadership says no." Administration had said that if she wasn't safe to do shower self-cares with a treating therapist, she's not safe to do them with him. They further expressed that if she *was* safe and he was able to complete self-cares with Delaney, as her caregiver, then it would indicate she was higher functioning and could likely have a shorter length-of-stay. Not being clinicians themselves, they didn't seem to grasp the concept that she wasn't yet walking with a portable walking device or that patients tended to show quicker progress with self-cares.

Or that there was more to Occupational Therapy than self-care management. It bothered him more than anything that he hadn't been able to honor her request, one of the only things she'd asked for since being able to communicate.

"That's so ridiculous."

Jack shrugged. "I get it, I guess. For any other patient, if the treating OT hasn't said they're safe, they'd never let the husband just jump in there." He froze, catching himself say 'husband.'

Sarah grinned, glancing to Delaney, who was staring down at her hands, pushing together her wrinkled fingertips. It wasn't obvious whether or not she had heard Jack. "*Well*, Jenna is on at least."

Jack crouched at Delaney's side after finding the tablet was drained of battery. Her face looked stern. "Poke, burgers, or pizza?" He asked, presenting each option with a corresponding finger on his hand.

It didn't surprise him when she chose pizza. Of the options, it required no utensils and was the easiest for her to eat without assistance. He placed his hand on her cheek, wiping away a stream of pool water flowing from the shaved stubble on the left side of her head. His eyes drifted to her parted lips before kissing her forehead again.

When he arrived to her room with a large pizza box and a pair of fountain drinks, she was sitting in the wheelchair gazing out the dark window. There was no indication she was actually looking at anything, her eyes appearing vacant and glossed over. She would have a difficult time seeing outside as the window mainly reflected the interior lights and hid anything outside.

There was a jarring manner to her motions. She was using her left foot to roll forward, then she would abruptly stop and roll backward again. She did this over and over, jaw tensely clenched, seemingly unaware he was there despite the door squeaking loudly as he pushed it open.

"Well, would you like the British narrator, or that American character tonight?" He asked, placing the food and drinks on the meal tray by her bed.

Delaney didn't respond, continuing to stare straight at the window, rolling back and then, with more force, forward again.

"*Hey*, everything alright?"

He received no response. Instead, she continued the motion of the wheelchair with the rhythm of a metronome.

"Delaney," he said softly.

Nothing.

He stepped toward her and spoke her name again, louder this time.

She frowned, but didn't stop and didn't look up.

Jack squatted to her level, trying to keep his calm. He took a breath. "D, I'm here."

She immediately jolted, like waking from a dream, and turned toward him. Her eyes were filled with tears, but she gave a small nod.

# 15
# day eleven

"Well, hello, hello," Dr. Schuler said cheerfully, pausing in the doorway of the group room to receive full acknowledgement. He smiled narrowly, walking casually to his seat.

"Good morning, Dr. Schuler. You look happy this morning," Teresa commented from behind her laptop, sweeping the ash blonde hair out of her eyes.

"You should have seen me our last couple conferences."

There were some nods around the table.

"No really, you should have seen me. We've *needed* you. I've already spoken with your boss about never letting you have another day off."

She shrugged, dismissively.

"I hear your dad is doing better?"

"Yeah he's doing fine. Hopefully he'll follow the cardiac diet restrictions. My sister is with him the next couple of weeks and then he'll be going to outpatient."

"Well we're all very happy to have you back. As are our patients. *One* in particular."

"Laney," she said, affectionately. "She's improving so much from what I hear."

"No disrespect, but it's not due to your backup. We've had some PTs, OTs, even an Anesthesiologist crossing over to make up for the mediocre Speech she's been getting."

"Alice is great for schools."

"Not good for ischemic stroke with severe apraxia of speech."

"Understood. I agree."

"But as you mentioned, she is making gains. As our commander-in-chief would say--'bigly.'"

There were some collective laughs from the group.

"And Laney *knows* he's the President now," he added.

"That must have been a *shocker*," Teresa said, disdainfully. She frequently made political references and it wasn't a secret how she voted.

"Evidently one of her last memories was watching that golden escalator descent in Trump Tower."

Teresa scoffed.

"She also remembers when she told me, quite confidently, that he would be the next President." He perked his eyebrows. "I gave her such a hard time for that--Which is why I now have his portrait on my wall--*again*. It only seemed right since she doesn't remember getting to gloat the first time around, plus it brought a smile to her face," Dr. Schuler said fondly, nudging Teresa's arm. "Great to see. Nobody smiles like Laney, *believe* me."

Grant choked a little on his coffee.

"I know there were some concerns at the start of having Dr. Mathison involved as a highly skilled *significant other* and stand-in OT. Hopefully, those concerns have been eased a bit? I purposely asked him not to attend conference so we could freely talk behind his back." He waited for some acknowledgement of his wit, then waved off his comment. "He's actually on call with Labor & Delivery this morning, but still. Let's hear it."

"He's amazing with her," Julie said. "No concerns here. At all."

Jenna nodded. "I agree."

Dr. Schuler tilted his head toward Grant. "OT?"

"She responds really well to him. He knows safety precautions. No concerns." He swallowed hard. "I was asked to meet with Sheryl Sellers tomorrow morning. *One* of the agenda items is Jack providing OT skilled services."

There was some uneasiness at the mention of the Administrator.

"Well, she values your opinion."

"Well, my opinion is that Jack is still a licensed OT and is more than qualified."

"Wait, I don't get it. What is she questioning—?" Jenna asked.

"I'm under a little scrutiny right now," Dr. Schuler explained.

"For Laney?"

He raised his eyebrows at the paperwork before him. "Sometimes in your life, your career, you have to make some waves in the spirit of doing what is right." He paused. "In the spirit of helping a person who deserves to be helped."

"They're giving you a hassle over *Laney*?"

His eyes crinkled slightly. "They're scrutinizing a few of my recent decisions—"

"For Jack to help her with self-cares," Grant clarified for the room.

"He's an OT," Jenna said, in disbelief.

"Before we had him just updating our communication card for any pertinent updates, but not doing notes or anything. Well, they put a stop to that. They want us to view him as any other 'caregiver'. They were questioning if we had enough other things to work on if he's capable of safely doing ADLs with her."

"Uh-*yeah*," Teresa gasped. "Of course we do."

"Exactly. Just be sure to document that."

"She asked for him, right?" Jenna asked. "To do shower ADLs, specifically?"

Grant reached for his coffee cup, lowering his eyes.

"She did. I haven't been able to honor that request. I'm assuming she's still getting showers--am I mistaken?"

"She's getting showers," Jenna confirmed.

"Good, because that chlorine is very drying to the skin," he said, trying to lighten his tone.

"Dr. Schuler, she needs him to do shower ADLs. She's *getting* showers, I did her shower last night, but--"

"But what?"

"She's a total assist."

"How can that be? She's what? A mod assist for upper body dressing now?"

"She's not participating for showers."

"That doesn't sound like Laney," Julie interjected.

"No, it doesn't," Jenna said. "It's not her. I don't want to overstep here, but she's pretty comfortable with me, right?" She paused. "Dr. Schuler, may I sidebar with you?"

The Physiatrist said nothing, but slid his chair back from the table, motioning toward the hallway. "Don't be too noisy," he chimed, attempting to lighten the suddenly tense conference room.

Jenna followed, her face serious. Dr. Schuler stepped across into Room 90, whose occupant had vacated the space for the time being.

"What's on your mind, Jenna?"

It had been an unspoken understanding that Jack Mathison was occupying 90 while Maintenance tried to resolve the persistent bathroom plumbing issue, which had made the room uninhabitable for patients. No one had gone into the room. Now that she was inside, Jenna couldn't help but peer around. She took in the sight of his neatly stacked belongings, extra pair of tennis shoes, his tightly made bed, a tiny gold elephant statue, the lone item on the bedside table.

"Messy guy. I don't know how Laney stands it," he said, flatly.

"Yeah. What a slob."

"Jenna? I want to hear what you have to say."

She took a breath. "My uncle suffers from PTSD. Some triggers will just freeze him up. He'll go into a trance-like state. I saw something like that with Laney last night."

"In the shower."

"Yes. I'm not saying Laney *has* PTSD, per say. What I've observed is--the shower turns on and she shuts down. Her hands shake. She doesn't respond to me. I have to repeat myself more than once for her to even hear me and then she just--it's like she's not there."

He moved toward the bed, rubbing at his eyes with his thick fingers. When he dropped his hand, his eyes found the same gold elephant statue Jenna had spotted. He swallowed hard, turning back to Jenna. "Thank you for sharing this with me."

She stood quietly then awkwardly angled toward the door. "Well we should get back in there."

He nodded and followed her back across the hallway. The room of Rehab staff turned at once, abandoning their side conversations.

"Let's have everybody come back now," Dr. Schuler announced as he took his seat. He pulled out his phone, squinted at the screen, then pressed it to his ear. "Jack, it's Martin. She's fine. She's swimming, I think, right?"

Julie nodded.

"Jack, you're on for Laney's showers." He nodded reassuringly toward Grant. "I'll deal with Administration. Just know if you screw it up, I'll probably be fired."

There was a short response on the other end.

"Like, *without pension*, Jack." He winked to the room, but there was a level of truth in his tone. "Yeah, she should be done at the top of the hour. Great. Don't worry about it. Thanks, Buddy." He hung up and placed his phone conclusively on the table. "I'm pretty sure I'll have a job next week."

There was a collective laughter from everyone except Grant, who seemed more concerned than Dr. Schuler about his career outlook.

"What's the minutes breakdown right now? Minimums. I know some of you--" he glanced over to Julie, "are putting in extra time."

"Minimum 90," Julie replied. 90 was already over the standard 60 per discipline.

"Realistically?"

"As much as she can tolerate. She's motivated. Terrence works with her almost daily, too, so maybe 90-120 minimum total for PT."

"Yesterday's minutes?"

"180. She asked to go for an evening swim and it was Terrence's late day."

Dr. Schuler gave a half-smile. "I love that she's asking for things."

"Right?" Jenna said. "I love it. Though she keeps changing the voice on the tablet. A couple days ago she used this demanding German voice. Scared the *shi*—daylights out of me."

"Speech? OT?"

"Alice was doing 60. I can do more," Teresa offered.

"I don't know what your caseload is, but if you can manage it. At least give her some homework, if you could?"

"Absolutely."

"Alright, so how's she doing?"

Teresa sat up in her chair. "Lots of things to do with her. Ja--Dr. Mathison was awesome to get us hooked up with the tablet and some pretty spendy apps. I guess it was enough to get leadership wanting to get a few more of them to circulate with our patients, which is great." She flipped through her papers. "I have never seen this level of apraxia of speech while still having such high level cognitive function. Her brain still can't quite make the connection sometimes with her body, which makes sense given the location of the bleed. Lots of that intermittently. She has some encoding issues, which has impacted her short-term memory. She reports that keeping notes on the tablet is helping. That's probably how she was able to remember her *voting history*." She pursed her lips. "She reviews those most days, but is becoming less dependent on them." She paused to sigh. "Longer term memory issues, as you know. Last in, first out, which is unfortunate. Especially for Jack--er--Dr. Mathison, since her last solid memory was from about four years ago and they didn't start seeing each other until more recently--three years ago I think? But he's incredibly supportive. *Incredibly* supportive."

"She lights up when she sees him," Jenna remarked.

"She does do that, doesn't she?" Dr. Schuler asked rhetorically.

"She was having a really off morning yesterday." Grant cleared his throat. "I saw her sitting out there after I came in. She--wasn't herself. Very, very down. Tearful. Hadn't slept."

Teresa frowned, clasping her chest. "Poor girl. She's dealing with so much."

"Luckily Jack was in ninety--his—"

"Temporary accommodations?" Dr. Schuler finished.

Grant nodded. "She did better once he went out there."

Julie beamed. "He was *singing* to her."

"Oh that's sweet," Teresa said, clutching her chest. "Is he a good singer?"

"He sang and did theater through college."

Teresa's jaw dropped. "What plays?"

"A lot of the big ones--he was in *Phantom, Newsies, Les Mis.*"

"Seems a waste to have him as the Phantom. With the mask?"

The room turned to Teresa.

"I'm just saying. He's an attractive man—" She put a hand over her mouth. "Oh God, that sounded--"

"Alright, I think we're off topic," Dr. Schuler said half-heartedly.

"We need a staff talent show, for charity, or new equipment or something."

Julie smiled. "He was Raoul in *Phantom.*"

"*Ohhh,*" Teresa said, reflexively. "They've really done an injustice to Raoul in some versions--he was definitely a better choice--"

Dr. Schuler smiled. "Dr. Mathison is a dreamboat, we get it."

"You have your good qualities, too, Dr. S," Teresa said, encouragingly. "Does *Laney* sing, too?"

"Well she isn't going to win American Idol, but she rocked it at karaoke."

"What'd she sing?"

"*These Boots Are Made For Walking.* We picked it for her."

"Oh she could pull that off."

"And she did," Julie remarked.

Grant scoffed, his eyebrows raised.

"Maybe we'll try sound generation with lyrics. I'll have to ask her about what music she likes," Teresa said, making a note.

"Any other observations?"

"For memory--she seems to be making some connections there. Hopefully we can build on that and maybe recover other things. Emotions, feelings, all seem to be there. They just don't all seem to have the memories attached, like those connections were broken and the memories are just drifting out on their own."

"It's interesting," Dr. Schuler remarked. "The feeling remains but the memory that created it is gone...or at least missing."

"Well I have a theory," the speech therapist said, sitting taller. "It's not based on clinical theory or anything."

"Let's hear it."

"You know how muscle memory is better than cognitive memory sometimes? Your fingers remember a phone number automatically, but you really have to think through the number to tell someone?"

Dr. Schumer nodded. "Sure."

"Well, the heart is considered a *muscular* organ." She paused as her theory resonated with the group.

"Her brain doesn't remember, but her heart does," Jenna interpreted.

Julie's mouth fell open. "I'm going to cry."

"Maybe you can write greeting cards for these unique circumstances," Dr. Schuler suggested.

Teresa glanced through her notes, waving off his remark. "You're a softy deep down, Dr. S. You're not fooling anybody."

Dr. Schuler scanned the room. "Am I not fooling anybody?"

Several staff shook their heads.

Teresa smiled. "Okay, let's see--she's very distractible. Very difficult time multi-tasking, which is very far from her baseline. If there's a loud noise or a flickering light or too much activity, she won't hear most of what you say."

"She's improving, but the distractibility is still there," Julie added. "I was going to try using the goggles with her when we're walking. Do you think she'd do OK with that?"

Teresa thought about that. "The virtual reality ones?"

"We just have the ones that block out everything. Neuro has the VR ones, which are amazing. I wish we could get them."

Dr. Schuler frowned at his paperwork.

"That'd be great for her. Also doing sessions in quieter areas so she can focus, turning down the lights, making sure she's comfortable, should all help her to focus. I'm planning to slowly build outside stimulation in our sessions so she can hopefully improve. Otherwise, yeah, very hard worker. Smart. She knows what's going on, she has great insight--only a couple days into working with her so I can't comment too much on her carryover," Teresa added.

"Carry-over is improving with me in the past week. She's in there," Julie said with an optimistic smile. "Some reminders and cueing, but then she's got it."

"Again, so good to have you back, Teresa," Dr. Schuler said. "OT?"

Grant sat a little more comfortably in his chair. "As my most recent note will reflect: Caregiver education provided for self-care ADLs. Much left to work on from a fine motor, occupational, and visual training perspective with excellent prognosis to meet goals." He made eye contact with Dr. Schuler and they seemed to share a congenial agreement.

"Model patient," Dr. Schuler said, smiling lightly. The pun went unacknowledged.

Grant nodded. "We're working on getting some more flexibility in her hands. We have her in the contracture gloves to help with spasticity. We also ran some visual testing with her. Her vision seems pretty good, though she's having more trouble on the right--it didn't seem to be there last week. It seems to be impacting her balance on that side."

"I was thinking that, too," Julie said. "Before I wasn't sure, but I notice some difficulty when she's walking."

Dr. Schuler jotted something down. "That's new?"

"I've seen her squint that eye in the last couple of days when I'm working with her," Jenna added. "No dizziness, but I was wondering if she was having vision problems."

Dr. Schuler was thoughtful for a moment, nodded to himself, then glanced around the room. "Anyone else?"

"We've been doing relaxation and meditation with her," the curly haired Recreational Therapist, Sarah mentioned. "Her request. I got an email from her."

"She's emailing?" Dr. Schuler sat back a little in his chair, frowning. "She hasn't written me."

"Yeah, that was a surprise. She also asked about hypnosis. It seems like her brain almost tenses so she thinks hypnosis might break through that. We did a bit of that yesterday."

"I like it for relaxation--let's not use it for memory retrieval though. A lot of controversy there."

"That was the plan."

"Is she participating in other activities with you?"

"She stopped attending most activities. It's tough because she can't interact verbally at this point. I think it makes her feel more isolated."

"It does," Julie said. "She hated breakfast group. The distractibility plus not being able to hold utensils very well--and our other patients could have been more tactful."

"I'd hate to just have her cooped up in her room," the senior resident, a man that fashioned corduroy pants, elbow patch jacket, and an ironic bushy beard chimed in. He would have pulled off appearing sincerely concerned if it hadn't been for a widely circulated account of the day about six months earlier Delaney confronted him about being condescending with her patient's mother. He had told her matter-of-factly that he would have her fired for talking to a doctor that way.

She was not only *not* fired, Dr. Schuler had made a point of putting him through what could only be described as hazing rituals.

"She's hardly in her room," Jenna corrected, raising an eyebrow.

"Lots to work on," Dr. Schuler concluded, looking over his notes. "Length of stay? Originally I was thinking 3-4 weeks at least, but she is making progress. I'll keep her as long as she needs, but I don't want to keep her too long if she'd do better at home, especially for memory issues."

"I'd like to get her to the EVA, then hopefully to a walker. She won't be happy with that goal, but it's too early to be thinking a cane or walking sticks."

"I agree. She won't like a walker. You really think walking sticks are a possibility?"

"She has the strength. She's athletic. Even if she doesn't reach that level here, she'll definitely get to that point eventually. At a minimum."

"What's your goal date for a walker?"

"Two to two and a half weeks?"

"2 and a half weeks from today you'll have her walking, supervision to modified independent?"

Julie hesitated, then put her shoulders back. "Yes. It'll happen. We're going to get there."

"Speech?"

"I'm OK with that date. She'll be able to continue working on this stuff outpatient and at home, but I'd like to really zero in on getting her talking."

Dr. Schuler nodded.

Sarah sat up straighter. "We have tai chi scheduled for her tomorrow and again Monday."

"I might join you all," Dr. Schuler said as he jotted down a few notes. "She's had trouble sleeping. How'd she do last night?" He looked up at Jenna.

"The night nurse said better than the night before."

Dr. Schuler nodded regretfully. "I spoke with Jack about it. The tablet is great, but she's having access to information she hadn't quite remembered yet."

"There's too much information out there with social media," Teresa said.

"This one was significant. Her dad passed away about a year ago."

Jenna's jaw dropped a little. "And now it's almost like she's experiencing the loss again."

"It's expected she feel grief, but if you all notice anything more serious, let me know?" His eyes scanned over the table occupants, pausing at Jenna. To her, he gave an almost imperceptible nod of approval.

Julie rubbed at her face in exhaustion. "I didn't even think of that--"

"How's her physical pain?"

"Some pain issues, but she absolutely doesn't want to take the Gabapentin," Jenna reported.

"I can lower it. We had bumped her up--maybe we overdid it--"

"She took care of that."

"Pardon?"

"She gave me a little cup of them this morning to throw away. By the look of it, she hasn't taken them most of the week."

Dr. Schuler stared at her.

"The Gabapentin made her feel drunk, she said. She didn't do it out of disrespect for you."

"She knew I'd make her take it," he said, shaking his head. "What seems to cause her the most pain?"

"The shoulders and the hip. It really bothers her when she sits for too long."

"Old injury in her hip," he murmured. "She had pins placed. Plus the neurological pain from the stroke."

"She said if we could obtain some pool floaties, she'll just chill out in there all day."

"Did she really?"

"She did. In a British male accent no less."

"Nigel," Julie said. "She startled me the first time she switched to that voice."

"What about the muscle relaxer? I have it PRN--is she taking it at all?"

"She asks for it most nights. It seems to help her sleep."

"Maybe an extended release would help her sleep longer." Dr. Schuler scratched at his eyebrow. "Guess I'll discontinue the order for Gabapentin," he made a note, then he dropped his pen. "My God. She's really in there."

"Yes, she is," Julie and Jenna said together.

"Willful, stubborn ass girl." He laughed silently, shaking his head.

"What about a cooking task? Outing?" Sarah suggested.

"She thankfully doesn't seem to have the fatigue of some of our patients who have been in a hospital for a long time. I've thought about a pass for her to try out going home, identify any barriers there, but we're not quite there yet. She seems to get enough social interaction, despite her apraxia, between all of us."

"She's been talking with 85 a lot, too. Well, she texts. He talks."

"Mr. Personality?" Dr. Schuler asked, fondly.

Jenna sighed. "Yeah they do get along well."

"He gave y'all a hard time when he first came over?"

Julie rolled her eyes. "He just seems really unhappy with his situation."

"I don't blame him," Dr. Schuler replied.

"He's been much nicer to everyone since they sparked a friendship. They play games on the tablet. Chess, I think," Jenna said.

"We have rehab patients playing *chess*." Dr. Schuler chuckled, shaking his head as he signed off on the conference form. "Brings back memories."

"Of playing chess?" Teresa asked, confused.

He smiled in his way that said he wasn't going to elaborate further. "Perfect segue. How is Mr. Harwell doing?"

***

The care team had just finished rounding with Quinn and had moved onto the liver transplant patient. When he rolled his wheelchair out toward the hall, he could see them all gathered outside the room across the corridor, donning yellow contact precautions safety suits. He hadn't seen much of the patient simply because of the fear of infection.

One of the nurses peered over her computer monitor at him as he wheeled himself toward the therapy courtyard. He felt his heart ease a bit seeing Laney sitting in the shade by the water feature. She glanced up upon hearing the automatic door open, squinting into the sun.

"Hey Laney, what'cha doing?"

She showed him the tablet screen.

"Ah, sudoku." He observed. "*Expert* level. No cognitive deficits here, folks."

She smirked, turning back to the screen. Her hair was sopping wet, a pool of water collected on the ground behind the chair.

"Did they round with you today, too?" he asked, looking uneasy.

There was a small shake of her head and she turned the tablet toward him. *"They skip the formalities with me."*

"They're planning to gear my discharge goals to be from a wheelchair base." Her forehead creased.

"I guess they've given up on me walking out of here after all."

*"Who told you that? Was it Julie?"*

"No, it was the social worker. She's working on getting authorization on a custom chair."

*"Then Julie isn't on-board with the wheelchair."*

"She did seem uncharacteristically quiet."

*"Trust her. Work hard."*

"You trained her?"

*"For stroke I did, but spinal cord injuries are her wheelhouse, not mine."*

He nodded, his body relaxing considerably with this new information. "Do you think Dr. Schuler remembers me from when you were in the hospital before? He said something about you being a 'mood stabilizer' for me."

She laughed, surprising both of them.

"Laney, that was a legitimate laugh. A little raspy, but still."

She seemed to be trying to test out mouthing basic words, but no sound came out.

He stared at the stream of water trickling down the wall. "What is it about water noise that's so peaceful?" He noticed she and Jack had sat out in the courtyard the night before. Jack had pulled a chair over by the bench so she could prop up her legs and was reading something to her. Laney was bundled up in a hoodie, cheek resting on his shoulder, studying the book jacket as he read. There had been nothing particularly sexual about the scene, but it had felt outwardly intimate and he found himself retreating.

She joined him in staring at the glass water wall and the long wispy plants below.

He exhaled deeply. "I never really take time out to just sit like this. It's nice."

She fiddled on the tablet screen then when she seemed to find what she was looking for, handed him the device.

On the screen was a photo of a waterfall set against dark angled stones and lush green trees. In the foreground was the silhouette of a girl staring at the falls, standing beneath an orange pagoda with dark, sloped rooftops.

When he glanced up at her, she nodded toward the water wall and closed her eyes.

"This is what you're picturing huh?" he said with a smile. "Is this Japan?"

She blinked intentionally.

"Do you have more photos of your world travels?"

She smiled, her eyes falling on the tablet.

He backed out of the photo and found himself looking at what seemed to be an endless tiling of vibrant, exotic places. He zoomed in on the first and started swiping rhythmically through. Her photographs transported him to Greece, to Japan, to the Great Wall, to riding on an elephant by the ocean, to grand landscapes and poor marketplaces, to monkey hot springs and wild deer parks, to ancient ruins and modern wonders. She was in some of them--it appeared at the destinations where her dad joined her. He stopped on one featuring the pair of them in the most unassuming of places. It looked like a cool day, both of them in light parkas. Her dad's arm was around her, squeezing her tightly, by the look of it. Her face was natural, void of even a hint of makeup. Behind them was a stone bridge set over a calm river, the space beyond filled with emerald green tones of grass and trees set beneath a contrasting gray sky. Her head leaned into her dad's cheek, her lips curled into a relaxed smile.

It was as he thought to ask about her dad that Quinn glanced up to see her breathing in a focused manner, eyes closed, hands relaxed and open in her lap.

# 16
# four years

It was one of those summer days when you could feel the heat rising up from the pavement, even at 7:04am. The jury shuttle bus had broken down and she was already late for her check-in so Delaney was huffing the twelve blocks from the court-approved parking garage. She was just starting to regret her choice of outfit, specifically heels, having seized the opportunity to wear something a bit dressier than scrubs when a sports car failed to yield at the crosswalk and nearly hit her.

She didn't need to have words with the driver--the water vendor on the corner was already taking that responsibility upon himself. He waved her along so Delaney continued down the sidewalk, her wide leg dressy gaucho pants swishing with each long stride. She thought she heard her name, but kept going.

Two blocks later, the sports car roared up along the sidewalk. Even in her peripheral vision, it reeked of overt boastfulness and entitlement and she had no interest in a conversation with whoever was driving it. The driver lowered the passenger window and called out "I'm sorry about that."

"Don't worry about it," she said dismissively.

"I almost turned my junior high school crush into a pancake. Of course I'm going to worry about it."

She turned her chin toward him.

He was crouched slightly to see her through the passenger side window and had taken off his sunglasses, but the window tinting darkened the entire interior and made it challenging to make out his face.

"Quinn?"

"Let me give you a ride."

"It's right there. I'm fine walking."

"Still."

She had assessed that continuing her walking course would certainly be more efficient, but a couple cars were starting to line up behind Quinn and they didn't look particularly patient. She hurried toward the passenger door. "You understand what this looks like, right?"

He smiled, shifting into drive. "Where to?"

"Right there," she replied, pointing to the next large building. "I think you can turn in here."

He pulled into one of the blue lined spaces of the handicapped and passenger pickup/drop off lot, sighed, turning toward her expectantly as though it was the awkward goodnight after a first date.

She reached for the door handle. "Well, thanks for the cardiac challenge."

"Hold on, that's it? It's been forever."

"Well I can't give you above a 4 star Uber rating, docking a star for obvious reasons."

"Jury cases won't start for a bit. You should be fine. You know there are about two thousand ways to get out of jury duty, right?"

"I was out of extensions. Plus it's our civic duty and all that. I just don't want them to make me repeat this."

"Understood. If you're still down this way midday, why don't I take you to lunch?"

She nodded. "That'd be nice, Quinn." She pulled out her phone and tapped out a message. "My last phone was evidently never linked to the cloud before I dropped it in the pool--what's your number?"

He watched as she created a contact, then he recited his number.

"I'll text you when I know. You have my number now, too, so we don't go years in between lunches."

His phone lit up in the console and he rushed to stop the car from reading out her text. The least of his concerns would be for her to find out he already had her in his contacts.

He chose the new Brazilian steakhouse on Central. She had told him she would walk, saying she needed to stretch her legs after sitting and working on the laptop for several hours. He timed his arrival to be just before she was due to arrive so he'd have a chance to be seated and then get to enjoy the view as she made her entrance. He visualized how he would smile at her as she approached in the way that made the most confident of women blush, stand and kiss her cheek.

The restaurant was packed for being before noon, as they were apparently hosting a corporate event. He stepped around some very boisterous groups of people wearing convention IDs and finally reached the host stand. "Reservation for two for Harwell. A young woman should be arriving in a few minutes."

"Ah yes, Harwell. Actually, the young woman has already arrived. Right this way."

She had her hair pulled up in an effortlessly elegant, yet relaxed bun, a few loose strands of dark hair falling lightly on her neck, and she had her usual impeccable posture. The waiter was paying especially close attention to her, leaning towards her as he spoke in a definitively flirtatious manner, but immediately straightened up when he saw Quinn approach, correctly assessing he was the source of his potential tip.

Delaney picked up on the social cues and in one fluid motion, rose to her feet and moved to greet him. She acted first and gave him a cordial hug. She laughed kindly at the 'formality' when he guided her back to the table and her cloth napkin was placed back in her lap by the attentive waiter. She glanced around the restaurant, at the chandeliers, the contemporary bar and lounge area. She contorted her face a bit. "I don't visit restaurants like this very often. You must be doing well."

"I've doing doing alright." He went to adjust his nine-piece vested suit as a means to draw attention to it and messed up the folded perfection of the handkerchief in his chest pocket.

"It looks nice without it," she offered. "You don't need a color pop."

He shoved the fabric into his lapel. "You look gorgeous, as always."

Her eye flickered, as though hearing an off-key note. "Oh I bet you say that to every girl you pick up on a street corner," she whispered, but the waiter was, of course, close at hand. She smiled tightly as the waiter's jaw dropped. "May I have an iced tea, please?" she offered.

"Same," Quinn added.

The waiter walked quickly away.

"Well at least we know he has standards. No streetwalkers." She rolled her shoulders. "I appreciate you taking me to such a nice lunch--the hot dog food truck would have been perfectly fine though."

Quinn took in the setting--the mahogany tables, the wine service before noon, the plethora of business suits and expensive haircuts, ironic beards--and contrasted it to the woman sitting across from him. She could easily fit in here with her easy elegance, but she was unimpressed by all of it. He thought of how uncomfortable he was in his suit, still an imposter.

"It's pretentious, isn't it?"

"It's just fancy. I'm sure it'll be delicious."

"Let's go to the food truck."

"I was being metaphorical."

"Oh there's a place just down the way." He stood, pulled out a twenty-dollar bill.

Delaney smiled, gathered up her laptop bag.

Quinn was pleased to have the opportunity to place his hand on her back to guide her toward the front door.

"Hey Harwell," an enthusiastic man greeted as they reached the door. When he noticed Delaney, he sized her up approvingly, raising a thick eyebrow. "Hey, who's she?"

"She's an old friend of Quinn's," she responded, holding out her hand. "Delaney. Who are you?"

"Chuck. I work with Quinn." His face flushed.

"Nice to meet you, Chuck."

"You all finish lunch already?"

Quinn quite enjoyed how flustered Chuck appeared to be. "No, we've decided to dine elsewhere today."

"Yeah this place gets tough on the budget. It's so good though. The price tag isn't for everybody." He smacked him on the back.

Before he knew what was happening, Delaney's hand was resting on Quinn's chest in, dare he say, a suggestive way. She tucked herself into him. "You ready, Quinn?" Her eyes were particularly wide, a mischievous little grin on her face.

Chuck had noticed, his mouth falling slightly open.

"Enjoy your lunch," Delaney said, as she let Quinn lead her out the door. They turned right with no destination in mind, walking as one unit, the valet thoroughly confused by the abbreviated dining excursion. Once they were out of view of the restaurant front, Delaney broke free, smiling in her effortless way. "Kind of a jerk, that one."

Quinn didn't want to tell her that Chuck was one of his more down-to-earth, less misogynistic colleagues. He was also feeling the absence of her body pressed to his. He wondered what she would do if he reached for her hand, tried to kiss her. Men did that, right? Bold moves? Hell, he did that most Friday and Saturday nights.

Delaney had whirled around on her heel, her laptop bag swinging with her.

It was clear he had missed what she said.

"I feel bad you paying $20 for air. We should have gotten to-go cups or something."

"Nah, the look on Chuck's face was worth it and I doubt they do to-go drinks."

She winced. "I don't know where they keep the food trucks, but I saw a Meditteranean place on my drive in. Then again, I'd also go for something smothered in cheese. What sounds good?"

"Mediterranean is good with me."

She nodded approvingly. "It was just up here on the right, I think." Her body language was infinitely more relaxed than it had been sitting in the restaurant. He had almost forgotten about the carefree way that she walked. Her trajectory was rarely a straight line as her eyes took in the sight of old buildings with their interesting architectural choices, the sky, as though wandering through a park. "At least there's a little breeze." She slowed to walk beside him, locking her hand on the bag strap--to keep him from reaching for her hand, he realized.

"So where are you living these days?" he asked.

"About ten minutes east on the river."

"Ah. I'm close. I'm in a loft in Old Town."

She peered over her shoulder as she stepped into the crosswalk. "There it is. So do you like this kind of food or are you just along for the ride?"

"It's hummus and pita, that kind of thing?"

"Basically, yes."

The restaurant had a wall-sized painted mural of the Parthenon and one side of the room was surrounded by silk plants and Christmas light wrapped trellises to simulate being outside. They were quickly ushered to a free table in the faux patio area. No one placed a fabric napkin on either of their laps. Actually, the hostess immediately started yelling to the kitchen as soon as they were seated. A bus boy, no older than 14, carried over two ice waters in red Coca-Cola tumblers and carefully placed one before each of them, then left.

"This is totally not your kind of place," she observed, grinning over her laminated menu.

"It's--quirky."

"That's what I like about it. Although I spent two months eating at establishments that had me order at a kiosk so maybe I'm not a great food critic."

"By kiosk? Like a vending machine?"

"No. Well, kind of. In Japan, kiosk order is huge and their ramen is cheap--keeps the food budget in check. You put through your order on a machine, but you go in and eat in the restaurant when it's ready."

"2 months in Japan?"

"Yeah. My dad's business associate has an AirBnB he usually rents out. I spent some time inTokyo, but I spent most of the time in Kyoto."

"Wow. How was that?"

"Tokyo is just crazy. Interesting, great people watching, but just busy. I loved the quieter parts of Kyoto the best. I'd usually go exploring really early in the morning and then late afternoon to avoid the crowds."

"Did you do the whole geisha thing?"

"I kind of thought it was an obligatory tourist thing. I also posed as a samurai." She struck a pose as though using a samurai sword to slice through the air, her face serious.

He smiled. "So did you like it?"

She took a long swig of water, nodding. "Kyoto is my favorite city in the world."

"I'd be worried about the language barrier."

"Hotondo no hyōshiki wa eigodesuga, soredemo tokidoki kurō shimashita."

"You learned Japanese?"

"Yosōijō ni kantandeshita."

He watched her check her phone briefly. "You're an impressive person, Delaney Adara."

She scrunched up her nose. "No, I'm a fortunate person. Not many people get to travel like I was able to."

"Have you gone back?"

"Twice so far. I've been lucky."

The hostess returned to take their order.

"So what do you do exactly, Quinn?"

He shrugged. "Investments. High yield holdings. Wealth advisement."

"High stakes."

"It *can* be--*if* you don't know what you're doing." He said this confidently, but hearing himself in this setting, it didn't seem to strike the right chord. The statement was usually something of an aphrodisiac at clubs. Here he just sounded arrogant.

"Well it's a good thing you know what you're doing." There was a flicker of something in her eyes, but he didn't see judgment.

"And what about you?"

"I'm a PT. I did my neuro residency two years ago, but now I'm working with our pediatric patients—I just started a pediatric residency to earn the credentials."

"Is it kind of like med school?"

"I rotate through the different care settings--inpatient, Rehab, skilled nursing, outpatient, there's an educational curriculum, I give presentations--"

"Isn't it pretty similar to what you would have learned in PT school?"

She shook her head. "Not quite. Treating a pediatric patient is a lot different than treating a grown up or geriatric."

"I wouldn't think many kids would need therapy."

Delaney's eyes widened a bit, almost imperceptibly. She inhaled quickly, a tell that she was choosing not to say something.

"That must be really fun working with them though."

"It definitely can be," she agreed, again not sharing what she was thinking.

"Are you seeing anyone?"

Delaney frowned, her eyebrow raised. "I don't really date. My friend, Julie— she's one of our therapists—she keeps trying to set me up though."

"Setups are the worst."

She shrugged. "She means well."

"Yeah, I'm not dating anyone either."

There was a silence, an awkward, long, painful silence.

"Well, not seriously."

She gave a slight wince, but quickly neutralized her expression. "I bet you do alright for yourself, Quinn."

The food arrived, a red plastic basket placed before each of them. Delaney sat up eagerly.

"This looks good," she remarked, inhaling the steam rising up from the basket. She picked out a homemade French fry and chomped into it. "I am going to be sluggish in the pool today after this, but it's so worth it."

"Still swimming?"

"Yeah. Almost everyday."

"No wonder."

"What?"

His eyes scanned over her. "You look *really* good, Laney."

"Thanks, Quinn." She still didn't look comfortable receiving the compliment.

"Going back to the dating thing—I think I don't end up dating seriously because I have a tendency to compare every woman I meet to the one who got away."

She looked up in time to see him jolt his eyebrow upward. "Is that right?"

"Would you let me take you on a proper date?"

She hesitated. "Quinn—" He could see her formulating the right words to say to let him down easy. "I don't think it would be a good idea for me to—"

"You don't have to do that. I get it. It's fine," he said sharply.

"I just—"

"No, no." He attempted to relax his posture, his facial expression. "It's okay, Delaney Adara," he said, smiling with forced kindness. "No explanation required."

There were more words sitting on the edge of her tongue. She frowned, seeming to swallow them down.

"How is it?" He asked.

She carefully took her first bite of gyro and nodded.

He suddenly became fixated on something on his cell phone screen. "I'm sorry to do this, but they need me back at the office." He waved to the hostess. "Excuse me, miss? May I have this wrapped up to go?" He stood.

Delaney had a dumbfounded expression on her face. "Investment emergency?"

"Yeah, client is jumpy about the market."

"Uncertainty with the election next year has a lot of people spooked," she said casually.

"Yeah," he said, a little dumbfounded that she had such insight.

"I'd stay away from the stocks until next fall, then buy bigly," she suggested. "Domestic, not foregin."

The hostess came by and angrily started assembling the to-go box.

"'*Bigly*?' Is that your election prediction?"

"We'll see how it turns out, but yes." She smiled tightly. "It was nice to see you, Quinn."

He gazed at this young woman, still his ideal woman, and felt two things: 1) insecurity, and 2) regret for having asked for the to-go box because he was certain he wouldn't touch the food and because waiting for the waitress to pack it up seemed petty.

It was clear Delaney didn't want anything romantic with him, but despite this, he longed to spend time with her. They could be friends, surely, but he'd never be satisfied with that arrangement. Instead of doing what he so desperately wanted to do: sit down and ask her about her world travels and her life, what made her choose such an unlikely Presidential candidate, he pulled out two twenty dollar bills, dropped them in the center of the table and said goodbye.

# 17

# water

The late morning sun was passing over the courtyard. Quinn had just returned to his room to call his parents, give them updates and Delaney had strategically positioned herself under one of the tree canopies, captivated by the intricate patterns on her skin from the sunlight breaking through the leaves. Her hair was still tied on top of her head, dripping chlorine water down her neck. Having been a swimmer since high school, she loved the challenge of the endless pool. She found it easier to move in the water and when she was permitted to float on her own, her pain melted away. Back in the wheelchair, her joints had started to ache almost immediately.

As she closed her eyes, she could imagine she was on vacation, simply taking a break from swimming to enjoy the surroundings. She could kick back on a cushioned chaise lounge in the shade and savor a day of relaxation, order a drink served with a mini umbrella and pineapple garnish, to savor as she read a book. Something light and funny, but not trashy.

She could see a cove of white sand, turquoise water, gorgeous reefs poking above the water when the waves flowed away. Crystal clear water. She couldn't decipher if it was a memory or something her mind had dreamed up. As she focused on the water, she knew she had gone wreck diving not that far off shore. She had ridden on a mo-ped through the winding roads of the island, wind whipping her hair. She had her arms wrapped around a strong torso. Her skin was tacky with aloe vera from treating her scorching sun burn.

Delaney breathed deeply, feeling nearly as weightless as she had felt in the pool. A gust of cold air swept around her and the images turned dark. She could hear the water wall again, the distant hospital construction. She opened her eyes and found Jack walking in her direction. Despite the distraction of his chiseled features, he still looked tired, like he hadn't had a good night's sleep in quite some time. Still, he appeared pleased to see her.

"How was the pool?"

The tablet sat on the side table, battery running low, but she didn't seem to even think to reach for it. She simply smiled in her lopsided way and willed herself to say hello. *Say it: Hello, Jack.*

"I don't want to interrupt; it looks like you're really relaxing out here." He frowned slightly at the displaced tablet as he sat down next to it to allow himself to be at her same level.

Meanwhile, Delaney had just noticed her nearly-flat palms. She wiggled her fingers, invigorated by their whimsical dance.

"We finally got the green light for shower ADLs. How about it? Want to get that chlorine out of your hair?"

She extended her arm upward toward him.

"A high five? I guess that's a 'yes'?"

She smiled, looking pointedly toward her outstretched hand, wiggled her fingers in the wave motion again.

"D," he said, grabbing her left palm gently. "You're doing it."

*Jack. Say it. Jaaack.* When he released her hand, she begrudgingly reached for the tablet, jabbed her fingers into the screen. *"Hi Jack."*

He narrowed his eyes questioningly.

She pointed toward her mouth then to the screen, sulking a bit.

"It'll come back. Look how far you've come just in the past week."

Julie emerged through the automatic doors on the other side of the courtyard. "Love the robe, Laney. You look like you're at a day spa," she said, taking in the sunny day.

"Hey Jules, check it out," Jack said, pointing to Delaney's hand on the armrest.

"Was there any doubt she'd be an all-star?"

Delaney nodded, raising her eyebrows. Only Jack noticed. Delaney adored Julie and hell, she was complimenting her, but the way she spoke across her was really starting to bother her. People spoke about her like they would a child, talking in code at times and with unearned praise at others.

"You *know*, Teresa is fond of *you*."

It took a moment for Jack to realize Julie was talking about him. "Me?"

"Yeah, Delaney fell a few notches because of her political views."

Delaney rolled her eyes.

"Our political views are pretty much the same."

"Don't tell her that."

"Why is she so fond of *me*?"

She grinned. "She was fascinated to learn of your Broadway days."

"College theater is not Broadway." Jack recognized something in Delaney's watchful, inquisitive eyes. He turned to Julie. "What'cha got there?"

"TENS for Mr. Harwell. Hoping it'll help his pain, but maybe we can wake up some of the nerves in his back. You know, I didn't think he liked me, but just now, he was a totally different person. They were going to put him with another PT and he insisted on working with me." She looked pointedly at Delaney. "He was *told* I was his best chance to get out of that wheelchair."

Delaney smiled lightly.

"Thanks, Laney. I was already losing sleep over this case--this doesn't add any pressure."

"*He's good people, Jules.*"

"He *has* been nicer. Your influence, I take it?"

Delaney shook her head, pointed back to her message, then started typing. "Who's Mr. Harwell?"

"Quinn. Young guy, car accident. Kind of a jerk, but Laney is evidently having a profound impact on him."

*"He likes classical music, sci-fi movies, comic books. Set him up with the therapy dogs. Big breeds. I remember there was a dog named Loki—he'd be perfect."*

Julie read the screen, frowned questioningly, and glanced up at Jack, who was having trouble with the glare on the tablet. Her eyes lifted. "Hey, speak of the devil."

Quinn appeared in the doorway in one of the sport model wheelchairs, dressed in cargo shorts and a polo shirt. He didn't look like he had any business in the chair. If it weren't for the leather flip flops, he looked more like he was getting ready to play nine holes. "'Devil' seems a little harsh."

Delaney turned her chair toward him, but she still wasn't able to propel herself with her right arm yet. Jack took over, started toward them.

"What's that?" Quinn asked, pointing to the TENS.

"Electro-stimulation therapy."

Quinn looked over at Delaney and Jack. "She's been wanting to electrocute me since I got here. Tell my dog I loved her."

Delaney grinned.

"Hey--" Quinn said, motioning to Delaney's hand then holding up a fist. She copied the gesture, her fist a bit looser. He tapped their knuckles together, then spread out his palm. She did the same and he made a small explosion sound as he retracted his hand back by his shoulder.

Then he took full notice of Jack. "Hi, I'm Quinn."

"Jack."

"Read a bit about you, Jack," Quinn said, motioning his brow to Delaney. "Good to meet you."

Jack released one handle and shook Quinn's hand. "You're in great hands with Julie."

"So I've been told." Quinn glanced expectantly over at Julie, who looked overtly tense. Her mind was likely racing AFO options, walker options, how she needed to get the DME rep in to evaluate Quinn.

"Well let's get to work then," she said, motioning toward the gym.

"Right behind you," he said, accelerating toward her. She waited for him to catch up then they continued side-by-side. "Now, a day or two ago you would have suggested electro-therapy and tried to lead me to the pool. This is progress. You know, I think this is the start of a beautiful friendship, Julie."

Delaney released a chuckle, which came out like a gurgle, then peered up at Jack, who she found had been watching her closely. He silently started pushing her back to her room.

She sat in the wheelchair watching Jack get her shower supplies situated on a low enough level for her to reach from the shower chair. She resented the presence of the shower chair, but she also knew with the way her right knee buckled randomly, it was probably a safer solution. She could always try a waterproof brace later on.

"OK, let's get that water heating up. I know you love your scalding showers."

The water gushed out of the shower faucet in loud splatters against the subway tile. Immediately she found her body had turned rigid, her hands balled into fists, her thoughts stiffened, and she found herself glaring at the shower drain. She took a breath, closed her eyes.

Sarah had unknowingly given her water noises as a relaxation tool and had even put a sound machine in the hospital room set to waterfall. Delaney had managed to switch it to waves instead after memories had prevented her from sleeping. Sarah had persisted with the waterfall noise during sessions and there wasn't much Delaney could do. She finally felt like she was making some progress, imagining herself next to the waterfall in Japan, surrounded by mossy cliffs and trees. It would sound similar, but it would be peaceful. Safe.

There was something different about how the water hit the tile. There was a harshness to it, a piercing quality to the way it clattered against the tile. Too familiar.

She tried in vain to visualize the space behind the waterfall, the curtain of water blocking out the rest of the world. The more she tried, the louder the water seemed to become, taunting her. She opened her eyes and stared at the shower tile.

She could see herself falling toward a similar tile. She could feel her arms being bound behind her back. She could feel the pain seething through her.

The pain.

The scuffing of plastic jolted her out of the trance. She blinked twice, took in the setting. It was just one of the Rehab room bathrooms. She had been in them countless times. So many patients inevitably found themselves needing to use the facilities at the start or end of her sessions. She had stared at this tile on so many occasions, allowing patients some privacy. Dr. Schuler had made the final decision about the tile. She looked up from the tile to find Jack removing the shower seat. "Don't tell anyone, but I hate those things."

She watched him tuck it next to the toilet.

"I want to try something." He lifted his eyebrows optimistically, placing his hand gently on her arm. "Are you OK?"

Delaney found herself briefly studying the contours of his muscular hand before nodding.

He pulled off his lab coat, removed his scrubs. Beneath was a pair of swim trunks and a rashguard. "I know, like Superman, right?"

She smiled, but she found herself staring at his biceps, pronounced under the spandex/nylon blend.

"I'll tell you something. Superman has an eternal wedgie."

She smiled, but suddenly the noise of the shower and the intimacy of the moment put her on guard. She felt her body, her mind tightening again. *Waterfall.* Her eyes focused on Jack. She watched him make final preparations, moving the shampoo to the higher shelf again. He looked a little funny in a swimsuit in the shower, but she liked seeing him in the swimsuit. With his tan skin and broad shoulders, he looked athletic and strong. She wondered if he had continued to work out while she was in the hospital, if it had been a stress reliever for him.

Having determined the shower was the right temperature after letting the water pour over one of his muscular hands, he looked over at her. It was a kind expression. Patient. The skin on her neck tingled.

He said something, but he sounded a thousand miles away.

She managed to block out the images, but she couldn't stop the noises from overtaking her mind again, phantom pain from years shooting through her again.

The pain.

The pain.

*Waterfall*, she persisted. She took a breath and a voice from deep in her mind replied: *Jack*.

She opened her eyes, not remembering she had closed them, when only the sound of a single shower remained. And Jack was there, crouched immediately before her. He was there, waiting patiently. *Jack*. The memory of the pain started to recede, like a wave pulling away from the shore. *Jack*.

*Jack*.

He nodded, as though to prompt her.

She wiggled out of the waffle robe Terrence had her wear after pool therapy. Underneath was a navy blue two-piece--a racerback tankini top and high waist brief style bottoms, which was easier to get on instead of the one piece she was used to swimming laps in. Both were a bit too big, bought by Julie, who upon seeing the size discrepancy, waved her off and said she was too thin to begin with.

She flexed her hands as she looked down at the polyester material, remembering how awkward it had been getting it over her head in the first place. She attempted to grasp the material with her hand, but found she couldn't get a firm enough pinch.

"What about between your fingers, or maybe your knuckles?" he suggested, squatting beside her.

Laney focused all efforts on squeezing her knuckles around the material and watched in amazement as she was able to lift it all the way to her chest. At that point the material caught and she dropped the hem.

"Oh, this has one of those built in sports bras, doesn't it? That's why."

*My ample bosom has thwarted my progress.*

"Let me help you," he said, reaching forward and tugging the swim top upwards, pulling the bra band away from her skin to be more gentle. He kept in close proximity, as to avoid having her sit topless and exposed in the wheelchair, she realized. He had turned his body a bit toward the door, seemingly to shield her from anyone who might burst into the bathroom.

It was one of those moments when the feelings she sensed he had for her, the love, was palpable, another presence in the room.

"OK, let's get you standing," he said next to her ear.

At first she assumed he had just moved closer, but she found it was her who had leaned forward considerably, breathing steadily into his neck. She nodded, settling back.

"I know this is still a challenge." He held out his forearm, trying to give her as little assistance as possible. She winced as she gripped his arm with one hand, one hand pushing firmly off the wheelchair. As she pulled herself upright, she wobbled a bit. He had to scoop his arm around her lower back to stabilize her. She steadied herself, placing a hand on each of his upper arms. As she focused on her hand placement, she grinned. *I found this humerus*, she said silently.

He didn't hear the silent reference, but he noticed her attentiveness to his arms, his shoulders. "Try putting your arms around my neck. Like a junior high school slow dance."

She did as instructed, breathing deeply and following his lead to move into the shower. She hesitated to move right, staring at his arm as she focused on feeling something in her right leg. It was still numb. Most of the time she only got sharp tingles out of it. She found herself resting her left foot flat and only balancing on the toes and pads of her right foot.

"If you'd like, you can use the grab bar for more support?"

Her eyes scanned over to the brushed stainless steel bar, so cold and so institutional, and tightened her hold on him.

"I'm OK with this, but we do probably need to slip you out of those bottoms at some point." He stopped their natural sway. "I did not mean for that to come off like a bad porno script."

She smiled slightly.

He pressed his lips together. "Not that I have *any* experience with those."

She raised an eyebrow, looked pointedly toward the floor.

"The bottoms, right."

Laney reached for the grab bar and stood as steadily as possible, staring off toward the tiled walls as he eased the bottoms down her hips. With the weight of the water, they dropped to the floor without any additional encouragement.

He chuckled. "How did those stay on while you were in the pool? They're huge on you.

"Here, lift your right foot. And now for the left." She leaned more heavily on him as he pulled the swim bottoms out of the way with his foot. He stood upright and encouraged her to resume her hand positions, trying to maintain a neutral facial expression. "I peeked. I'm sorry."

Her lips stretched into a slanted smile.

"OK, let's just sway a bit, see if that right leg wants to wake up."

She sent out a signal to her right leg, which returned little more than a pin prick in her foot in response. The feeling of helplessness triggered a flood of senses from that day in the locker room--the thick, humid air, the staleness of sweat and dirt, the creaking of the air conditioner as it fought to start up, the unforgiving tile and its deep grout lines digging into her back, the forcefulness of hands squeezing the bones in her arms, her breasts. The pain.

The pain.

"Just dance with me, D."

Jack's voice caught her by surprise. His face was focused, but serene. She found herself gazing up into his eyes, shifting side to side, following the gradients of blue, grey, and green in his eyes, like floating along a gentle sea.

The images continued to push their way forward--the chaos of bodies intertwined with the clattering of the showers, the forced contortions of her body. The seething pain. She squeezed her eyes closed again, hoping to suffocate the memories, but they were persistent. The cackling, the taunting, the gasps of pleasure contrasted to her own agony. She fought, she writhed, she tried to scream.

Everything hurt.

*Waterfall*, she pleaded silently, desperate to push the thoughts away, her hands trembling against Jack's thick shoulder. She desperately tried to summon images she'd been given to use in meditation, but her brain refused to be overridden.

And then he began to sing.

Her eyes, burning with tears stared straight ahead at his polyester rash guard. She concentrated on the gentle loop his arms had made her back, his warm skin a stark contrast to her own. She listened to his smooth, baritone voice that he maintained to just above a whisper, like a lullaby. She could recall going to the Vegas version of the Broadway production. She remembered being caught up in the grandeur, the drama. She understood that most were caught up in the mystery of the Phantom, but she had been attracted to the steadiness of Raoul, how it had taken a second look to realize what he had almost missed in Christine.

She suddenly wasn't scared. She wasn't in that locker room shower. She was with Jack and she was safe.

She choked slightly with that glorious sensation of long-awaited release, finding herself wrapping her arms tightly around him. She let him lead her body back into a gentle swaying motion. A rhythmic, lulling dance. The water crashing beside them blocked out the rest of the world. Her only indication they had moved was when the water started pouring down her back. She let her forehead rest on his collarbone, exhaling deeply in the rhythmic motion.

He let his voice fade off, stroking the bare skin of her back. His touch was the most intimate he had allowed himself since the stroke. He exhaled deeply into her hair, kissed her forehead.

After an indulgent few minutes, Delaney felt him shift his stance, but he kept a firm hold on her. "D, look at your feet," he whispered into her ear. There was something in his voice, having him so close, that sent chills through her neck, even in the warm water.

She opened her eyes. Both feet, paler than normal, bony and unpolished, were planted solidly. She looked back up at him, noticing her right hand had a more relaxed hold on his neck. She watched the fingers of her left hand stroking his neck, tickling his hairline of their own accord. There was subdued bewilderment in his eyes. Happiness. Love.

She pushed upward through her feet and kissed him. Once. *Jack*. Twice. *Jack*. Three times. *Jack*.

He pulled back slightly after the third kiss, his eyes wide and brimmed with tears. "Say that again."

She was slightly dizzy, but she focused on the features of his face so close to hers and breathed: "*Jack*."

# 18
# river

The hospital lobby was deceptively festive. There were towering trees filled with glowing lights, spiral gold tree picks, ornate Victorian star toppers, and the base was surrounded by a white velvet skirt, perfectly wrapped presents. It was more like the atrium of a grand hotel than a hospital. A volunteer was playing classic Christmas songs on the grand piano and nodded approvingly upon seeing the large bag of presents Jack carried toward the visitor elevators. When he reached the 7th floor, the ambiance was entirely different. The hallways were lined with colorful paper ring garlands, framed kid artwork and the trees and decorations were much more whimsical, as though decorated by Dr. Seuss himself.

A guitarist was situated in the multi-purpose room with a dozen or so children gathered around him, singing along to carefree songs like *"Up on the Rooftop."* Some kids were in wheelchairs, many were wearing masks, one was in a hospital bed, some were connected to IV poles, more than a few didn't have hair. Parents were strewn around the room as well, soaking up the moment, some singing along. There was a bittersweet sense to the occasion. He could feel the weight of parental worry that hung in the air.

He didn't see Delaney sitting in the group room so he moved onto the nurse's station to ask where he could find her. They pointed toward the patient room in the far corner.

"Is that Kai's room?"

The women glanced at each other. "Is is. Sweet Kai."

"Why isn't he in with the group?"

The nurse that was sipping her hot chocolate stopped. "Kai's been having a really tough time. He doesn't like to be around many people."

Her coworker sat down, nodding. "He *loves* Laney though."

"What's going on with him?"

"Bone cancer," she said, regrettably.

Jack felt his stomach turn, despite knowing this fact. The weight of it hadn't struck him until he saw the look on the nurse's face.

"He had surgery to remove the cells since it hadn't spread, but I think it was more than his mom expected. She hasn't been back for over a week."

Delaney had been staying late with him, sometimes until he fell asleep. This schedule had led to her turning up in the Anesthesiology sleep room on more than one occasion, too tired to drive herself home. Even exhausted, she struggled to sleep, the crease between her eyebrows deep as she dreamed.

Her world had started to revolve around this young child--her work schedule, as she justified needing two treatments per day instead of one, she was visiting with him when she wasn't working, and now he had started to overtake her dreams.

A few nights prior, she had left the Anesthesiology "holiday" event early after getting a call from one of his nurses. There had been razzing from some of the senior physicians that he had been abandoned by his date. At the time, their opinions held weighted meaning to him. There was also something that bothered him about their use of the word "date," how it belittled what she truly meant to him. He had been researching how to get a ring size when someone doesn't wear rings, keeping a small slip of paper both at home and the sleep room to wrap around her finger while she slept. The trouble was that she was struggling with sleep and if she did find what seemed like peaceful sleep, he feared waking her from it.

All of this--feeling separated from her, living parallel, but seemingly separate lives, the nervous excitement of knowing in spite of this, he had found the woman he would spend the rest of his life with the embarrassment he felt at his colleagues remarks--metamorphosed into a frustration that overtook him. Jack concluded that she needed to distance herself from her patients, that she cared too much. He lectured her, becoming aware that as he did, that she was filling his kitchen with groceries, having taken the time to go pick them up. His brain registered how comical the argument was, faulting her for being too good a person, but then she had stopped what she was doing, stood quietly and calmly, listening to him ramble on. He had started to get flustered, angry at her composure. He started rearranging things she had already put away, acting dissatisfied with where she had chosen to put the vegetables in the refrigerator, closing cabinet doors with too much force, angrily emptying a bag of apples into the fruit bowl. Through it all, she observed him with interest, but not judgment or opposing anger.

Once it seemed he was finished, Delaney crossed the kitchen and kissed him gently on the cheek. She continued past him to gather her bag, having already expressed her intent to return to the hospital.

"Do you agree?" he had asked, a little flabbergasted by this action.

She shook her head calmly, not turning back around. "No."

When he pushed open the door, the hospital room was dreamily lit by a small tree in the corner, covered with colorful light strands, paper cut out ornaments hastily colored with crayons. There was a fishing line hanging from the ceiling tiles that held mixes of snowflakes--some beautiful and intricate, others with too many holes cut that hung awkwardly. A small pizza box sat on the side table with an unwrapped clothing box.

Finally his eyes fell upon Delaney sitting in the oversized vinyl recliner facing the wall of windows. The city sat below with its array of lights and based on the darkness of the rest of the windows, he determined the room must face the mountains. A small boy with the biggest brown eyes he'd ever seen was snuggled beside her, his face smashed into her chest. He was wearing a pair of flannel dinosaur pajamas with the tag still attached to his wrist. There was a cozy blanket pulled over their legs. They both looked up at him as he approached.

"Merry Christmas," Jack whispered.

Delaney smiled. "Merry Christmas." She flinched her eyebrow questioningly. "You must be Kai?"

Kai nodded, clinging tighter to Delaney.

"I'm Jack."

Kai was clearly not wanting to make conversation and tucked himself even further behind her. Delaney stroked his back, reassuringly. "We're watching for Santa," she explained. "They've tracked him to the East coast so we're going to try to stay up."

Jack smiled lightly. "Well, I don't want to interrupt, but I brought you a few presents, Kai. It looks like you opened a couple already?" He nodded to the Brontosaurus the boy had clutched in his small hand.

Kai held it out for him to see.

"Oh, I like it. I always liked the plant eaters. It seemed like they'd make better pets."

The small boy's eyes lit up a bit.

"Would you like to open *these*?" Jack asked, stepping toward the tree. "Or would you like to save them until the morning?"

Kai wiggled toward the end of the recliner.

"Hold on, Buddy. I'm not as young as you. It takes me a while to get my butt out of this chair."

Kai smiled broadly and waited. As she sat up with ease and helped him scoot to the floor, Jack noticed one of his pant legs was empty from the knee down. The excess fabric bounced as he moved. He made quick eye contact with Delaney and felt tremendous guilt for minimizing the importance of her spending Christmas Eve with Kai. He had remarked about him taking priority when his dad and sister would be in town, despite her reassuring him she would have Christmas Day dinner with them. In his anger, he had scoffed about--

"Bailing on them like you did the holiday party." There had been a flicker of something in her eye when he said it.

He remembered saying something during their ridiculous argument about how Kai would have the nurses around, "he won't even remember it," "he's only three." Now, as soon as Delaney sat on the floor, he watched Kai clamor into her lap, kissing her cheek sweetly.

It all quietly came firing back at Jack. He's three. He will remember. He would have had no one.

"Look at all those presents, Kai," Delaney said, leaning in close to his cheek. "You must have been really good this year."

"*Wow*," Kai said with almost comical enthusiasm. "These for me?"

"All for you."

He sat there looking over each package, a funny little grin on his face.

"Let's open them," Delaney whispered conspiratorially.

He giggled and grabbed the one closest to him. With each present, he clarified that it was, in fact, for *him*, smiled, then as he revealed the contents, stared at it in wonder: Coloring books [of his very own], race cars, and a choo-choo train. Swept up in the moment, he stood and leapt toward Jack to thank him with no thought of his own safety.

Once they convinced him to go to bed, it took almost no time for him to fall asleep. Jack watched Delaney tenderly tuck him in, whispering something to him, kissing his cheekbone like she had done it a thousand times before. It was a magnificent thing to behold, actually, seeing the woman he loved in an entirely new light.

She walked quietly to where Jack waited at the foot of the bed. He held out his hand and led her toward the hallway, squinting against the LED overhead lights as they emerged. From there, they walked down the now quiet corridor to the elevator. It was once they were inside that he pulled her to him tightly.

He tucked her hair on the right side behind her ear gently. "Three things," he said in a low voice. "One, I love you. Like, more than you can fathom, love you."

"I like this list," her muffled voice said into his chest.

"Two, I was wrong. Unequivocally wrong."

She gave a small, almost imperceptible nod.

"Three, I'm sorry for being a jerk whilst being so unequivocally wrong."

The elevator doors opened to the lobby, the piano quietly playing itself now. She followed him to one of the sofas facing the main tree, sighed as she sat down, reluctant to relax too comfortably.

"I know you want to get back to him. I just wanted to sit with you for awhile, if that's OK?"

She nodded, looking exhausted.

"Is it strange that the hospital feels like one of the most festive places for Christmas?" he observed.

"Like you can feel it more here?"

"*Yeah*, why is that?"

"Raw human experience happens here. Babies are born. People die. Critical life events. The things that give life value and meaning."

He pondered this. "What made you start volunteering on Christmas?"

"Christmas never felt like Christmas after my parents got divorced," she explained, stretching. "It just made me sad. We'd go through the motions of it, but we didn't linger over comfort food or hot chocolate Christmas morning. It sort of became something we did because we felt pressured to, check the boxes, you know? I didn't realize how much I missed Christmas until I spent the one after the accident in the hospital." She swallowed hard. "My dad was called to an emergency meeting so it was just me."

Jack furrowed his forehead. "On Christmas?"

"He was secretly dating a woman at the time. I suspect she threw a fit and insisted he still go on their trip to Aspen that I was never supposed to know about. He stopped in earlier on Christmas Eve when I was in PT, but that was it."

"That doesn't seem like your dad."

Her eyebrows perked a little. "He changed a lot once I moved in. The girlfriend vanished, for one thing. I think he regretted--" She seemed to be choosing her words wisely. "Being such a 'passive' presence in my life for so long."

He could see her father, with his sandy colored hair, a stark contrast to hers, giving Jack an intentionally formal handshake, standing outside Security at the airport, smiling knowingly at him. He had spent a long weekend in town and had been quietly observing the pair of them in a manner not unlike his daughter. As a voice over the intercom made a warning about unattended baggage, he had pulled him in with one arm and hugged him.

"Be good to my little girl," he whispered. Then he had turned and pulled Delaney in rather energetically for a hug, wrapping both arms around her. He had kissed her repeatedly on the top of the head, tears glistening in his creased blue eyes, his nose red. He took in a deep breath of her hair, squeezing once more before moving briskly away. It would have the outward appearance of being dismissive if not for his tear streaked face. He turned back once he was a distance away, though the emotion was evident on his face. He had his briefcase bag swinging on his shoulder, walking backwards, and had mouthed the words "I love you." He blew her a kiss with both hands before turning on his heel and disappearing behind a frosted partition.

He died of a heart attack the next day.

She sighed. "I had convinced myself I was too old for all of the Christmas festivities, but being alone that Christmas--Caprice was unavailable--" she added, for clarity. "--and it just kind of hit me--everything that had gone on, all that emotional repression got released. Suddenly? I felt *really* sorry for myself--" She sat up a little.

Jack tried to listen like he had seen her do--without interjection, without judgment.

"--and then I didn't. I looked around and saw all the little kids who weren't getting to enjoy it like they should, like I had gotten to at their age. So I started volunteering every Christmas after that. Most Christmases it's just a few hours, giving the parents a chance to have some time with their other kids at home, especially with the contact precautions kids who can't have regular visitors. This year was a different though--"

"*Kai.*"

"Kai," she echoed. "I couldn't leave him, Jack."

"I wish you'd--" He stopped himself. "I wish I'd taken the time to know."

She lowered her eyes, her forehead furrowed. "I have a confession."

His stomach dropped.

"The social worker had mentioned the idea of fostering him and I had been considering it."

Jack tensed involuntarily.

She sat at the edge of the couch, shaking her hand as though waving away his thoughts. "His dad is going to take him. I found out earlier today."

He surprised himself by feeling a little disappointed suddenly, a little protective. "Has he spent any time with him?"

Delaney looked regretful. "For the first few days after he was born, then no."

Jack felt an ache in his heart. He looked at Delaney and suddenly he could see her taking care of that sweet boy. They were a perfect match, really. She was incredible with kids--she just had a way when she was working with them. She'd attend to the parents, of course, but she truly engaged with the kids. He remembered walking into the pediatrics therapy gym one day and found her cross-legged on the floor mat. A little girl, about eight years old, with impossibly bright blonde curls (a wig), sat focused behind her. In exchange for doing her session with a good attitude (after refusing three other therapists), the girl was getting to do Delaney's hair however she pleased. How she pleased was dozens of tiny, and based on Delaney's occasional silent wince, painful braids. She was in the gym for over an hour.

He was rounding with the Residents on the Maternity wing while she was wrapping up her salon session. He was explaining a procedure in his most professional way when she strolled by, looping around the opposite side of the nurse's station, shoulders back, grinning sideways at him.

The little girl--Abby--had used every color hair band and had finished off her masterpiece with about two dozen plastic flower and butterfly clips.

He thought of how she must be with Kai. Knowing her, she was probably working feverishly to get him up and moving on a prosthetic. She'd have that kind, personable tone on the phone with the prosthetics vendor, reviewing the details, adamant they check it's right. In her sessions, they'd make silly faces at each other. He thought of how she kissed him goodnight so tenderly. He thought of how Kai looked at her, filled with trust and adoration...and now he was going to live with a man he didn't even know, who abandoned his child, who probably had a limited knowledge of the care Kai needed. Would he get proper medical care? Would he put in the needed effort? Why wasn't he spending Christmas with his son?

He suppressed his anger once he saw Delaney was picking up on it in his expression. She seemed to correctly read that it wasn't directed at her.

"I'm sorry, D," he said, running his hand over hers.

"He lives nearby, so maybe he'll still bring him here for doctor visits. He doesn't have insurance, but maybe the hospital will work something out since Kai's already established as a patient," Delaney said, gazing off toward the Christmas tree. "I can't imagine living that close to your son and never seeing him. I don't care what the situation was with his mother." She seemed unaware of the parallel with her own dad, who she adored.

Jack shook his head angrily. "Neither can I."

She settled into his chest as tears started to fall from her eyes. "Did I see a little panic in your eyes at first?"

He cleared his throat. "Maybe a little."

"It'd be a huge change, I know."

"It would be."

"And you, not even sure you're going to keep me around," she teased, shifting the subject.

He squeezed her tightly, kissing the top of her head. "Are you citing the dinner w/ Cappy again?"

"I am."

"In my defense, she and I have limited mutual interests and I was unprepared for her aggressive line of questioning while you were in the restroom."

Caprice had flat-out asked if he was going to propose and he told her that neither of them felt any rush. He had meant to clarify further that, as far as he was concerned, they had the rest of their lives anyway, but Delaney had returned from the restroom and he thought adding that important piece of information with her sitting there would take away what he was planning to say in his impending proposal. Caprice had looked satisfied, smirking throughout dessert. She had been strategic in waiting until after the bill was paid when Jack had to take a call from the hospital to question Delaney about how after three years, they still weren't that serious.

"That woman has some serious jealousy issues with you. Was she always like that?"

Delaney shrugged into him.

"What was it you said in response to her nonsense?" He asked.

" *'Tis better to have loved and lost than never to have loved at all.'*"

"That's Lord Tennyson, right?"

"It is. It's a wonder I could think so quickly when I was so emotionally distraught." She stretched, smirking.

"Oh stop it. You know I'd rather be half-eaten by a shark than be without you," he said, kissing the freckles on her cheek.

"Oh Lord. What half?"

He grinned, pulling her closer. "*So*, Tennyson."

"Yes. He's a classic."

He leaned in close to her ear. "'If I had a flower for every time I thought of you, I could walk in my garden forever.'"

She turned toward him, her eyes glowing with the reflection of the lights on the trees. "Man I am *really* glad it was you in the sleep room bed that night."

"Yeah?"

"*Best* impulse decision I've ever made."

"Best *impulse* decision? What would you say was the best overall decision?"

She thought for a moment, scrunching up her nose. "*Oh*, I went to the food truck frenzy event in the fall," she said, dreamily. "Remember that? I was debating about the salmon club sandwich. I wondered if the salmon/cheese/bacon combo was too much and as it turns out, it's really pretty amazing." She had summoned an incredible amount of enthusiasm.

He shook his head, laughing silently. "And people think I have an obnoxious sense of humor," he murmured.

"Well I *have* been pushing that message pretty hard lately."

He suppressed a laugh. "Well despite that, I do have one of your presents to give you."

"Here? You don't want to wait until tomorrow?"

"No, here's good."

She furrowed her eyebrow. "I know this looks cozy and living room-like, but this can't be your own naked room, Jack."

"That would qualify as a gift?"

"Uh, yeah." Recognizing his bemusement, she added: "We could add a bow."

"You can open that one tomorrow."

Her eyebrows jumped, but he could still see the worry about Kai persisting behind her enthusiasm.

He sat up, searching his pockets. "Well last Christmas you mentioned those *Lifetime* movies, the quintessential 'perfect' Christmas scene, complete with an adorable puppy in a box?"

"You didn't get me a puppy."

He squinted. "No, we're not home enough to tackle housetraining." He pulled out his phone. "Maybe down the road, but in the meantime, I thought you should still have a sweet face greeting you when you get home. You know, beside me, if I happen to be there." He flipped the phone around and on the screen was a photo of his front hallway, which now housed a Bombay bloodhound entry table.

She clasped her hand to her mouth. "And no howling."

"It's silly."

"No, it's adorable. I love him." She shook her head, smiling widely. "So how do we handle this? Does he switch off between our places or will he be living at your house full-time?"

"Well I was kind of hoping you would both be living with me full-time."

She suddenly looked at the screen with a focused stare.

"D."

She said nothing.

"D."

"I was just wondering how sold you are on that wall color. If I'm going to be living there, I might want to make a few changes." She smirked.

"Is that a yes?"

She returned his phone, conclusively. "Yes, I would love to steal your covers on a nightly basis."

"So you admit you do that."

"It's my one glaring flaw," she said, eyes wide, daring him to disagree.

"I wouldn't even call it a flaw--you look so *cute* when you do it, king-sized sheets wound around you so tightly. It's like my very own long, sexy Delaney burrito."

"You're saying I'm bad at my one glaring flaw?"

"Horrible."

"Dammit."

"I could offer some fall-back flaws I've observed."

"That could be helpful. Not now though. I don't want to start off living together on a negative note." She turned and settled deeper into his arms. "Alright, say something sweet. The flaws thing sort of stings."

# 19

# delicate

Securing two full weeks off work required some unfortunate trades that had resulted in four back-to-back overnight on-call shifts. Jack decided to take a break from his documentation, desperate for food and caffeination. He was yawning widely as he walked into the scarcely populated cafeteria, stopping halfway through the entrance when he saw Delaney standing at the grill line with Allie, one of the pediatric nurses.

He was so pleasantly surprised to see her, his heart racing a bit at the sight, that it didn't occur to him in that moment how odd it was to find her in the cafeteria, let alone during prime treatment hours. He pressed his finger to his lips, intending to sneak up on Delaney, but Allie shook her head, frowning.

Delaney turned around slowly. To anyone else she probably just looked a little disoriented, but he knew immediately something was very wrong.

"D, what's wrong?"

"Hey Stranger," she said, smiling lightly. "Headache."

Her face didn't look quite right. He placed a hand on either cheek, looked back and forth between her eyes, checking to see if either pupil was dilated. If there was even a miniscule variation between them, he didn't see it. "When did it start?"

Allie perked up to answer. "She looks off, right? It started this morning after that *visitor*. She's not one to complain so when she mentioned it, I knew it must be bad. I told her to go home."

Jack recognized the emphasis Allie placed on "visitor" and wondered fleetingly who it had been, but there was a knot in his stomach suddenly.

Delaney stiffened, raising her hand to her forehead. "They would have pulled Brittany to cover. Terrence is on paternity leave."

Allie rolled her eyes. "We could have survived one day with Brittany."

"Brittany shouldn't be allowed within a football field length of children. She smokes and she swears." It seemed to be taking a superhuman effort for her to stay upright, but she continued making her point. "And she told a five year old that Santa was actually her parents."

Allie nodded, reluctantly, in agreement.

"Did you take something already?" Jack asked, trying to assess again if one pupil was larger than the other. The left was starting to swell, it seemed.

"I took a headache cocktail."

"Didn't help at all?"

She leaned into his palm, her eyes exhausted. "Not yet. It was 15 minutes ago or so."

"I told her she should try eating," Allie added, finishing up ordering her food.

"Follow my finger," he said, moving his index finger from side to side in front of her eyes. She seemed to follow it well enough.

"We get it, you're a doctor," Delaney said in her joking manner, though she was having trouble hiding her pained expression. Her attention seemed to be drifting, distracted by the line cooks' banter, the sizzle of bacon on the griddle, the dropping of coins from the register change dispenser.

"Raise your arms."

She humored him. "Just don't tickle me. You know I hate that."

"You love it," he said, half-playing along.

"Do you want to join us for breakfast?" Allie asked.

Jack exhaled deeply, exhausted from the overnight shift, wondering if maybe it was sleep deprivation that was making him paranoid. She was 29 years old. Healthy. Active. She was allowed to have an off day. He was just being paranoid. "I was just going to finish some notes. Have some packing to do before tomorrow."

"That's right--Hawaii!" Allie chimed, seemingly in an effort to energize Delaney.

"I'm fine, Jack. Go do your doctor thing."

He brushed the hair out of her eyes. "I'm probably just being overprotective, but call me if your headache doesn't go away, okay?" He glanced up to the menu, about to say something casual to lighten the mood when her hand grabbed his forearm.

The same crystal blue eyes that danced when she laughed, the eyes that gazed at him sleepily from across their silky king sheets in the mornings, the eyes that threw daggers when she was angry looked unlike he had ever seen them. They looked terrified.

"D?"

She looked pointedly down to her idle, slightly ajar mouth, which had started to slope to the right, before she fell forward in his arms.

"Omelet with cheese, chicken sausage, mushrooms, spinach?" the line cook announced, unaware.

Allie looked uncertain whether she should take the box.

Jack held out his phone, trying to balance Delaney. "Call a stroke alert. Tell the team to meet us at Radiology." With his hand free, he hoisted Delaney into his arms. He beelined out the cafeteria entrance, weaving around people taking their trays to the trash, people lightheartedly walking down the hallway. The stroke alert operator answered immediately and Allie managed to give them the correct information.

"Say something, D. Say 'Jack's an asshole.'"

"Jack's an asshole!" Allie said enthusiastically, running to catch up.

"Great, now D, you say it."

Delaney's eyes no longer focused and there was a distinct limpness to her body, her face nuzzled into his neck.

By the end of the evening, rather than finishing packing for their trip to Hawaii, she was lying in ICU, a half-dozen machines humming and beeping around her.

*** 

Jack stood at a wheeled computer station, inputting notes on the five epidurals he'd performed that morning. A styrofoam cup of Freddy Prinze, Jr., or some other middle-aged celebrity brand of Keurig coffee was sitting on the surface next to the keyboard. It seemed like every celebrity thought they could slap their name on k-cups. K-cups were the new stinky mass-produced perfume. It all tasted like Folgers to him.

"I didn't know you were working again," Allie said, coming off the elevator holding a styrofoam to-go box. Her dark brown hair was now mostly blonde, fading up to dark roots and was left naturally curly. She also had a large round belly.

"I didn't know you were expecting."

"Expecting *what?*" She asked coyly, then modeled her belly's side profile. "How's our girl?"

He blinked, then did an automatic nod. "Much better. Really making progress." For the first time, it wasn't an exaggeration.

"Really? That's so good to hear. You tell her I'm going to come see her."

Jack did the mental calculation to determine if Delaney might remember her. She wouldn't. Allie came on as a new grad night nurse after they started dating.

"I still can't believe this happened. She's so young."

"She's tough," he replied, his automated response.

"Do they know why this happened? I mean, to someone so young?"

"She had a concussion as a teenager. They think that may have weakened the blood vessel." Another stock answer.

"Oh, so stress *can't* cause it?" It sounded like a follow-up question.

"It could contribute," he said with a frown, "but it would probably have to be chronic stress." *Was she chronically stressed and he just never noticed?*

"Oh she deals with stress better than anyone I know."

He relaxed his shoulders. "I agree."

"She was really upset though. That day."

"About what?"

"Some guy came to see her."

"*Who?*"

"I don't know. Big guy--he looked like a big, burly country singer, like a young Trace Adkins. God, does that age me? So many male country singers now seem so--*not* masculine."

"Was he a patient? Patient's family member?"

"I don't think so. He seemed nice enough from what I could tell."

"What was his name?"

"Don't know." She checked the styrofoam box to be sure she remembered to get a fork. The box appeared to contain a salad. "No, I *do* know. Timothy Something--Timothy--" She seemed to really be straining to find the last name in the back of her mind. "I'm sorry. Pregnancy brain. He had come to the nurse's station looking for her."

He dismissed his thought that the man could have been Kai's father, whose name was Keith. "They argued?"

"No, that's the thing. They seemed to get along okay. Actually, they sat outside for awhile. He even kissed her goodbye." She tried to read the expression on his face. "It was just a kiss on the cheek--*well*, he kissed her, she didn't kiss him--"

"You said she was upset."

"No, no, no--she didn't get upset until *after* he left." She picked a crouton out of the box, munched it loudly.

"What happened?" Jack asked impatiently.

"She said goodbye to him, but when she turned around toward the nurse's station, she looked like she had seen a ghost. She took off for the restroom, I went in to check on her and she was throwing up."

"*What?*" His voice was firmer than he meant it to be. "You didn't say anything about this."

"Well everything happened so fast. And I kind of thought--" She seemed to be regretting starting this line of conversation. "Maybe he was an ex-boyfriend."

Jack focused on breathing. *She wouldn't have had a chance to tell you if an ex-boyfriend stopped by.* He decided to switch gears. "She vomited?"

"Yeah, she was a mess--I thought she was hyperventilating. The walls are super thin in the nurse's lounge."

"Allie, you're still on lunch, right?" another nurse Jack didn't recognize asked, passing them carrying a patient lunch tray.

"Yeah--15 more minutes, Lynn." She turned back to Jack, as casual as if they had been discussing a recent movie release: "It's good to see you, Jack. I better go gobble this down. Give Laney my love."

And she was gone.

He stood watching her grow smaller down the hallway, finally disappearing into the nurse's lounge.

"Hey, Doc, are you about done with that COW?"

Jack jolted to consciousness. "Sorry?"

"COW. Computer on Wheels," one of the Internal Medicine physicians clarified.

He thought to correct him, that IT had officially changed the name due to a patient complaint, but decided he didn't particularly care. "Yeah, all yours," he said, stepping slowly away.

He spent hours wrapping up documentation, sitting in the all too familiar sleep room, rather than retreating to his current accomodations on Rehab. With the overhead fluorescents on, it gave off a far different ambiance than when Delaney used to join him. Back then, they would, at most, have the bedside lamp on. He remembered how it never made a difference to him what her intent, if she'd undress and start kissing him, if she'd undress and snuggle in against him, or if it was all she could do to even collapse exhausted in bed, he was never disappointed. There was an ease that draped over him when she was near.

He stared into the computer monitor, the glare straining his eyes. He wondered if he had imagined it all, if he had built up this image of her and despite competing evidence, hadn't questioned anything and had refused to see anything too negatively.

He pictured her looking at him, her eyes vibrant, trusting, kind. When she said goodbye in the mornings, she'd place a palm on each of his cheeks and gaze into his face before kissing him, pressing through her toes to make herself taller. He remembered feeling her cheeks constricting against his skin so that he knew she was smiling.

*Remember the flaws*, he told himself.

She fell asleep during movies, but only at home. There'd be something he'd want her to see and he would know as soon as she tucked herself a little too comfortably against him, she would be dozing in minutes. He'd warn her and she'd assure him that she was wide awake and inevitably her hand would go limp, her eyes would close and he'd be left to watch the movie alone. *There.* He was satisfied to have unpacked this flaw. *But is it a dealbreaker flaw?*

Occasionally he'd decide to spend the night out on the couch, holding her close, the moonlight shining brightly into the living room. That was pretty magical, in its own way. Or sometimes he would lift her, carry her to bed. Usually she was a sound sleeper, but there were times she'd wake and sleepily murmur something about his strength or "Prince Charming," or "The only thing that would make this more perfect is if you'd sing to me."

She was always trying to get him to sing.

In those instances, she'd wrap herself around him and continue to plead until he kissed or tickled her into unbridled laughter.

*Flaws*, he thought. *See her realistically.*

He kept trying to force feed himself synthetic images of her being kissed by another man, laughing with another man, resting her head against the chest of another man, but his brain instead returned memories that pulsed with life and authenticity.

He saw Delaney watching the fireworks on the Fourth of July, her eyes widening, her smile broadening slightly with each burst.

He saw her sipping gingerly from an enamel mug, campfire flames illuminating her face in a warm orange glow, a beanie pulled down over her ears.

He saw her as he returned to the stands during a Cubs road game they attended with his dad. It was the first time his dad had met her, but their shoulders dipped toward one another as they conversed. His dad spoke with animated hand gestures, explaining about the difference between the National League and American League, and she listened intently, an engaged audience. As he handed them each their beer from concessions, his dad had remarked about Jack's high school baseball career with fondness. Jack remembered looking at Delaney, rolling his eyes lightly, as he sat in his end seat. His dad nudged her in the arm twice before the close of the inning to point out some positioning of the pitcher's feet giving away the pitch he intended to throw.

Delaney no longer remembered his dad telling her how Jack had taken a returned fastball in the nose, which had resulted in a permanent dent. She wouldn't recollect how later that evening when they were back home, she had paid special attention to the old injury, kissing his nose repeatedly. She wouldn't remember inside jokes or road trips they'd taken or that when he made her breakfast in bed for the first time, he had created a smiley face flower out of a pancake, blueberries serving as the face, sliced strawberries as the petals. She didn't remember that when she first moved in, she had reached a moment of surreality and--panic, that he had tugged her out to the moonlit backyard for some fresh air and a dance.

Jack didn't find his way to Rehab until later in the evening. It was unlike him to miss having dinner with Delaney, a fact Jenna pointed out as she saw him coming down the hallway. He fumbled through a response.

"Are you OK?"

"Long day," he said.

She lowered her chin regretfully, probably assuming something had gone wrong during a surgery. She wasn't the type to press further. "Well Laney just got back from the pool a little while ago. She's been out in the courtyard with Quinn—"

"Quinn?"

"85."

He nodded absentmindedly. His mind now seemed more capable of accepting the synthetic, dramatized images and it reeled an image of the man Allie had described. He thought of how Grant had been enamored with Delaney, how they had gone on a "non-date." He thought of Caprice mentioning "the other doctor" before they even started dating. He wondered about Quinn. This carousel of men whirled in his mind, blurring, distorting his image of her.

"She asked about you," Jenna offered.

His heart swelled.

"You must not have had your phone with you?"

The slope of her eyebrow told him he should probably check his phone.

An audio message in his texts. He stared at the icon.

"She worked on it during Speech. It took all session to get a good take." Jenna smiled and turned on her heel. "She's in her room."

He hit play. Delaney's voice was raspy and uneven, like the recovery period after laryngitis. "*Hey good lookin', what'cha got cookin'--*" The message ended with a click.

"*How's about cookin' something up with me?*" he whispered, his eyes welling with tears.

"Oh and she had you evicted from 90," Jenna called out as he approached, a broad smile on her face.

"She did what?"

"Mmhmm," she replied, her eyes panning to Delaney's room.

Her eyes were closed as he entered, turned onto her right side, facing the small lamp and sound machine set to ocean waves. He moved quietly across the room, finding his duffel placed next to the bedside table. He removed his lab coat, hanging it over the footboard, and pulled out his standard basketball shorts and t-shirt to change into, along with his last pair of clean underwear. He'd need to run to the house tomorrow, which was probably a good thing. The house plants were probably all shriveled.

As he resituated the duffel, he glanced upon her sleeping face and he thought of the basset hound entry table and the woman for whom he'd bought it. She seemed to have appreciated the gift, seemed to have been enthusiastic about living together before and after her temporary panic. He knew her--and yet he had allowed a hallway conversation to warp his thoughts, challenge his view of her, make him question if he truly knew her at all, if there was more she hadn't told him. And now, she didn't remember their relationship, didn't remember the table, didn't remember Allie, didn't remember the encounter that may or may not have triggered the stroke.

He moved to the bathroom, where he shed his scrubs and let the shower try to drown out his thoughts. When the shower shut off, they returned. He had used her body wash, having forgotten his own, the smell of citrus and vanilla taking him back to their encounter at the gym so long before.

That night hadn't ended as he expected. She revealed so much, the feelings he had about her appreciating by the minute, and he had resolved to be a gentleman, walk her to get her bag, make sure she got to her car safely. When they reached her old car, the light from the streetlamp illuminated her face and he found himself kissing her once, twice, three times. *Like she did in the shower.*

He replayed the moment from the parking lot, how she had pressed through her toes to follow him each time he retreated slightly from the kiss. He thought of how she had followed the same pattern in the same shower where he now found himself, how the first thing she had managed to speak was his whispered name.

When he emerged from the bathroom shaking his hair dry with a towel, she was sitting upright, chin pressed to her chest, stretching her neck. Her eyes opened slowly as she released the stretch and looked at him, her smile sweet. She read his face in an instant, her smile turning hesitant, questioning.

He shook his head slightly, answering her unspoken question, crossing to her bedside. She didn't move, her posture tall and straight. He kissed her, bracing her face in his hands, intending for the kiss to be brief, but he found himself leaning further into her, interlocking their lips, so that they fell back into the pillows. His stubble rubbed against her soft skin, but she didn't seem to mind, her arms wrapped around his neck, encouraging him to continue. So he did. He kissed her lopsided smile, he kissed her neck, he kissed along her old, faded scars, and the healing surgical wound behind her ear.

He knew her.

He knew every inch.

He knew every scar.

"*I love you,*" he breathed. He said it again and again, sometimes silently, sometimes in whispers between passionate tangles of their lips, their fingers.

"Well *now* I know why your heart rate spiked, Laney." The bright hallway light silently flooded the room and glared in Delaney's eyes and Jeff's silhouette stood in the doorway.

"They WD-40'd that hinge, did they?" Jack said, catching his breath. He hadn't noticed on his way in.

"I'll just go ahead and turn off the alarm so you don't get any other visitors. Maybe remove it while you're--*intertwined* like that."

Jack looked in her eyes as the door closed and they were left again in the dim light of her room. The interruption seemed to have sobered them both a bit, the hospital room setting coming more into focus. He reached to her left hand and gently pulled the fingertip sensor from her index finger, wrapped it around the bed rail on that side.

"Hi," he said, touching the red stubble-burned skin of her chin, her lips with the tips of his fingers.

"Hi," she replied simply, her brilliant blue eyes focused intently on him.

He exhaled and rotated onto the bed beside her; a snug fit. He watched her survey him. She wore a soft gray t-shirt with a logo for a surf shop the neckline falling over her shoulder. She had slight pink dent marks on her nose from wearing her glasses. Her long hair was pulled into a messy knot on the top of her head, the loose ends wild. She smiled tightly when he patted his chest, beckoning her to lie down with him. He wrapped his arms around her, kissing her hair.

"Jack?" Her voice was shaky. Rebuilding her speech seemed to follow a similar path to rebuilding physical strength. Even still, he loved hearing her again.

"D?"

She moved in close to his ear, whispering: "Stay with me."

He turned so they were nose to nose. "Yes." It wasn't clear if she meant to stay for the night or something else, but it didn't really matter to him. He squeezed her gently. "I'm not going anywhere."

# 20

# omissions

There were three missed calls, two missed tone pages, and a text message from Julie when he got to the lockers after wrapping up a complicated transplant surgery. He had been stretching too casually, a calm sweeping over him, thinking of what dinner he could get to share with Delaney.

He had been entirely unprepared for what this could mean. Another stroke? Did she have a bad fall? Julie's text was vague, just instructing him to call her immediately, which he did. Twice. At the point her phone rolled once again to an overly cheerful voicemail greeting, he slammed his locker door shut and took off for the elevators.

"What a surgery, huh? Bet you're glad to be off maternity," Ian Richter, the transplant surgeon said, just swiping his badge for the sleep rooms as Jack came barreling out, not stopping to hold the door.

Jack went straight for the stairwell, taking the steps two at a time. There was a crowd collecting on the first floor entrance. Someone said his name, but he ignored them, pushed through to the corridor. Once there, he started running toward the Rehab building.

Julie called back as he reached the central corridor. "I'm here," he blurted out.

She appeared before him, just inside from the courtyard. She held her hand up. "Woah, take a breath. You're going to need it."

"What happened?" His eyes scanned the windows and found Terrence pushing Delaney in a wheelchair through the opposite exit, which led to the back entrance of the gym and the pool. There wasn't anything distinctly unusual to the act, to the positioning of her in the chair. Jack exhaled deeply. "She's OK? Julie, if your plan was to give me a heart attack--" Movement on the courtyard drew his attention. "*Caprice.*"

"Caprice," Julie repeated.

He pushed the button and stepped into the overcast late afternoon.

Caprice was pacing back and forth jabbering on about how "sometimes the truth hurts."

Quinn was glaring at her from the water wall. "Do you want some truth?" he asked, suddenly.

Caprice snapped to attention. "This was a private conversation, thank you." She saw Jack approaching and cackled. "Oh. My. God. You're *still* here."

"I am."

"Still waiting for her to remember you after all this time?"

"Why are you here, Caprice?"

"I'm her sister and clearly *someone* has to tell her which way is up. She didn't even remember her own dad died."

"You rubbed that one in her face, did you?" Jack spat, his body rigid.

"Apparently she messaged our aunt. I can't *believe* you didn't tell her he died."

"*Do you want some truth?*" Quinn repeated. He was practically shouting.

He had Jack's attention and Caprice's followed.

"You said it's Delaney's fault Jeremiah dumped you?" Quinn glanced across at Jack as he spoke.

She narrowed her eyes. "Wait--You weren't always in a wheelchair, were you?" There was a look of disgust in her eyes, like the wheelchair was a poorly chosen fashion accessory.

"No, the chair is new. You said it was Delaney's fault Jeremiah dumped you?"

"It was. Apparently she came onto him, threw herself at him. So desperate. He said it was just too uncomfortable."

"Who's Jeremiah?" Jack asked.

"My boyfriend."

"In *high school*," Quinn clarified.

"We'd probably be married with a couple kids right now if it weren't for her," she said matter-of-factly.

"Tell me you don't actually believe that," Quinn antagonized.

"It wasn't enough she was the favorite child and had her whole modeling life--'*Oh your sister is just so beautiful!*'" she mimicked, rolling her eyes. "She *always* had to be the center of attention."

Jack found himself muted, a silent observer.

"She was always jealous of us."

Quinn shook his head.

"She *was*. For once, I had something she didn't and she couldn't stand it."

Quinn shut his eyes, silently contemplating his next words.

"I don't have time for this," Caprice scoffed, locating her purse.

"He told her you were crying in the girls locker room." His words were solid, precise.

Caprice stood upright, narrowed her eyes. "What are you talking about?"

"Jeremiah went and found her at track practice, told her you were crying in the locker room and were asking for her." He took a short breath, his words slow. "Inside the locker room, six of his friends were waiting."

She was frozen pointing at him, recognizing him at last.

"They locked the doors, pinned her in the shower, and raped her."

Caprice wasn't blinking. "You're that guy who hung out after our mother died," she said quietly. "How do you—did she tell you--"

"I was in the hall. I saw her go in." He exhaled. "I heard what was going on."

"You *let it happen?*" Jack said so abruptly he startled them both.

"They locked the doors."

Jack leaned forward, disbelieving, hands outstretched. "You didn't do *anything?* Call for help? Try to break in?"

"There wasn't any—" Quinn stopped short because he knew what he was about to stammer out wasn't true. He could have immediately pulled the alarm. He could have ran down to the field, gotten the track coach. He could have tried the art building. He could have found someone. He could have called 911.

"But you don't know for sure what happened," Caprice bargained.

Quinn peered over at Jack and spoke softly. "I know what I heard--and I know what I saw after."

"You weren't actually there though." Her voice was weak.

"Caprice, it's time you left," Jack said without looking at her. He was clenching his jaw, breathing heavily, staring down Quinn.

"I'm her sister."

Jack stood firm, gave her one brief glare and she quickly gathered her handbag and left. Then he turned back to Quinn.

Quinn sat in his wheelchair, not quite sure what to do with himself. Jack's broad stature suddenly seemed far more intimidating than minutes prior.

"What did you see?"

Quinn furrowed his forehead. "It won't help you or her to know--"

Jack seemed to agree, but he continued to stare at him.

***

He could hear her call out to her sister just as Jeremiah locked the door.

There was a back entrance to the locker rooms through the JV gymnasium, he remembered, so he took off through the boy's side, not really certain what he was planning to do. There were at least 7 decent sized senior boys and he was a small sophomore who no one was about to mistake for being strong—or athletic.

The door was locked on that side, too, but the gymnasium side was closer to the showers. There were a number of voices inside. None belonged to Delaney. All were male.

"Just us here, sweetheart," he heard someone say.

Jeremiah spoke next. "To think I'll get to be the first in both you *and* your sister." There was a shuffling of bodies, then swearing.

"She was aiming for you, asshole. I think she broke my fucking nose."

"She's stronger than she looks," someone laughed. There was the crinkly rip of duct tape. "There. I don't trust her not to scream."

"Hold onto her. I can't wait any longer."

Quinn heard her muffled protests, the squeak of a tennis shoe, then a long groan.

"See? You like that, don't you?"

"My turn, Jeremiah."

"Fuck off, Matt. So *Laney*, your sister told me you're modeling wedding dresses tomorrow." Another exaggerated groan. "Ironic since now you won't be able to wear white at your own wedding."

Inside, he heard the clattering of the showers, which seemed to be getting louder. It was otherwise eerily void of other noises. It was then his arm brushed the fire alarm box. He opened the top of the alarm and gripped the pull handle. *Pull and run*, he thought.

"Oh my God, she's so damn tight," Jeremiah said, his voice strained.

"Not for long."

Quinn stood listening to the horrible noises inside as the boys switched places and became more aggressive. He felt incapable of moving, then it sounded like something cracked against the wall.

"Oh shit," someone said, laughing nervously.

"You couldn't keep her from hitting the wall?"

"Damn, Dude, you're so new to sex you should have training wheels."

"I think she hit the shower handle."

"Great, I get to bang a corpse."

"Well, she won't struggle at least."

Quinn pushed his ear closer to the door.

"I don't think she's breathing, Jeremiah."

"You fucked her to death," someone said, amused.

"Shut up, Matt. I'm serious."

Quinn flinched and pulled the alarm in the process. He froze for a moment before ducking into the boy's bathroom. Just after he did, the lock next door unlatched and a swarm of boys darted out.

Once he heard the outside gymnasium doors slam shut, he quickly moved next door. The girls' showers looked like a mirror image of the boys' side. The showers were all running, to drown out noises, he suspected, paling in comparison to the screeching of the fire alarm. In their hasty exit, the boys had thought to close the curtain for the shower stall she was in—like that would keep anyone from finding her.

He crept forward, trying to fathom that he was about to see a dead body. The fingers of her right hand were visible beneath the shower curtain, limp but a vibrant pink, from struggling, he realized.

He saw her hand retract as he approached, like a hermit crab ducking into its shell.

He slowly pulled the curtain to one side. "Delaney?"

She was just sitting up, soaking wet, her gray track shirt ripped and discarded beside her. She pulled her knees close, folding her naked body in half, not looking up. The duct tape from her mouth was flapping in the stream of water.

Quinn glanced around frantically, finding what appeared to be a hand towel hanging on a nearby rod. He offered it to her, trying not to look at her too much, though he couldn't help but notice the blood streaked across the shower floor, across her thighs. There was blood dripping from her head. Too much blood.

She was taking some deep breaths, trying in vain to keep the hair from her eyes.

The fire alarm stopped. The sound of water now seemed deafening, echoing around the bathroom, sounding like a raging waterfall clapping against rocks. He said her name again, turned off the shower. She squeezed her eyes, wincing.

"The noise?" he asked, quickly running to turn off the other seven shower faucets. Having less sound competing in his brain, it finally occurred to him to remove his shirt and offer it to her, leaving his undershirt.

"Thanks, Quinn."

He pushed aside the shock that she would know his name and knelt beside her. "We need to get you to a hospital."

She didn't respond as she got herself off the white tiled floor, a white knuckle grip on the shower handle. Her legs were wobbly and she blinked quite a bit. She used his shirt as a pseudo towel, holding it up under her armpits. She had nothing to cover her backside as she staggered across the locker room. He tried not to look, but he did. Her skin was red and indented and there was still blood trickling from her wet hair, down her legs.

"You hit your head. I'm not sure you--" he began, once she had reached her locker.

Her eyes focused on him, silently telling him to stop talking. She ruffled through her locker, not aware or not caring that a pool of red water was collecting by her feet, that her back was entirely exposed. She removed her backpack from its hook and dug out what looked to be a different outfit. She bent down and in one fluid motion, mopped up the excess water and blood from her body, then launched the hand towel and his shirt to the hamper. Her track shorts and underwear were nowhere to be found. He thought to retrieve the shirt, then decided he didn't like it much anyway.

Quinn had fantasized about the moment of seeing Delaney with less clothes on--he had found himself searching the internet for her modeling photos. There had been the wedding dresses, but not the smiling, happy bride sort of photos. They had her drowning, they had her strewn across a bed, arms poised over her head, they had her pose in something that looked like a bikini, a lacy sheer train providing little coverage. Most of the others were the intimidating sort of photography, like the model was clinically depressed or otherwise angry, judging the viewer. There had been a few that gave the illusion of nudity, but there was something in her face in those photos--in her huge eyes, that bothered him.

Seeing bits of her naked body wasn't what he imagined. Her skin was taut over her ribs—excessively so. This was not apparent when she was dressed. There was a slightly opaque quality to it; he could see a power grid of faint veins. Her shoulders suddenly looked too bony, frail even, and her shoulder blades jutted out at too sharp of an angle. Without a word, she pulled on her jeans and stood upright. He briskly turned his head away, sorry that he hadn't given her privacy and had been just standing there watching her dress.

He spotted a gray towel hanging inside one of the lockers and pulled it out, mopped up the floor.

She slipped on the navy v-neck tee she had on earlier in Calculus and he thought it was safe to turn around. She looked more like the girl he had tried to strategically place himself near since 7th grade. He silently scolded himself for this bringing him some relief.

As she picked up her backpack and slid it on her shoulder, she made eye contact with him again. She didn't have eye makeup to smear so besides the wet hair and droplets of water on her shirt and very tired eyes, she looked remarkably--normal. She dropped a pair of flip flops to the floor and stepped into them. "I'll check for people in the hall."

He frowned.

"Would be strange to see you coming out of the girls' locker room."

He nodded awkwardly, mouth slightly agape.

She pointed in the direction of his locker and he followed her to the door. She cursed under her breath when she had to unlock the door. The facilities director who was checking on the fire alarm was dismissing it as a false alarm through the walkie talkie. He exited toward the football field when they emerged. To Quinn's surprise, Delaney went directly for his locker.

"Are you OK?" he asked, slowly doing the combination. The director must have spotted the open lock.

She stared down the hallway. Her breathing was hollow as her fingers gingerly touched the place where the shower handle must have hit her head near her right temple.

"Did they—" he stopped short. It was a stupid question. He thought of her ripped clothes, her naked body, the blood. He scowled at himself. He had his hand on the fire alarm for too long. *I should have pulled it sooner.* "I'm sorry. I tried to get in—"

"It's happened before." She shook her head, seemingly to get her mind back on track, blinked several times.

He gasped. "This has happened before?"

"Not *that*. The modeling thing —men try things. Well, they do things."

"You're 15."

"I don't look 15 the way they doll me up." She shrugged, tried to clear her throat. "I should go."

"I'm walking with you. You need to go to the hospital or the police." He thought he sounded pretty bossy for someone who did nothing to help her.

"I'm going to my dad's place. It's close."

"I'll walk you."

She seemed to understand that he wasn't going to be deterred. Or she was simply too tired to say no.

She led him out the back of the school into the student parking lot, which only contained a dozen cars. There were two freshmen waiting to be picked up, but no one else.

"I don't see any of them."

"Cars are gone," she observed, wincing behind her veil of wet hair. She placed her palm up to her temple again, delicately feeling the area around it, closing her eyes. She immediately fell forward toward the pavement and fortunately, he managed to catch her.

"Laney?"

Her head was hanging sideways like a rag doll. He angled her so gravity encouraged her head forward to what appeared to be a more comfortable angle.

She stirred, looking around at her surroundings. When she saw who was holding her upright, she looked mildly startled.

"You probably shouldn't be walking around."

Her body went rigid and she broke away. "I'm fine." She felt her wet hair as she walked, frowning.

He caught up with her easily. She kept slowing her gait unsteadily, then, upon seeing him closing in on her, sped up again. She had the sense to wait at the first main road for the crosswalk lights to blink. "You hit your head, Laney. That could be really serious."

She wrinkled her forehead in concentration, like she was trying to translate a foreign language.

"Will you please have your dad take you?"

She half-nodded.

After walking in hurried silence for another two streets, he cleared his throat, locking his thumbs around the straps of his backpack by his hips. "Your parents are divorced?"

"Yeah. A long time ago."

"Just didn't get along?"

"That's kind of what it came down to."

"That's tough. He'll be there, right?"

She nodded, stopping at the gated entrance to an upscale condominium complex. "I can take it from here."

"I'll see you tomorrow? I can meet you here if you're walking."

"I'm not at school tomorrow. Photo shoot."

"You're still going?"

She shrugged.

"Do you like modeling?"

"No." Her answer was immediate and precise.

He frowned, shuffling his feet awkwardly. "You're really okay?"

She squinted one eye, the glare of the sunset illuminating her face with an orange glow. She gave a slight nod, then moved toward the gate.

***

He described the scene in limited detail--omitting the fact he'd just stood by, practically a fly on the wall, that Delaney may as well have been alone in the locker room.

"There's more." He went on: "She hit her head in the shower--well, they hit her head on accident."

Jack raised his eyebrows.

"It knocked her out. They thought she was dead--that's why they stopped. They ran out, left her there."

Images began forming in Jack's mind, images he tried to force away.

"This happened in the shower?" Julie said, mouth agape. "That's probably why she froze up for showers here—she'd feel so helpless since she couldn't—" She clasped her hand over her mouth. "Oh my God."

"What happened to them?" Jack's voice broke. He swallowed hard. "After they did this to her. What *happened* to them?"

Quinn had a concerned look on his face. "I don't know too much even with social media. I think Jeremiah does something in telecom. Tim took over his family's business. Paul was kicked out of the Army. Something with drugs or pain meds. I don't know for the others."

Jack stared at him, disbelieving.

"They didn't go to prison?" Julie demanded.

"I tried to get her to go to the police, but she insisted she was OK." Quinn's cheeks reddened. "I was a stupid, scared shitless kid," he said quietly then shook his head, lowering his eyes. "She was just a kid, too."

"How old was she?" Julie asked.

"15."

*The same year her mom died,* Jack thought.

"If there was a day I could go back and change, it would be that one."

Jack shook his head conclusively. "You found her in the shower. Then what?"

Begrudgingly, Quinn told him about how they walked out together after she dressed.

"She got up and just *walked home?*"

Quinn decided to also omit the fact that she collapsed in the parking lot. "I was going to try to get her to talk to the police the next day. The more I thought of it, something needed to happen to them—"

Jack thought of Delaney having to endure a police interview, a doctor's exam after what she'd already been through, how her story would be scrutinized.

"—but *then*—well, you know about the accident."

Jack's eyes widened. His body was suddenly less steady than seconds earlier. "You're saying one day she was raped by *seven*--" His voice caught in his throat. "And the *next* day--" His eyes burned with tears. "The next day, she watched her mom die? That's what you're telling me?"

Quinn nodded slowly, as though realizing the weight of this for the first time.

Jack remembered her dad telling him how it took firefighters 50 minutes to get her out of the car; that they said she was conscious during that time. He thought of her scars, how she had revealed them to him with so much resilience. He had most closely examined the ones on her face, paying close attention to the one near her temple. Suddenly all other thoughts fell away. "They hit her head," Jack echoed, his words slow and reflective. "On the right side."

"Yeah." Quinn motioned to the place just behind his own temple directly above the cheekbone.

"She's been having vision problems on that side," Julie said urgently, looking back and forth between them. "Just over the past couple days."

"Could it cause another stroke?" Quinn asked.

"I'll talk to Dr. Schuler," Jack said, steadying himself again. He reset his posture, straightening his back, but he still looked rigid. Angry. "You were *friends?*"

"We didn't know each other very well before that day. I visited her at the hospital after the car accident." Quinn shrugged. "She didn't say much, but she seemed okay with me being around to keep her company." He seemed to find some amusement in that statement.

"I'm glad she had someone around--to be there for her."

Something eased in Quinn's posture. "You know, I used to have a major crush on her." He immediately regretted the statement as he was no physical match for the man standing before him, a half-foot taller than anyone else.

Jack's eyebrows snapped upward. "I doubt you were the only one."

"The thing is--in my mind, I would have done anything for her, be her knight in shining armor or whatever. When it came down to it, I didn't do anything to help her that day." He let a few moments of quiet pass and he thought of how she had literally picked herself up that day in the locker room, blood trails streaming down her face, her legs. "She didn't have *anyone*."

"You've helped her here," Julie offered. "Your arrival seemed to spark something in her."

Jack looked back and forth between them. "When were you admitted?"

"The weekend Tabitha got married," Julie replied.

Jack was quiet, then nodded in agreement. "The timing--" his face contorted into conflicted thought. "Dr. Schuler knew you back then," he said, answering an unspoken question.

"He pulled some strings, I guess," Quinn said. "A 'synchronicity' is what he called it. 'A meaningful coincidence,' I had to look it up—" he added. "And while I appreciate you saying that, Julie, Laney's the one helping me. Not the other way around."

"I can't believe what she went through," Julie remarked, then caught Jack's eye. "Did you know any of that, besides the accident?"

He briefly closed his eyes and shook his head. He couldn't manage a verbal response.

"It doesn't surprise me she didn't tell you," Quinn said.

Jack's heart lurched.

"Up until a couple of days ago, I didn't even think she remembered it," Quinn said. "She told me things were very foggy after she blacked out in the parking lot leaving school." He had to ignore their disbelieving glares. "It was all surreal, like a bad dream. A few days after the accident, it all came back."

"Did she think no one would believe her?" Julie asked no one in particular. "Why did she just let them--" She stopped short when she saw the wide-eyed expression on Jack's face. It wasn't meant for her, she assumed.

Quinn grimaced, visibly constructing what he was about to say. "I asked her about that."

"Tell me it wasn't because of Caprice," Julie pleaded.

"One main reason was Caprice. She didn't want Caprice having to think of her first boyfriend that way. This is a guy she thought she loved, he was her first--"

"Well he was Laney's first, too--" Julie began, then clasped her hand to her mouth.

This fact struck deep within Jack's chest. He thought of how she would catch his gaze when they were making love, search his eyes for something, smiling lightly when she found what she was looking for.

"The other reason--" Quinn began, clearing his throat. "Delaney had a best friend when she was young, up until middle school. Timothy Sellers."

*Timothy Something,* Jack thought solidly.

"Shy kid. His house burned down when he was a baby, his mom didn't make it out, although I think she may have started it. Anyway, he had these big scars from it--on his arms, legs, going up his neck. Anyway, he and Laney struck up a friendship. Kids teased the pair of them--called them 'Beauty and the Beast'."

Jack silently replayed the conversation he had with Allie in the hallway the day before, about Delaney's "visitor," how she had become physically ill after he left.

"Because he was a big, strong kid, the 'cool kids' eventually accepted him. He became an offensive lineman for the Varsity team in 9th grade and he and Laney grew apart." He paused. "That day in the locker room, Jeremiah had one of the boys--*restrain* her."

It was clear from their faces, their widening eyes that they were following along.

"He didn't actually *do* anything--not like--"

"Oh he did plenty," Julie stammered, tears streaming down her cheeks.

"She recognized his arms."

A small squeak emerged from Julie's mouth.

"That gets me. He was her best friend--" Quinn shook his head, his voice low. "And in the middle of everything, she recognized his arms around her."

Jack narrowed his eyes, questioningly.

"When I found her in the locker room, she knew what happened. I didn't know this about Timothy, but I knew then she wasn't going to turn them in. She wasn't even considering it."

"She wasn't—" Jack began, then stopped, shaking his head. "She was going to protect him," Jack concluded.

"Timothy had a rough childhood. His mom died, his dad was gone all the time, drank, beat him up sometimes. Her response two days ago when I asked? 'Turning him in would have destroyed any chance he had for a good life'."

Julie threw out her arms. "I'm sorry, she was protecting the guy that held her down--"

Jack stopped pacing abruptly. "Timothy came to see her--the day of the stroke."

Quinn stared silently, then swallowed hard. "*That's* why he called me."

It was a random Thursday when Holly, the new receptionist sent him a notification that 'Timothy Sellers called, looking for contact info for Dulaney Road.' Good business practice was to return calls so he did. It had stung a bit to tell him that he hadn't had contact with Delaney for years, but had speculated about where she worked. At the time, Quinn didn't know Timothy had been in the locker room at all so he had been friendly enough and they had carried on a fifteen minute conversation. Quinn sighed. "He's on Step 8. Seeking forgiveness."

Julie shook her head. "He still became a Goddamn alcoholic?"

"Like his father before him."

*He even kissed her goodbye.* Jack's throat constricted. "She forgave him."

"*What?*" Julie demanded. "How do you know?"

Jack thought of Allie's question about stress, how she described Delaney hyperventilating in the bathroom. He pictured her in the cafeteria, dazed, how tired she looked when he was doing an impromptu neurological exam. How she even joked with him. *We get it. You're a doctor.*

Allie's voice echoed in his head: *Could stress cause a stroke?* He found himself answering her question aloud. "It was a weaker blood vessel. A big spike in her blood pressure probably could have caused--" He fell silent. *She even joked with him.* Jack shook his head sharply. "Dammit, D."

Quinn propelled himself toward the exit. He stopped short, turning to Jack, whose hands were subconsciously clenched into fists, his eyes glazed, staring off toward the water wall. "Is there any truth to what Caprice said? That you didn't want to marry Laney?"

Jack could imagine that wasn't all she said, given her tendency to editorialize. Delaney's words rang particularly true. "'*Just because someone says something doesn't make it true.*' And no. *Zero* truth to that."

"She said once she never saw herself being in a relationship, getting married, any of that. That could have been a brush-off to me in hindsight, but she seemed—resolved about it." He exhaled. "I still hoped she would end up with someone who deserved her."

Jack's face was hard, his eyes bloodshot and brimmed with tears.

"It seems she did after all." He paused to take a breath, suppress something internally, "I don't know you very well, Jack, but I suspect that *you're* the type of guy that would have broken down that door to get to her."

With that, he moved for the exit. Julie watched him go down the hallway, nodding slightly to him.

Jack dropped his chin to his chest, his eyes closed, breathing. Julie stood behind him saying nothing in the quiet courtyard, the sky split between what promised to be a glorious sunset to the west or a terrible storm brewing to the east. The courtyard lights came on, giving the odds to stormy weather, along with the spotlights illuminating the water wall.

When he opened his eyes, his voice was low, calm. "*What else did Caprice say to her?*"

# 21

# words will never

Julie reluctantly shared the details--how Caprice seemed supportive and caring at first. She was enthusiastic to take her to the coffee bar. As soon as Julie saw Delaney's face when they returned to go in the courtyard, she knew things had changed. Caprice talked endlessly through the halls--about herself mainly. Delaney had looked like a prisoner, trapped in that wheelchair.

When Julie went to the courtyard to get Quinn, Caprice had been touching Delaney's face, talking about the droop of the right side. She seemed pleased when she told her she looked less like their mom since the stroke, but not to worry, she was still pretty on the left. She had grasped at her right cheek and tried pulling it upward, as if it were made of modeling clay.

She told her she guessed now Delaney would have to see what life was like for "everybody else," but offered to help her figure out makeup to make the droop look less obvious. She said she heard Jack had stuck around, that she guessed it was out of sympathy and guilt, that it doesn't make any sense if he didn't want to marry her before. "Big of him, but kind of seems like a waste of his time. If he didn't love you before, I'm sorry, but this--" she had motioned to Delaney's face, eyeing her sitting in the wheelchair, "isn't going to help."

Terrence had come up beside Julie at that point and took off jogging toward Delaney, who was desperately trying to unlock her wheelchair brakes.

"She wasn't crying," Julie said, "but the look on her face? Jack, it was heartbreaking. I was stunned. I'm not used to seeing her like that. She's so—"

"Resilient?"

She nodded, regretfully. "Terrence was trying to help her. She loves him, but she was so hurt and frustrated she actually shouted at him."

"She--shouted?"

"Yeah. I was shocked since she hasn't been able to project her voice. And it wasn't really at *him*."

"What did she say?"

Julie lowered her voice and bellowed as best she could in whisper form: "'I can do it.' Terrence rolled with it and said something about just wanting to get them both away from the crazy lady."

Jack shook his head. "I don't see how the two of them share any amount of DNA."

"They're just half-sisters, right? The demon spawn part must have come from the other side."

Jack exhaled, his breathing staggered. "I want to help her, but I don't know how."

"I think we can both agree that Laney doesn't typically ask for help."

Jack raised his eyebrows in agreement.

"*Except* when she really needs it. She speaks up."

Jack remembered when her dad died. A heart attack at a conference. She had received a call from his business partner, who had the emotional warmth of an electric stapler.

Jack had tried to be there with her around the clock. He thought that's what she needed. He had taken himself off the surgery schedule and was readily available, practically her shadow.

As kindly as possible, she had approached him and told him she needed to spend the day on her own. She had clearly not slept, despite lying in bed all night—since 8pm when he insisted she 'try to get some sleep.' It was a busy surgical day so the other anesthesiologists were more than happy to have him come in and promptly sent him to cover maternity. He felt tremendous guilt leaving for the hospital. He had kissed her and watched her go to the backyard with her coffee to sit on the porch swing.

He didn't get home until close to 11. The house was quiet and he didn't want to disturb her, wherever she was. He went to the bedroom and stretched out on the bed. The door creaked open soon after. It was clear she had been crying for the better part of the day, her eyes practically swollen closed, but she seemed more at peace, her body was more relaxed. She crawled in beside him, snuggled in with him and slept for a solid 12 hours.

"Did you know it was her idea for hypnosis?" Julie asked.

"That doesn't seem like her." She was far too private a person.

"But she knew it would help her. TR was doing relaxation with her, but it wasn't working very well. She was too tensed up. She knew she had a block in her mind and that was the way to break through it."

He thought of how she asked to help her with shower tasks, shutting down when anyone else attempted them after that initial fall with Grant. He imagined the scene Quinn had just described, but he pushed it from his mind again. He could not bear the thought of what had happened to her, knowing how her attackers were still free, how years later, she was still dealing with the consequences, how she had dealt with it on her own all this time.

Another image came to mind--He had just gotten home from a long shift not long after they started dating. She had been sleeping so he went to take a shower. The glass door had been overtaken by steam when she appeared in the bathroom doorway wearing just his blue Cubs shirt and a pair of hipster panties. She had wordlessly removed her clothes and joined him.

"Well if it isn't my favorite consonant," he had said, letting the water slick back his hair.

She had been intentional as she moved into the stream of water with him, kissing him, running her hands slowly, gently across his chest, his arms. She seemed to be leading him, showing him how she wanted him to touch her.

"She asks for what she needs," Julie said softly, as though through telepathic narration. "In her own way."

Jack sat at the edge of the bench, burying his face in his hands. He felt tremendous anger, but suddenly, an incredible sense of relief poured over him. *She asks for what she needs.* She had found a way through the crippling fear and had guided him through what she needed. When she woke and couldn't remember their relationship, whatever peace she had found in that late-night shower with him had disappeared. She had to cope with it all over again.

*She asks for what she needs.*

He leaned over his knees and began to cry.

*Jack Mathison does not cry,* Julie thought, watching him in helpless horror. She wondered if she should hug him, or pat his back, or something else noncommittal. Fortunately his light sobs lasted a brief few moments. It stopped as suddenly as it had started and he stood, rubbing his face roughly as he beelined for the door. "What is it?" she practically shouted, running to catch up.

His face was distraught, but it was resolute with an undefined excitement behind his eyes.

"Jack, what?"

"She needs me."

He pretended he didn't see Julie roll her eyes and throw her arms out like an annoyed teenager, her version of: *Well, duuuuuuuh.*

He turned without a word, rounding the corner to Delaney's room, but found it empty. The wind outside was picking up, the tree tapping loudly against the window. Her bedside lamp was on, illuminating his duffel bag stored next to the window. *She asks for what she needs. In her own way.*

"Gym," Jeffrey said from the nurse's station, dangling the desk phone by his ear.

In the early evening, the gym was deserted, mostly therapists sitting along the wall in the back busily tapping away at keyboards to complete their documentation for the day. Terrence was standing alongside the parallel bars looking like a football coach, wearing a headset and padded microphone. Beside him was a very tall, lean brunette with her back to them. She had her hair pulled back in a ponytail and she wore a giant pair of black goggles that wrapped around her ears.

Julie glanced down at the neoprene sleeve around her right knee.

"She requested it," Terrence explained, making sure his microphone was muted. "She said she has a fear of her knee buckling. It's a *'psychological barrier.'*"

"She said that?"

"Every syllable. God I missed that voice."

"What are the goggles?"

"Virtual reality. Dr. Schuler has them on loan from Neuro." He stopped to watch her adjust her balance. "We're getting to pull a lot of strings these days, have you noticed?" He handed Julie a tablet, which looked as though it were a live feed of a beach. The horizon adjusted based on if Delaney was looking up or down. She seemed to be focused on the sand immediately before her, the sky toward the top of the screen. "Not a bad place to be."

It was then Jack noticed she wasn't wearing shoes. He nudged Julie and pointed out the fact that her right foot was firmly placed on the platform as she walked and she was focused on letting every inch of skin settle into the wood platform with each step.

Julie was about to squeal with delight, but both men waved her off. She and Jack backed away to watch from the treatment table behind them, each perched on the edge of their seat. Julie had started to gnaw at her nails, quietly chanting encouragement.

Delaney had a determined look on her face, focusing on placing one foot in front of the other. She reached the end, confirming it by sliding her toes along the beveled edge. She slowly managed the pivot to turn around, and continued toward the other side.

"You're looking good, girl. Need a rest break?"

She shook her head.

"How about trying the EVA walker with a gait belt," Julie suggested, unable to stand on the sidelines. "We can do a stock AFO to stabilize Delaney's knee a little better."

"Delaney's knee feels OK as it is."

Everyone snapped to attention, including a few of the therapists in the back of the gym, recognizing the familiar voice.

Julie clasped her hand to her mouth.

"But I like the idea of the EVA," Delaney added. "Can't exactly take parallel bars with me."

"You can hear us?"

"Not soundproof, guys."

Nervous, disbelieving laughter echoed in the gym.

"Alright then. You heard the Boss. Jack, you spot your girl there, I'll get the EVA. Julie, continue standing there with that dumbstruck look on your face."

Jack quickly moved to the end of the bars.

Delaney stopped once she felt the edge with her toes. She waited, looking straight ahead. "Where *am I*?"

"The gym?" Julie said, slightly panicked.

Delaney's chin rotated toward her with a jolt. "I meant in the goggles."

Julie patted her chest. "Thank God. I was going to say--uh--" She looked at the screen. "Well it looks like Hawaii. Hey Terrence, what places do they have in here?"

"All over the world. It's pretty sweet."

"Where's Laney?"

"Oh. Our girl is in *Fiji*."

Delaney rolled her shoulders, her face at ease. "Fiji."

Terrence rolled the EVA toward them. "Laney, what do you think about keeping the goggles on for the EVA?"

"Well given my distractibility and current visual deficiencies on the right side, I think it's probably a good idea."

"OK, now you're just showing off," Terrence remarked, kneeling to adjust the height.

"Good beach weather today?" Jack asked softly, leaning close to her ear.

She gave him a wide, lopsided smile, her cheeks tight. "Hi Jack."

Terrence clapped his hands as he rounded to the parallel bars opening. "Beast mode activated. I love it. Laney, step forward then feel for the arm rests. Wow, I forgot how tall you are." He adjusted the height again. "Better. OK, you know how these work. Just focus on your beach and your steps."

Several of the therapists had collected at the back of the gym to watch her, silently motioning to anyone just coming into the gym to be quiet. Julie walked alongside her, laughing under her breath, whispering to someone Delaney couldn't see.

"Please tell me there are lots of people staring at me right now."

Some excited chuckles confirmed her suspicions.

"Just a dozen or so," Terrence replied. "And here comes some nurses."

The nurses were far less quiet. Jeffrey actually let out a woot-woot.

"Awesome. Thanks for the support, Jeff."

There were a few gasps.

"Yes, y'all, I'm talking now."

Dr. Schuler appeared then, his eyes as wide and bright as a child on Christmas morning. "OK, *this* is one of my favorite moments of all time."

She smiled. "Ah, my swim coach."

"Say *what?*" Terrence asked.

"Backup swim coach," Dr. Schuler corrected. "OK, let's hear it. I'm sure you've saved up choice words to say to me," he challenged, though there were whispers about the tears in his eyes.

"Can I take these goggles off now? I feel a little ridiculous."

Terrence handed off the gait belt to Julie, then helped Delaney remove the goggles.

Her smile broadened upon seeing Dr. Schuler, her face lined with the red outline of the goggles, her eyes squinting in the bright lights. "#1, the food here has *way* too much salt. Way too much. No wonder we spend a small fortune on compression stockings for patients. #2, you keep it too damn cold in this gym. I know it's you who adjusts the thermostat so don't even deny it. Not all of us have a football player build like yourself. #3?" Her face softened. "You need to take a day off." Her voice caught a bit at the end. There was more to what she was going to say, it was clear in her eyes, but Dr. Schuler had given her a very purposeful look.

"Not while you're a patient." He swallowed hard. "I will claim a hug later, but can you spare a high-five?" He strategically held up his left hand.

She stretched out her hand fully and clapped their palms together, grinning. She immediately grabbed for the hand grip of the walker to steady herself.

"You are something amazing, Kiddo." He leaned over the arm rests and kissed her forehead. Turning toward the crowd, he threw his arms out to his sides, his eyes overflowing with tears. "Why *yes*, I do have a favorite. I'll just say it." He waved his hand toward the spectating therapists with a grin as he walked through the back of the department.

She took the turn into the hallway, more apprehensive about her movements.

"You're doing great," Jack said, encouragingly.

"Good because I need to sit," she winced. She did not appear too thrilled with the idea.

"What's going on?"

Julie scanned her legs. "Right leg is spasming?"

Delaney muttered some garbled expletives under her breath, squeezing her eyes shut.

"That leg's probably finally waking up," Julie guessed, tightening her grip on the gait belt, just in case.

"Alright, that's good for today," Terrence said, jogging to the corridor housing some spare transport chairs.

Delaney beat at the arm rest lightly with her fist then reluctantly applied more weight on the right leg. She continued forward.

Terrence abandoned the transport chair next to a meal cart.

"20 feet," Jack whispered.

She nodded sharply, trying to unclench her jaw. "Is this the EVA with the wide base that won't fit through doorways?"

"It is."

She nodded, problem-solving. There was a collection of staff observing from the nurse's station who she tried to ignore. A speech patient down the hallway was being taught voice projection by singing *Hey Jude*. The floor had been waxed recently and sharply reflected the overhead fluorescent lights into her eyes. A dinner cart was just arriving, rumbling and clattering behind her. Someone had ordered meatloaf, potatoes, broccoli...another plate must have been an Italian dish. Quinn had said the lasagna was surprisingly good.

*Focus.*

Delaney closed her eyes, chin to her chest. She attempted to block out all her senses except for what she needed in that moment. She felt Julie's death grip on the gait belt intensify, sensed the close proximity of Jack on her right side, recognized the secure placement of her bare feet solid on the linoleum floors. She fought off disgust and added a task item to wash her feet as soon as possible.

"When I get to the doorway, will you dance me in?" She took a shallow breath. "I'm sorry that sounds like a demand through gritted teeth."

"Oh sure, I can do that," Julie said pleasantly.

"Pretty sure she's talking to Jack."

"Oh. Right. That makes sense."

"*Almost* there--let's stop here so we can slide out the walker," Terrence directed.

Delaney was still visibly in pain as they moved the EVA away and Jack stepped in. She placed one hand on each of his biceps, breathing deeply, preparing herself for the rest of the journey.

"Junior high dance," he cued, sliding her left hand up to his neck while keeping hold of her waist.

"I can serenade--a little Al Green perhaps?" Terrence offered. "Hell, I'll even do some Buble."

"I've got this, Terrence," Jack said, kindly.

"*Yeah* you do," Terrence replied without skipping a beat, his smile wide.

Even with her eyes closed, she sensed the darker lighting in her room as they swayed inside. It sounded like rain was starting to slap against the window. She focused her thoughts on relaxing her tense muscles, resting her forehead gently on his shoulder so she could see her feet. The hospital linoleum made to look like hardwood was far different than the sand in the VR goggles and she was only slightly less disgusted by the cleanliness of the floors in her room, but it felt like less of a priority now that Jack's dark blue cross trainers were standing opposite her bare feet.

"You smell like coconut," she whispered.

He smiled audibly, resting his cheek against the side of her head.

"Hey Jack, let me take over there," Jeff said, bringing in a rush of hallway air. "You're needed at the nurse's station."

Delaney felt her right hand tighten involuntarily, pausing their swaying motion.

Jeff raised his eyebrows apologetically at Jack, as though to say: *Yes, really.*

Jack distanced himself a bit physically. "I'll be right back, I promise."

She nodded, smiled politely to Jeff.

"Laney, my sweet," Jeff said, arms outstretched. "You know, I'll have some serious bragging rights for getting to be the first nurse to talk to you. Like meeting a celebrity."

"No dipping," Jack warned as he allowed Jeff to slide into position.

"How about a little waltz? A little mambo?" Jeff suggested.

"How about a little sitting?"

"A little anticlimactic--much like a *true* celebrity encounter."

Jack thought he heard her laugh, a scoff really, and he could have sworn she called Jeff an ass.

# 22
# almost

D
r. Schuler was typically a mountain of calm, but there was an aura of anxiety even as he leaned, seemingly striking a casual pose, against the nurse's station counter. As he turned to Jack, his head tilted toward Delaney's room, his eyes exhausted behind his glasses. "I was going to come over here to give Laney a pass for tonight, try out going home."

Jack stopped in his tracks. Home passes were typically only given to ambulatory, perhaps supervision level patients.

"I'm assuming that would be with you?" A half-joke.

He nodded slowly.

"Thought you both could use a night away from here."

Jack vaguely remembered meeting the protective father of one of the girls he dated in high school, who made a point of having the more intimidating portion of his gun collection out when he came by to pick her up. Dr. Schuler had a naturally level demeanor, but there was the same desperate worry in his eyes, perhaps a step beyond that.

"I wish that's what I was doing."

"Hey, Dr. S., quite a day!" Jenna exclaimed, having just come in early for her night shift. "I'm sorry I missed it."

Dr. Schuler nodded, smiling in a disconcerting, nondescript way. He motioned to the case management room behind the nurse's station.

Once there, he discreetly asked the social worker to step out. She seemed to understand without further explanation.

The physiatrist took a breath, reached up and touched his head near his ear—where Quinn had indicated Delaney had hit her head in the locker room shower, the place he himself was going to discuss with Dr. Schuler.

Jack stared at him.

"Her vision on the right side has been getting worse. Therapy, nursing, even Laney herself expressed some concern about it. I had her go for a scan earlier this afternoon." His voice was low and gentle. "There is an unruptured aneurysm--"

Jack exhaled. With it, a series of expletives exploded from his mouth. He paced, running his fingers roughly through his hair. He'd been the Anesthesiologist for brain aneurysm clipping surgeries, which was inevitably what they would recommend. Of the five surgeries, one of the patients died.

Samantha.

He thought of the tiny pink bundle in the newborn nursery that she could hardly wait to hold. He thought of how he had gone to the nursery while the rest of the family members grieved with the news and placed his hand on the baby's back, felt her breathing, and told her how her mother had loved her so very much, how her name was the last thing she would ever say: *Eve.*

"They couldn't see this on previous scans?"

"It was there, but it was small." His voice was a distant buzz in the back of Jack's ears. Dr. Schuler finished his explanation and waited.

"Hasn't she been through enough?" Jack demanded. "It's not--you, Dr. S— but goddamn it, hasn't she been through *enough?*"

"I get it. I'm going to have a hell of a time explaining the broken computer monitor in my office." Dr. Schuler sighed. "I think we're close enough for you to call me Martin."

"Dammit," Jack growled, then glanced up. "*Martin.*"

"I was thinking of blaming the Russians. For the computer. That seems like the thing to do now."

Jack grabbed the back of his neck, stretched. "Or say it contained incriminating information on the Clintons."

"It was *suicided*," Dr. Schuler said, widening his eyes.

He shook his head. "She has to have the surgery, Jack."

He decided not to elaborate that the Neurologist who reviewed the scan called him directly--he said it was some sort of miracle the blood vessel hadn't burst yet. Dr. Schuler put a hand on Jack's back. "I wanted to give you a chance to get some of this out and then we need to go talk to your girl." He offered him a stapler to throw, then thought better of it and presented him with a spongy unicorn stress reliever instead. "Do we have fourth graders working here?" He examined the creature and placed it back on the desk.

Jack shook his head. "You're recommending the clipping."

"Yes. Coiling is less invasive, but it's not reliable."

The surgeon would cut Delaney's skull in a broad, half circle shape. The surgical suite would look like a welding shop with the tools required. He could see the thick seam that would be left behind, secured with narrowly spaced staples.

"There has been better success recently by having the patient awake during the clipping. She'd be able to talk and wiggle her toes and they would know if there was an issue. They can make sure they're not causing any inadvertent problems and make corrections right then."

Jack remembered when Delaney had become squeamish when he talked about c-sections. "*To be awake and know they're cutting into your body?*" She had shuddered--and he had continued sharing details until she covered his mouth with the entirety of her palm.

"*I suppose I'd feel okay if you were there,*" she had said a few minutes later, when she had returned to reading, her head on his chest, and he had returned to shopping for camping supplies on his laptop. "*You're calm in those situations. You'd make me calm.*"

She had casually moved on and pointed to the laptop screen. "*I like the blue one. You look amazing in blue. Blue is lucky you were born to wear it.*"

It was a sleeping bag.

"Being awake during the clipping makes sense," Jack said, his voice collaborative if not a bit flat. "Which surgeon?"

"Isaac."

Jack nodded. "No resident. I understand this is a teaching hospital, but--"

"No resident. I agree. Anesthesiologist?"

"Freeman or Shaw." He tried to picture the department whiteboard schedule. "One should be on call."

"OK," Dr. Schuler concluded, starting for the door.

When they returned to her room, Delaney and Jeff were sitting together discussing Jeff's love life. She looked a little amused, more so repulsed by the fact that he'd managed a breakfast date and a dinner date on the same day he worked a 12-hour shift--and that both had ended "successfully," as he put it.

Jeff turned to the new arrivals, but when it was obvious he wasn't going to get commended on his displayed attempt at masculinity, he took his cue and left.

Delaney read their faces immediately, her eyes widening a bit and she waited for Dr. Schuler to speak first.

He explained the situation carefully, but briefly, presented the two options of surgery--one, invasive, but effective, the second, non-invasive, as far as a procedure in the brain goes, but less effective. He recommended the first and she nodded in agreement.

"There's been recent research to suggest that patients who are awake--" He wavered a bit, seeing the fear flash across her eyes. "Have better outcomes."

Jack swallowed reflexively. He hoped no one heard, but Delaney immediately looked up at him. "Nicely done, Dr. S. You've spooked the Anesthesiologist."

Dr. Schuler glanced over his shoulder at Jack.

"It makes sense," she said, calmly, though her hands were starting to tremble. Her choice of words made Jack wonder if somehow she had heard their discussion.

"You'd be asleep for the craniotomy and you'd be sedated but conscious for the clipping," Dr. Schuler said.

She looked at Dr. Schuler, then over to Jack. "How long is the surgery?"

"3-5 hours," Jack replied.

"The last thing I ate was around 11." She furrowed her eyebrows.

"It should be fine," Dr. Schuler replied.

"Turkey burger has really gone downhill here. Some sort of soy filler, I think. I only ate a bite or two." She swallowed, then whispered: "I'm *really* hungry."

Neither man spoke.

She gave a regretful smile.

"It's going to be okay," Dr. Schuler said.

"I know—but I am. *Really* hungry."

"I'll get you something really good for breakfast," Jack offered, putting his shoulders back to look more confident.

"Pancakes," she said so forcefully it was almost comical. She waited for their faces to turn a little less serious. When they didn't, she dropped her chin to her chest, closed her eyes, and breathed. When she looked up again, her brilliantly blue eyes were filled with tears. "I'd make a goofy face at the two of you to ease the tension, but with the droop it'll just look sort of sad and creepy."

Her chest heaved with a giant gulp of air. "Papa Schuler—"

"I love you, kiddo," he interrupted, his face blotchy and eyes bloodshot. "I'm saying that because I should have before, not because—" his voice broke.

"I love you, too," she said softly.

He furrowed his brow. "I'll be there for your surgery, but am I also invited for pancakes?"

She gave a small tilt of her head. He stepped forward, kissed her head, then turned away quickly, saying something about lighting a fire under Neurosurgery's asses.

Delaney suddenly looked incredibly small sitting on the hospital bed. Her fingers reached to touch her right temple, as though trying to feel the ballooned, damaged blood vessel. Jack carefully sat beside her, watching her. She seemed to think better of prodding around too much.

"Where?" she whispered, her voice raspy. "Where will they cut?"

He took her hand, gently guided her index finger from just behind her ear up and around to just where her skull rounded and continued forward toward her hairline.

Her breathing intensified, her chest rising and falling heavily as she stared forward, focused on the JoJo Moyes book on the tray table of the recliner. He had been reading it to her, the third book since she'd been hospitalized. She thought of how he looked in the light cast from the little lamp on her bedside table each night, how the bulb illuminated his face in a soft, orange glow. She thought of how when he started reading it, he had come out with a truly convincing accent. She imagined her eyes had widened in surprise and she remembered wanting so desperately to laugh. *She's British*, he had explained, and had gone immediately back to reading aloud.

She knew his expression then without remembering she'd seen it before—a small half smile—was both hopeful and tremendously sad at the same time. She knew even the playfulness he intended was causing him pain. She knew he had been crying recently, his eyes set within swollen lids. She knew that the thought had occurred to him that all he was doing for her might turn out to be for nothing. She could also see the resolve, that he knew he needed to do it anyway.

"Jack," she said quietly--and before she could tell him, before she could say that she didn't need to remember everything to know that she loved him, he had turned her face gently with his hands, his strong, capable hands, and kissed her.

# 23
# solitude

The limitations of a three-pack of crayons was becoming too much. Caprice sighed, slouching back in her chair the way only four year olds can, her puffy parka that hung on her chair crunching under her neck. She stared up at the ceiling, at a half-deflated balloon that no one had bothered to retrieve.

"Here he is," her mother, Edie, announced, standing and straightening her outfit.

Caprice didn't stand, but she knew to sit up straight and she resisted the urge to rest her elbows on the table. She watched as her mother, a tall woman with thin features, stepped toward the bald, stocky man with dents in his face and half rim glasses that made him look like he worked for the FBI in the 60s. He took in the sight of her mother with possessive interest. His hand rested lower on her back than any other adult that she'd seen embrace her. His eyes showed disappointment simultaneously with attraction. Her mom seemed to be coaxing him toward the table. When he saw Caprice, she felt a surge of excitement, as a four year old should when she sees her father. He sat across from her, his face softening a bit.

"You're getting big. Are you six, seven now?"

She giggled. "I'm four, silly." It didn't occur to her that he wasn't joking, that he really couldn't distinguish between a four year old and a seven year old.

"Oh God, she has my teeth," he grumbled.

"*Alec*," Edie whispered.

"Oh. Well that's what braces are for," he said lightly.

Caprice didn't know what braces were, but interpreted his change of speech pattern as being positive.

"I hear you have a baby sister now. How's that working out?"

"She's sweet," Caprice said affectionately. "She doesn't cry much."

He nodded, glanced over to Edie. His eyes scanned over her with the same level of possession as when he walked in. "You look decent for having just had a baby, Edie."

"Mommy feeds the baby from her boobs," Caprice reported.

Alec rolled his eyes. "I probably wouldn't even recognize them."

"No one's asking you to identify them, Alec," she said through gritted teeth. "You're here for your daughter."

"I told you before, Edie, I'm no good with children."

"You work with them."

"*No*. I represent models and actors." He scoffed, reaching a tailored sleeve across the table. "Why do they include a yellow crayon?"

"Right?" Caprice said dramatically. "I don't always *need* to draw a sun."

Alec chuckled. "What's good to eat here, kid?"

"Mac and cheese."

His disgust returned. "No wonder kids are obese these days."

"What's 'obese'?"

"Don't worry about it," Edie replied. "Do you want fruit with yours?"

"French fries!" Caprice declared.

Alec scribbled in the restaurant mascot's Napoleon-like hat, rolling his eyes.

"Will I get to see you more now?" Caprice asked.

"Well—my job keeps me busy."

"What's your job? My friend Cora's daddy is a firefighter."

"Good for him." He proceeded to try to explain what a modeling agent does. When he drew correlation with her mother, he seemed to get uncomfortable.

"You knew Mommy when she was little?"

He glanced across the table, his eyes scanning Edie again. "We met when she was a little older. Not like your age."

With his eyes upon her, Edie's cheeks reddened seemingly in spite of herself.

"And you fell in love?"

Alec frowned, pleased when the server came to take their order. Caprice ordered her mac and cheese with certainty and asked for a fruit punch to accompany it. Alec ordered a double cheeseburger, justifying that he hadn't eaten all day. When it came Edie's turn, she seemed suddenly self-conscious. She ordered a salad loaded with vegetables and a vinaigrette dressing on the side. Alec's face was pleased as he handed over his menu.

"So Mommy used to work for you?"

"I represented her. As I explained, agents help models be famous."

"Mommy was famous?"

His expression turned stern.

Caprice was thoughtful for a moment. "You thought she was pretty."

"Very much so."

"So you fell in love."

"Edie was only--what? Sixteen when you signed with me?"

"Thirteen."

He shrugged, dismissively.

"How old are *you*?"

Alec stared at his daughter. "Age isn't everything."

"Mommy is 22. I'm almost 5."

"Which means she was--" He stopped short, the math not quite resulting in the answer he would have preferred to make his point. "She looked older than her age."

"After I was born, she stopped being a model."

"Yeah." He thought longingly of an alternative universe where Edie had become the world-famous model everyone said she could be--with him as her agent. "She *chose* to be your mom instead."

Caprice failed to pick up on the resentfulness in his words or the glare of his eye. She twirled a small crayon in her fingers. "Laney could be a model. She's really cute. Everyone thinks so."

"Is that right? Laney's your sister?"

"Show him her picture, Mommy."

Edie pulled out her wallet, slid out a couple of photos. One was the pair of girls giggling on the carpet. The other was a family photo she hesitated to let him see.

"I see the resemblance," he said, shuffling between the two photos. "What's his name?"

"Thomas."

He seemed to favor the one of the girls, his thumb sliding over Delaney's face. Then, with an inquisitive jump of his eyebrow: "Have you thought of modeling her?"

"No. Only if she wanted to. When she's older, obvioulsy."

"She would do better the younger you start her." He looked closer at the photo of the two girls. "Not to insult myself, but you took a dip in a better gene pool the second time around, Edie."

Edie glanced across at Caprice, her mind lost in thought. It took her entirely off-guard when he continued, this time sweetening his tone and speaking with skillful determination directly toward Caprice.

"What do you think, Caprice? To have your baby sister as a model? We'd get to see each other *a lot* more often," he offered, leaning conspiratorially across the table.

***

*Thirteen years later...*

Jeremiah returned to Caprice's bedroom, zipping his pants and belching. He smirked when he saw that she was still strewn naked across her bed, her position intentional and meant to be seductive.

"You look like you're ready for another round," he remarked. "You'll have to give me a few minutes." He ran his fingers along her desk, his eyes scanning the tiled photo prints on her wall as he approached the bed. Her room was an array of colors, photo collages, and band posters. She had been trying to remove evidence of her childhood—no stuffed animals or figurines, nothing that wasn't current, age-appropriate and otherwise socially acceptable. He picked up a photo album and dropped to the mattress beside her.

Caprice wrapped herself around his side.

"Why don't you clean yourself a little. I don't want to be wearing myself."

She pulled a blanket over her body and searched for tissues or a towel.

"Is this your *dad?*"

Caprice glanced over the top of the album. "Yes," she said automatically, then retracted. "Well, step dad."

"Laney's dad."

She decided in that moment there wouldn't be 'another round' that night. She found an oversized t-shirt and pulled it over her head, relieved to have something to cover her body.

"They're divorced?"

"Yeah. He and my mom got divorced when I was 10."

"Do you have a picture of *your* dad?"

"Somewhere, yes."

"Did he die or something?"

"No. They were never married." She pulled on a fresh pair of underwear and sat on the edge of the bed. "He's there." She pointed to the photo that had been taken at a fashion show a couple years earlier. He had one arm wrapped solidly around Laney's torso, one far less enthusiastic arm around her own shoulder. The background was a runway designed to look like a darkened forest. She remembered how the outfits had started off looking more whimsical--Laney had started the show looking like a fairy ballerina, spiraling onto the stage on her tiptoes. She had dabbled in a wide range of things to increase her attractiveness as a model, including ballet, drama, and for a time, hip hop.

Throughout the show, things had turned dark and Laney had ended the show in a high collared bustier gown, her hair wildly teased, golden butterfly clips holding it back from her face, her youthfulness contoured away, her blue eyes set in intense, dark shadows. In the photo, Laney wasn't smiling, her dark lips pressed together, her eyes focused, owning the camera.

"Is this your *sister?*"

She nodded. "They did this dark fairies theme, that's why her makeup is like that." Caprice glanced to the opposite page where Laney was hugging her neck enthusiastically. Her face was clean and makeup free and pulled into an uninhibitedly wide smile. She looked like a 13 year old should minus the wild crimped hair. "She was the featured model, which was a pretty big deal." She smiled fondly at the photo of the two of them again.

"You do realize that your dad is totally copping a feel, right?" He pointed to the placement of her dad's hand on Laney. It could be dismissed as unintentional--a quick pose, but his wrist was extended a bit to allow his thumb and index finger to rest on the side of her budding chest beneath the contoured bustier top.

"He didn't mean to. It's not like she had much there. She was only 13."

"Does she now?"

Caprice glared at him.

"Well it's not like she's *his* daughter." Jeremiah flipped to the back of the album, started thumbing backward. "Oh here he goes again."

A more recent photo: It was the 20s/flapper dancer inspired show. Delaney wore a silver cropped, tinseled top and skirt. There was no denying her cleavage, as the top pushed her breasts upward. Caprice's dad had photobombed, wrapping his arms around her from behind, this time his hands a bit lower than appropriate.

"Not that I blame him. I wouldn't mind if the two of you teamed up."

"You're being gross."

"Oh, come on. It's totally natural for a guy to fantasize about sisters. Don't act so innocent--because--what *you* just did, was the opposite of innocent."

"It's just--"

Jeremiah closed the album and tossed it to the floor. "You're a knockout, Caprice. You know that." He touched her cheek beneath the hair that had fallen in her face. His voice perked up. "Say it."

She laughed nervously. "What?"

"That you're hot. Say it."

It took a bit more encouragement for her to actually say it and when she did, he immediately ran his hands up her shirt, squeezed her breasts roughly.

"And *you* definitely have plenty here."

It was a compliment, she thought.

"And I want to see plenty more of you, Caprice."

To that, she smiled lightly.

# 24

# mr. blue sky

J ack sat in a metal chair in the hallway just outside the surgical suites. He was bent down over his knees, his face dug into his hands. He had sat like this for so long, his eyes squeezed shut, picturing Delaney's face so intently that when Dr. Schuler touched his shoulder, he felt like he had been startled from a deep sleep. He jolted, glanced at his wrist watch and sighed.

"They're just getting scrubbed in. She's sleeping soundly," Dr. Schuler said, straining slightly as he took the chair beside him.

Jack nodded.

Both men leaned their heads against the wall, watching the various staff moving about the hallway. Jack knew the surgical schedule. A liver transplant was underway just down the hall, an appendectomy across from there, an overflow ortho patient--ankle, he thought, was just behind him. He had positioned himself to know the instant someone emerged from the surgical suite for Delaney.

They sat in silence for a few minutes, then Dr. Schuler said rather bluntly: "I never did like you much."

Jack turned to him, slowly.

"As an OT you were tolerable I suppose." His eyes scanned the hallway. "When you came back as a doctor, you had the persona of a doctor though." He shrugged. "I was the same way, to be honest--still that way sometimes. Being a doctor goes over well at happy hour, I suppose." He indulged himself a bit, but his face turned sad, like it no longer gave him the same adrenaline rush as when he was younger. "When you get to be my age, things do change. You start to wonder who's going to be there--" He shook off the thought. "When I heard she was dating you, I didn't like it."

Jack wasn't sure if he'd ever sat side-by-side with Dr. Schuler. He always seemed huge with his broad frame, obvious that he had once played professional football, but now, he looked smaller somehow. Not small, but perhaps more equal in size to himself than he realized.

"I wondered--why would a girl like that go for a guy like you? She's always been so smart. She had to have seen what I saw, right?"

There was a long enough silence for Jack to question his treating the question as rhetorical. He watched the man turn a silver flip phone over in his hands. It was easily decade old technology despite Dr. Schuler always being the first to secure the latest phone model.

"I met that girl when she was 15. She was--is--smart, kind, witty. Getting to mentor her, help her along with school, her career--she's the closest thing I'll ever have to a child of my own." The weight of the statement lingered. Dr. Schuler handed him his cell phone. "One of the nurses sent me that."

Jack looked down at the screen. On it was a photo taken in the parallel bars. It was hard to believe that it was only a couple of hours earlier. The photo was taken from behind Delaney. A faint smile was just visible on the left side of her face under the enormous VR goggles, but his own face was clear just beyond her. His smile was exuberant as he gazed at her, mesmerized, his eyes filled with tears.

"Turns out she saw a whole lot more than me." Dr. Schuler sighed, smacked him hard on the shoulder as he stood. "*That* is something extraordinary," he said and stepped back into the surgical suite scrub room.

Dr. Schuler reemerged close to ninety minutes later, waving him in. He immediately turned back inside, holding the door for him.

Jack's body seemed to have molded into the shape of the chair. His back throbbed as he stood. He was about to protest going inside, but Delaney's voice echoed through the doorway. He rushed forward, glancing briefly at the speaker where her raspy voice emerged, and without thinking, gazed toward the surgical table. There were just four main figures in the center of the room--there was Delaney, her face visible beneath a large clear drape, beyond which her head was secured in a three-prong clamp contraption to be sure she didn't move. Sitting on her left side was the Anesthesiologist, Dr. Francis Freeman, one gloved hand resting on her shoulder, and an accompanying nurse. Standing over the surgical site, watching a crisp image on a flat screen directly across from her was Katarina Isaac, MD of Neurosurgery, her crimson hair knotted at the base of her neck. The screen showed the aneurysm--a large bubbled sac, branched off from an otherwise healthy blood vessel. With the magnification, it looked like a small, heavily filled water balloon. Beyond it, there were peachy folds, which in a surreal realization, Jack recognized as Delaney's brain.

Dr. Isaac was having Delaney count 1 to 10, then 10 to 1. She gave her simple instructions--to wiggle her toes, to identify objects in the photos Jack was familiar with, as they were adhered to the ceiling of the surgical suite. The nurse held a laminated flashcard version since Delaney was only partially reclined.

Past the arm of Shaw, he could see Delaney's eyes peering at the photographs he himself had looked at so often. She blinked, slowly and sleepily. She described snowcapped mountains and a turquoise lake. The screen showed Dr. Isaac's skillful gloved hands with an extremely steady grip, securing the first clip in place. "That sounds like somewhere I'd like to visit."

"It looks peaceful," Delaney murmured.

"Okay, Laney, let's try something else. Do you sing?"

Delaney's voice chuckled lightly. "You don't want me to sing."

"I do. Just a few lines."

Delaney took a lengthy breath, swallowed hard--searching her mind for a song to sing perhaps. Her eyes squinted in concentration, like trying to solve a riddle.

Silence fell for a brief few moments and then, a new voice, soft and deep came through the speakers in the surgical suite, originating from the intercom on the opposite side of the observation glass. Her lips curled at the corners when she recognized Jack's voice crooning an upbeat Frank Sinatra song.

Delaney's voice joined in with a slightly constricted quality from being reclined.

Dr. Isaac nodded approvingly as Delaney's voice trailed off, smiling beneath her blue surgical mask. "That's good." She secured another clip, her gaze intent on the screen. "You've got that soulful raspy voice happening right now."

Delaney blinked slowly.

"I wasn't expecting a duet though," Dr. Isaac remarked, unable to resist glancing momentarily to the observation room, then back to the monitor.

"Jack sings to me sometimes," Delaney remarked.

He could actually see her smile wholeheartedly now as he stood upright, his arms squeezed tightly over his chest. He was watching the screen as the last clip, according to a whisper from Dr. Schuler, was being placed.

"His mom and dad used to dance to that song."

Jack stood straighter, turning his attention back to Delaney, who was watching him now.

*She doesn't remember that.*

His eyes jumped to the ballooned sac, slightly less pressurized than moments earlier.

As though showing off, now knowing he was there and could hear her, she continued: "He took me to Havasu Canyon for our first date. We camped out. He pointed out constellations. He explained how the Big Dipper isn't a constellation at all, but a part of the Great Bear."

Jack could picture the dark domed sky overhead, the shimmering stars. His original plan had been to camp out in a hammock, as he had planned it to be more of a backpacking trip, but he researched last minute and found a suitable place they could camp. He bought a queen air mattress the morning they left, unable to shake the feeling he would be ill-prepared and the trip, and by extension, their relationship, would ultimately be a disaster. The presumptuous appearance of the mattress didn't occur to him until he saw their campsite all set up with pillows, sheets and blankets. He had left her sitting by the fire to set up camp and she returned just as he surveyed his work. "I can sleep in the hammock," he had blurted out.

Dr. Schuler was now standing shoulder to shoulder with him with his nose practically pressed to the glass. Jack followed his gaze to the screen and watched as the clipped sac seemed to be shrinking before their eyes.

"You went camping for your first date? That's pretty adventurous. What did you do for your second date? Skydiving?"

"We played Scrabble and Battleship at a coffeehouse."

"Third date?" Dr. Isaac's eyes floated over to the observation room, a smile clearly hiding behind her surgical mask.

"A hockey game. We were going to go ice skating, but there was a peewee league championship that had taken over all the rinks."

Jack's smile broadened and Dr. Schuler smacked him on the arm.

"Good memory," Dr. Freeman remarked, nodding to the Neurosurgeon. "I can hardly remember what I had for lunch."

"*Oh*, that was Ber*muda*," Delaney murmured, sighing in relief.

"What was?"

"I've been having dreams about being on a beach—before. I didn't know where I was or if I had really been there," she smiled, sleepily.

"And?"

"A few months after Jack and I started dating, he was invited to speak at a conference in Bermuda and I tagged along."

"Is it nice?"

"Very much so. Everybody drives mopeds on these winding roads. It's crazy—it's like being on a speeder in the Ewok forest."

Dr. Isaac's eyes scanned over her work carefully. Once she was finished, her shoulders relaxed considerably. "Well, that, my dear, should do it for your part,"

Dr. Isaac's smooth voice said. "Dr. Freeman is going to have you float off to sleep again, alright?"

Dr. Freeman adjusted the drip, moved in closer to Delaney's cheek. "Let's revisit that lake, shall we?" He motioned to the photograph.

"Your name is Francis Freeman?"

"Yes, ma'am."

"Do you ever go by the name Ajax?" Delaney's face was serious. Inquisitive.

Dr. Freeman looked abruptly to Dr. Isaac, who chuckled behind her surgical mask. Her eyes slid back up to the screen as she checked her work again.

"Can't say I do."

"Do you have a good middle name? Francis Freeman is a *terrifying* name to read on the nametag of someone sticking needles in your veins."

Dr. Isaac took a half step back to compose herself.

"*What's my name?*" Delaney said, mimicking a demanding British man, her eyelids impossibly heavy. Then she settled back. "I'm sorry. You don't look a thing like him. You have a much kinder bedside manner, also." Her words slurred, her eyes drifting to her Neurosurgeon. "If I never see you again, I want you to know that I love you very much.'" There was an upward tilt of her lips.

Dr. Freeman watched the monitors. "Just about--"

Delaney sighed so deeply her whole body seemed to melt a little into the table.

"Sleeping like a baby," he confirmed, placing his hand back on her shoulder. He shook his head at his sleeping patient. "What was she talking about--Ajax?"

"*Deadpool,*" Dr. Isaac explained, chuckling, the team around the table multiplying. She held her hands out before her, a statue, as tools were carefully exchanged. "Good luck."

Dr. Freeman was at a loss while a couple of the nurses were clearly amused. "That's what I get for only getting to watch kid movies."

"Yeah, definitely *not* a movie for kids. I didn't have her pegged as a fan."

"You either."

"Oh I'm a Comic Con regular." Dr. Isaac peered over to the pair of men in the observation room. Jack seemed to be explaining something to the Physiatrist, who started laughing in an overtly animated fashion. "Is it just the anesthetic or is she normally that funny?" She asked.

Jack pressed the intercom button. "This is totally normal behavior for her."

Dr. Isaac nodded approvingly as she stepped toward her patient. "I'll have her to Recovery by midnight, if you'd like to wait for us there?"

The nurse coordinator moved into observation to further usher them out the door and into the hallway.

"Can we tee up some music please? Probably not *Deadpool* though. How about *Guardians Volume 2.*"

A few moments later, *Mr. Blue Sky* started echoing through the surgical chamber, and Dr. Isaac began the work of closing Delaney's skull with skillful precision.

# 25

# interlude

The coffee barista now had a fondness for one of the Neurosurgery residents. He greeted Jack as "Doctor," but he no longer used the fluctuation in his tone that implied some sort of innuendo. He was still unbelievably energetic, even at 9:58pm, and remarked unknowingly about Jack's request for a double shot cappuccino: "Quite a night ahead, hmm?"

He didn't seem offended when Jack just smiled absentmindedly and took his cup. His head was blurred, his body drained, but his chest felt inflated with the knowledge that Delaney remembered. She had laid there and described their first date. Second date. Third date. She remembered a movie they had watched a year and a half earlier. It all seemed to have come back to her.

She remembered.

He released a long sigh as he took in the sight of the near empty cafeteria.

He found himself moving toward the lobby without prior thought to do so. It was quiet and peacefully lit with its separated conversation sets and greenery. Jack had just identified a loveseat by the vertical garden wall as the most ideal place to sit when he noticed a young woman shift in the club chair just to his left.

He didn't need to turn to know who it was.

"Is she out of surgery already?" Caprice's voice was high and concerned.

Jack felt his hand tighten around his cup. He silently reminded himself that, for whatever reason, Delaney seemed to have saint-like patience for this woman. *Everyone is fighting their own battle*, she had explained. *Everyone.*

"She will be soon." He loosened his clenched jaw. "How did you find out she was in surgery?"

"One of the nurses. I came back to see her—"

He nodded, almost imperceptibly. "They're finishing up--that can take some time. It went well." As he took a sip, his mouth turned up at the corners, thinking of how she had smiled from beneath the drape, how she had sung along with him. It was surreal to think that there had been a recent time when it was uncertain if her speech would return, if he'd have a place in her life anymore.

Caprice stood. "I would have never forgiven myself if the last thing I said to my sister--"

He shook his head, not wanting to allow the thought of what could have happened to percolate too long in his brain. "She's going to be OK."

"Can we talk? Would that--what time will she be done?"

"We've got time. I was going to head to Recovery in a little while." Jack motioned toward the sea of empty tables. "Can I get you a coffee?" he began, then noticed the lights off inside the small coffee house. "Well, there's just the main cafeteria now. There's a dirt-like quality, but it's tolerable. There's hot water if you like tea?"

"I'm fine. Not a big coffee or tea drinker."

"OK," he said, stepping toward a table. He pulled out a chair and waited for Caprice to sit before taking his place on the booth side.

She seemed a bit flabbergasted by the gesture. "Wow, you're old school."

"Meaning?"

"Holding out chairs, things like that--"

"I've also been known to say 'Bless you' when people sneeze."

"What does 'kazoo tide' mean anyway?"

"Pardon?"

"When people sneeze."

Jack pursed his lips, resisting the urge to laugh. "I guess you don't hear that one much anymore, do you?"

She took a breath. "I love my sister," she said, defensively, but then she sank into her seat. "I haven't shown it, but I do."

He nodded slowly.

"It was tough to hear that Jeremiah would—" She noticed when he flinched. "I didn't want to believe it."

Jack stared at her, attempting neutrality. He took in the lines by her eyes and mouth from focused chain smoking, more recently obsessive vaping, the puffiness around her eyes from a recent cry. Then he took in her rounded nose, the arch of her eyebrows, both similar to Delaney's--he could see more of an underlaid resemblance than he had allowed himself before.

Caprice spoke toward her hands, intertwined and resting on the tabletop. "It makes sense--hearing it. What he said happened—Laney wouldn't--" She frowned inwardly. "She never even liked him."

Leaning back into the cushioned booth, Jack focused his breathing. "But you *did* believe him."

She nodded, regretfully. "I was going through a lot at the time."

Jack released an audible scoff.

"I lost my mom in that car, too," she said, her eyebrows raised assertively, channeling Delaney to apply forcefulness through her words.

The words plunked at something deep in his chest. "I'm sorry. I know you did, Caprice."

"Laney went to live with her dad. For not seeing much of him in 8-9 years, they became really close. She had that other guy hanging around as her friend or whatever, too."

"Quinn."

"Right. Quinn. She was one of the top kids in her class. She graduated a year early. From my perspective, she was doing really well, all things considered."

He took a sip of his coffee to keep from putting the phrase "all things considered" into context.

She shifted in her seat. "I, on the other hand, barely graduated from high school after already being *held back* a year, I lived with friends--"

"I thought you moved in with your dad?"

"I stopped speaking to my dad before our mom died. Not that he was around for, like, my entire life anyway."

"Why did you stop talking to him?"

She pressed her lips together firmly before speaking, as though bracing herself. "The only reason he ever spent time with me was when Laney was around."

Jack frowned.

"He was a modeling agent--for our mom and then for Laney. I think she hoped he'd spend time with me once she signed Laney on with him."

"I take it that didn't happen?"

She rigidly shook her head. "He was only interested in Laney—and he was *very* interested in her."

He tried to digest this, his stomach suddenly knotted. "Are you saying—"

She shrugged. "Laney wouldn't have done anything willingly. I don't know for sure what happened. I got rid of the photos, but if he did that openly—"

"Did what?"

Caprice shifted in her seat. "When they were posing for photos at events--his hands would be where they shouldn't have been."

He thought of Delaney positioned under the surgical tent joking with Dr. Freeman. In the midst of brain surgery, cracking jokes.

"I begged my mom to pull Laney from modeling."

Jack exhaled. "And?"

"I think at that point she was pretty invested in the idea of Laney being a model. She was seventeen when she got pregnant with me and had to stop. Living vicariously and all that."

Jack set down his coffee cup, rubbed roughly at his stubbled cheeks and chin.

"She told me I was being jealous—as well as some other things I would rather not repeat."

Jack stopped mid-chin rub, gazing across the table at this woman who had morphed, in just a few minutes, from someone he disliked intensely to someone he felt tremendous sympathy.

"I had no idea what happened to her. If I had known-" she pulled in her breath, her jaw clenched, her hands pulled into fists. "For all I knew, if I *didn't* accept what Jeremiah told me, the only alternative was that he was rejecting me."

"Like everyone else seemed to have done."

There was a small, hopeful upturn of her chin, as someone seemed to finally understand. "I never even approached her about it until today—"

He narrowed his eyes at her use of the word "approached."

She stared at him, her eyes glistening with tears. "I don't know what came over me."

He shook his head. "You realize she never intended for you to know the truth."

It was clear from the stunned expression that this hadn't translated to Caprice. "I'd choose my sister over Jeremiah."

"*Now* you would. Because you know. Because you believed Quinn. What if she had told you the truth back then and you hadn't believed her?"

She was thoughtful for a moment. "We wouldn't have a relationship."

He thought he had understood, but the weight of her words resonated deep within him. *We wouldn't have a relationship.*

"I wish I'd never met him. I wish I'd never brought him into her life. *Either* of them," she said, desperation filling her voice.

"You can't do that to yourself, Caprice," he said quietly.

"I've been terrible to her."

He resisted the urge to agree wholeheartedly with her. He checked his watch and cleared his throat. "Delaney once told me one of her best childhood memories was coming home from a photoshoot with her hair all done in some crazy number of braids—"

Caprice's eyes widened.

"And having you help take them all down."

"Her hair ended up looking like she stuck her finger in a light socket," Caprice said, her mouth turning up at the corners, her forehead furrowed in disbelief. "That's one of her favorite memories?"

Jack scratched at his eyebrow. It was the memory she had cited after yet another frustrating dinner they shared with Caprice. He had said "I don't know why you put up with her." *Because somewhere in there is the big sister that sat and de-braided my hair for 2 hours,* Delaney had replied with a small shrug.

He watched Caprice sit up a little straighter, her face brightening at the memory. She reached into her bag and retrieved her phone. "I've been working on scanning in old photos." It only took her a moment to find what she was looking for: a photo of a fresh faced, 13 year old Delaney with a wild mane of crimped hair, crossing her eyes and making a fish face at the camera. She was sitting in a bedroom with aqua walls covered in sketches and he recalled her sharing that Caprice drew a lot as a child. Jack gazed at the photo, taking the phone in his palm. He was captivated by the sparkle in Delaney's eye, the warm glow in her youthful cheeks. He couldn't help but smile along with her.

"We hadn't really spent much time together, but she came home and was trying to take down her hair in the bathroom. She just looked so—helpless." Caprice reached for the screen and swiped left twice. "It looked pretty neat all done up though." The complete look had the braids wrapped around her head, sculpted into an abstract wave pattern like some sort of Star Wars royalty. She wore a full length gown with flared shoulders that looked like they were made from reptile skin.

"Here's what she looked like when I found her." She swiped right.

The mini braid updo looked like some sort of tangled mohawk. Delaney was hidden behind the chaos, giving a distraught, age and situationally appropriate pout.

"Oh Jesus. Where do you even start with that?"

"It took forever to get them all out." She took the phone and swiped ahead to the original that she showed him, then onto the next photo, smiling fondly at it before presenting to him.

Delaney had her face smashed into her sister's cheek, arms wrapped around her neck. Caprice didn't have any makeup on, which revealed a light affliction of teenage acne, and her hair appeared to be a natural golden brown. They both wore broad, open mouthed smiles.

"I love that photo. She didn't smile much growing up so it makes me happy to see."

Jack saw the effortless way Delaney smiled in the photo. He knew the deep, unrestrained laugh that probably accompanied it. He looked at Caprice eyeing the photo with such affection and heard himself saying: "You mean a lot to her, Caprice."

She swallowed hard.

"Go get some sleep," he said softly. "I'll let you know how she's doing."

"Do you need my number?" She asked, flabbergasted by the turn of events.

"I have it, Caprice." He glanced up at the surgery monitor—the room status for the OR suite was still showing as in-progress, but he was eager to get to Recovery.

"Jack?" she called, just as he took a step away. She took a breath. "I'm really glad she met you."

He thought for a moment. "Me, too."

# 26
# almost

A steady beep of a monitor. The chill of fluids steaming into her hand. A very warm, heavy blanket holding in an abundance of body heat. She let her eyes open ever so slightly, but even the dim light through her eyelashes made her head thump.

She could feel a pressure where they cut. Just pressure, mercifully.

Compared to her overly insulated body, her head felt cold, despite being snugly bound in some sort of medical gauze wrap.

They had shaved her head, she remembered. They were going to do it once she was under anesthesia. For her prior surgery, they had shaved just around the incision. For this, they advised shaving the whole thing, as to limit infection risk, etc. It made sense. "I'll just channel GI Jane," she had added with a smirk.

She hadn't let herself think twice about it. Now she did. She felt the strange smoothness of her scalp against the wrap. No friction or scraping of hair as the wrap slid on the pillow.

She thought to lift her hand to feel the bald ridges, but the anesthetic hadn't completely worn off and she was afraid of causing damage.. Plus there was something heavy and warm holding her hand. Peeking through her eyelashes, she confirmed that it was Jack's hand.

Her eyes drifted up the length of his arm. He was wearing his weathered Wrigley Field shirt, the one she liked to steal to sleep it when he was working overnight.

*When he was working overnight,* she thought with a smile, marveling at the simple ability to remember something.

She remembered how his bedroom had a grand, luxurious quality, like it belonged at a resort. He had bought the house fresh off a remodel, and had the designer from the upscale furniture retailer fill it with selections that ultimately made it look like a Tommy Bahama catalog locale. When she first moved in, he had told her to feel free to add personal touches, that it was her home, too. To that end, she had purchased a ruffled duvet cover with a pastel floral pattern, and gone on about how she'd always wanted it, doesn't it look contemporary, but also shabby chic? He had gazed over at it, a sore thumb in his sophisticated, simplistic bedroom, and said: "I was going to say French Country," then he kissed her, moved to change clothes.

"You don't think it's too much?" She had asked, dramatically sprawling across it.

"Are you kidding me?" he said, returning from the closet, having traded jeans for basketball shorts. He was just pulling on a t-shirt. "You're laying on it. It's my favorite comforter in the world."

She smiled lightly. "I got it to torture you."

He cocked his head to the side, framed by the door. "Now that you mention it, it is sort of burning my retinas right now," he conceded, moving toward the bed. She sat up and he took a seat beside her at the base of the mattress. "By 'torture,' do you mean 'test'? As in, to test if buying a comforter would alter my feelings for you enough to regret living together?"

"Maybe subconsciously. Or--semi-consciously? Is that a thing?"

He looked at his hands. "Well. We're keeping it."

"What? No. It looks like—"

"Our new comforter," he said, peering over his shoulder. "Like a bed and breakfast—somewhere without electricity or running water."

"I'm returning it."

He stood, starting to search the hem. "Where is that 'Under Penalty of Law' tag?"

"Don't you dare," she said, jumping up.

Jack had searched half of the perimeter of the duvet when Delaney wrapped herself around him, toppling the pair of them to the bed. He kissed her again and again, purposely choosing her neck, her ear, as they were particularly ticklish.

"We shouldn't do this here. I have to be able to return this."

"We're keeping it."

"It was $400. I didn't even bother with the 20% off coupon knowing I was just going to return it. It went against everything I hold to be dear in retail shopping."

He stared at her, pondering. "You win," he concluded, lifting her and settling her on the chaise lounge. "How about we pick something out together?"

"Now?" She grinned.

"No, what I have planned will take at *least* 20 minutes. *Then* we can go."

She laughed silently.

"We can get some breakfast, go shopping, come home and break in the *new* bedspread."

"I like that 'home' is the same place for both of us."

He gazed into her eyes in that introspective way he did sometimes. "I'm glad to hear it, because I--" he paused to kiss her. "Am not--" Kiss. "Letting you--" Kiss. "get away."

"So you're saying it's *The Point of No Return*?"

He pondered this *Phantom of the Opera* reference, deciding against responding to it. "I was about to *do* something--"

"Sing to me?"

"No, I don't sing anymore."

"What if I asked nicely?" Her eyes widened, playfully.

"You're never going to let the singing thing go, are you?"

"Just sing to me," she whispered, pleading. "Not all the time—just daily when you get home from work, if you want to wake me, if I'm having a bad day, randomly for no reason at all, two, maybe three times a day. Max."

He shook his head, matter-of-factly.

She sighed, rolling her eyes. "Fine. Well at least tell me something sweet."

"I love you."

She crooked an eyebrow. "In French?"

He kissed her neck, letting his breath tickle her skin. "Tu es mon amour. Tu rends mon monde magnifique et je ne pouvais imaginer ma vie sans toi." She arched her back, stretching, as he kissed his way from her chest to her navel. Then he stopped, retracing his way to her lips. "Je t'aime," he whispered, like some romance novel love interest.

"Wow," she said, dreamily. "You could have been telling me where the restroom is and it sounded unbelievably sexy."

"Didn't know you liked French guys."

"I don't. I think France, as a whole, is tremendously overrated, socialism is a severely flawed leftist ideology--but you speaking French?"

"That does it for you, huh?"

"To the point I'm wondering why we're still talking." She tugged him toward her, kissing him. "Don't stop," she breathed.

"En outre, c'est la couette la plus moche que j'ai jamais vue."

"What did you just say?"

"Also, this is the ugliest comforter I have ever seen."

She stopped, pulled back to look at him. "OK, the French is totally working. Add it to the regular rotation."

"Vous ronflez comme un ours aux narines très enflammées." He kissed her, their exhaled breaths hot and erratic. His hands urged her closer.

"Oh that's good. What does it mean?"

"You snore like a bear with severely inflamed nostrils." His hand slid down her torso, backtracking upward as it reached her thigh. "Oh wait. That's me." He shrugged and continued.

She laughed, her body pulsed, her back arched, hands, arms, legs, every inch of her wanting him.

She remembered.

She remembered their first date, camping at Havasu Falls. She remembered how they had made the long drive home and he had to drag himself in to work the overnight shift.

He had pulled into a parking spot in front of her building and shifted into park, gazing across the cab of his pickup truck. His lips curled up at the corner, his eyes telling of thoughts he wasn't sharing.

Delaney had managed the weekend with just the backpack that rested between her feet and glanced up at the tall condominium complex.

"I'll walk you in," he had offered, but before he knew what was happening, she had released her seat belt and was sliding across the bench seat. She turned, braced his face in her hands and pulled him toward her to get better positioning to kiss him. She pushed their lips together gently then with increasing intensity, then slowly parted their lips, exhaling deeply.

"Have a good night at work," she said softly.

"I was going to walk you to your door."

She shook her head lightly. "If you do that, you'll be late."

His smile tightened as he leaned back into the headrest. "Until tomorrow?"

"Until tomorrow." She kissed him again, then quickly gathered her bag and let herself out of the cab. It took every effort to move forward. Every impulse in her body wanted to jump back in that cab, feel his hands embrace her. She wanted to melt into him, like she had on that air mattress in the moonlight. She actually felt disoriented by the pull she felt toward him.

She stopped by the headlight, peering over her shoulder. She felt the left side of her mouth creeping upward, her cheeks hot as she saw him grinning at her.

She remembered how full her heart felt, how it burned with certainty that from that moment forward, it belonged to Jack Mathison.

***

The weight of the blanket was becoming too warm. The cold hospital air beyond it, she had decided, would feel amazing on her skin.

She wiggled her arms, instructing them to free themselves. The left managed movement. She felt it nudge Jack, she assumed, and he sat up. Her right side still needed some focused attention.

"Are you too warm?" Jack asked, folding down the blanket. His voice was a whisper.

Delaney relaxed into the bed, breathing deeply, the frigid air instantly refreshing. She swallowed repeatedly, trying to clear her cottonmouth, keeping her eyes closed. After less than a minute, she instinctively grasped for the blanket, chills shooting through her limbs.

He tucked her back in, gently, his hand resting on her cheek. She nudged against it, pulling her left hand free so she could reciprocate. Her fingers found his face immediately.

She rubbed at the stubble on his cheek. She blindly felt the rest of his face, as though to make sure it was really him, even letting her fingers glide over his eye sockets and nose before settling back on his cheek. She had done this exact thing a few times in the sleep room, after snuggling into him, after kissing him passionately for several minutes. She'd inevitably breathe a dramatic sigh of relief when she had resolved that it was, in fact, him. His cheek tensed into a small smile beneath her palm.

"I'm here."

She inhaled and exhaled solidly then felt her body being coaxed back to sleep.

When she woke again, the light from the sunny window pressed persistently at her eyelids. It was morning, but she was immensely disoriented and couldn't resolve the day of the week. She let out a quick whimper as the light translated into a pain in her skull.

Jack wasn't there. He would have never opened the blinds.

At this point she noticed her head wasn't situated back on the pillow. It was lifted slightly by what felt like plastic. Her head also felt confined within something--and sweaty.

"Good morning," a cheerful female voice whispered loudly from her left. "I'm Sadie. I'll be taking care of you today. Can I get you anything?"

"I'm--" She swallowed. "--having pain."

Sadie's voice was growing incrementally louder. "What level would you say you're at?" There was a shake of a laminated strip of card stock—the pain scale.

The pain increased exponentially. Cracking--she was certain her skull was cracking like a warming glacial lake.

"Sadie," another voice scolded from the side wall. There was a muffle of activity in the hallway. "We don't do handoffs here like other floors."

"Just getting her pain rating."

"She has pain level: post-craniotomy." The angel of mercy crossed the room. "*These* were closed."

"Thought she'd like to see the sunrise to help her wake up."

Mercifully cool darkness fell across her eyelids.

"I've been a nurse for two years—" She made this sound like this made her a veteran. "I've never not done bedside—" her voice cut out.

Delaney suspected she was getting silently scolded. After a moment passed, she felt a light hand on her shoulder.

"I put her helmet on, I figured she needed that--"

A more audible shush. A rush of air. "22 year old nitwit—" the angelic nurse said, her voice trailing off into mutters. "I'm going to remove this helmet, OK? Someone from Neuro dropped it off, but you're not supposed to wear it yet."

Delaney lifted and lowered her chin. Some kind of gel had been applied to her incision so the helmet was resistant to being removed. She cringed.

"I'm so sorry, sweetie. It's off. I'll get some more cream to put on there."

Her head was chilled again. She tried to picture what she would look like without hair. This wasn't her first brain surgery in a matter of a few months so at this point her scalp was probably starting to look like a toddler had drawn squiggle art across her head.

There had been times before the car accident that she thought of cutting her hair short in rebellion, but it would do nothing but complicate modeling and disappoint her mother. There had been times after the accident that she'd stared at her dad's hair and beard trimmer in his bathroom--she had been restricted to taking baths and her bathroom only offered a walk-in shower. She had stared at the trimmer and pondered buzzing her head. She had determined that would draw more attention, which was the opposite of her intent. She didn't want to make a statement. She just wanted to exist where her appearance had a neutral impact. She had determined shaving her head would fail to accomplish this goal.

And now, fourteen years later, it had been done.

They offered to minimize the amount of hair that needed to be shaved, but at the time, she had put on a brave face and dismissed the importance of hair. It would make everyone's job easier to just shave it all. It had sounded like a winning thing to say--and she had wholeheartedly believed it.

The tears were thick and warm as they filled her eyes and began streaming down her cheeks. She sniffled and gulped. *This is ridiculous*, she thought, using her left hand to wipe her face.

With her hand already so close, she slid it further upward, staying on the left side of her head to avoid the fresh incision. Her fingers touched the smooth, taut skin. She inhaled. She could picture the width of the incision on the same spot on the opposite side--about pinky width with some swelling. She knew there were tightly inserted staples that looked far too raw of materials to be securing a scalp together. The number of staples would be in the twenties, at least. She could not think of the staple removal process, could not imagine even looking at the incision.

Tears seeped through her eyelashes and her nose burned. She pinched her face as she tried to hold back a sob.

A shoe squeak made her eyes fly open.

Jack was standing in the doorway, carrying in his duffel bag and Dr. Schuler was behind him carrying takeout containers. When they saw her, they froze, faced braced in both concern and excitement to see her conscious.

"I'm sorry," she blurted out, dropping her hand from her head. "I'm--I'll be fine." She studied each of them through her tears, focusing on Jack's expression, his worry, his overgrown blonde waves shaved to the root. Suddenly, her chin fell to her chest and she squeezed her eyes shut. She couldn't control her breathing or the chokes of sobs.

Jack dropped the duffel to the floor, moved toward her. "I should have been here when you woke up. I'm sorry."

She seemed torn between a negative and positive response. "Don't apologize for that."

"No, I should have waited—"

She slowly raised her eyes. "Apologize for shaving that beautiful hair." She reached out her hand and slid her palm against his head, a pained expression on her face. "What the hell, Jack? Those hair follicles did nothing wrong."

His lips spread into an affectionate smile.

Delaney hiccuped on lingering sobs, trying to take a full breath.

"I told him not every man can pull this off," Dr. Schuler said, modeling his own bald head. "I'm sorry, kiddo. I was on Laney patrol, but got a page. I was only gone a few minutes."

Delaney focused her gaze on her hand resting on Jack's cheek, her more cooperative fingers, on the flattened portion of his nose, a result of taking a fastball to the nose. She examined the broadness of his chin, the gentleness of his eyes. She reveled at her vivid recollection of the first time she spent time studying his face in that way. "You have a *really* weird shaped head," she whispered, eyeing what was actually a marvel of symmetry, her eyes brimmed with tears. "Was it always this *pointy*?"

"There's a flat spot back here," Dr. Schuler offered.

"They didn't have those baby helmets when he grew up," she remarked, her eyes brightening.

"I'm going to go hit up the nurse's station for some forks and knives."

Once Dr. Schuler was gone, Jack moved close. "D?" His voice broke on that single syllable, his hands bracing her face. "I *love* you."

She nodded repeatedly, trying to hold back tears. She felt joy for her returned memories, but shock and fear over what she had endured, what had been stripped away from her and what had been thrust back into her possession. So much at once. She tried to focus on the man before her, but her brain was submerged in a vat of blended images. "Do you want to know the bright side to all this?" she managed to say, though her voice was trembling and uncertain.

"What's that?"

"I got to experience falling in love with you twice." She smiled lightly.

Jack looked back and forth between her eyes. He studied the variation of each shade of blue, of gray, of green.

"D, *you*--" His voice broke.

She could see the moment when the fear, the tension that he had been carrying around, fell away. His shoulders lifted, his face brightened, and his eyes flooded with tears. He kissed her once. Twice. Three times.

"I can leave," Dr. Schuler announced, returning with utensils. "Just say the word." He didn't seem to have any intention to leave as he settled in with his styrofoam box in the recliner.

"I love you," she whispered toward Jack's ear.

Jack kissed her left eyebrow, took a step back toward the takeout bags.

"Don't even think about it, Martin," he said, turning toward Delaney as though to say *I get to call him Martin now!*, "but what kind of person orders blueberry syrup for pancakes?"

"Don't knock it unless you try it."

Nursing assignments were evidently reshuffled, as a different nurse, this one with natural blonde hair pulled up like Heidi, came in to dispense pain, anti-seizure, and antibiotic medications. Delaney tried to be patient, watching her box of buttermilk pancakes become colder, her stomach growling furiously. Jack had noticed her eyelids becoming lazy. It was once Heidi-Collette decided she needed to check her vitals and wrapped the blood pressure cuff around her arm that Delaney's chin slowly dropped and her body seemed to settle into the mattress. Even as the cuff continuously strangled her upper arm, her breathing deepened until soft, breathy snores emerged.

Heidi-Collette pulled off the cuff with a loud rip of velcro. She placed the pulse monitor on Delaney's fingertip and tucked the blood pressure monitor stand into the corner. "We'll try again later." Then she left.

"Poor kid," Dr. Schuler said, shaking his head. "She just wanted some pancakes."

"I'll get her fresh ones when she wakes up."

Dr. Schuler gave a small, amused smile then turned neutral. "She has a bed on Rehab whenever she needs it. Dr. Bordeaux already agreed to take her case even if I'm gone by then."

Jack set his unopened to-go box aside.

"You really should eat."

"What's the story, Papa Schuler?" Jack asked, echoing Delaney's nickname for the doctor.

Dr. Schuler raised his eyebrows pointedly at the to-go container and waited until Jack had started to eat to continue. "I've decided to retire."

"*Oh?* When's the big day?"

There was a small flicker in the fifty-six year old's eye. "Next Friday."

"That's soon."

"Quinn Harwell's discharge date. I wanted to see his case through. *Administration* wanted me to see his case through as well." He was thoughtful for a moment. "He's min assist for transfers now. Julie's going to try to get him in the harness today or tomorrow. He'll hopefully be set up or modified independent by discharge."

"That's good progress for him since I saw him." Jack was thoughtful. "In what? 3-4 days?"

"Really good progress." Dr. Schuler nodded, leaning back in his chair. "Kid might even walk short household distances by the time he leaves. Julie's working on AFO's."

Jack dropped his fork back in the box. "Are you being forced out?"

"No one's saying that."

"But that's what's happening."

Dr. Schuler inhaled, gazing over at Delaney. "They admitted I did right by my patient--so I can live with it."

"So this isn't about clinical decisions--" Jack said, frowning.

Dr. Schuler stabbed a piece of pancake, shaking his head. As he chewed, he motioned toward the beige padded vinyl helmet on the side table. "You realize she is *not* going to be compliant with the helmet."

"Yeah, well. Neurosurg doesn't know conscious Delaney very well," Jack replied, accepting the change of subject.

They ate in silence for several minutes, the only sounds in the room the steady beep of the monitors, the icemaker in the nurse's station, and Delaney's gentle snore.

# 27
## "wa"

The rental apartment was situated just outside the entrance of Fushimi Inari. Thomas Rhodes had taken an early morning shinkansen train from Osaka with just a clamshell style backpack, a departure from his typical rolling carryon. He followed the instructions, taking the JR Nara Line from Kyoto Station, a contemporary and hectic railway station a short seven minute ride to Fushimi Inari Station, which featured red beams and fox silhouettes and was an entire escape from the modern persona of the city. From there, he walked along the congested neighborhood streets, taking in the food aromas from various street vendors.

She had said she was constantly getting lost when she first arrived so she had added something to the house sign so she could find her way home easier. He checked the address and peered up at the gates. Two driveways down, he understood what she meant. Above the number 7, she had added a four-leaf clover.

The front door of the simple wood slat townhouse opened. Through it emerged a young woman in wide black linen pants, a simple white v-neck tee and sandals. Her dark hair was long and cascaded around her shoulders in waves. She was unaware of his arrival, taking in the sight of the day with a natural, rhythmic interest as she crossed the shared driveway to the next door holding a small container of food. The woman who answered the door was dwarfed by Delaney's height. She was no more than 4 foot 5, her eyes folding inward as she smiled upon seeing her neighbor. Delaney bent forward and hugged the woman, who had to be 95 years old, and appeared to be politely declining an invitation to come inside. Finally the woman relented and Delaney crossed back over the driveway.

She raised her eyes and smiled broadly at the sight of her father standing twenty yards away.

Her long strides and quickened pace got her to him in no time and she let him sweep her into a tight hug. "I wasn't expecting you until later!"

"I switched from Haneda to Osaka during my connection. Saved like 5 hours."

She took a step back. "Why didn't you call me from the train? I would have met you at the station." She was fresh faced and it appeared her natural complexion had seen a lot of sunshine.

"SIM card was acting up."

"There's WIFI on the train. You can make calls with that."

He shrugged. "You know I'm not good with technology." His eyes scanned over her. There was a relaxed way about her, an ease to her presence.

"I'm glad I made extra food. I went on a hike this morning, came home and made biscuits and gravy."

"With sausage?"

"Yes, which is tough to find. Japanese breakfast sausage is very different from what we're used to."

"I won't turn that down. You brought some over to your neighbors?"

"Mrs. Ikeda," Delaney said fondly, peering across the driveway to the empty screen door. "She's great. I told her how you used to make them." She started to lead him inside.

To say biscuits and gravy caused the downfall of his marriage to Edie would be naive, but his brain had connected the two things.

It was Christmas morning when Delaney was five. After opening the presents from Santa, they took a break to get coffee and breakfast going. Edie had been affectionate as he prepared the homemade gravy, slipping her slender hands up the sleeves of his robe as they embraced. She said she loved the warmth of his arms, often resting the palms on his forearms. Everything seemed blissful, actually, until the moment the girls finished eating, having enjoyed the meal so much that Caprice had licked her plate. Delaney had giggled at the sight and copied her.

Thomas had gathered their plates, dismissing them to go play when he noticed his wife was as white as a sheet. When he asked her what was wrong, she didn't answer, staring at the girls climbing into the big toy boxes.

"Edie."

"Would you have Caprice help you drag out those boxes, Tom? I'm going to get Delaney cleaned up."

"But they're having so much fun with them," he mused.

"Oh they have plenty of actual toys to play with. Please, darling?"

'Darling' was her stern term of endearment for him. He did as he was told. When he returned, Dell was scurrying down the hallway toward her room, pajama top bundled in her arms, back bare.

"Is she OK?"

"Oh, her pajamas got wet. She was just going to change." Edie smiled, relaxed suddenly, and moved toward the living room.

The sound was so small he wouldn't have heard it if he were any further away from his daughter's bedroom. He moved inside. Delaney was standing inside staring at her laundry hamper, her back to him. She sniffled and then thrust her shirt into the hamper.

"What's going on, Dell? Need some help?"

She peered over her shoulder, her crystal blue eyes filled with tears. Second only to when she told him that she knew the exact moment her mother died in that car—when her unconscious body let out one final exhale—this was the most heartbreaking moment he'd experienced with his daughter.

"Are you not feeling good, pumpkin?"

"I'm sorry," she managed, her face braced in sadness.

"For what, baby?"

"I loved breakfast."

He moved forward, embracing her. "What are you sorry for?" Being in such close proximity, he picked up on a pungent, spoilt odor. "Did you get sick?"

She shook her head.

Thomas dropped his hand into the hamper and pulled out her shirt. "You threw up?"

She nodded.

"Did your tummy hurt?"

She frowned, shook her head again. "Mommy told me I had to."

His heart dropped, his mind in a state of bewilderment. He had known Edie had an eating disorder growing up and he had even observed her anxiety over the food Delaney ate--no five year old ate the ratio of vegetables that she did, but they had a conversation and agreed that it was important Delaney be allowed to be a kid. "There has to be a balance," she had agreed.

His next moves came quick and instinctively--he helped Delaney dress then carried her out to his car, saying they were retrieving a surprise as they passed through the living room. Instead, he drove them to his parents house. They were gone a couple of hours, but Edie had elaborated this in the court proceedings that followed a couple months later, framing the situation to resemble kidnapping. Her tearful recollection, along with his angry voicemail recording from a few days later and Delaney altogether denying the vomiting incident when asked by the judge, and Edie was granted sole custody. He was given an every other weekend visitation plan.

It was remarkable to him that she didn't have a negative association with the breakfast. One morning soon after she moved in with him at the age of fifteen, he found her stretched out on the couch, which she had said was more comfortable for her hip than the bed. He had kissed the top of her head on his way to make coffee and she had stirred.

"Hey Dad?" she had said softly, sweetly.

"Hey Dell," he whispered, watching her face tense as she readjusted her body in the cushions. "Need the morning dose?"

She exhaled. "Probably, but I was wondering--would you maybe make biscuits and gravy this morning?" Her eyes had widened optimistically.

He had probably gazed at her a little too long, searching her face for some sort of subliminal message, but her eyes were youthful and good-intended.

"It's supposed to rain all day and I thought it would be nice if we stayed all cozy inside, maybe watch *Goblet of Fire*?"

He ran his fingers over her cheek and smiled. "I love that idea."

"I hope I'm not interrupting your day too much getting here early," he said as they arrived at the front entrance of the Japanese townhouse. He took in the bamboo-surrounded step, the ornate wooden door, the koi pond river that divided the entrance of the home from Mrs. Ikeda's front walk.

Delaney turned quickly. "Are you kidding? I'm so glad you're here." She narrowed her eyes, reading something in his expression. "Daddy? Why are you crying?"

She hadn't called him 'Daddy' since she was nine.

"I'm just happy to see you," he managed, nodding.

In the time since she graduated and started traveling, he had found his condo unbearably quiet. In the relatively short time she'd lived there, she'd become its identity, with at least two of her books always positioned on the coffee table, a fresh batch of cold brew coffee in a glass pitcher in the fridge, thriving house plants, fragrant vanilla bean candles, and he was constantly tripping over a pair of her sneakers or a misplaced backpack. With her gone, leftovers from corporate dinners tended to pile up and spoil in the fridge. When she lived there, he would find her dining on cold pad thai for breakfast the next day. He had observed a healthy balancing act--her weight rising to a normal level while his weight had dropped to the divide between healthy and overweight.

She had a steady unpredictability. Some days he'd arrive home and she would be sitting in the hammock chair on the patio reading. Other days, she'd have travel books strewn across the kitchen table, pouring herself into the exotic destinations she could explore, or she'd be tensed over a textbook, her hair pulled up in a messy knot, or she had just returned home from swimming laps, her hair still dripping and smelling strongly of chlorine, humming in the kitchen as she prepared dinner.

Now she was standing in a foreign land, looking equally, if not more so, at home. She smiled lightly, stepped toward him and hugged him.

Late that afternoon, they found themselves in Northern Kyoto, in a restaurant made of bamboo and reed mats and constructed next to a waterfall over a roaring stream. Their server was explaining the process of food delivery, most of the patrons lined up at the bar nodding along.

"I didn't review the Tripadvisor listing," he whispered to his daughter when the server had finished instructions. "What is happening right now?"

Delaney smiled, a pink azalea tucked behind her ear. "They're going to send cold noodles down the bamboo chutes. We have to catch them with our chopsticks."

He frowned. "Well, alright then."

When they had returned to their table and tatami mat seats, Delaney sipped her tea and watched her father take in the surroundings, his long legs jutting out from beneath the table.

"What?" he said. "I look like a giant here, don't I?"

She pressed her lips together. "No," she said, suppressing a laugh. "A little. It's okay though. We both do. I can't tell you how many times I've been told how large I am. 'Pretty girl, *big* feet.'" Her cheeks were tense as she stabbed her chopsticks into noodles.

He was thoughtful for a moment. "I ran into Quinn the other day."

"Oh yeah?" she said, her mouth full. She swallowed. "How is Quinn?"

"He has his elevator speech down."

"His what now?"

"It's a business thing. Get your point across concisely, like the length of an average elevator ride."

She nodded, wincing a bit. "What's his elevator speech?"

"He's doing an internship with his dad over the summer, then he'll be going to UCLA, pre-law. He'll be able to work with one of the sports teams out there, plus the rental he'll share is near the water so he'll finally get to learn to surf, and 'let's face it,' who doesn't want to be in LA?"

Delaney covered her mouth as she attempted to finish swallowing her water then raised her hand. "Me."

The server moved quickly to their table, misinterpreting the gesture. "More tea?"

"Yes, arigatou gozaimasu," she responded automatically, then turned back to her dad. "In his email, he failed to mention he'd be *sharing* his rental."

"It would be a lie if I told you that I didn't enjoy the fact that you're not easily impressed by boys."

She wrinkled her nose. "Still holding my spot at the nunnery?"

"It's very nice and somewhat progressive. They even get to wear pants while gardening."

Delaney laughed. "Praise Jesus."

"Well that's generally the idea."

She grinned widely. "You don't have to worry about meeting any boys."

"I don't, huh?"

"Well generally there's no meet the dad requirement when it's just *casual*."

His face fell and he stabbed his chopsticks into his rice.

She lunged over the table to retrieve them. "Never leave your chopsticks in your food, Dad." She released them into his hand. "Geez Louise, I was joking."

He exhaled deeply, staring at her. His serious demeanor broke. "Actually, that was a fair joke. Uncomfortable, but fair." He went back to eating casually.

"I actually have no interest in dating or getting married though."

He frowned. "You have plenty of time for all that."

"When I get back, I'll be so busy." She shrugged. "I'm not eliminating the possibility of meeting someone and having a family eventually, but if I don't? That'd be OK, too."

Thomas thought of the loneliness he had felt in his life--the nights coming home to a dark condo, waking up to silence. Imagining Delaney having that experience in life made his heart ache.

"Not everyone falls in love," she continued, filling the void. "Right?"

It was clear from her eyes, her hand gesture, that she was drawing some lesson from him.

He situated his chopsticks next to his rice bowl, raising his eyebrows. "Is that acceptable chopsticks placement?"

She nodded.

"Of all the life experiences you can have, falling in love is not one I'd want you to skip.

"Love is what life's all about, baby. We want to make our mark on the world, and you will be a phenomenal physical therapist. You'll help so many people, you'll teach new grads, you'll publish papers, present at national and international conferences--"

She squinted at him.

"Martin Schuler and I do lunch."

"You and Dr. Schuler do lunch?"

"Or dinner. A couple times a month."

"I didn't know that."

"You're so smart--brilliant, actually--and you'll have a fantastic career."

"Thanks for the flattery—But?"

"But there's nothing like loving someone. I want you to experience that."

She frowned. "But you and mom--it ended so badly."

"It did."

"And she said it wasn't love--"

It looked like she shot him. He peered across the restaurant at a young boy abandoning his chopsticks to grab at the noodles with his hands. When he looked back at her, his eyes were brimmed with tears. "I wish she had felt differently." He wiped his mouth with his cloth napkin, shrugging. "Did I ever tell you how I met your mom?"

"No."

Thomas had stopped off at Walgreens to pick up an anniversary card for his parents--he had just finished lunch at the restaurant that shared the same parking lot. He was thumbing through the section when 2-year-old Caprice walked up to him, with her two blonde sprouts and a big puffy jacket. He had hesitated to say anything, but as the store was fairly deserted and her mom wasn't tearing around the corner looking for her, he put the card back and said hello. She greeted him in return.

"Where's your mommy?" he had asked, crouching down to her level. She pointed toward the back of the store. He had a sinking feeling about what he might find, thinking perhaps she was shooting up heroine in the bathroom or something, but he followed Caprice back to the in-pharmacy clinic.

Edie was slumped over a plastic chair arm, dark hair unkempt and unwashed, body bundled in an oversized hoodie, mouth agape. Caprice had climbed up beside her, startling Edie awake. She apologized to her daughter for dozing off, sitting up straight. It was then she noticed Thomas for the first time.

"Oh. Are you the doctor?" she asked, eyeing his business suit. She was devastated to learn that Caprice had wandered so far away and thanked him for making sure she got back safely.

He could see her visibly shaking with chills. "I think you need an actual hospital, Miss."

"My insurance has like a $2000 deductible. I can't—" She looked absolutely defeated. "I just can't shake this. It's been over a week."

Thomas glanced over at Caprice stroking her mom's hair. "I'll help cover it, but you need to go. For her sake."

Edie squinted up at him. "Why would you help me?"

"Whenever I've needed help I've been fortunate to have someone be there for me. Consider this paying it forward."

When they arrived at the emergency room triage, Edie's temperature was 105.4 and her breathing was labored, her blood pressure alarmingly high. The nurse had her immediately put on a gurney and wheeled away. She had already lost consciousness.

"What was wrong with her?" Delaney asked, her forehead tense.

"Sepsis. She thought she had a respiratory infection, but it was pneumonia, which had turned into sepsis."

When he received the first update, after taking Caprice to the cafeteria and quarantining her to the empty children's play area, the doctor wasn't confident she'd make it. The social worker was able to contact Edie's adoptive mother, who met him at the hospital and was able to take Caprice home with her.

Edie's mom had been surprised by his appearance, his business suit. He'd long removed his jacket and rolled his sleeves. Their brief conversation seemed to have reduced her suspicions that perhaps her daughter was a sex worker. The following day when she came to the hospital after dropping Caprice off at daycare and found him sleeping in the recliner in Edie's room, she had decided they must have been dating for some time.

Thomas found himself drawn to the hospital, visiting every day. Edie had stabilized after a few days of antibiotics, but remained in the hospital for two weeks. The infection had left her so physically and mentally weak that she required help to eat, to transfer in and out of bed, and for the first week, she was unable to safely ambulate so he would push her in a wheelchair (and drag the IV pole) to the patient courtyard.

"The worst part of it for her was not being able to see Caprice. I kind of served as the messenger between them--I brought in drawings and crafts Caprice made and Edie would share stories she wanted me to tell Caprice. I could never do the stories justice, but I tried. Your mom had a way of telling stories—"

Delaney gazed at him. "You didn't even know her—why would you do all that?"

"I loved her," he said, matter-of-factly, then lowered his eyes. "I know how that sounds. I just—I needed to be near her." His breaths were becoming heavy. He smiled distantly, summoning a memory of her drawing with chalk on the front sidewalk with Caprice when he got home from work, her belly large and protruding in front of her like a torpedo. When she had stood to greet him, her jaw was lined with smudges of orange and pink.

She hadn't wanted to find out if they were having a boy or girl, but she often referred to the baby as a boy. "Oh I hope he has your eyes," "I hope he's as mellow as you."

When Delaney was born, she had the swollen, mushed appearance of a newborn and Edie seemed comforted by her splotchy skin, her wild, thick hair. Within a day, nurses, doctors, hospital staff were gushing over her and Edie became increasingly uncomfortable. Delaney rarely cried or fussed, but Edie struggled, blaming her behavior on feeling guilty for splitting her attention from Caprice.

Her lack of initial attachment to Delaney grew over time to resemble resentment, and it had made him uneasy. Eventually the sweet infant won her over, but the trade-off was a perpetual tension and insecurity in Edie. Thomas recalled his building sadness as the version of Edie he fell in love with faded and was overtaken by one who needed to look a particular way, dress a particular way, be seen a particular way.

Delaney watched him closely, but didn't push for him to share his thoughts. Instead, she lowered her gaze.

He frowned. Her defeated posture reminded him of when they told her about their divorce. Mid-explanation, Edie had risen up from her chair and disappeared down the hallway. It was just as Delaney appeared to be processing the news, her face pinching into sobs, that Edie returned, noisily wheeling his packed suitcase.

It was in that moment that he knew he would never forgive Edie. He looked across at the devastation in his daughter's face. Suddenly she felt further away somehow, out of reach. As he saw the placement of his suitcase, the expectation that he was to make his exit clear, it struck him how his intent to make things better somehow for Delaney through divorce was falling short. It felt more like he was abandoning her and if he left, he'd lose her forever. Not a day went by that he didn't regret fighting harder for her.

"I never felt like she cared about me," Delaney said with a huff of her chest. "She treated me like I was her show pony."

He was impressed by Dell's bluntness. He wanted to argue that Edie did care, but the case was weak. She had confessed she feared a modeling lifestyle for Delaney and then a few months later, pronounced she had signed her with an agency, nervously fidgety when she talked about the agent being Caprice's estranged father. They had fought a lot after Delaney's birth, but that argument had revealed to him that he had been viewing her with rose colored glasses. He had credited her for being a strong, resilient single mother, but as he watched her impulsivity in action, her lack of sound judgement, he realized she was abundantly naive and immature. He had been so blinded in his adoration of her, that he failed to realize the truth before bringing a child into the situation.

"Actually, the day of the accident was the first time I felt like I had a mom."

Thomas looked up into the wide, tear-filled eyes of his daughter. Something inside felt like it had split apart. There were so many things he wanted to apologize for. He wanted to tell her how he fought for custody, but that he probably approached things in the wrong way. He wanted to tell her how he felt like he was living a half-life without her, that there was a constant hole in his heart, and since she came back in his life, he felt renewed. It was nothing he ever would have wanted for his daughter, to have her mother die, let alone before her eyes, but it was one of those situations that felt like it was ultimately for Dell's benefit. He had assumed Edie hadn't responded well to hearing her intent to quit, that she had perhaps driven recklessly. It had helped him cope to think that Edie was at least partially to blame for the accident, but that Delaney had been mercifully saved. "She supported your decision."

Delaney nodded, her bloodshot eyes panning away to the stream. "Despite everything, I felt happy, driving home that night. She had told off the director even, at the shoot."

He wondered what had gone on in the shoot that had made Edie see the light, but he wasn't about to ask.

"I'm sorry me modeling drove a wedge between the two of you."

He stared at her in disbelief. "Your 'modeling drove a wedge,'" he echoed, questioningly.

"She said you were against it and she really pushed." Delaney's eyes narrowed.

Thomas exhaled, looking into the bright blue eyes of his daughter. It was not her fault. He told himself he would not share details that would imply it was. At the same time, it didn't feel right to divulge all the details about Edie. Delaney's last interaction with her had been positive--he risked hurting her more by sharing too much, but he refused to lie to her either, so instead, he shared a truth: "I'm not the easiest man to live with."

She cocked her head to one side. Several games of chess had revealed this maneuver as her tell, indicating she had figured out a key part of his strategy. "It was very wrong what she did. To you." She swallowed. "To me. She was hurtful and manipulative and selfish."

He was once again in awe of his daughter's directness.

Her face intensified as she organized her thoughts. "I don't let people get close to me. That's something I get from her. I just think that with that being hard-wired in my brain, along with experiences to reinforce it--" Her voice trailed off.

"You don't think you're capable of loving someone?"

She half shook her head. "Maybe. I think it's not letting someone in."

"So you know what you have to do."

"Avoid all human interaction and replace human relationships with an apartment full of cats?"

He paused. "Yes. That exactly."

She managed a small smile. "It's scary stuff, Dad."

"Hell yeah, it's scary. A part of me *would* rather stick you in a nunnery."

She rolled her eyes.

"I don't regret loving your mom. Not for a second. Even if she didn't love me."

"But you wound up with nothing."

"No. I didn't," he said, raising his eyebrows. He was quiet, then added: "I got the toaster oven."

Delaney snorted, then found herself clutching her chest as she laughed. "At least I have an explanation for my really twisted sense of humor."

He smiled into the beautiful face of his daughter. "I got you, Dell. There is nothing in this world better than that to me."

She swallowed hard, trying unsuccessfully to hold back tears. She inconspicuously wiped her nose on her napkin and exhaled deeply.

His face turned serious as he placed his hand on her arm across the table. "You've only just begun, Baby."

***

The local news called the storm a monsoon, but the torrential winds and endless rain was looking more like a hurricane in the desert. Thomas took a sip from his water glass as an explosion of lightning bursts lit up the sky outside the window. There was a collective "ooh" from the restaurant occupants. It was a barbecue restaurant close to Delaney's hospital. When she had justified the selection, he had assumed it was because it was her assigned weekend to work, but she had become uncharacteristically quiet and had explained that there was someone she wanted him to meet and he would be coming straight from the hospital.

He had waited until he could see her in person, when she met him at the airport, to ask any questions. The questioning was complicated by the loud clatter on the car roof and the wild windshield wipers. What he was able to learn was that his name was Jack Mathison--Delaney's cheeks had tightened involuntarily as she said his name--they had worked together previously, but he wasn't clear on this, and he was now an Anesthesiologist.

Thomas scanned over the menu then glanced up to see Delaney approaching the table from the restroom. They had both been pummeled by rain on their run around the building from the parking lot, Thomas having refused to be dropped off at the door, and after they discovered Delaney had forgotten her umbrella at home. When she had excused herself to the bathroom, he had worried she might be applying makeup or otherwise "fixing" her appearance, but she returned looking decidedly unchanged apart from perhaps her hair being wrung out. She smiled at him as she approached the dining area, but her eyes veered to the left suddenly, and her smile broadened wider than he had ever seen.

She turned on her heel, gliding across the restaurant. Thomas followed her gaze to a tall, broad-shouldered man standing beside the hostess stand, securing his umbrella. He laughed upon taking in her disheveled appearance.

Jack Mathison was intimidating in stature and had a polished look to him, dressed simply but fashionably in dark wash jeans, a pale blue button down shirt and a dark grey v-neck sweater. When he hugged Delaney, he wrapped one arm around her shoulder and the other around her waist. He saw how he closed his eyes for a brief, indulgent moment as he rested his cheek against her neck.

Thomas watched Jack whisper something to her that made her arch backward and grin, arms still tightly wrapped around his neck.

Delaney released her hold, pushed her lips firmly to his cheek. When she rotated to walk beside him, they both immediately reached for the other's hand and when they walked toward the dining area, they moved as one.

Her smile.

Thomas could not take his eyes off the exuberance of her smile.

The brightness and hope in her eyes.

"Dad, I'd like you to meet Jack Mathison," she said, her mouth turning upward with each syllable.

Thomas glanced back and forth between them as he stood. When Jack extended his arm to shake his hand, Thomas frowned at it and moved in for a hug instead. He found himself tearing up and tried to silently sniffle, but he caught Delaney's eye as he patted Jack on the back to end the hug.

Thomas nodded to her.

"Oh stop that." She lowered her voice and gritted her teeth. "Now he *knows* I'm crazy for him."

"Is that a secret?"

Her eyes widened as she tucked herself conspiratorially next to her dad. "*Yes,*" she said in loud whispers. "I think we can salvage this though. Be cool, Dad. Be cool."

# 28

# day three

E veryone sat rigidly around the conference room table. Julie picked at the laminate siding on the table edge and had just inadvertently chipped off a large piece when Dr. Bordeaux stepped in carrying three boxes of fresh bakery donuts. He arranged the boxes side-by-side and flipped open the lids.

The scent of warm sugar was so rich that it was obvious when the aroma had wafted to each team member. Their eyes widened and they took in the sight of the puffy pastries with captivated interest.

"Aside from fresh beignets on BourbonStreet, these are the best breakfast pastries in North America," the doctor said, taking a seat. Nurse Sandy slid him some lab results and he slipped on his readers to examine them, leaving everyone to sit and deliberate if taking a donut was equivalent to some form of disloyalty to Dr. Schuler.

Dr. Bordeaux debated the significance of the lab results, speaking quietly to Sandy about fluid intake. He made an intense effort not to look up when staff started to invade the donuts boxes, but there was a small jump of his mouth as he spoke. He had a solid, squared face, clean-shaven as though he had visited a barber shop for a straight edge shave that very morning and short, spiked brown hair. He typically wore a suit, and a complicated, vested suit at that, but he sat in the conference room with impeccable, but somehow still casual posture, wearing navy scrubs, crisp new cross trainers, and a stethoscope around his neck, tapping his fingers together.

He spontaneously reached for one of the boxes, took out a chocolate glazed donut and a napkin and placed them before himself. "Oh, we'll get started in a second." He rose from the table and left, returning a few moments later with a very large blended coffee drink with a whipped cream dollop and caramel drizzle. He sat with a sigh, taking a long, satisfying swig. He appeared pleased when he noticed the boxes were more empty than before he stepped out.

"I've met everyone now at this point, I think. If I haven't, I apologize. I'm really trying to reach out to everyone. Please come introduce yourself." Previously when other doctors covered, they were provided a cheat sheet reviewing all pertinent information about each patient. Dr. Mike Bordeaux was certainly told about it, as he looked up and down the table expectantly. When it was clear no one was going to be providing such a lifeline, he nodded. "I believe we have close to a dozen patients to round with today."

The case coordinator, keeper of the lifeline, nodded tightly.

"Alright then, well I'm going to start with dear sweet Laney."

The faces of several staff softened considerably upon hearing her name.

"She's a warrior. No other way to describe her. I've worked with professional athletes and I'm not sure I've ever met someone who's made as great of a comeback as Laney." He glanced up at Julie, eyebrows raised.

There was a resonating agreement around the table.

"So she's 5 days post-ICU since she had a brief stint on acute. As I understand, she had significant deficits when she was on Rehab that had started to resolve when the unruptured aneurysm was discovered. Evidently the aneurysm had been impacting primarily her memory. On that front, the clipping procedure effectively reversed the memory effects. It's--amazing--from what I've heard from  Dr. Mathison."

Jenna smiled.

"She didn't start off recovery like other young clipping patients since she had the residual effects of the bleed, which was clear back in--March? Wow."

"That girl needs to get home," Sandy said, conclusively.

"I agree. Since she discharged from us to Neuro to have the craniotomy, she spent 8 days in ICU, took a short tour of acute until she was medically cleared, and now she's back on Rehab."

"Thank you for making sure she was brought back over," Julie chimed in. "I know there was some pushback."

Dr. Bordeaux blinked in acknowledgment. "There was concern from others, but my stance was non-negotiable. She's one of our own."

The air in the conference room lightened significantly.

"I missed her the first time around—" he didn't mention it was because their beloved Dr. Schuler had refused to let anyone else cover Rehab. "But in the short time she's been here, I've seen her in the pool, I've seen her making laps in the hallways, doing reps on the weight machines--"

"Laney gonna Laney," Grant said, raising his eyebrow.

He smiled.

"She does fatigue after activity," Jenna remarked.

"I barely got her back to her room before she passed out yesterday. *Not literally*. She was just really tired. She's sleeping a lot more than she had been," Julie added, questioningly.

"Well she did have someone poking around in her brain not too long ago. Most craniotomy patients get extremely tired with even light activity. Plus she has the brain bleed she's still recovering from. From that perspective?" He shrugged and sipped his coffee, making a dramatically impressed face.

"She's a warrior."

"Precisely. She had total independence before, obviously. I read we had been considering a cane for her?"

"Yes, or walking sticks. She's not going to be happy with either," Julie said, "but she's realistic. She knows she's limited because of her activity tolerance and she wants to get home."

"I get that impression, too."

"I think it's going to be best to have her with a walker or cane to start and a wheelchair as a backup option. Give her a chance to recover. In her case, I think she's going to recover better at home."

Dr. Bordeaux pushed back in his chair back. "Despite the complication she faced, I know how much progress she made before, how hard you all worked with her, how hard your work with all your patients. The work done here on Inpatient Rehab is remarkable. I recognize it, the many people over me recognize it. We're very proud of the work that you do to take care of our patients—and you should be, too."

There was silence around the table, some confused glances.

"You bet your ass we're proud," Jeff pronounced from the open conference door, startling half the room into suppressed chuckles. "I was told there were donuts."

***

"How did I do?" Mike Bordeaux asked, once back in his new office.

Julie shrugged. "Better than I expected."

"Ouch."

"I just mean that people are really unhappy about Dr. S. Considering that--" She gestured loosely toward the freshly painted office wall.

"Considering that, what?" he asked, wrapping his arm around her waist and turning her toward him.

"Anyone could walk in here."

"They're raiding the donut boxes," he said smoothly. He kissed her cheek.

"I *told* you not to get yourself a fancy coffee."

"I need the caffeine."

"So drink regular coffee."

He pulled up his nose. "Gross."

"You are *such* a snob."

"So you don't want yours then?"

Her cheeks reddened. "You bought me one? Really?"

"No, but who's a snob again?"

She smacked his chest. "That would have been a nice gesture."

He reached to his desk and grabbed his cup. "You may have mine."

"It says your name on it."

"So?"

"*So*, we said we were going to keep this under wraps."

"Fine, fine, fine."

"Alright, I have to go see a patient." She kissed him quickly on the mouth, then stole a large swig of his coffee. "Are we running into each other for lunch?"

"11:45. Beat the rush."

She nodded. "OK, thanks Dr. B," she said loudly as she exited the office. "I'll let him know." Julie glanced toward the nurse's station to make sure no one suspected anything, but there were only two nurses seated and they were fixated on their computer monitors.

"Let who know?" a woman's voice said from just behind her.

Julie let out a small squeal, clutching her chest, as she turned to find Delaney approaching. She was hesitantly walking with a front-wheeled walker and an attentive Terrence at her side.

"Who are you going to tell? Mr. Powers?"

"Who's that?"

"You know. Mr. *Austin* Powers?"

Julie blushed, her mouth falling open. "Stop! You know, your memory coming back is not without its downsides!"

"What are you two talking about, now?" Terrence asked.

"Nothing," they both said in unison.

"Took you long enough," Delaney said in a sing-song voice.

"I didn't do anything. It was totally out of the blue—he--" Julie's eyes widened. "*You*," she said, accusingly, pointing at her friend.

Delaney shrugged.

"Is this about Dr. B and Julie doing the horizontal rumba?" Terrence asked casually, placing his hand on Delaney's back to provide more support.

"What?!" Julie screeched, her cheeks beet red.

"They haven't been subtle?" Delaney asked between giggles.

"I'm very observant."

"Well that's true," Delaney acknowledged they turned back to Julie. "You have whipped cream on your lip, General."

"That's what you get for drinking my coffee," Mike Bordeaux muttered through the door.

"Hey Dr. B, Mr. Kline will need a custom wheelchair for discharge. Could you print a prescription?"

"What specs?"

"Lightweight, removable footrests and cushion."

"Pick it up after your session. I'll leave it on my keyboard."

"Thank you, Sir."

"I heard there were donuts?" Delaney said toward the door.

The door creaked open and a plate of two chocolate glazed donuts appeared.

Terrence took the plate, suppressing a laugh.

"Yeah, baby, *yeah*," Delaney added, grinning at Julie. She continued pushing along the walker, which made a squeaky noise as it slid across the floor.

"Don't push so hard," Julie called after her.

"Oh *behave.*"

# 28
# refresh

J ack sat on the pool decking, his legs dropped in the water, watching Delaney swim. The length of the pool was not ideal for laps, but she made do. Occasionally she stopped to let her body drift upward, gazing at the early morning sky as she floated.

Her discharge instructions said to wait two weeks after she was discharged to submerge her head, but due to seizure risk, she should not swim unsupervised. This was why at the fourteen day mark, she had woken him at 6am, already changed into her swimsuit. The surgery had presented a setback for her mobility, hence her eagerness to start rebuilding her strength. She had become proficient at bed to wheelchair transfers and propelled herself around with ease. She tried not to complain about requiring the wheelchair for now. She did grumble about it, if she turned too quickly, or otherwise struggled with the limitations of the chair, but for the most part, she had accepted her need for it until she could build some strength and endurance.

In the warm chlorinated water, Jack yawned widely. His sleep schedule had become erratic these past few weeks. He anticipated he might sleep better after her craniotomy, after her memory had returned, but he found himself with increasing anxiety as they prepared for her discharge. He had been tense preparing the house for her, but he thought it might subside once she was home. It hadn't.

Typically he would wake in a panic in the middle of the night, search for her in the sheets and exhale deeply when his hand found her. More often than not, he wouldn't be able to sleep the rest of the night.

She napped a lot so it wasn't as though he didn't have the opportunity to play catch up on sleep. He'd inevitably fall asleep if he sat down with her to read or watch an occasional movie, but he kept busy with other tasks instead. Waking from sleep seemed to be linked to a feeling of anxiety, which drained any energy he'd managed to accumulate while he was sleeping.

When he opened his eyes, not realizing he'd closed them, she was upright in the pool, eyes just above the water.

"You're a human alligator," he said with a small smile.

She stood taller, the water coming to just above her waist, like a grand tulle skirt, and stepped smoothly across the shallow end of the pool. Months in the hospital had removed the taut tone in her shoulders, but she had started to regain the weight she lost in the hospital, thanks to casseroles and lasagnas colleagues had dropped off, so she didn't look quite as emaciated as she had after ICU. His eyes scanned over her—her balance outside the pool was still shaky at times, but she stood solidly in the water.

They would start at the gym on some seated weight machines soon. She could probably do the rower to build up her arms and back, but she would need to start slow as quick movements often brought on headaches and dizziness.

He allowed himself the memory of the day she approached him as he waited for the rowing machine. She had effortlessly good posture—*Pilates*, he noted silently. *Pilates would be good, gentle muscle building exercise.*

There had been something vulnerable about her that day in the gym. She always seemed to have an easy confidence, but there was a wider set to her eyes, a hopeful, yet fearful gaze. She had been slightly fidgety, twisting her earbuds cord around her fingertips.

Before him was an entirely different image. More vulnerable, weakened—and yet, stronger.

She tilted her head to the side, her dark hair stubby and unruly. "Penny for your thoughts."

Jack raised his eyebrows.

"Your thoughts are worth much more than that, but I'm on long-term disability. It's all I can afford."

He gave another small smile, indicating he wasn't going to share.

She furrowed her forehead, moving closer to him. "Despite all evidence to the contrary, I'm not going to fall apart on you again. Think of me like a certified pre-owned car."

"I will do no such thing."

"Soon you won't even see these scars. In a short several years time, I'll have long flowing hair again. Not as lustrous as your locks of course--" The slant of her lip due to the initial facial droop was still present, but far less prominent since she had been vigilant about doing her homework to correct it.

He dropped into the pool, waded over to her. She sank into the water so he could wrap his arms around her. "I don't see the scars now."

"What about the giant staples in the shape of a fish hook?"

He shook his head, exhaling. "All I see is my future wife," he said, gazing into her eyes. "*If* you'll have me."

***

Jack stood in the warm sunshine of the driveway, tucking the gym duffel into the backseat, when he heard the crunch of gravel under tires. The white compact car eased to a stop in front of the curb and a woman with medium brown hair chopped at her shoulders climbed out. She wore blue mirrored sunglasses, but removed them quickly when she saw him.

"Caprice. You look different."

She wore dark wash jeans, a plain navy v-neck, and navy Converse, and carried a slouchy leather purse. She seemed to be making an effort to look friendly, but there was an overtly nervous expression on her face. "How is she?" she asked, her forehead furrowed.

He considered his response, then decided on: "She's Delaney."

This brought a small, reflective smile to her lips. "Do you think she'd talk to me? I don't want to intrude--were you going somewhere? I could stay with her while you go."

He excused that she just implied Delaney needed a babysitter. "We were heading out to the gym," he said, closing the car door. "But we can go later."

She nodded, her eyes bright. "So she really is doing well?"

He motioned toward the garage door. "She's inside." He stepped in first, expecting to find Delaney filling her water in the kitchen in preparation to leave, but the house was silent, her turquoise stainless water bottle disassembled on the counter. "D?" he called, stepping across the kitchen.

Through the back patio windows, he saw her holding the phone to her ear, gazing across the grassy backyard, leaning solidly into her cane. She had a short-term goal to switch to hiking poles that week for short distances, but for now reasoned that the cane offered more stability. She was still using a wheelchair for longer distances and when she fatigued since she still lacked endurance.

He read the words "thank you" on her lips and then she stood stunned. The impact of the conversation seemed to destabilize her and she moved quickly to sit in the waiting wheelchair. She dropped her hand holding her phone into her lap, staring ahead, breathing heavily.

As though prompted by her inner task list, she suddenly rolled the wheelchair in reverse, spinning so she was facing toward the door, her face a blur of uncertainty and exhilaration.

She frowned when she saw him, reading his expression immediately. Then she saw Caprice over his shoulder. Where he would have expected dread to appear, he saw kind neutrality emerge. In a matter of seconds, the neutrality evaporated and Delaney's face was filled with only kindness and love. Her lips were pressed together, but she pulled them upwards at both ends, motioning for Caprice to join her on the patio.

Caprice stepped outside apprehensively, first unsure of whether she should hug her sister. She decided against it, then debated about whether to sit or stand, walking awkwardly in a circle. She reasoned it wasn't fair she stand since Delaney didn't have a choice in the matter. The words flew out of her mouth and then she immediately clapped her hand over her mouth. "I'm sure you'll be out of the wheelchair soon." She quickly decided this made matters worse. "But if not, that's OK, too--" She shook her head. "Oh God, I'm terrible at this--"

"Caprice," Delaney said solidly, the first word she'd spoken since seeing her sister.

Caprice froze, her eyes filled with tears.

"Sit here," she said, softer, pulling out one of the outdoor dining chairs. When her sister did as she was told, Delaney shifted the bench seat from under the table, applied the wheelchair brakes, and maneuvered the transfer expertly. It was smoother than any transfer she'd done in the time since she'd been out of the hospital and as her eyes met Jack's, he could see her silent celebration. Then she lowered her chin, the slightest acknowledgement that she would handle the conversation on her own.

Jack closed the patio door and began to pace in front of the refrigerator. He glanced at his phone, noting the time: 2:38. He put the phone screen down on the counter and resolved to cutting up the watermelon a neighbor had dropped off, pulling down a large cutting board and selecting an appropriate knife. He distracted himself with thoughts of it being late in the season for watermelon, what were the indicators for a sweet watermelon? Did they say a yellow spot is a good sign? He lined up the knife, stopped, glanced out the window--Delaney was sitting with her impeccable posture, listening. Her face gave nothing away about what Caprice was saying. He went back to the cutting board, lined up the knife along the curve of the watermelon and started slicing.

Delaney sat quietly. Months of being aphasic had given her a certain comfort level with periods of silence, where previously she would have felt pressure to fill the void.

Thankfully she had been keeping herself on regimented dosing of Tylenol, which helped take the edge off, so her ever-present headache was dull and less-intrusive than it could have been.

She watched as her sister resituated herself in her chair. Caprice had always tried to project an image of confidence--overconfidence really, but years of

Delaney having the most minute gestures, ticks, micro bits of body language pointed out to her as a means of critical analysis had given her a heightened sensitivity to their presence in others. She watched Caprice fix her hair, touch her face, cross and uncross her legs. She watched as her eyes darted toward the door. Finally, she took a deep breath.

"I forget to breathe fully sometimes. My counselor pointed it out."

Delaney nodded.

Caprice seemed to have found a starting place. "I see a counselor now. A couple times a week. It seems excessive, maybe, but it helps. She thought it was best for me to work some things out for myself before getting in touch with you. I still have a long way to go, but that's why I didn't reach out sooner--even though I've wanted to." She paused. "There's no excuse for my behavior, especially the visits when you were in the hospital. I have been very selfish and immature. I've blamed you for things that you are not responsible for." She seemed to be reciting lines. Delaney imagined her sitting before her mirror speaking them to her own reflection, her brow severe and furrowed. "I've had-- and still have--a lot of anger. You've been the easy target for that, but it's-- *displaced*," she said, stating the word like a child interpreting the word in a spelling bee. "What I felt before for you was jealousy to some degree, I think, but mainly anger toward myself."

Delaney swallowed, her throat dry.

"I was angry at myself for a number of reasons--and a lot of that I'm finding is displaced anger that I have toward other people. I know now that you didn't do anything wrong. You're not to blame and I think I--" She was speaking quicker, more like her normal speech pattern. There was a sense with the quickening pace that her words would barrel off the rails.

"Caprice, it's just me. *Breathe.*"

Caprice looked her sister in the eyes, took a slow, deliberate breath. "I'm sorry, Laney. I'm so sorry. For my behavior. For what you've been through--"

Delaney inhaled and exhaled purposefully.

Caprice paused to do the same. "I failed as your big sister. I should have protected you. It was because of me that you even were roped into modeling in the first place."

Delaney squinted thoughtfully. "I never blamed you--and I never thought you failed."

***

He had just cleaned up the scraps of every piece of fruit in the house when he heard the scraping of the outdoor dining chair. He turned around quickly to find Caprice stooping to hug Delaney, who seemed to be straining to make it less of an awkward sideways angle. The sun was set low in the sky, triggering the automatic sensor on the globe lights on the patio to turn on.

It was then the doorbell rang. In his quest to stay busy, Jack had ordered in food. He hesitated knowing that Delaney would be uncomfortable from sitting so long and still needed help transferring at times and the conversation finally seemed to be wrapping up. He checked the clock-5:52pm.

He answered the door, briskly grabbed the food bags, mumbled a quick thank you, and jogged back to the kitchen, dropping the bags on the counter.

Caprice was sitting again, leaning forward and speaking closely to her sister over the pair of now empty lemonade glasses he'd brought out to them, knowing it was warm and knowing how important it was for Delaney to take in enough fluids. He was taken back by how natural Caprice's expression had appeared--he had become accustomed to the synthetic smile she wore when she was being insincere. Now she spoke conspiratorially, like catching up with an old friend.

Delaney had always given off the impression of being the older sibling, the mature one—looking out for her, loaning her money, letting her stay at her condo. He had assumed she just tolerated her sister. Now he found that she had angled herself toward Caprice, her face filled with relief, something she thought had been lost forever, suddenly found. Her eyes glistened and her breath seemed to catch every few seconds as she inhaled, followed by what seemed to be a methodical release of sadness as she exhaled.

Caprice glanced toward the door, waving toward him just as she caught Jack about to step further inside. "I should get going," he heard her say, and she started to stand.

Jack pushed open the patio door and stepped immediately to Delaney, who seemed jarred by the sudden activity.

"Are you free on Saturday? I'm supposed to sign the papers on an apartment--I'd love for you to see it. I won't have furniture, but maybe we can go to dinner?"

Jack looked to Delaney, who was smiling lightly. He waited for her to reply.

Delaney frowned in his direction. "You work that night, I think?"

"How about lunch? Or brunch?" Caprice asked. "I just want you to see the place. I need help coming up with decorating ideas."
Delaney began to speak, but had to clear her throat a few times. "Maybe we can find some nice wall frames. Do some justice to your artwork."

Caprice rolled her shoulders back, smiling tensely, holding back tears it seemed.

Once Caprice had pulled away in her generic white rental car, waving out the passenger window, Jack turned back toward the front door. Delaney remained sitting idly in the wheelchair, staring down the road. Her breaths were heavy.

"We can still go to the gym if you want, but I figured it was getting late. I ordered some food from Cha."

That's when he saw the flare of her nostrils, the quiver of her lip, and the tears beginning to stream from her eyes.

Jack crouched down next to her. "D?"

"I'm sorry," she said urgently, turning her chin toward him. "If she knows about Jeremiah, that means you know, too."

"D, listen to me—"

"I should have told you." In the orange hue of the sunset, her face had a pained, sorrowful expression. "I'm sorry you found out that way." She reached her hand to his cheek instinctively, her eyes pleading--though it wasn't clear if she was pleading for forgiveness, for release from the memory, or both.

His heart ached for her having to carry not only the burden of the memory, but of having to share the memory. How many times had she planned to tell him? How many times had she mentally prepared herself for the conversation and backed down? Maybe she had been set to tell him and he had made a move on her or not been receptive in one way or another.

"I know it's something I should have told you—"

Jack sighed, not able to disagree with her. "I wish I could just—" He wasn't quite sure how to finish the sentence. He wanted to erase the event from her life, but saying that seemed like a superficial remark.

Her eyes seemed to understand. "Everything that happens, good or bad, shapes who we are and where we are, who we end up with. Change one thing—"

"Everything else changes, too," he said quietly.

"No more Ja-Laney." She pulled up her nose as soon as she said it. "Sorry, mashed up couple name. Jeff started coming up with them at the end of my IRF stay."

"D-Jack," he offered.

"That's so obvious--how did he not come up with that?" She smiled weakly.

"Let's go inside," he suggested, having just squashed a mosquito on her arm and brushed it off gently. He stood and Delaney moved to lock the wheelchair brakes so she could stand as well. She pushed the cane heavily into the ground and focused on her steps as she moved into the house. He followed her inside with the wheelchair, but left it by the front door across from the dog butler table.

Delaney had already reached the couch and was waiting for him as he put the takeout in the refrigerator.

"So if you change one thing, everything else changes, too," he prompted, sitting beside her.

She nodded. "No one wants to go through the bad stuff, obviously, but there's always something good or meaningful that comes out of the bad."

"That's a really positive outlook."

"If what happened in high school *didn't* happen, I would never have put my foot down about modeling, I wouldn't have figured things out with my mom--" She frowned at that. "I'm not sure if I would have had the relationship I had with my dad if not for the accident--even with a better situation with my mom. If I hadn't been in the accident, I wouldn't have met Dr. S and I would have never become a physical therapist. I would like to think I would have met you, but I don't know how exactly we would have crossed paths."

"It's really something to think about all the things that had to line up for us to meet."

"Twice."

His eyebrows jumped briefly. "It wasn't the right time the first time around."

"I think our life experiences shaped us to be just who the other needed."

He nodded, looking down at her hands laying flat in her lap. It was still a surreal sight after months of clenched fists. When he spoke, his voice was gentle. "Why do you think you didn't tell me?"

She waited for him to make eye contact. When he did, her eyes were filled with tears again. "I should have told you, but I--I didn't feel like I *needed* to." She sighed. "I never ever thought I'd be in a relationship. With every man before you--*and there were several.*" Delaney slapped her palm to her face. "I meant that as a joke, but it just came off like I was a--never mind. You know my number."

"Two. Including Michael Bordeaux."

"Yes, future husband of Julie." She cleared her throat, her face turning serious. "Dating was torture for me. I felt so anxious. I tried to get past what happened, but there was always something--something in how they acted or something they said that reminded me of that day. I hated sex. I didn't want to date. I was done.

"And then I met you. I was nervous, but in a good way. In a being on the brink of something wonderful kind of nervous. I had given up on the idea of dating because I thought I would have this huge obstacle to overcome, needing to get over what had happened or deal with those memories and thoughts whenever I was intimate with someone.

"But with you, all of that went away. It wasn't you, me, and all these bad memories. It was just you and me." Jack watched her lips as she spoke, how her lips pulled up at the corners with each syllable. "I feel free from it. With you."

He hesitated in his response. He knew there was more to the story. He knew there was more explanation as to why she wouldn't say anything. He knew she had protected others at her own expense. He wanted to tell her that he'd been in contact with Charlie, a friend of his from high school, who was now a criminal prosecutor. He said that if they got Tim's cooperation and testimony, supplemented by Quinn, he could likely get a conviction for, at last, Jeremiah, even without actual DNA evidence.

He wanted to tell her about it, but she just looked so exhausted. Her face pinched and she dropped her chin to her chest. "I'm sorry."

He exhaled loudly. "You have nothing to be sorry for."

"Yes, I do."

"Delaney? You don't."

His expression hardened for a brief moment, but Delaney saw it. Had he put an emphasis on the word "you" just then?

"Jack?"

"They should have to answer for what they did to you."

"If I don't press charges are you going to deliver justice yourself?"

"I'm already working on my alibis."

She shook her head. "No need for that."

"What do you mean?"

"Which lawyer friend have you talked to? Not Blake--he went into politics, right? Charlie?"

"Yeah, you met Charlie."

"4th of July last year."

Jack smiled lightly. He knew her memories had returned, but sometimes it still caught him by surprise in an entirely pleasant way.

"Would he take the case?"

"Yes. He said he absolutely would."

"OK." She was thoughtful a moment. "Quinn would testify. Caprice is on board, though I don't know if she'd be helpful for testimony."

Jack could feel the relief of reconciliation radiating off her.

"I don't know how much you know about what happened," she continued, reluctantly. "I'd want to talk to Charlie about someone else who could be a witness. He'd probably be charged with something, accessory or something, but maybe he could work out a plea bargain."

"Timothy?"

Her eyes widened. "You know more than Caprice then."

"Quinn and I talked after Caprice left."

"Ah." She searched his eyes for some indication of support.

He released a breath. "I don't understand why you want to protect him. He was your friend when you were younger, but--" He couldn't bring himself to say it, to describe to her what she had gone through. She looked down at her hands, stretching her fingers.

When she looked up, her forehead furrowed. She tried to piece together words that would articulate the tangle of emotions she felt. She went on to describe their friendship, how they shared adventures that gave them both a sense of freedom from their otherwise isolated captivities--"Let the wild rumpus start!" was their catchphrase before going to a movie or miniature golfing or any number of decidedly mild activities. She smiled as she explained this, still able to reflect with affection on the memories. He could see the darkness of what was to happen shade the memories. Her face fell. "He didn't want to be in that locker room any more than I did."

Jack thought of how Quinn had described Delaney recognizing the scars on Timothy's arms in the midst of it all. He imagined how it would disarm her.

"Modeling had exposed me to a lot of things too young," she said, swallowing hard. Her eyes were hesitant to focus too long on him and the rate of her fidgeting increased.

She had been afraid she might be raped. Both men and women would touch her in ways that maintained some level of deniability, but they were getting more bold. Timothy tried to get her to quit, but she said it wasn't an option. (Her mother had become reliant on the income.) At the age of fourteen, she had asked him to have sex with her--not because she truly wanted to or because she had romantic feelings for him, but because she wanted her first time to be with someone she loved.

Timothy had taken her gently in his arms and painted a story with his words about how her first time would be in some picturesque setting and she would be in love. He said he refused to take that away from her.

Jack noticed how her hands had started to tremble.

It was both a comfort and a cruel nightmare to recognize his arms in the locker room shower. Despite having put up a good fight to that point, the inevitability of the situation had just impressed itself upon her brain. She had actually taken momentary solace in his arms.

She was having trouble taking a breath, her pupils starting to overtake the blue rings of her eyes.

"D," Jack whispered.

Her eyes focused on him and she started to take slow, steady breaths. She reached her hand up to his cheek, taking in the details of his face, paying close attention to the furrow of his brow. She ran her thumb over it, trying to smooth out the wrinkles.

"I know this isn't going to be easy for you so please tell me what I can do."

She smiled lightly. "You can take me for a dance."

"I can do that."

Her gait was unsteady as they made their way from the living room, through the kitchen and out into the backyard, but her face filled with childlike wonder as he turned on the globe lights. She leaned on one of the lounge chairs as she waited for Jack to put music on the speakers. He scrolled through his extensive collection on his phone and grinned when he had made his selection. "Ready?"

The tune was lighthearted and playful. And upbeat. "You have more confidence in my balance tonight than me."

"Come on, Mathison," he said, smirking, taking her hand. He immediately twirled her and watched as her feet took over, as though programmed with the moves.

As she spun toward him, her hands instinctively landed on his arms.

He started singing the lyrics with his best Garth Brooks impersonation, leading her through the quick steps and several more twirling sequences. With each stanza, with each fiddle accompaniment, with each misstep, her smile broadened. "*And I'd be sad and lonely if there were no yoooooooou-ooooooooo---*" he sang, dipping her to be perpendicular with the floor, then popped them both back up.

When it was apparent her body was tiring, he wrapped his arms around her and he supported her weight in doing a simple sway. They were out of beat with the music, but neither of them seemed to mind.

## 29
## over and over

Exiting the jam-packed department store, Jack took a gulp of chilly city air. It was not refreshing as he'd hoped. It contained an unhealthy helping of exhaust fumes, fried food, and nicotine. There were the expected crowds, but having not lived in a city for a couple of decades, he found he had taken for granted the luxury of personal space. He stepped across the sidewalk, swarms of people moving in all directions colliding with him at varying speeds. He scanned the sea of faces for Delaney. She had made tremendous gains with her mobility, but she still fatigued. Navigating the crowds the day after Thanksgiving was certainly not advisable, but Tabitha had begged them to help outfit their new house for their baby, due to arrive in March.

They had woken with the crows and strategized a number of retailers for discounted gear. When last he saw Delaney, she was perusing clothing racks filled with miniature clothes, everything half off.

He had just retrieved his cell phone when he spotted Delaney standing alongside a police horse, gently stroking its head, seemingly talking to the animal.

The chestnut horse with a brilliant white muzzle was nuzzling insistently at her as she spoke. Jack took in the surreal sight, the empty saddle, the trekking pole leaning against the trash can, Delaney standing as solidly as anyone.

Delaney caught his eye mid-sentence, transitioned her mouth to a smile.

"How are you planning on getting him on the airplane?"

"Jack, meet Jack. His partner needed to check on a situation in the jewelry store. I offered to keep Jack company."

"Of course you did." Jack let the horse sniff his hand. "A little crazy out here today, huh Jack?"

The officer was just emerging from the store, still carrying on a conversation, but all seemed to be well.

"I figured we'd head back to the house soon, maybe stop and get lunch first? Tabitha has a couple more places she's going to go."

"One more deep dish pizza before we go home?"

"Well since you suggested it."

She smiled, her bright blue eyes peering out from beneath a grey knit beanie.

"Thank you so much," the young officer who looked no more than 24 said. He eyed human Jack, noting the position of his hand on Delaney's back. "Your wife was nice enough to help us out, huh buddy? Normally I just hitch him to a bench or a tree, but it's so busy out here today and I was just around the corner when the call came in."

"All is well?"

He ran his hand over his slicked hair. "Yeah, teenage kid tried to shoplift and things got tense."

Delaney kissed the horse between his eyes. "Thanks for the good conversation, Jack."

The officer extended his hand to Jack. "Thanks to you both." Jack shook his hand and the officer moved on to Delaney, giving her an extended but respectful gaze.

As Jack and Officer Castillo rode off toward Cloud Gate, Jack lifted the trekking pole from its resting position on the trash can a man was now utilizing as a table for his platter of chili cheese dog and fries, raising an eyebrow at her.

"*You* try to pet a horse and hold onto that at the same time."

"Yeah, yeah. It's probably more of a hazard out here anyway," he said, guiding her down the sidewalk. "Now let's get you that deep dish pizza."

"I prefer thin crust. You know this," she said with an eye roll, looping her arm around his elbow. She hadn't yet been able to shake a slight limp when she applied weight to her right leg and her gait speed was snail-like compared to her normal long strides.

Jack surveyed the traffic situation that was at an absolute standstill. "Are you OK to walk? We can catch the Red Line at Monroe."

"I'm with you, but I am *not* racing the Google Maps walking estimates."

"OK, but I'm going to ask that you find the following romantic and not dehumanizing."

Before she'd had a chance to interpret this, or respond, he had swept her up, wrapping his arm around her hips and lifting her against his shoulder. He immediately started weaving in and out of cars, jay-walking to get to the opposite side of the street.

"Jack, I am perfectly capable," she said as he placed her back on solid ground. She quickly surveyed her surroundings and the stairs that now confronted them. "Was that absolutely necessary?"

"Train leaves in three minutes."

"Then why did you put me down?" She said urgently. "Just be careful. People might think you're kidnapping me."

"The giggling might tell them otherwise."

The train was mercifully less packed than the streets and they were able to sit side-by-side.

"So what'd you talk to Officer Jack about?" he asked, placing his hand on her knee.

"The typical—he's being picked on in the barn so I gave him some advice. He listened to me ramble on about what I should do with my career life since my life as a therapist is essentially over."

"Not necessarily."

"I know my limitations. I wouldn't be safe to walk any patient for a 10 meter walk test, let alone be able to support them if they lost their balance."

"You're getting stronger everyday."

"You just hoisted my butt over your shoulder so we wouldn't miss the train."

"Well that's speed, not strength."

She shrugged, leaning back into his arm. "I'm not giving up. I just feel down about that right now. I'll play some 'Eye of the Tiger' at the gym tomorrow and I'll be fine."

Jack squeezed his hand around her shoulder, kissed the top of her head.

It was the day before they left for Chicago at a stroke support group that Delaney had shared the advice of her Neurologist--that she was at extreme risk for complications if she became pregnant. A spikey-haired sixty-one year old divorced Biology professor had agreed whole-heartedly, stopping just shy of telling her that she would be signing her unborn child's death warrant, along with possibly her own.

Delaney had gritted her teeth, fighting back tears as she told Jack about the encounter, even defending that the woman was being realistic and hadn't been vindictive. The woman had endured three second trimester miscarriages herself after suffering a stroke at the age of thirty-two.

Tabitha didn't know this when she tasked them with shopping for baby gear and clothes and Delaney had quietly told him not to say anything. She had beamed at Tabitha as she filled Thanksgiving conversation with tales of visiting her obstetrician, feeling the baby move. Delaney had even sat with her, her palm braced over the tiniest of baby bumps, talking to the itty bitty Tabitha clone inside until she felt a definitive kick.

Jack watched as she reached her hand toward his, running her fingers back and forth across his palm before interlocking their fingers.

"Why don't men wear engagement rings?"

He chuckled. "I'm not sure. Are we about to have a walk through modern day feminism?"

"Lord, no. I don't have the energy for it. Forget I said anything."

"Engagement is sort of a weird phase."

"It is, isn't it? It's such a public proclamation declaring you're basically a step above dating and that for all intents and purposes, you're decided to spend an exorbitant amount of time and money planning a wedding and dieting and exercising excessively."

"Like us?"

"Precisely. I felt off those *entire* five days." She smiled widely, running her finger over his simple tungsten band. "I love your hands," she said, dreamily.

Jack was about to respond when Delaney's phone lit up with the hospital switchboard number calling. "Who do you think that is?"

"Probably an appointment reminder," she mumbled, answering it, seeming to expect a robo-caller. She sat up straighter almost immediately. "Happy Thanksgiving to you, too." Her eyes widened at first, then her face turned solemn. "Well, she would know him pretty well so if she thinks it's a good fit--" She pressed her lips together, staring blankly out the windows. "Yes, please do. Thanks. No, I'm building back some strength, but I'm a ways from being able to come back. How's--oh wow, congratulations! That's amazing. I'm so happy for you." She swallowed hard, wiping at her eyes quickly.

After she said goodbye, she exhaled, looking ahead as the train pulled into the station, purposefully avoiding Jack's gaze.

The crisp winter air was unforgiving of Delaney's tear-streaked cheeks as they stepped onto the platform. Rather than moving toward the exit, she stepped toward a bench to get out of the way of exiting passengers. Her breaths bellowed out in thick puffs.

"Delaney?"

"This station has no elevator," she said flatly.

"Permission to sweep my lady off her feet?"

She hesitated. "Permission granted. Careful on the stairs--they could be slippery."

As he carried her down the steps, he noticed how she kept her face turned away. It was once he situated her back on her feet and she stood, pushing firmly into the walking stick, that she looked him in the eyes.

"That was Renee, the pediatric social worker." She took a deep breath. "She heard I was doing better so she wanted to update me about Kai. Remember from—" She waved her hand. "Of course you remember. She had called that day Caprice came over, but there was nothing definite. He had come in for some appointments." She took a breath. "His dad was arrested for DUI and three counts of involuntary manslaughter--he killed--" She straightened her hand before her, indicating she wasn't finishing that story. "They moved Kai into a group home until he could get a foster placement."

He found himself noticing the small details as she spoke—her focused expression, her sad eyes, the slight quiver of her lip.

"He's been at the group home since early September. It's really actually good news that he's been matched so quickly. Some can wait years and they get moved around--with his medical concerns, I'm surprised it all happened so fast." Her positive facial expression, the forced upward motion of her lips was a sheer veil of the devastation she was trying to hide. "She said the foster had gone through all the classes, is financially stable--"

He grimaced.

"That's something we'd have to make a decision about together--I know that. We have a lot going on anyway. And this is probably the best thing for Kai. I just--" She looked at the ground.

"What?"

"I just--really love that kid--"

"I know you do, D."

"I know this is going to sound crazy or something, but--" She closed her eyes slowly, then as she opened them again, the crystal blue had turned silvery, glistening with tears. "I felt a connection with him, like--someone else had given birth to *my son*." She let out a single laugh at that and the tears started streaming from her eyes. "That sounds ridiculous. I sound ridiculous. I'm sorry." She moved to join the flow of pedestrian traffic. "Gino's is this way, right?" When he didn't respond, she turned to find him with his phone to his ear.

"Hi, Trish. Jack Mathison. I got your text."

Delaney watched him closely, trying to decipher what was happening.

"I just wanted to confirm. Everything is set? OK, good, so when--tomorrow at 10. Perfect. Thank you so much. Yes, we'll both be there. Thank you." He gazed back at her, a little dazed.

The confusion and the breeze had dried her tears, or at the very least, frozen them to her face. "What was that about?"

Jack was smiling lightly.

"Jack? Where are we going tomorrow at 10?"

"To get our son."

"What?"

"Kai's foster? Is us--I applied when I found out what was going on with him--it was while you were in ICU. I'm sorry. I should have told you what I did. They removed him from his dad's custody and then put him back. Then his dad was arrested so he was put in emergency care. Then there were delays because they were required to try to reach out to his mother and they didn't know what she would do."

"Did they reach her?"

"She got back to them today. Trish—that's his case worker—had called me earlier. I wanted it to be a sure thing before I told you."

Her eyes were filled with tears again.

"They could only do foster before, but his case worker is going to change our application from foster to adoption--and add you. There's still a few steps, but--"

She burst forward, wrapping her arms around his neck. The walking stick clattered to the sidewalk. "Thank you, thank you, thank you."

He tightened his hold on her. Even through the thick jacket layer, he could feel the moment when her body tensed.

"This is crazy, right? We're crazy? We don't have enough going on already, let's jump into parenthood?"

"Oh we're absolutely insane," he said with a smile.

"We're going to be parents."

He smiled tightly. "Yes, we are."

Her eyes widened. "Oh my God, 10am? We have so much to do."

"Let's get somewhere warm--" he began, studying her face--her big eyes, prominent freckled cheekbones, her lopsided mouth, the right side with only a slightly less enthusiastic curve now. "We'll eat and *then* the panic can set in."

# 30
# merry

J ack quietly pushed open the bedroom door, quickly shedding his thick hoodie on the chaise lounge. In the early morning light, he set his eyes on the sight of Delaney sleeping with the upturned hand of a four-year-old resting across her face. Besides the crinkle of her forehead, she seemed unphased by its presence and the fact that Kai's finger was pulling at her nostril, her sleep mask propped up on her forehead, probably from when he first climbed in their bed. While she typically ended up wrapping herself in the covers, he found the covers in twisted disarray, tossed hastily over the pair of them.

In her excitement building for Christmas, Delaney had matching shirts made featuring the Christmas Vacation car logo and framed with the text: "Mathison Family Christmas. Her version was red and was pulled snugly over her rounded stomach. About two weeks earlier, her belly had "popped" and they had decided to spread the word about her being pregnant.

There were mixed reactions—those who were oblivious to the risks after having a stroke and an aneurysm clamping, who were elated, and those who were well aware of the risks and frankly, shocked that they were so reckless. It was almost easier to ease the concerns of the latter than explain why she would be on bed rest for much of the remainder of the pregnancy to those naive to the risks. It was a bit disheartening to watch the giddiness fade from their faces.

They had taken all recommended precautions--the pill was not an option due to drug interactions so she had an IUD placed, and even though the doctor had assured them it should have been effective immediately, they had elected to use condoms for the first two months. The chance of conceiving was virtually zero.

They weren't planning to have children, not so soon, and hadn't gotten around to formal discussions about opting for adoption when they found out about Kai after Thanksgiving. It was the day after Kai came home that Jack observed Delaney subconsciously rubbing at her breasts in the bathroom. He had teased her, asked if he could help and she whispered back how sore they were.

"Well, maybe your cycle is getting fired up again," he had suggested. She hadn't had a period for months, which had been attributed to all the medical issues she was facing.

"At least I'm not having cramps. Those used to be awful."

He had allowed this information to percolate, recalling that they had been forewarned that periods tended to intensify with the copper IUD, not ease like with hormone based birth control. He continued to observe her go about the day. Eventually she changed into a strong support sports bra to apply compression and he couldn't help but notice that her midsection looked swollen. It was after they put Kai to bed in his Iron Man pajamas that Jack approached her with a pregnancy test he picked up when he went out to get dinner.

She hadn't seemed surprised that he made the suggestion, seemingly having made the connection as well, but she stared at the box, her eyes glassed over. "I got an IUD, we used condoms," she said quietly. "My body isn't even--"

"I know," he replied calmly.

When she took the box, her hand started to shake.

The test was merely a formality. They both seemed to know what the result would be. As it was, they didn't have to wait the three minutes specified on the box, the word "pregnant" appearing immediately, the corresponding box filling in with two solid lines.

Delaney had moved to the sink, quietly washed her hands. She looked up as Jack took a step toward the test and nodded. "I would like to snuggle with you on the couch and watch a movie."

"Okay," he agreed, leaving the test untouched on the bathroom counter. "Popcorn?"

"Yes, white cheddar."

"My favorite."

Her breathing was punctuated. "I would like you to grab my boobs at least twice."

"Don't they hurt?"

"Good point. Please do not grab my boobs as you normally would."

"What if my hand just lingered there throughout the movie?"

She frowned. "No. It should be stealthy, like all of a sudden I look down and boom, your hand is on my boob."

"If that's what you want."

Her face broke, eyes filling with fear. She moved forward quickly, colliding into his shoulder. "I'm not going back to that f-ing support group."

He wrapped his arms around her, squeezing her snugly.

The next day, one of the OBs agreed to see her. Her lab work was remarkably good, her blood pressure was normal, and there were two very healthy, very active 12 week babies on the ultrasound.

Dr. Pomeroy had assessed that the IUD had pierced the uterine wall and shifted. It had to be removed or risk causing pregnancy complications. As the shock set in, he paused to don gloves and pull out the t-shaped contraption. He returned quickly to the ultrasound, not allowing the potential awkwardness of the procedure with the wife of his colleague set in.

"Typically we worry about ectopic pregnancies with IUDs. The chance of having a pregnancy with IUD is so low, let alone twins," he remarked, his widening mouth curling up at the corners. "Let alone twins that appear to be perfectly healthy." He tapped the keyboard, freeze framing on the babies cuddling like otters.

He had then read the social cues and excused himself to go see another patient. He was to set her up for a more detailed scan the following week.

Jack squeezed her hand gently and she raised her chin to look at him, her blue eyes filled with tears. "Jack?" she began, her voice breaking. It appeared she was about to sob.

He wasn't sure what she was about to say. He could only imagine all the things going through her head—the woman at the support group who lost babies due to complications after her stroke, her blunt warnings, feeling overwhelmed by having three children, perhaps feeling worried, guilty even, about Kai, since he had just come to live with them—but his wife combed her fingers through her stubby dark locks and started to laugh.

The tears flowed from her eyes as she hiccuped with laughter. "Of course it's twins!"

He watched her in suppressed amusement. Then he joined in. "Next thing will be the ultrasound technician telling us Dale missed the two babies hiding behind these," he said, lifting up one of the ultrasound printouts.

She froze. "Too far, Mathison. Too far."

"Well we're officially outnumbered, D."

She stared at him, serious suddenly. "I don't know which of your little Generals was leading the condom breech mission and managed the hostile copper infused world, but he was a determined little dude."

He shook his head. "Didn't they say the copper actually separated the head from the tail on the sperm?"

"They did! I felt so sorry for them! They must have fashioned some sort of protective gear."

She was trying desperately to maintain her calm, but he watched a glistening tear trickle out the corner of her eye. "I'll be good. Whatever they recommend. I'll take precautions." She had started to nod as she spoke. "This—we can do this."

"Hey--" he coaxed, bracing her face in his hands. "It's going to be okay."

In the early Christmas morning light, he placed his palm lightly on Delaney's side, closed his eyes and prayed silently.

When he opened his eyes again, Delaney was still sleeping, but Kai was watching him, his face tucked under her chin. Jack motioned to him to stay quiet. Kai looked to where Jack's hand rested and quickly sat up, pulled back the hem of Delaney's red shirt. His brown eyes widened as he motioned to her protruding stomach.

"There are *babies* in there. Two babies."

"I know. It's amazing, isn't it?"

Kai kissed her stomach gently. Twice.

Jack noticed how the pull on her abdominal skin was starting to stretch some of her scars from the accident.

Kai quickly pulled the shirt back down over her stomach, stirring Delaney from sleep. She rolled on her back, eyeing the pair of them. "How bad was the snoring?"

"Symphonic."

She grinned.

Kai dove back into her, yelling "Mommy!"

The first time he said it, Delaney had been beside herself, unable to speak. His adoption was moving forward, but things weren't official yet and they were both scared about something changing, a relative coming forward, Delaney constantly worried her medical history would be brought up. When Kai called her "Mommy," she had embraced him, kissed his head, his cheeks, his ears in staccato fashion until he was in hysterical giggles.

There was a shift then. Delaney had explained that she had to push all the fear she felt aside and be who Kai needed, be brave, fight, advocate for him if something did come up.

She rubbed his back gently. "Merry Christmas, buddy."

"It's Christmas!" he cheered, rolling himself off the bed.

"Should we go see what Santa brought us?" Jack suggested. He helped Delaney come to a sitting position. She stretched out her ankles and calves before attempting to stand.

"I already got what I wanted," Kai said, standing matter-of-factly before them.

Both Delaney and Jack observed that the other was holding their breath.

"I got a whole entire family." Kai smiled.

"You *know*, I already got what I wanted, too," Jack said, rubbing her shoulders. "Maybe we don't need to unwrap presents."

Delaney twisted her face, exchanging a look with Kai. They said "Nah" simultaneously, then Delaney added: "I'm hoping to get compression socks from Santa."

"Shrek and Donkey angry already?" he teased, motioning toward her feet.

"Not yet, but as soon as I'm vertical for long enough, the swelling shall return."

Jack smirked widely, watching Kai beeline for the bathroom. He had a nonsensical ritual when using the bathroom, which included pulling down his bottoms and underwear *then* turning the light on *then* closing the door. Once the door was finally closed, Jack turned to Delaney. "You know, I'd be willing to extend our *horizontal* activities, if that'll help."

"Wow, you'd do that for me?"

His cheeks reddened. "Of *course*. I'm here for you, darlin'."

"So stunning and brave. I'm touched."

He pinched his face, his lips tightening. "Nah, that's bait right there."

Delaney smiled. "Props on waiting until the little guy was behind a closed door to make the sexual innuendo."

His eyes widened. "Oh that was pure torture."

***

Jack's dad had just left for the airport to fly to Chicago to finish off Christmas with Tabitha, who was restricted from traveling during her third trimester, and Kai had just fallen asleep under his train table when a black town car pulled up along the curb in front of the house.

"I wonder who this could be," Jack observed, drying the cast iron pan they had used with breakfast.

Delaney yawned, peering out the window. "I hope it's Publisher's Clearing House." She frowned. "No, I don't see balloons or a camera crew."

He chuckled to himself, replacing the towel on the oven handle.

When she saw who was emerging from the backseat, carrying just a weekender bag, she smiled broadly. Delaney moved toward the front door, wincing. "Shut up, round ligament, you're fine."

"Easy," Jack called, moving quickly toward her. He stood behind her as she opened the door and grinned at the man walking casually up the front walk wearing a collarless shirt, dress pants and a three-quarter length matching blazer. "You look like an extra from *Miami Vice*, Martin."

"How *old* are you?" Delaney said, giving Jack a jeering look.

"They made a movie recently--"

She perked an eyebrow.

*"Fairly* recently."

"Like 14 years ago. Were you referring to the clothing in the movie or the show though?"

"The show," he admitted.

"Mmhmm." She turned abruptly, a broad smile returning to her face. "Papa Schuler!"

Martin dropped his bag abruptly. "I'm gone for a few months and look what trouble you get into." He motioned to her stomach before stretching open his arms to hug her. He kissed the top of her head and Jack couldn't help but notice that his eyes looked misty. "Merry Christmas, Sweet Girl."

Delaney tightened her hold on him.

He kissed her head again. "You look fantastic."

"So do you."

"Lies! I've put on 20 pounds." Martin kept one arm around her and turned them both toward Jack. "You really married this guy? *This* guy?"

"I did."

"That was a good choice," he said, speaking conspiratorially to her. "He's really a good guy. The best. Just don't tell him I said that." Martin stepped away from Delaney to shake Jack's hand and pull him into a hug. "I'm happy for you, Jack," he said quietly, smacking him on the back.

"Come inside," Delaney exclaimed, then clapped her hand over her mouth. "Oh, we do have Kai sleeping in the playroom," she said, lowering her voice and motioning toward the open double doors off the family room and kitchen.

Jack moved outside to retrieve Martin's bag and when he returned, they were just getting settled on the couch and Martin had a hand on her belly. "Hey Martin, it's a little soon--if you feel anything, it's probably the breakfast skillet talking," Jack said.

Delaney shrugged as he moved his hand away.

"It must happen a lot? People getting handsy with the belly? It's just so-- pronounced."

"Julie hugs my belly when she sees me, so yeah."

"Everyone's good? Healthy?"

"Yeah, my doctor wants me to limit activity, but both babies are right on schedule, measuring a little big at this point, about 17 weeks right now."

Martin kept glancing at her belly, smiling.

"So what's going on with Ms. Ponte Vedra Beach?"

Martin grinned. "Ms. Ponte Vedra Beach is wonderful. She's spending Christmas with her son and daughter. Vivian and I thought it would be too soon to introduce me."

"Well I'm happy you're here," Delaney said. "It means a lot to me."

"Well, you know, it works. She's with her kids, I'm with mine."

Jack froze in place as he silently closed the playroom doors. Delaney watched him push his lips together and turn back toward the kitchen.

"I think you made Jack cry."

"I'm not crying, *you're* crying," he said quickly, smiling.

Delaney and Jack shared all the details, how Kai's eyes had turned as wide as saucers looking at all the presents, the twinkling white lights, how he had stripped down in the middle of the family room when he unwrapped his Captain America costume. He had asked about Kai's "big" present and, as though on cue, the pudgy yellow lab puppy emerged from the playroom, where she had been snuggling Kai. This led to a long explanation of the back story for her name, Lloyd, and why they pronounced it "La-Lloyd." (Named for a character in his favorite movie.) Kai followed soon after and had been thoroughly amused by Martin's playful conversation.

The sun turned the sky orange and they dined on Asian fusion takeout after changing back into pajamas. Later, they video chatted with Caprice, who was working, then with Julie and Mike, the two physiatrists sharing an awkward, but cordial greeting. Kai had requested to watch his new favorite movie, and one of his gifts from Santa, resulting first in Martin falling asleep with Kai snuggled to his side, much to Jack and Delaney's amusement. They finished *Lego: Ninjago* on their own, watched as the flames on the fire slowly faded.

The credits woke the sleeping pair. Martin was supposed to sleep in the guest room, but Kai convinced him to sleep on the trundle bed in his room, where he was joined by Lloyd.

Once they were tucked in, Delaney shuffled her feet toward the kitchen with Jack just behind her. As she stepped into view of the Christmas tree, shimmering with nine strands of white lights, she stopped, her hand delicately rubbing her stomach.

"Everything OK?"

She smiled lightly. "Today was a good day."

There was so much context to the sentence. There were so many days from the year to contrast with this one, but in the moment, with his son sleeping down the hall, with Delaney standing before him, her belly silhouetted in the glow of Christmas tree, he felt only gratitude. "It was a *very* good day."

# epilogue

Jack & Delaney officially adopted Kai the following April. Three weeks later, they welcomed two healthy babies--Thomas Jackson Mathison & Annabel Martin Mathison, nicknamed TJ & Annie. Jack still works at the hospital, but has secured more family-friendly shifts. Delaney has been a contributing author for several publications, but was never able to return to the clinical setting.

Martin Schuler moved to Florida and married Vivian. He was recruited to be Medical Director of a Rehabilitation Hospital in Collier County. He declined and now operates a scuba shop in the Florida Keys.

Julie married Mike Bordeaux. She had suffered from PCOS for years, but had never told anyone. After three failed in vitro procedures, they are currently in the process of adopting their first child.

Quinn bought a bar in Old Town. During a follow-up scan after experiencing pain and unsteadiness in his left leg, a tumor was discovered in Quinn's kneecap. He had the leg amputated, went through a cycle of chemotherapy and is currently thought to be cancer-free. When he went to get fitted for his prosthetic, he met a woman named Mallory. They are engaged to be married.

Caprice works two jobs, including at Quinn's bar. She just completed illustrations for a children's book, written by Delaney.

Jeff is still single.

Delaney met with the prosecutor just prior to Kai coming to live with them. Rape and aggravated assault charges were brought against three of her attackers. Timothy testified as a witness, reducing his own charge to aggravated assault. Dr. Schuler testified, as he had ordered pregnancy testing for her and she had shared what had happened at the time. Quinn also provided testimony. Investigators matched DNA to the three charged with rape from Delaney's school clothes, which she had stored in a Ziploc since that day. Quinn's account of how the boys, led by Jeremiah, had set the trap for her, along with her stroke being attributed to injuries caused by the attack, the judge was particularly strict with sentencing. Two of the attackers were 18 at time of the attack and were tried as adults. The third had a skilled lawyer who spared him from the same. Jeremiah was given the maximum sentence of 21 years plus 3 years for aggravated assault. Paul was given 13 total, with a chance for parole after 5. Matt, who was tried as a minor, was given 2 years probation with 1000 hours of community service. Timothy was fined and did not serve jail time.